DEADLY VISION

DEADLY VISION

A NOVEL
BY

T.D. SEVERIN

www.penmorepress.com

Title: Deadly Vision

Author: T.D. Severin

Copyright © 2025 T. D. Severin

ISBN: 978-1-957851-93-8(EBOOK)
ISBN: 978-1-957851-94-5(Paperback)

BISAC Subject Headings:
FIC031040 FICTION / Thrillers / Medical
FIC031060 FICTION / Thrillers / Political
FIC036000 FICTION / Thrillers / Technological
FIC015000 FICTION / Horror
FIC028020 FICTION / Science Fiction / Hard Science Fiction

This novel is a work of fiction. Any resemblance to real persons or events is purely coincidental.

Editor: Chris Wozney

Book Cover Art : Mark Aceves http://www.markaceves.com

Please send all correspondence to:
Penmore Press LLC
920 N Javelina Pl
Tucson AZ 85748

PRAISE FOR DEADLY VISION
BY T.D. SEVERN:

"Deadly Vision is a gripping novel of suspense ingeniously plotted. Dr. Severin writes with an expert's hand in virtual reality and medicine, creating a unique, intriguing and intelligent medical/techno thriller that blew me away from its opening page."
—Robert Dugoni, New York Times Bestselling Author of *The Jury Master* and the Tracy Crosswhite series.

"A Blockbuster! This gripping novel grabs you on page one and never lets up! Dr. Severin's storytelling is seductive; it compels us to understand the intricacies of mysterious medical issues and the unique world of cyberspace, a powerful formula that leaves our brains buzzing with awe! A rollercoaster ride of suspense. This book is as provocative as they come! It should easily be a best-seller!"

—Robert Litman, M.D., critically acclaimed author of the medical thrillers *Allergy Shots* and *The Treblinka Virus*

"An idea so powerful, unique and riveting that I'm shivering! Tension builds steadily with exceptional crafting. Vivid characters. Intriguing, compelling premise. Virtual reality and medicine: unique, timely. The hero physician plagued by a tribunal of horrors; hallucinations, big bad medicine and big bad government. Absolutely superior work! It hooked me!"

—Kathleen Dougherty, best-selling author of
Moth to the Flame and *Double Vision*

"Groundbreaking! A brand-new fresh voice. With this novel, TD Severin breathes new life into the medical/techno thriller, tearing down the boundaries and creating a whole new genre of scientific suspense. A non-stop, terrifying book! Timely and intensely compelling in its examination of technology and medical ethics. Intriguing characters, devilish plot and head-first, non-stop action! I can already see the movie and it will be very, very hot! Look out Robin Cook, there's a new doctor in town and he means business!"

—Smadar Hansen, Actress (*The Usual Suspects, Nash Bridges*) and screenwriter of *Do or Die* and *Stock Car Dreams*

"Dr Severin's Deadly Vision is one of the best techno-thrillers I have read. He may be the new, improved Michael Crichton. This fast-paced novel smoothly combines the author's fluency in both the medical field and the science of computer technology to escort the reader into the expanding world of virtual reality. Add to that some very surprising twists, well-developed and quirky characters, Machiavellian politics, corporate espionage and murder and you have a novel the reader doesn't want to put down. A first-rate thriller. I was highly entertained."

—Janet M. Bank, Senior Editor, The Pen Cushion

"Fascinating premise! Riveting, scary, powerful and dynamic. Just the right mixture of creativity and expertise. This novel is very hot."

—Mimi Albert, critically acclaimed author of *Skirts*

and *Second Story Man*

"We are intrigued with mysteries of the body and mind. In the American landscape, we have explored this fascination through the works of Chandler, Hammett, Grafton, Spillane, Clancy, and Macdonald. TD Severin's Deadly Vision is an intense, modern twist upon this exploration, cut from the same cloth of the American literary tradition that precedes it."

—SV Brown, author of *Carnival Songs*

"Terrific! Fast action, surprises, great complications. Very exciting stuff."

—James N. Frey, Edgar Award Nominated author of
The Long Way to Die

"Excellent! Dynamic action and an impressive eye for minute and telling detail. The characters are individuals, not puppets. A distinct voice. The setting is excellent with strong description. Wonderful conflict and great action!"

—Jacqueline Simon, finalist National Magazine Award for Fiction, winner Texas Writer Recognition award

"Memorable! Interesting premise. Terrific details and story about the duality of existence and virtual reality. Intensely visual. Excellent!"

—Venkatesh Kulkarni, award-winning author of *Naked in Deccan*, Winner of the American Book Award and Chairperson of the World Literature Center

For Corinne. . .

. . . walk with me

ACKNOWLEDGMENTS

Tess Gerritsen, Michael Palmer, Robert Dugoni, Gary Bierken, Kathleen Dougherty, James Frey, Mimi Albert, Robert Litman, Venkatesh Kulkarni, Don Gerrard, and Joel Saltzman, my teachers one and all, for their expert professional guidance and advice.

Michael James and Chris Wozney and the family at Penmore Press for their belief in my story.

Ron Gross, M.D. and Silvia Orengo-Nania, M.D. for allowing me to be writing when I was supposed to have been working, and Baruch Kupperman, M.D. for his early support and encouragement.

Neil White, M.D. and the staff at San Ramon Regional Medical Center Cardiac Cath Lab.

Seal, John Grisham, Tiger Woods, Bruce Springsteen, Michael Crichton, and Paw for inspiration.

John Rancik, Andre Taylor and my friends at Liberty Entertainment for the endless brainstorming sessions that fueled my imagination.

Gregg Campbell, Tina Glueck, and Les Bloch, all writers in their own right, without whom this book wouldn't be half the story that it is.

Mark Aceves for the cover art. Thanks for making it look great!

Paul Chevez, Steve Grace, Katie Magnus Rebarber, Tammy Carson, Deborah Valentine, Chara Hoe, Mark Aceves, Nadine Naumu, and Charles Yoakum for their endless support; and my friends for telling me that I was crazy but never getting around to actually committing me.

Corinne Severin, my beautiful wife and inspiration, without whom, none of this would have been possible.

Chad, my son, for coming into my life and teaching me to be a better dad and a better man.

Kimo, Milo, Sofi, Gigi, Grits, Nalani, Bosco, and Kimchi for endless laughs, walks and love.

PROLOGUE

Thursday, October 12 , 4:59 p.m.
Robert Chan froze in place, staring at the shadows in his hallway.

From the bedroom where he stood, Chan couldn't see the shadows' origin, just the elliptical darkness, spreading across the walls, creeping down the hall. As the sun descended beyond the distant Golden Gate Bridge, a chill seized the air, but Chan didn't feel it. His eyes were fixed on the hallway, studying the growing shadows, searching for signs of movement, or a flicker.

A sign they came from something alive.

Shadows had always terrified Chan. As a child, long after his parents had gone to sleep, he'd lie motionless in bed, his face half-hidden by the blankets, staring at the ceiling. Moonlight, filtering through the branches scratching outside his window, cast a dance of light and darkness above him. Lurking within the specter of shadows, he'd see the spirits of his grandmother's tales, the *kuei-shen*—the phantoms of the deceased trapped between the world of the living and the dead. Too frightened to move, he'd lay immobilized, watching as the shape-shifting *kuei* transformed, taking the forms of lions and dragons. He'd see the *kuei-shen* as they descended upon him, feel them as they entered his flesh, melting into his soul. The chill of their deathly presence within.

He'd carried those visions throughout his adult life.

Still, no number of childhood nightmares could prepare him for what he faced now.

Chan's eyes shot from the hallway to the suitcase lying upon his bed, lid propped half-open, socks and underwear dangling over the edge. He rushed to the case, stuffed in two pairs of grey slacks, then dashed back to the closet. Glancing at the rows of cotton shirts, he shoved the stripes aside and grabbed the white Oxfords. *Less eye catching*, he thought, *more anonymous.*

Anonymity had never been one of Chan's concerns before. As a young and hungry engineer in the Medical Applications Division of CyberTech Systems, he'd done everything in his power to avoid it. In the cutthroat world of Silicon Valley, anonymity in the corporate workplace was the high-tech kiss of death. In order to advance to the high-paying executive levels, Chan had to stand out, be noticed. And he did. Clocking in a string of over fifty consecutive 80-hour weeks, his work habits routinely drew the notice of the upper levels of CTS management. His ascent through the ranks of engineers was unprecedented.

But that was before he found the files.

Now, all he hoped for was to get out alive.

Shoving the Oxfords into the suitcase, Chan glared at the manila envelope on his bed. His stomach tightened. The envelope looked so mundane, so ordinary, like it contained IKEA catalogs or Publisher's Clearing House winner entries. There were no outward clues as to what lay inside. The deception. The hidden discovery that was causing his once carved-in-granite life to crumble around his ears.

He wanted to grab that envelope and rip it to pieces, shred it; pretend he'd never found the files; get back to his life of deadlines and coding assignments, his twice daily visit to Starbucks with Elizabeth, his routine afternoon stop at the Porsche dealer where he'd been eyeing the new Boxster, dreaming of himself behind the wheel.

But it was too late for that. He'd been working on AI programing for a team of researchers at San Francisco University Medical Center, a special project assigned to him by the CEO himself, Reginald Erickson. All the engineers knew he was working on this assignment. His cyber-trail through the

CTS database was easily traceable. Every keystroke monitored and replicated. Each step readily apparent to someone who knew where to look.

The ringing of the phone snapped Chan to attention. He jerked from the bed, his eyes darting to the receiver then beyond to the digital clock on the far wall.

It was 5:00 P.M.

Panic seized him. No one should be trying to reach him at this hour. Not here. Normally, he'd still be at CyberTech logging in another eighteen-hour day pounding out code. No one should know he was home.

The phone rang again. Chan winced. His eyes shot to the envelope. He had to get out of there. Get the files to the Federal Building; get the evidence into the hands of the Justice Department or the FBI or whoever, get filtered into the witness protection program and hope to start a new life as an elementary school teacher in Wichita or Amarillo, or someplace else he'd never even heard of. Let the Attorney General, the world, see what he'd discovered before it was too late. Maybe they could put a stop to this.

But how do you stop a Presidential election?

The phone rang a third time. Chan ignored it, shoved the folder deep into the suitcase, covered it with a sweatshirt and slammed the lid closed. Yanking the suitcase off the bed, he rushed to the front door.

At the doorway, he paused, for just a second, turning to take one last glance at his apartment, his home for the last six years. The delicate Chinese watercolors, the bonsai he'd trimmed each morning, the wooden crucifix above his bed for his daily prayer. It all seemed like such a waste of time now. His plans to become a chief engineer, create his own start-up, propose to Elizabeth next Valentine's Day were worthless. Vanished like rain drops that never reached the ground.

He swallowed hard and ran into the hall.

He didn't get more than two steps before the first shot rocked him. The force of the gunfire lifted him off the ground and sent him hurling backwards through the open doorway. He collapsed onto his back, his vision dimming, descending into a miasma of swirling reds and greys. Pain, like fire, ripped across his belly. A metallic smell filled his nostrils followed by the coppery taste of his own blood.

Chan tried to swallow the liquid bubbling into his mouth. He became vaguely aware of the gaping hole that now occupied his lower abdomen. Warmth flooded down his flank, collecting at the small of his back. Pools of blood gathered on the white carpet. Chan turned his head, eyes half-focused, and watched as each crimson pool began to morph into vague shapes, like clouds taking patterns. In the blood, he saw the faces of his mother and his father, both dead for years. He saw the face of a long-lost uncle, and his childhood friend, Wong, who'd died in a car accident.

The pain sank deeper into his belly. He fought for breath. With the last of his strength, he craned his head towards the door, where he could just make out the silhouette of a lone figure, a bald man. He concentrated hard, trying to resolve the image. Slowly, details took form. Chan's eyes locked on the muzzle of the silenced 40 caliber H&K pistol now aimed at his chest.

Chan sighed and allowed his head to fall back. Around him, the bloody pools gathered into new shapes, like the shadows of his youth, forming lions and dragons.

Despite himself, Chan smiled. He closed his eyes and allowed the darkness to seep into his veins, bringing with it a quiet peace, the realization that he wouldn't have to run anymore.

The *kuei-shen* had arrived.

INITIATION

*STUNNING RESEARCH OFFERS NEW VISION ON
HEART DISEASE*

Researchers at San Francisco University announced the development of a revolutionary new treatment for heart disease. Employing high-resolution MRI scans with real-time, digital ultrasound, doctors will transport themselves into the virtual world of a beating human heart. There, they will perform life-saving surgery entirely within the realm of virtual reality.

"With virtual reality," said Dr. Taylor Abrahms, lead researcher for the Virtual Heart Project, "I'll be inside the human heart, seeing the ventricles contract, hearing the heart valves snap as the blood surges down the coronary arteries. As I move through the virtual heart, my movements will be translated to micro-robotic lasers, surgically placed inside the patient's real artery. These micro-lasers will follow my movements exactly to the plaque blocking the artery and obliterate it. Restoring blood flow. We'll be able to heal the heart entirely within the realm of virtual reality. This will forever change how we treat heart disease."

Not everyone was supportive of the new technology. Senator Randolph Henry McIntyre, the Republican Presidential nominee, has campaigned vigorously against medical hyper-technology as "dangerous and prohibitively expensive." Despite these attacks, Dr. Abrahms remained optimistic. "Medicine is about to enter an era of computerized reality, and I doubt it will ever be the same again."

—The Washington Post
Special Technology Review

CHAPTER 1

When Dr. Taylor Abrahms arrived at the nursing desk at the San Francisco University Hospital Emergency Room, he had no way of knowing that his life would never be the same again. Reaching the tail end of a 24-hour shift, it had been one hell of a day, made more complicated by the Hospital's insistence that he squeeze a press conference in amongst his daily barrage of ER patients. Speaking on the latest advances in his research, the Virtual Heart Project, the conference had gone well, the networks and newspapers devouring the story about artificial intelligence and robot medicine. But at that moment, Taylor didn't care. After another brutal shift in the ER then the hospital show-and-tell, all he wanted were a few precious moments of sleep. Sweet, beautiful sleep.

Unfortunately, that wasn't going to happen.

SFU Hospital reigned as the major trauma center for the San Francisco area. A busy Thursday night brought seventeen to twenty priority-one trauma cases through the electric ER doors. Gunshot wounds, motor vehicle accidents, and gangbangers. Drunks and drug addicts. This Thursday was no exception.

Taylor, still dressed for the news conference in his off-the-rack suit and pretend red power tie, made his way passed the line of loaded gurneys towards the nursing desk. Six red lights flashed above the main board, indicating new arrivals. A young mother calmed the cries of her bleeding child in the waiting area while two drunks battled to be next in line for admission.

An ambulance team raced by, heading towards the exit and another load. The air reeked of antiseptic, urine, and the sourness of unbathed human skin.

Mary, the twenty-year veteran head nurse, a black woman with coppery complexion, red hair and freckles, sat behind the counter. She scribbled orders into a patient chart with one hand while she pointed directions to a nurse with the other. Eight charts lay sprawled across her desk. The telephone was glued to her ear.

"What the hell do you think I'm talking about? We ordered 80 milligrams of Gentamicin IV and you sent us a piggyback with 800 mg in it. What are we supposed to do with that? Blow out the kidneys of every damn patient down here? Get me the proper order and I mean now, as in yesterday."

Mary slammed down the phone. "Amy, get that IV started in room six. Jean, check in the head wound for room eight, and somebody call the lab. I've got ten tubes of blood here."

People scurried in all directions.

"Another quiet night on the job?" Taylor asked.

Mary looked up, the tension in her eyes relaxing just a bit as she saw Taylor. "Just another night," she said, a wry smile forming her lips. "But it's always a pleasure to see you here, all dolled up in your Sunday best, just like you were still on TV."

Taylor blushed, knowing his $250 no-name suit was hardly an Armani. "Don't tell me you saw the news conference."

"Hell, yes," Mary smiled. "We had every TV in the ER broadcasting your pretty face. You think we're going to ignore it when CNN comes to our little hospital? It isn't often we get a glimmer of hope here. You're our big chance."

Taylor pulled on his collar, loosening his tie. He thought that he'd be used to all the attention by now, but that wasn't going to happen. Ever since the hospital made a grand announcement of the Virtual Heart Project, the media had descended upon him like locust on a corn field, besieging him with requests to appear on talk shows—Good Morning America, Cuomo, 60 Minutes—to discuss the future of "robot medicine." He would have been a natural too. His dark hair, penetrating brown eyes and broad-shouldered frame were perfectly suited for television.

But characteristically, he refused to take their calls. None of the awards or fanfare mattered to him. Even this early in his medical career, Taylor had seen too many scientists get caught up in the media game. No matter how much coverage he got from the popular press, in the world of academic medicine he was only as good as his last paper. No amount of television exposure was going to help him realize his dream.

Mary looked at her watch. "What brings you back?" I thought you just finished a twenty-four hour this afternoon."

Taylor was grateful for the change of subject. "Nancy's out sick. I wanted to see how things were running without her."

"You're off-duty and you're still worried about the ER?"

"This place is my responsibility."

Mary raised her eyebrows. "The last several Chiefs couldn't get out of here fast enough. You couldn't even see them sprinting for the door, just feel the breeze in their wake."

"Not my style."

"I can see that," Mary smiled. "But we're doing fine. Go home. I'm sure your wife's not too happy about your work habits."

Taylor rubbed his eyes and looked at the clock behind the desk. Coming up on 5:30. He'd been at the hospital nearly 34 straight hours. He'd meant to get home to Sherilyn early that night, grab a nice dinner, a glass of red, and just relax together. It seemed like forever since they'd had some time together, alone, without beepers or cell phones or interruptions. But with his ER shifts, his VHP research, the news conference....

"You might say it's a sore point."

Mary nodded. "I'd imagine. Go home to her now. We're doing okay here."

"I'll wait. I heard there's a bad trauma heading in."

"I'll get Peter to take it."

Taylor stuck his thumb towards the main admissions board. "He's tied up with a GI bleeder."

Mary squinted in agreement, but shook her head. "We'll handle it. You're not supposed to be here. Go home."

Suddenly, the cacophony of beeping monitors and shouting voices burst through the double glass door entranceway as paramedics rushed the fresh trauma victim down the main corridor. Running along side the gurney, one paramedic held down the patient's convulsing legs while his partner pressed a dressing against the wounded man's chest with one hand, squeezing an Ambubag ventilator with the other. Blood soaked through the bandage, seeping onto the gurney. The paramedic's eyes glared with panic.

"We need a doctor now!"

Taylor glanced at Mary and gave her a wink. "Duty calls." He grabbed a stethoscope off the nursing counter before she could stop him and sprinted towards the gurney.

"What've we got?" Taylor asked.

"A mess," the paramedic said, panic in his eyes. "Home invasion robbery. Gunshots chest and abdomen. We did everything we could just to get him this far. I don't know how he's still alive."

Taylor leaned forward, his eyes scanning, triaging the extent of trauma. Beneath the pallor and shock, Taylor could make out the man's rounded features. Distinctly Asian. And young. No more than thirty.

Taylor's pulse began to race, his fatigue melting away as adrenaline shot through his veins.

"Do we have a name?" he asked.

The paramedic hesitated.

"A name?" Taylor repeated. "Do we have a name?"

"Uhm... it's Chan. Robert Chan."

"I'm taking over." Taylor shifted his gaze to the waiting nurses. "Shock Room One! Prepare for immediate intubation. Give me two 16-gauge IVs, Lactated Ringers wide open. Type and cross for six units of blood. And call cardiothoracic surgery STAT!"

The ER team responded in unison, rushing Chan to the Shock Room and prepping him for resus. Cardiac monitors, oxygen saturation computers and electronic defibrillators pumped out vital data on Chan's cardiovascular and respiratory status. Respiratory therapists readied their ventilator by a row of green oxygen tanks. Nurses ripped open packages of surgical instruments, lining them up on a sterile tray. Discarded sterile wrappers and excess tubing littered the gleaming white floor. The team moved with choreographed precision, like dancers in a macabre ballet.

"Hang in there, Mr. Chan," Taylor said.

Mary rushed to Taylor's side and began inserting an I.V. An assistant nurse catheterized Chan's bladder while a pharmacist readied the Shock Cart of medicines.

Taylor positioned himself at the head of the table and took stock of the situation. He snapped on a pair of latex gloves, grabbed an overhead light and pulled it into position, peering down at the bloody mess that was his patient. He'd seen many gunshots in his years as an ER resident, but nothing like this. Chan was bleeding from everywhere—every wound, every orifice, seemingly every pore. Gaping holes of torn flesh bore through his abdomen. And from the size of the exit wounds, Taylor knew that the bullets used hadn't been standard issue rounds. These were hollow points.

Something struck Taylor as being terribly wrong. He'd been in the ER long enough to earn his badge of honor in the knife-and-gun club of inner-city San Francisco, and one thing he'd learned was that hollow-points weren't used to commit random crimes. They were too expensive, too unpredictable. Crimes were committed with .38's or .22's.

Hollow points were used when you wanted someone dead.

Taylor filed that information away. Leaning over, he probed the man's chest. The gurgling sounds of Chan's gasping filled the room.

"We need airway stabilization!" he yelled. Mary responded instantly, thrusting a fiber-optic scope into his hand. Taylor snatched it and peered down Chan's throat, searching for the opening into his lungs. The oral passage was filled with blood. Taylor swept his finger into Chan's mouth, fishing out the clots while he searched for the white flesh of the glottis—the opening to the trachea. Finding it, he slid the breathing tube into Chan's throat and hooked it to an Ambubag. Immediately, a nurse began pumping air into his wounded lungs.

Taylor's eyes darted up from his bleeding patient. The EKG monitor beeped out Chan's uncertain pulse. The IVs were running. Blood was on the way.

"Vitals?" he called out.

Mary glared at the monitors. "Blood pressure's dropping, 90 over 45. Pulse weak and thready."

Chan's heart wasn't beating strongly enough to hold a pulse.

"Epinephrine now." Taylor ordered. "Ten ml bolus."

Mary grabbed the syringe and quickly injected the medicine into the IV. "It's in."

"Vitals?" Taylor asked again.

"No good," Mary's voice edged with urgency. "Blood pressure's still falling. We got V Tach."

Taylor's eyes shot to the monitor, studying the erratic, irregular beating of the heart. Ventricular Tachycardia. The EKG alarm screeched in his ears. "Damn it! He's bleeding out on us. Where's the blood?"

"On the way. Six units."

"Not enough. Get six more. Repeat epi and prepare lidocaine bolus!"

"Epi's in," Mary pulled the needle from the I.V. "It's not working. BP's still falling. 70/35."

"I can't ventilate him!" a nurse yelled, struggling to compress the manual ventilator bag. "There's too much resistance."

"Must be a hemothorax," Taylor swore under his breath. Experience told him that blood had flooded into the membranes lining Chan's lungs, impairing their ability to expand. He had to get the blood out or else it'd make ventilation impossible.

"We've got to open him up," Taylor ordered. "Get a chest tube; keep the Ringers Lactate wide open. Repeat Epi, now!"

Chan's body convulsed on the gurney, flailing out in spasm. The paramedics tightened their grip on his quivering legs while Taylor grabbed a scalpel and stabbed an incision into the side of Chan's chest by the fifth rib. Using a hemostat, he pried open the wound, separating the muscles from the lining of the lung.

"Tube," he called out.

Mary thrust the thick plastic tube into Taylor's hand. Clamping it with the hemostat, he forced the tube into the space between Chan's chest wall and his lungs. Instantly, a rush of blood shot down the tube into the plastic collecting compartment.

Taylor shook the blood off his hands onto the splattered floor. "Vitals?"

"BP's still falling, 60 over palp!" Mary yelled back.

Taylor shot a glance. The cardiac monitor showed ventricular fibrillation, the last dying beats of a critically-wounded heart.

"We're losing him!" Mary yelled.

"Start CPR!" Taylor tore off the remains of the Chan's shirt. "Defibrillator on full charge!"

A nervous silence ran through the Shock room.

"CPR now!" he yelled again.

"I... can't," Mary hesitated, her eyes wide, her voice stuttering. "There's no chest wall for compression."

Taylor stopped and glared at the patient. She was right; the chest wall was shattered. His ribs and sternum bisected. All Taylor could see were the heaving strain of his dying lungs.

Flatline.

"He's going!" Mary yelled.

Taylor pounced on the gurney. Without hesitation, he straddled the dying man, spread apart his shattered ribs and thrust his hands into the open chest cavity. The biting aroma of blood rushed to his nostrils and he snorted to clear his lungs. He stumbled for a moment, his hands groping amidst the wetness, until he felt the firm, muscular mass that was his patient's heart. He grasped it in both hands, squeezing it, forcing the dying myocardium to send blood to the brain. He opened his hands to allow blood to refill the ventricles, then squeezed again.

Open. Squeeze.

Open. Squeeze.

"Repeat epi now!" he yelled. "Get amiodarone ready and keep ventilating him. For God's sake, keep ventilating him!"

The nurses scattered to fill the orders.

Sweat matted Taylor's shirt to his back. He glared down into the vacant eyes of his patient. "Hang in there, Mr. Chan," he panted, squeezing Chan's dying heart in his hands. "I'll do this all night if I have to. All night!"

Blood splashed across Taylor's hands.

Open. Squeeze.

Open. Squeeze.

CHAPTER 2

The Caucus Room, located one block off Pennsylvania Avenue, exactly halfway between Capital Hill and the White House, was the kind of restaurant few people received an invitation to dine at, and those who did knew better than to boast about it afterwards. This made it the ideal place for the quintessential late-night Washingtonian strategy session. Co-owned by a Democratic lobbyist and a former Republican National Committee Chairman, the restaurant was frequented by power-pushers and lobbyists from all political persuasions, searching for common ground amongst a bottle of fine Cabernet and a perfectly seared steak.

Senator Randolph Henry McIntyre took a measured bite of his filet then leaned back from his private table against the rear wall, taking it all in. Cell phone conversations crackled as lobbyists drove home their client's points. Heated debates echoed between congressmen. Waiters dashed about filling glasses and uncorking bottles. The room smelled of garlic and cigars and power.

To the Senator, the Caucus Room was the perfect place for him to be dining. Not because of the protection the exclusive restaurant provided against the hordes of press and newshounds outside, but because of its location. Halfway between Capital Hill and the White House was exactly where

McIntyre saw himself. Riding high on the momentum of his devastating series of primary victories and his subsequent Republican Party nomination, the Senator was a fifteen-point favorite in the polls to become the next President of the United States. After serving with distinction for twelve years in the Senate, two years as the majority leader, he was now halfway to the Oval Office.

"CNN has asked for an appearance on the Washington Insider tomorrow," his aide Jennifer Langston was saying, "but we're already committed to the Rotary Benefit dinner. What would you like to do?"

The Senator snapped his attention back to his meeting and took in his aide. Twenty-eight years old, blonde hair down to her shoulders and the stunning looks of a swimsuit model, the Senator knew he'd chosen her well. Many people could perform the duties required of his personal assistant, but few could do them while looking so striking standing next to him. The Senator was keenly aware that every person within his inner ranks was seen by the public as a representation of the Senator himself. Being constantly seen and photographed in the presence of such a lovely young lady made the Senator appear younger and more vital, enhancing his reputation as a man desired by women, and envied by men.

"Cancel the benefit," he said.

"They've planned this dinner for more than a year. It's for their battered woman's shelter and you're the guest of honor."

The Senator smiled smugly. "The dinner will be attended by a few hundred; CNN will be seen by millions. You do the math."

Jennifer nodded. "What should I tell them?"

"Send them my regards and best wishes. Promise them a grant once I'm in the White House."

Jennifer nodded and handed the senator a neatly typed sheet of paper. "The CNN show will be a call-in. Expect callers from all over the country."

The Senator folded the paper without looking at it and placed it in his breast pocket. "Any surprises?"

"The focus will be on your health care plan. That's still your number one strength in the polls."

Jennifer made a notation in her iPad calendar, making the necessary adjustment to the Senator's schedule. McIntyre smiled. He knew that she'd be doing a lot of schedule adjusting in the weeks to come. In the wake of the latest polls declaring his overwhelming lead against his rival, Congressman Snead O'Neil, the Democrat from New Hampshire, every news, political and charitable group wanted face time with Senator McIntyre. Face time was a powerful currency in power-hungry Washington. Everybody wanted to be seen with a winner.

The Senator flashed his patented, perfectly-capped smile and ran his fingers through his thick, salt and pepper hair. Fifty-eight years old and on the verge of stepping into the most powerful office in the world. As a former All-American quarterback at Georgia Tech, he still carried a strong athletic build. Combined with his sophisticated good looks and cool grey eyes, he knew he'd create an impressive photo opportunity standing next to the Presidential Seal.

"Working or eating?" a deep southern voice boomed out.

The Senator looked up into the smiling face of Roderick Stevens, his Republican Campaign Manager from Arkansas, his reddened, bulbous W.C. Fields nose protruding out from his puffy cheeks. His shock of grey hair unsuccessfully kept in place with a glob of Vitalis gel.

"Just finishing," the Senator said. He turned towards Jennifer. "If you'll excuse us."

"But sir, we still need to talk about—"

The Senator cut her off with a wave of his hand. "We'll finish later."

Jennifer knew better than to argue. She nodded briskly, gathered her iPad and papers and walked away. Roderick sat down in her still warm seat and picked up a fork.

"Good kid," he said, taking a bite of the unfinished steak on her plate. "You do her yet?"

The Senator frowned and took a sip of wine. "I don't 'do' any one. I'm a married man, remember?"

"Yeah, that's right," Roderick laughed. "You do your wife and fuck the rest."

Both men laughed. Roderick chomped on another fork-full of steak. "Good stuff. Too bad she didn't have time to finish." He looked at the Senator's plate; the steak cut in two halves, one half cut into precise one-inch cubes, the other gracefully pushed aside, untouched. "Is that all you're eating?"

"My calories are carefully monitored. I can't afford to let the cameras make me look heavy."

Roderick reached over and stabbed the Senator's uneaten portion, pulling it over to Jennifer's now finished plate. "Good thing I'm behind the camera."

"Is this why you came by, to grab a free dinner?"

Roderick wiped his mouth with the napkin. "Have you seen the evening edition?" Roderick handed the Senator a copy of the Post. "You're not going to like it."

The Senator took the paper, scanning the headlines until he reached the yellow highlighted title.

STUNNING RESEARCH OFFERS NEW VISION
ON HEART DISEASE

The Senator read the contents, feeling his blood pressure rising with each word.

"Damn," he finally said.

Roderick swallowed his last bite of steak, red wine sauce dribbling down his chin. "I thought you'd say that."

"Is this in every newspaper?" McIntyre asked.

"Don't know, but it's hit the wire. Anyone can pick it up."

The Senator's eyes narrowed, his forehead furrowing.

"That's his project, isn't it?" Roderick asked.

The Senator nodded.

"Your son-in-law? Taylor Abrahms?"

"That's him."

Roderick took a sip from Jennifer's wine glass. "What'cha going to do? This will be very humiliating for you once the press makes the connection."

"I realize that," McIntyre folded his hands before his face and took a deep breath. His eyes scanned the headline while his mind raced forward. He knew one day this would come, there was no way to avoid it. Not with the press digging through his past like grave robbers excavating a cemetery. Over the course of his campaign, McIntyre had built his reputation by attacking the medical establishment, targeting medical costs as the cause of the country's ills. At each town hall meeting, news conference, or meet-and-greet, McIntyre never failed to drive home his point that the cost of health care was destroying the country, devouring more than 17% of the nation's gross domestic product. Twice the amount spent on education. With his photo blazoned across the cover of Time Magazine, McIntyre was quoted as saying, 'health care reform is the foundation upon which this country will once again right itself.'

He'd done everything in his power to avoid the embarrassment of his dirty, little secret, and so far, had been successful. Until now.

"This is going to get messy," Roderick was saying, "You've managed to keep your daughter's personal life out of the press so far, but once they make the connection between you and Abrahms—"

McIntyre looked up from the paper. "Nothing is going to happen."

Roderick crossed his arms over his chest. "All it takes is one issue to break an election. Just look at Hilary and the "basket of deplorables" fiasco. That one comment gave the opposition all the ammo they needed to bust her campaign. Voters can be very unforgiving."

McIntyre's eyes flared. "I don't need a history lesson from you."

Roderick swallowed and wiped his mouth with his hand. "You've talked to him about stopping. At least postponing until the election?"

McIntyre shook his head. "He's not worth my time."

"Randolph, the election is less than four weeks away. You've got to talk to him. Reason with him. Charges of nepotism and favoritism at this late date could be very damaging for you. Now that it's public, it's only a matter of time before the press seize on it."

"I'm aware of that." McIntyre placed his palms firmly on the table. "We'd foreseen this possibility since day one."

Roderick paused, giving the Senator an opportunity to reconsider. To stop before things were set into motion that could never be undone. He wiped his chin with a napkin and eyed the Senator carefully.

"Are you sure? This is your daughter's husband we're talking about."

McIntyre lifted his glass and took a slow, deliberate sip of wine. He looked about the Caucus Room, watching the minor political pundits jostling with each other for their meager position in the power pecking order.

Halfway between Capital Hill and the White House, he thought. *Halfway.*

"Let's win this election," he said.

CHAPTER 3

Taylor Abrahms stood alone in the Shock Room.

Only minutes had passed since the Cardiothoracic Team had rushed Robert Chan to emergency surgery but already the ER staff had been called off to other duties. An ambulance crew raced a head injury to the minor room from an auto versus motorcycle accident. A croupy child wheezed at the Admissions Desk while a mentally ill homeless man ran around in circles, declaring the end of the world. Shouting voices and screams echoed down the corridors as security ran in with restraints. In an inner-city ER, time waited for no one.

Taylor rubbed the fatigue from his eyes and surveyed the detritus around him. Discarded medical wrappers, oxygen tanks and syringes littered the Shock Room floor, silent witnesses to the horror that had just unfolded. Blood splattered the walls, reaching to the ceiling, grisly patterns splashed out like a Rorschach test from the mind of a deranged killer. The bitter stench of plasma hung heavy in the air.

Peeling the latex gloves off his hands, Taylor massaged the circulation back into his cramped fingers, still locked in the shape of Chan's heart. Somehow, through the transfusions, medicines, and open-heart massage, Chan had clung to life.

Taylor looked down at his best suit, now a hazmat-stained mess. Dropping the blood-soaked gloves to the floor, he stepped to the corridor. He avoided being run over by two orderlies whisking oxygen tanks to Room Six then stepped through the doorway of the On-call Room.

Inside, Dr. Norman Browne, the Chairman of the ER Department, was holding court. An icon to the ER staff; Browne was a world-renowned educator and researcher with over three-hundred publications in the medical literature and enough textbook chapters to fill a bookcase. In the ER he was known as "the firefighter", drifting from room to room and stamping out smoldering crises like a fireman stomping out a blaze.

One hand resting on his large belly, Browne gestured with the other towards a chest X-ray. Resident Dr. Peter Ketchem, stood at attention, his eyes riveted on the film.

"A pulmonary embolus," Dr. Browne was saying, stabbing the X-ray with his meaty finger. "How many times must I tell you? Chest pain, acute shortness of breath and blood in the sputum spells embolus. E-M-B-O-L-U-S. Embolus."

Peter nodded. "But a pneumonia could mimic the signs-"

"A pneumonia couldn't mimic anything but a pneumonia. Look at this film." Browne pointed again. "Do you see a pneumonia?"

"Well—"

"Of course, you don't. Why not? Because it isn't there! Embolus. Should I spell it again? E-M-B-O—"

Peter nodded, the lesson drilled into his head. Browne cut off and turned his large mass away from the X-ray view box, spotting Taylor standing at the doorway. A smile filled Browne's face, partially masked by his bushy beard.

"Taylor, my boy, do come in." He waved his beefy hand. "Peter and I were just discussing the finer points of the differential diagnosis of chest pain with shortness of breath. Anything to add?"

Taylor smiled and shook his head. "No, sir. You gave me the same spelling lesson last year."

"Splendid." Browne shot his gaze at Peter. "Now that we all know how to spell embolus," he thrust his index finger towards the door, "Get out there and diagnose it."

Peter nodded, scampering for the exit, he shot Taylor a glance. They were both familiar with Dr. Browne's spelling lessons.

"Don't be too hard on Peter, he does a good job." Taylor said.

"The jury is still out on that one," Browne huffed, turning back towards Taylor. "Nice work out there." He nodded towards the Shock Room. "I'm beginning to believe I've taught you something over the years."

Taylor managed a weary smile. "Only how to spell fatigue."

"As I recall, you were the one who requested the double duty of residency and research—" he let his words linger.

"Don't remind me," Taylor said, fully aware of the unusual request he'd made and the warning that immediately followed not to let his ER duties suffer. But that was what Taylor expected from Browne. Over the three years of his residency, Taylor had found Dr. Browne to be the perfect ally. As a teacher, Browne thrived on imparting to Taylor the intricacies of emergency medicine, and as an advisor, Browne did his best to protect Taylor from the warring egos that raged through the academic halls.

Taylor shoved his thumb towards the Shock Room. "Did you get a good look at that last trauma?"

Browne shook his head. "I was tied up with a rudimentary spelling lesson."

"There was something strange about him."

Browne raised an eyebrow.

"This wasn't a random robbery."

"And why is this your concern?"

"What I saw didn't fit the paramedic's story."

Browne shrugged. "So, the paramedic was wrong. It wouldn't be the first time, won't be the last. Under the conditions they find these victims, I'm amazed they ever get the story straight. But again, I fail to see why it's your concern."

Taylor shrugged. "It's not, it's just that—"

"Let the Police handle it." Browne cut Taylor off with a slashing motion of his hand. "You have something much more important to worry about."

Taylor was taken aback by Browne's bluntness. He watched as Browne reached into his breast pocket and pulled out a letter, the San Francisco University Medical Center logo blazing across the top. Silently, he unfolded it and handed it to Taylor.

On Friday, October 13th, the Departments of Medicine and Surgery will discuss your proposed research, The Virtual Heart Project, at weekly Grand Rounds. Be prepared to present your research thesis in a forty-minute presentation. Also include any relevant ancillary information for discussion.

Call extension 2423 to arrange your necessary audio/ visual materials.

Taylor's eyes widened. The blood drained from his face. "This can't be right. That's tomorrow." He shook his head, not comprehending. "We're supposed to have three weeks until Grand Rounds."

Browne shook his head. "Plans changed. Dr. Preston pushed the VHP up the docket. You're on the clock now, due to take the stage in exactly," he paused to look at his watch, "seventeen hours."

Taylor's breath tightened. He ran his fingers through his sweat-matted hair. Grand Rounds, the most important scientific meeting of academic medicine, was what he and his research partners had been working towards for years. A chance to stand up on stage and show the entire faculty what the VHP could do. The way it would forever revolutionize surgery.

But that was supposed to be in November, weeks from now. Not tomorrow.

Malcomb was going to freak!

"Can he do that?" Taylor asked. "Move us forward anytime he wants?"

"He's Chair of the Committee that's evaluating your project," Browne said, "Dr. Preston can do anything he damn well pleases."

Taylor exhaled, wondering what had suddenly changed that pushed the date forward. He turned the letter over in his hands, searching for a clue. The only thing that stood out was the date.

Friday the 13th.

"This letter reads like the medical equivalent of a draft notice."

Browne nodded. "You should expect the veiled threats by now. Your research is ruffling quite a few feathers."

"Whatever happened to a fair and impartial jury?"

Browne shook his head. "This is a medical center, my boy, not a court of law. All eyes are on you."

That's the understatement of the year, Taylor thought.

Ever since he'd announced his research, faculty from all departments, many of whom he'd never met, took turns catching Taylor in the hallways, warning him about the battle he was about to enter. Browne had warned him earlier as well. Life inside the Medical Center was a minefield that required expert navigation through the egos and cancerous personalities. Each Chairman ran their department with all the subtlety of a feudal overlord. Grand Rounds was the front lines, where the chairs clashed on the academic battlefield, with Taylor holding fort in the middle.

"Any idea what I can expect?" Taylor asked.

Browne shot Taylor a cautious look. "The introduction of new technology always comes down to one thing. Who's going to pay for this and where's the money coming from." Browne spread his arms wide. "The medical system in this country is bankrupt. Just look at this place. We barely have enough money to turn the lights on."

Taylor noted that half the on-call room fluorescents were out. He took in the yellowed walls, the cracked x-ray view box, and the battered metal desk that was their only workstation. The room reeked of ancient mildew. SF City, like most inner-city hospitals, functioned on the brink of insolvency.

"Legislators and insurers," Browne continued, "are fighting for any way to cut costs. All new technology is placed under unbearable scrutiny for need, equitable access and cost. PSCM is screaming for it. And then you bring about a project as radical as what you're proposing—"

Browne let his words hang in the air.

Taylor grimaced. He'd heard the arguments before. Each month in the mail, he received letters from Physicians for Socially Conscious Medicine, demanding a moratorium on costly new biotech until the failing medical system could right itself. With the recent national economic collapse, those cries had only grown louder.

"And our very own Drs. Preston and Crawford are the heads of PSCM," Taylor shrugged. "I'm aware of that."

Browne pulled the x-ray down from the view box and walked to the metal desk. He glanced over his shoulder. "There are some very powerful parties with a vested interest in seeing you fail."

Browne's directness caught Taylor by surprise. He squinted at his director. "You're not suggesting I stop?"

Browne sat at the desk and tented his hands before his mouth. "Blind idealism is a death sentence, Taylor. You can't walk into Grand Rounds expecting the faculty to be amazed and bow at your feet. It won't happen. This is a zero-sum situation. If your project gets funding, someone else's won't. They will fight you every step of the way."

Taylor steeled his gaze. "All I need is one chance to show them what the VHP can do, Dr Browne. One chance. If I get past Rounds—"

"That's a mighty big if." Browne cut him off. "This meeting was pushed forward for one reason—to put you at a disadvantage. They're stacking the deck against you, Taylor. It can be devastating up there, alone on stage, nowhere to hide. Attacks will come from all sides. It can get very ugly, very fast. You wouldn't be the first resident I've seen get crushed at Rounds. I've watched some of the brightest scientific minds stumble under the pressure. Entire careers have been destroyed under the scrutiny."

"I'll be ready, Dr Browne."

Browne's arms crossed over his chest. "You really think you have something?"

"I do, sir. I really do."

Browne looked down at his watch. "Then you have 17 hours to prove it. Be ready to expect the unexpected. They'll question your methodology, your protocols, your null hypothesis. Anticipate everything."

Taylor took in Browne's warning. He glanced down at the letter in his hands.

Friday the 13th.

He half expected a crazed maniac in a hockey mask to be sitting in the auditorium waiting for him.

A final fleeting image of Robert Chan's bloodied chest raced through his mind, but he forced those thoughts aside.

The most important meeting of his career was due to take place in less than 24 hours, his one chance to show what they could do, and the truth was, they were nowhere near prepared.

Taylor bit his upper lip and looked at his mentor.

"We'll be ready."

CHAPTER 4

Dr. Bennington Crawford looked like a man whose world had just come to an end.

As the first African-American to be named Chief of Staff at San Francisco University Medical Center, Crawford had successfully guided the hospital through every major crisis that had confronted the institution over the last seventeen years. He'd handled malpractice attorneys, indigent rights protesters and corporate buyout CEO's all with dignified calm and political savvy. As one of the nations' leading medical ethicists, and the President of Physicians for Socially Conscious Medicine, he'd gained a reputation for skillfully running the hospital in the face of dwindling medical funds. Now, with his age edging past sixty, he thought he'd finally fought his last battle in the name of medicine and could look forward to spending his time fly fishing with his grandchildren on his south Montana ranch.

But now he knew his fighting days were far from over.

"I just can't believe this," he whispered, collapsing into the leather chair. He gazed across the darkly-paneled medical library at his friend and tried to take in the magnitude of what he'd just heard.

Dr. William Preston, Chairman of the Cardiovascular Surgery Department, stood by the fireplace, balancing his scotch on the antique marble mantel of the Doctor's Club. He swirled the glass, spinning the ice in a whirlpool of amber. His thinning black hair, lacquered across his forehead in a great sweep, couldn't disguise the tell-tale signs of Preston's advancing years. His small black eyes, deep set with almost no pupils, never left Crawford's face while he waited for a response.

"Right here, in our own backyard?" Crawford asked.

Preston nodded. "His name is Taylor Abrahms. He's the Emergency Room Chief Resident with grants from the CompSci and Cardiology departments."

"Why haven't I heard of this until now?"

"Are you kidding? He's just a resident. He's so far off the radar I didn't even know he existed. Then from out of nowhere, the Hospital Brass shine their shoes all pretty, put on a Press Conference and suddenly he's lead story on every God-damned newscast in the country."

"Jesus," Crawford said.

Preston strode over from the fireplace and sat in the leather chair opposite Crawford. The Doctor's Club occupied the top floor of the medical library on the Medical Center Campus, up the hill from SF City Hospital. Italian leather chairs, arranged in a semi-circle, fanned out in front of the fireplace. Two grey-haired endocrinologists conversed in the corner by the display of antique surgical tools. The cry of an ambulance siren echoed in the distance but was effectively camouflaged by the soft sounds of Handel playing in the background.

Preston lifted a bell resting on the marble table and rang it briskly.

Shortly, a man appeared, dressed in a black tuxedo, his thin grey hair slicked back from his forehead.

"Yes, sir?"

"Get me another scotch," Preston ordered.

"Yes, sir." He turned towards Crawford. "And for you, sir?"

"No, thank you, Martin. Nothing for me."

The waiter turned back towards the bar. Crawford watched him recede across the Persian carpets to the back of the Doctor's Club, just as he had done everyday for the last seventeen years. Martin was one of the last vestiges of the glory days of this institution. Once a staple of all major Medical Centers, most Doctor's Clubs had closed years ago, the space converted into computer rooms or file storage. In these days of cost containment and capitated health care plans, there was no place, the administrators claimed, for the ostentatious displays of wealth that the Doctor's Clubs represented.

But Crawford loved the Club. He loved the camaraderie he developed with his medical colleagues, discussing diagnoses amongst the aroma of fine pipe tobacco. He loved the privacy the Club afforded him, away from the constant strain of life-and-death decisions on the Medical Floors. In the Doctor's Club, the world made sense. It represented a time when doctors were revered and respected and handled their patients with compassion and an awe for the delicate balance of nature.

But that wasn't the way medicine was anymore. In the dawning decades of the twenty-first century, when cost-containment became the key phrase, complex medical decisions were stripped away from the capable minds of physicians conversing in the Club and were dealt out by faceless clerks with high school diplomas, lost in a warren of desks at an insurance company corporate office. Letters to him were no longer addressed to "Dear Doctor" or "Dear Physician," they merely said "Dear Health Care Provider," reducing him to just another cog in the corporate takeover of "Health Care."

Medicine, as Crawford knew it, was dying.

Martin returned, carrying a fresh glass of scotch. Preston took it and dismissed him with a wave of his hand.

"How's Georgia," Preston asked, patting his thin hair into place.

"She's well. How's Ashley?"

Preston sipped his scotch. "Ashley was the last one. It's Denise now."

Crawford blushed. "I'm sorry. I guess it's been a long time."

Preston clinked the ice against his glass. "Did you hear about the budget cuts at City Hospital, Ben? They're dismantling the pediatric ICU, it isn't cost-effective. For God's sake, this is the pediatric ICU we're talking about! The same ICU that saved your grandson's life."

Crawford frowned. "I'm aware of that."

"Then you know where I'm coming from. Medicine is dying around us. We have no choice. We have to fight this."

"I don't know," Crawford said.

"Look, Ben, I know you're looking forward to retirement. I'd retire too if I didn't have so damn much alimony to fork out."

Crawford shook his head. "I'm getting too old for all the politics, William."

"That's bullshit!"

The force of Preston's outburst startled Crawford. He glanced over his shoulder. The endocrinologists, broken from their conversation, were staring at him. Crawford nodded politely then turned back towards Preston.

"For God's sakes, keep your voice down."

"I don't care if they hear me. I want the whole damn Medical Center to hear this."

"I told you. I'm too old for this now."

"You're no older than I am. You're just feeling old."

"No, William. I am old."

Preston took a sip of scotch. "A fight like this will rejuvenate you, Ben. This is exactly what you need. It'll make you feel young again. Like when we were kids. You remember that, don't you? When we were young medical students and thought we could change the world?"

Crawford folded his hands before his face and took in his oldest and dearest friend. Yes, he remembered those days, back at Harvard with William, in the heyday of medicine, learning the fundamentals of diagnosis from the grandfathers of Hematology, Pulmonology and Critical Care. Medicine was an honorable profession then, an art, with deep reverence to the volumes of academic knowledge devoted to understanding the human body.

"Why me, William? Surely you can handle this."

"I'll show you why." Preston took a careful glance over his shoulders, then reached into his briefcase and pulled out a stack of papers.

Preston lowered his voice to a whisper. "This is just the beginning, Ben. Take a look at this."

Crawford took the papers. The first one: "Computer Chip Implantation for Augmentation of Visual Response in Patients with Degenerative Retinal Disease." The rest were similar.

Crawford couldn't believe what he was seeing. "These are unpublished research papers from labs all over the world. Where did you get these?"

Preston's eyes darkened. "That's not important. Our platform has been clear since the inception of PSCM; we can't afford the uncontrolled growth of medical biotech. The system is collapsing under the costs. We need to take a stand."

Crawford shuddered under the intensity of Preston's glare. He gazed down at the next paper, "Artificial Renal Function Simulation in Primates Using Computerized High-Perfusion Filters." He wiped his mouth then took a sip of scotch which burned all the way down his throat.

Preston snatched the papers from Crawford's hand and stuffed them into his briefcase. He closed the lid and slapped the metallic locks into place.

"Join us, Ben. Abrahms' project is on Grand Rounds tomorrow."

Crawford shifted uncomfortably in his chair. "Maybe his project has merit. Are you sure you're not just worried about your own department? "

"Of course I am, I'd be a fool not to. But that isn't the point. You know where this can lead. My God, just look at the hemodialysis fiasco!"

Crawford winced. He knew all too well the ethical crisis that consumed the nation with the advent of hemodialysis. Suddenly there was treatment to save the lives of millions of Americans dying from kidney disease. But there was one problem; there weren't enough dialysis units for everyone. Those who received dialysis lived, those who didn't died. In an effort to choose applicants in a morally defensible way, states established selection committees whose job it was to weed through the thousands of applicants and decide who would get dialysis and who wouldn't.

Preston sneered. "You don't want a return to the God Committees, do you?"

Crawford's eyes narrowed. "You know that I don't."

"Then something's got to be done." Preston slammed his glass down on the table. "Remember what happened when the media got their fangs into that one?"

Crawford rested his chin on his hand. When the press published news of the God Committees, the American public flew into an outrage. They refused to accept the concept of rationing health care. Finally, Congress bowed to overwhelming pressure and voted to provide full payment for the treatment of any person suffering from renal disease. Within just a few years, the hemodialysis budget ballooned to greater than $2 billion a year.

"We've got to stop this!" Preston was saying. "It's exactly what you've spent the last thirty years of your career fighting against."

Crawford took a measured sip of scotch. "Maybe it's time for someone else to take up the fight."

Preston huffed. He leaned forward, mere inches from Crawford's face, his breath sour with the smell of scotch. "There's something else you need to know."

Crawford pulled back, creating space between them. He gauged the look of intent in his friend's eyes. "Yes?"

"Senator McIntyre has lent his name to our cause."

Crawford tensed. "Senator McInytre? *The* Senator McInytre?"

"He's campaigning on a medical reform platform. He feels strongly that this case needs to be made an example of hyper-technology gone out of control."

Crawford was suddenly very uneasy. "Why this project?"

"Because health care is bankrupting the country, and it's the continual reach for more advanced technology that's driving the stake through its heart. Damn it, Ben, you know the numbers. We can't go on like this."

"I know that," Crawford said, "but why now? Why this project?"

"Who the hell cares why? He's dominating the election, and he's on our side. Next month he'll be the President. With power like that behind us we can't lose."

Crawford shook his head. "Don't ask me to do this, William. Not now."

Preston's gaze deepened. "I am asking. And so is the Senator."

Crawford felt his uneasiness growing. He didn't want any part of this conversation. He rose from the chair. Bookshelves, heavy with leather-bound medical tomes, filled the wall before him. Scanning the titles on the well-worn spines, Crawford identified the classics: *Harrison's Principles of Internal Medicine,* Stanbury's *Metabolic Basis of Inherited Disease.* Finally, his eyes came across his own book, the one he'd written with Preston when they were young professors at Northwestern: *The Essentials of Physical Diagnosis of the Heart.* He reached out, his fingers caressing the cracked leather spine. In its day that book had really mattered, teaching thousands of young doctors how to touch a patient and diagnose his failing heart.

Overhead, the hospital operator paged Preston to the Operating Room.

Preston scowled. "They're calling me, Ben. I need an answer. Do I have your support?"

Crawford lowered his eyes, his hand lingering on the spine of his beloved text. He and Georgia had just completed their purchase of the twenty acres of riverfront property in Montana; a patch of land where the sky glowed blue mid-morning and rainbow trout snapped all day long. He'd even picked up an extra fly-rod should his grandchildren take up the sport. There was no part of him that wanted to take on the cauldron of politics that faced him.

And the Senator getting involved? Why would the presidential frontrunner become enmeshed in a resident's research project? It didn't make sense. A knot formed in Crawford's gut. Deep down, he knew there was more to William's story than he was saying. Something dark lurking beneath the surface.

But then an image of his grandchildren came and he wondered what future awaited them. A future where the medical needs of the nation bankrupted the country? Where health care rationing and God Committees reigned as a constant reminder of PSCM's failure?

"Do we have your support?" Preston asked sharply.

Finally, Crawford sighed. He crossed the library and collapsed into his leather chair.

"Yes," he whispered.

CHAPTER 5

Rising from the top of Parnassus Hill, the San Francisco University Medical Center presided over the City like a monarch over its domain. The complex—a maze of concrete clinics, hospitals, and laboratories—wasn't what Taylor would call an architectural marvel, but it didn't need to be. The Medical Center's reputation was based on excellence in medicine, not architecture. SFU was the recognized leader of the progressive West Coast philosophy of medicine, a leader in innovative medical science, a world-renowned institute for scientific discovery. It was a place where a man with a dream and enough energy could create anything.

Taylor parked his battered 1969 MGB roadster in Student Lot C and headed towards his lab, hidden in the basement of Anderson Hall, one of the many anonymous concrete structures on campus. He entered through the double glass doors, nodding to the guard at the entrance.

The guard, Lawrence, a bald, stocky black man, lit up when he saw him.

"Hey, hey. The T.V. boy!"

Taylor blushed. "You saw that?"

"You were great."

"Thanks."

"What're you doing back here?" the guard asked. "Don't you ever go home and sleep?"

"Science waits for no one," Taylor shrugged. "Is Malcomb in?"

"Don't you mean, did he ever leave yesterday?"

Taylor smiled, knowing his research partner's bizarre work habits. It wasn't unusual for him to spend two, sometimes even three days straight locked away in the lab.

"Did Malcomb leave yesterday?" Taylor asked.

"Don't you mean, did he ever leave the day before?"

Taylor nodded, getting the message, and headed down the central stairwell to the depths of the basement. At the bottom, he turned right and walked down the dark corridor, lined on both sides by rusty metal filing cabinets that housed generations of experimental data and records.

He turned right again down the back hallway, which looked like a construction afterthought. Bare lead pipes and aluminum ventilation ducts streaked across the unfinished ceiling. Puddles of water splashed beneath his feet, collecting from the thousands of leaky plumbing connections.

No other rooms branched off this hallway—further convincing Taylor that it was a contractor's error—just the one small lab at the end, lost amidst the water heaters and the boiler room.

On the door, written in faded and chipped red paint, were the words

VISUAL COMPUTER ENHANCEMENT LABORATORY

Malcomb waited inside.

*****

The small, windowless lab was a disaster. Shelves lined the walls, stuffed to overflowing with printers, hard drives and CPU units in various states of disrepair. Angioplasty catheters and fiberoptic scopes jutted out at impossible angles, seeming to defy gravity; each piece of equipment lost amongst the incredible tangled web of wires dangling down to the concrete floor. The smell of ozone and mildew draped the air.

To the right, a battered green metal desk was propped against the wall, littered with stacks of *Annals of Artificial Intelligence* journals and a slew of discarded Nestle Crunch chocolate wrappers. Above the desk, schematic drawings and mathematical equations splashed across the wall like a river of technical graffiti, scribbled directly onto the concrete blocks in flaming red Crayola.

Standing on the desk, writing frantically on the wall, was Malcomb.

"We really should invest in a chalk board someday," he said without turning.

"What? And cover up that masterpiece?" Taylor quipped. "Red Crayola, the preferred medium of crazed geniuses everywhere."

"Wait until you see the coronary blood flow schematic," Malcomb said. "I used chartreuse."

Taylor chuckled. Malcomb Bernard was indeed a genius. Mislabeled as learning impaired because he was dyslexic, he taught himself mathematic theory and quantum physics by the age of ten then earned a B.S. degree from M.I.T. and a doctorate from Cal Tech by the age of 16. Concentrating on three-dimensional programming and applied Artificial Intelligence, he was set to make a huge splash in the Academic world, but his incapacitating fear of public speaking halted those dreams. Unable to present his research or give lectures, Malcomb hid away in the basement laboratory, his self-imposed exile leaving him on the fringe of mainstream academics.

Taylor walked deeper into the office and studied the crayon scribblings that unraveled like a holy scripture across the wall. Malcomb had ripped each and every page out of his computer science textbooks and pasted the sheets together like a mosaic along the edges of the wall, producing a tattered frame for his creation. To Malcomb, computers were a religion and this wall was his shrine.

Taylor brushed aside a pile of Nestle Crunch wrappers, grabbed a chair and pulled it over.

"White pawn movement from E-2 to E-4," he said.

Malcomb glared down at him. "We don't have time for that right now, Taylor. There's work to do."

"White pawn movement from E-2 to E-4," Taylor repeated.

Malcomb lowered his red Crayola and frowned. "You're trying to pull Legal's mate on me again, aren't you? I can't believe I fell victim to it last time."

Taylor smiled. He and Malcomb had engaged in a continuous battle of mental chess games since they first partnered on their research three years ago. With the long hours spent together, cramped in the musty laboratory, besieged by grant request deadlines and inter-departmental politics, the chess matches were the only thing that eased the tension that swelled between them. Quick and brutal, the matches had only one rule: players could use no written props to remind them of the moves or the position of the pieces.

"It gets you every time," Taylor said.

Malcomb closed his eyes for a moment, making phantom hand movements across a mental chessboard. "Black pawn moves from E-7 to E-5."

"A power move if I ever saw one."

"It's enough to keep you at bay for now. In case you hadn't noticed, we've got a disaster on our hands."

Taylor propped his feet up. "You have no idea."

Malcomb looked down from his position on the desk. "Me first. We need to postpone Rounds next month. I need more time. At least another month. Maybe two."

"I got news for you. Rounds isn't next month anymore."

"Great!" Malcomb beamed. "When? Two months from now, three? That should be—"

Taylor cut him off. "Tomorrow."

Malcomb stopped; his words stuck in this throat. He gazed at Taylor, not comprehending. "Tomorrow? What tomorrow?"

Taylor steadied himself for the onslaught. "Tomorrow the day after today."

Malcomb's eyes gaped. "Good God, man! Are you serious?

Taylor held his hands up. "I don't make the rules."

"There's no way we'll be ready!" Malcomb threw his arms in the air in a frenzy. He paced a tight circle on his desktop, kicking up a shower of Nestle chocolate wrappers. "I've been working nonstop on this, Taylor. Nonstop. Day and night. I haven't been home in over a week. I smell so bad my cat won't even go near me. The mildew is so bad down here my sinuses may never recover. I'm a walking poster boy for nasal spray, and you tell me now it's tomorrow?"

Taylor looked at Malcomb, his springy mat of black hair bounding in all directions, his brown eyes and boyish face hidden behind thick black-framed glasses, his wire-thin body covered by an oversized cardigan sweater, mismatched in color with his brown corduroy pants. He looked like a lost pariah, standing on the desk, cradling his red crayon in his hand like it was his sole possession.

"I've mortgaged my entire shot at tenure for this," Malcomb said. "If you get ambushed at Rounds, my career is over."

"You and me, both. I'd postpone it if I could—"

"A videogram from IMVRA came this afternoon," Malcomb cut him off. "They're webcasting Grand Rounds live over the IMVRA Ethernet."

Taylor rubbed his forehead. "You're kidding me?"

"That's what I'm saying. We're walking into a minefield. The IMVRA Chairman and teams from Europe and Japan are covering this. Their tech crew is posting Rounds real-time on the Computer Assisted Surgery website. We're revolutionizing medicine, Taylor. The whole world will be watching!"

Taylor winced. IMVRA, the International Medical Virtual Reality Academy, was the leading organization for scientific investigation in medical virtual reality. Based in Stockholm, the IMVRA consisted of scientists and doctors from around the world with one simple platform: with computers and robotics, the dream of operating on previously unreachable parts of the human body was now a reality. And Taylor was about to prove it possible.

IMVRA's presence at Rounds just upped the ante. CNN and the networks were already scheduled to cover Rounds and now IMVRA.

How much pressure can they pile onto this one meeting?

Taylor refocused. "Where do we stand with the robotics?"

"I spoke with Yang today," Malcomb said. "The laser micro-robotics are set; she just needs to check the logic circuits."

"She'll be ready in time?"

Malcomb climbed down from the desk. He pulled a Nestle Crunch bar from his stash in the drawer and ripped it open, letting the wrapper drop to the growing pile on the floor.

He took a bite, chewing in rabbit-like nibbles. "I believe so, but you can never tell with her. She's a difficult woman to talk to."

Taylor gave a half smile. He'd heard Malcomb's complaints about Helen Yang—the biomechanical engineer and third member of the team—before, every day for the last year. "I think you like her."

Malcomb's eyes widened. "Just as I like the pox! She's a detestable woman. A sarcastic, razor-tongued Beelzebub."

"Beelzebub?"

"You know what I mean. I only tolerate working with her because she happens to be a brilliant biomechanical engineer." Malcomb spun around and faced his computer.

"And the fact that she's very cute never enters your consciousness?"

Malcomb began typing on his keyboard. "I'm ignoring you, Taylor."

Taylor suppressed a laugh, leaned forward and studied the screen.

```
/data system
/sys
/virtual heart project
/vr program
/enter code-print-eco
/run
```

Data streamed across the computer screen, three symmetric rows of numbers, scrolling too fast for the human eye to follow.

"Jesus, that's fast."

"Two billion floating-point operations per second," Malcomb said.

"A gigaflop?"

"Faster than that."

"Has the latest AI programming been installed?"

Malcomb nodded. "Yes, came in from CyberTech Systems this morning."

"So, then what's the problem?"

"I'm having trouble maintaining our response speed."

Taylor winced. "In English?"

"In order to provide complete sensory immersion for your surgery in the virtual program, I've set a rendering speed of 100 frames per second."

"Is that fast enough?"

"Should be. As a comparison, television only updates 30 frames a second."

Taylor nodded, satisfied. "Then what's the problem?"

Malcomb began entering data. "Our virtual program is constructed from three-dimensional scans of the patient's heart and coronary arteries. All views and positions inside the artery are referenced and stored. When you move inside the virtual artery, the computer uses the CTS AI predictive algorithm to continuously calculate your exact position and updates your view with real-time images from the artery. This requires major computing power and speed."

Taylor knew where Malcomb was going. "There can't be any compromise. I need a seamlessly smooth view of the artery."

"Understood. My computer-geekoid reputation is riding on this. The problem is I can't break the 100-millisecond barrier."

"Meaning what?"

"Meaning that less than every 100 milliseconds, the image will update. No matter where you turn your head, your view inside the artery will be updated instantly. To each one of your senses, it will be as if you are actually standing inside a blood vessel."

Taylor paused and took in Malcomb's words. He could already imagine what it would be like; standing inside the virtual world of a living patient's heart, seeing it from the inside. Feeling the plasma flowing around him. Hearing the heart valves snapping open and closed in perfectly timed rhythm.

"What about surgical manipulations?"

"No problem there. I've programmed the data input to be constantly updated by real-time echo-T ultrasounds and the laser's micro-camera. If Yang does her job, the micro-laser will follow your movements precisely to the plaque in your patient's artery and you can disintegrate it. Right before your eyes. You'll see it all."

"If the sensory lag is even a tenth of a second when I'm operating, I could burn right through the artery. This new vision of ours could be deadly."

"That's what I'm saying. I need more time."

"We've got sixteen hours before they shut us down and kiss your tenure goodbye."

Malcomb shook his head, shoving the remaining chocolate in his mouth. He wiped his hands on his brown corduroys. "I hate this. I really hate this."

"I'll take that as a yes?"

"What if my sinuses explode?"

"I'll name a decongestant after you."

Malcomb watched the numbers flash across the screen. He reached into the drawer and pulled out another Nestle Crunch bar, holding it up for Taylor to see. "This is my ninth of the day."

Taylor smiled thinly. "Death by chocolate?"

"It may be preferable to what awaits us tomorrow." Malcomb unwrapped the end of the chocolate, studied it for a long moment then looked at Taylor. "I only pray you can pull this off."

Taylor noted the trepidation in Malcomb's eyes. In truth, he felt it too. Everything they'd worked for over the last three years was boiling down to this. This one presentation. This one moment.

Tomorrow.

Friday the 13th.

Taylor took a deep breath. "Pray harder," he whispered.

CHAPTER 6

Sherilyn Abrahms closed the folder of advertising proofs, pushed the papers across her desk and exhaled a sigh of relief. Three months after first visualizing the concept for her new venture—CyberEscape, The Travel eMagazine for the Wired Generation—she could feel it all coming together. Her small, but efficient sales staff had secured advertising contracts with some of the biggest names in Silicon Valley—Apple, Meta, Oracle, and Google—while her marketing staff had blanketed TikTok and Instagram with Cyberscapes, advertising the many tours and dream vacations her company was promoting, each trip carefully designed to be perfectly "grammable" with ideal picture locations.

Sherilyn allowed herself a smile. After years of battling for independence from the domination of her father, the Senator, the first hint of her own success was in sight.

She turned from her desk and looked out from the fifth floor of her Embarcadero Plaza office. Lights from the City's skyscrapers reflected off the Bay like a billion stars glowing underwater. While some of her staff were hybrid, combining working from home with time in the office, Sherilyn preferred having a true work location and address. It made her feel more professional. Currently, she only commanded 800 square feet of office space, hardly an empire, but still, she felt like the queen of Camelot.

Sherilyn stepped away from the window, catching a glance of her reflection against the blackened night sky. Her auburn hair, neatly pulled back into a professional but playful ponytail, stood out against her tailored Akris cashmere suit. Inwardly, Sherilyn beamed. She had always prided herself on her former Miss Teen-Georgia looks, and her daily three-mile jog insured that she stayed fit, but looking at herself at that moment, she saw something new. Something even more beautiful. The beaming satisfaction of a young professional making it out on her own.

The knock on the door caught her attention. Turning, she saw Courtney, her new writer, waiting for her. Twenty-three years old, with golden blond hair and a face that hadn't aged since high school, Courtney came highly recommended from the journalism department at UC Berkeley.

"Excuse me," Courtney said shyly, "I don't mean to interrupt."

"Not at all," Sherilyn said, pulling her attention away from the window.

Courtney stammered. "I was wondering if, I mean, since you don't have an assignment for me, and there isn't anything for me to do right now, I was wondering if —"

Sherilyn smiled at the hesitancy in her new employee. "Courtney, are you asking if you can leave early tonight?"

"Well, I hate to ask, this being my first day on the job, and I know you were planning on staying until eight—"

Sherilyn held up her hands. "It's okay. Go home. Get your energy ready for tomorrow when we take on the Microsoft travel assignment."

"Great!" Courtney's face lit up. "It's just that my fiancé travels for work and he's home tonight, and on his free nights he likes to make me dinner and I really didn't want to be late."

Sherilyn smiled, enchanted by Courtney's school-girl-in-love aura. She remembered the days when her marriage was young and she couldn't wait to get home just to be with her husband. She remembered the heat that filled her simply by thinking of Taylor. Unfortunately, with Taylor being pulled in so many directions with the demands of research and residency, she couldn't remember the last time they'd shared that passion. If he wasn't in the lab, he was in the ER, or at a news conference or research meeting, and the rare times he actually made it home, he was so exhausted he could barely stay awake. She wondered when would they find the time for each other again? And a family. When would they find the time for that? Children with dark, sleepy eyes like Taylor's.

A pang of jealousy surged through her. "Go ahead home," Sherilyn said. "Have a great night."

"Thanks. But what about you? Didn't I hear you say your husband was off from the ER? I bet you want to celebrate his newsconference, don't you?"

Sherilyn nodded. Taylor was indeed off tonight. And the truth was—she was eager to see him. She'd watched his newsconference that morning with the entire CyberEscape staff cheering him on. Seeing his piercing brown eyes and childish smile on TV, the CNN banner blazing across the bottom of the screen, an enormous swell of pride filled her.

She gave Courtney a mischievous grin. "Maybe a bottle of champagne is in order."

Courtney's eyes lit up. "And a fire in the fireplace?"

"I could pick up some take-out Italian," Sherilyn said, her enthusiasm growing.

"And some strawberries, dipped in chocolate."

Sherilyn nodded, feeling like a school girl in love herself. She licked her lips. "What say we both go home early tonight?"

Courtney raised an eyebrow. "I think that's a great idea."

*****

Taylor arrived home just after seven-thirty.

He squeezed the battered roadster into a space in front of the Pacific Heights Queen Anne that had long ago been converted into four floors of apartments. The area, lined with renovated Victorians and city parks, was one of the higher rent districts in San Francisco, a yuppie haven. Taylor's meager residency checks barely covered the monthly bills. He would have preferred to live somewhere more reasonable, like the Sunset or Cow Hollow, but the small two-bedroom unit was the only one Sherilyn wanted. He knew that it was a stretch for her to be living in any apartment no matter what size, instead of her father's seven-thousand square foot mansion in Atlanta, and the last thing Taylor wanted was to get into another argument with the Senator accusing Taylor of not properly taking care of his little girl. So, each month he milked as much as he could out of his salary and dreamt of the day when a full professorship meant more prestige and status and more zeroes after the number on the deposit slip.

Grabbing his briefcase, he climbed the stairs to the fourth floor. Closing the door behind him, he kicked off his shoes and threw them into the corner.

The small two-bedroom apartment was furnished with Sherilyn's traditional country belongings and a few of Taylor's medical school hand-me-downs. The second bedroom—a room Taylor rarely ventured into—stored his medical school papers, books and the few childhood mementos he cared to own. He'd been promising Sherilyn for months that he'd finally clean out the closets and organize the room but somehow, he never found the time.

Taylor dropped his briefcase on the kitchen table. The blinking light on the answering machine was flashing, but he didn't care. After the press conference, the crisis in the ER, and

Grand Rounds pending tomorrow, there was only one thing on his mind.

Sleep.

Get to bed and go to sleep, preferably in that order.

*****

Sherilyn arrived home just before eight and found Taylor sound asleep, sprawled face down on the Persian rug on the floor of the bedroom. He was fully dressed except for the one sock that he'd managed to remove before he collapsed into slumber. He still held that sock tightly in his hand.

Sherilyn's heart sank. She found him like this often; passed out on the floor of the bedroom, or the kitchen, or the bathroom, once even on the front doorstep. He worked himself to the point of exhaustion then staggered home where sleep consumed him for a day at a time.

Deep in her heart, she knew Taylor had too much to prove to slow down. He had to prove to his faculty that he could handle the double workload of research and residency; he had to prove to her father, the Senator, that he was good enough to be his daughter's husband, and he had to prove to himself that a poor kid, with no family, could come from out of nowhere and change the way that everything was done.

She lowered her bag of take-out Italian, and crossed the wooden floor. Kneeling beside him, she studied his face. As always, he wore a five o'clock shadow that was headed well past six. His wavy brown hair was too long and desperately in need of a trim, but she knew Taylor would never take the time for that. She brushed the curls from his forehead.

He moaned and began to stir.

"Hey, sleepy," she said.

"Where am I?" He glanced around the room, confused, then smiled when he realized he'd been sleeping on the floor. "Hey, I almost made it to the bed this time."

As always, his boyish smile melted her. "And you almost managed to get both socks off too."

He looked at the sock clutched in his fist. "Guess I wasn't as tired as I thought. Maybe one day I'll actually get undressed."

"I doubt it," she said. "Now get off the floor. Let's get you to bed."

Taylor stumbled to his feet, holding Sherilyn's hand for support, too tired to walk on his own. He craned his neck, looking towards the kitchen. "What's that smell?" he asked, sniffing the air. "Is that garlic?"

The emptiness crawled back inside her.

"No," she said. "It's nothing."

CHAPTER 7

The grey Chrysler van, *Professional Perfect Plumbing* stenciled on the side, sat parked on the corner of Bush Street, one block east of Taylor's apartment. In the back of the van, Edgar Ross finished loading the digital photos onto his laptop. His lithe, muscular body, toned from the ritualistic two-hour daily workout, felt cramped. He stretched his arms and rubbed his shaved bald head while he waited for the photos to appear on the screen.

Encountering the rough feel of stubble beneath his fingers, Ross cursed. He hated when his scalp wasn't perfectly smooth. The growing stubble was a sign of his lack of discipline and attention to detail and he made a mental note to rectify that matter at the earliest opportunity.

The target reconnaissance of the Abrahms' apartment, or target recce as he'd been trained to call it, had gone well. Using an Olympus C-8080 camera with 10x optical zoom, he'd covered the front, back and both sides of the building, taking notes of all entry and exit points. He targeted the location of all external services, telephone, electric and cable. A quick examination revealed that the building electrical had been updated with high capacitance breakers. Ross smiled, knowing that would make his job easier.

With the photos spread out on the screen, Ross typed a note identifying the individual rooms inside the fourth-floor apartment, noting the size of the windows to locate the bedroom and the ventilation duct indicating the kitchen. He brought up photographs of the MG parked across the street and the grey Honda Accord that had parked behind it 45 minutes later, labeling them T-1 and T-3.

Ross lit an unfiltered Camel, his one vice, and inhaled deeply. Despite more than twenty years with the Agency and five years providing contract services, static surveillance was still the least favorite aspect of his chosen career. He preferred to be on the hunt. But he was well aware that any successful op started with diligent recce and data collection. Looking at the state-of-the-art surveillance and communication technology that filled the van—digital front and rear video camera, GPS/GSM target tracking, TACCS system and MAV aerial surveillance—Ross knew nothing would be overlooked.

As with all ops, Ross needed to understand his target's psychology to help him assess habits and patterns, routines that might tip him off on how to best complete his assignment. Data on Abrahms wasn't hard to find and filled an entire dossier. Ross flipped through the pages. Taylor's mother died of heart disease when Abrahms was eight, after which he and his younger brother spent time in and out of foster care while their father descended into a fugue of alcohol. Abrahms had been estranged from his father for the last ten years, ever since the day of his brother's suicide. Abrahms himself wrote in his medical school admissions essay that the deaths of his mother and brother were the driving force behind his passion for medicine and research. His drive to create a technology that could have saved his mother's life.

Sounds fucking pathetic, Ross thought.

Shifting to wireless LAN, he tapped into one of the many unsecured wireless networks around him and downloaded the satellite aerial photograph of the building and printed it out. He pulled the cap off a yellow highlighter with his teeth, and marked all crossing streets in a four-block radius, indicating the most likely routes from the apartment building to City Hospital and the Medical Center.

Overall, Ross was pleased. The 100-year-old Queen Anne held no surprises. It was straight forward, just like the apartment of the CTS computer engineer, Robert Chan.

He took another deep drag on his Camel, tapping the ash into the ashtray. A flicker of ash broke off, landing on the grip of his H&K.

"Damn," he muttered, reflexively picking up a dry cloth, wiping the grip clean. Bringing the pistol close to his eye, he inspected the grip and blew on it, making certain it was spotless. Like everything in Ross's world, it had to be clean.

Ross holstered the gun in his shoulder harness, closed the laptop and climbed into the driver's seat. Target Recce One was an unqualified success. Starting the ignition, he pulled the plumbing van away from the curb and headed down Divisidero towards the Medical Center.

Anderson Hall was next.

CHAPTER 8

Friday, October 13th., 7:24 am

"What do you think they have planned for me?" Taylor asked.

Taylor stood with Dr. Lynette Jensen, Chair of the Cardiology Department, while she scrubbed her hands in the sink outside the Cardiac Cath Lab on the sixth floor of SF City Hospital. She was dressed in her usual lavender-colored scrubs, covered by a lead vest and skirt, her shoulder-length cinnamon hair tucked under a hair cover.

"They'll attack you from any side possible," Jensen said with a hint of a French-Canadian accent. She dropped the scrub pad into the sink and started her rinse. "First, they will start on the scientific facts. Yes? If Crawford doesn't have the firepower there, he'll move to the area of bioethics. That is where you are most vulnerable."

Taylor shrugged as he slipped on his heavy lead vest and skirt, designed to protect him from the high doses of x-ray radiation in the Cath Lab. Taylor glanced at the clock over the scrub sink. Rounds was due to start in exactly 4 hours and thirty-six minutes. D-Day. He wished he could be home preparing for his presentation, but he'd been scheduled to assist Dr. Jensen for months, and knew he couldn't cancel on such short notice. He thought back to previous Rounds he'd attended, trying to recall the attack strategies the faculty had used. He remembered when Case Stevens presented years' worth of prostate therapy data, only to have his entire database rejected when Crawford detected an error in his null hypothesis. His project canceled. Back to ground zero.

"Grand Rounds didn't always have this much control over a scientist's career."

"Times change," Jensen said, completing the final rinse of her hands. "As less money is available for research, Grand Rounds will take on an even more powerful role in how that money should be used. It's all politics."

Taylor knew she was right. Politics ruled the academic forum. Over the last week, Taylor watched allegiances rise and fall around him as departmental heads calculated which side of the biotech debate would be the winning side. Even traditional enemies, like the heads of Plastics and ENT, who battled for facial reconstructive patients, put their differences aside and formed an alliance. In this case, supporting Taylor.

"You are treading some dangerous waters here," Jensen said. "Enemies are made quickly once you enter the world of scientific research."

Not the words Taylor wanted to hear. He looked into the eyes of his teacher. "What do you think my chances are?"

Jensen pulled her hands from the infrared faucet, turning off the sink. "Will Dr. Browne be there to support you?"

"Should be."

"With him, you might be okay. He's the only one with enough clout to go against Crawford and Preston."

Taylor fastened the Velcro on the lead skirt around his waist. "I was hoping you'd be there."

Jensen smiled. "I will. I don't relish the thought of going against Preston, but your research is fascinating. Certainly, better than what we'll be doing here today. Anything I can do to help move it forward, will be my pleasure."

Taylor breathed a sigh of relief. The more allies he had behind him when he took the Grand Rounds podium, the better. He fastened the lead thyroid protector around his neck. Jensen turned and backed into the Cath lab door, opening it without using her freshly-cleaned hands. A nurse greeted her, handing her a sterile towel.

Dr. Jensen took the towel and started drying her hands. She approached the cath table. "Are we prepped?"

The cath nurse nodded, gowned and gloved Jensen, then stepped aside.

"Valium, 5 mg I.V. push," Dr. Jensen said.

The Cardiac Cath lab looked like a small operating room with a massive x-ray unit rising from the floor. Called the C-arm, because of its C-shaped configuration, the x-ray imager could rotate on any axis around the patient, providing an infinite number of views of the heart and arteries. Sending X-rays from the lower arm, below the patient's bed, the images were captured on the upper arm above the patient, where they were fed to the digital recording units. Vital sign monitors filled one wall, while two fluoroscopy screens rested on a suspended arm. The atmosphere was serious, but not tense.

Taylor had been observing Dr. Jensen perform angioplasties for the past six months, preparing himself for the use of his virtual angioplasty system. He pulled up a stool in his usual vantage point in the corner, near the bank of plastic storage cabinets, keeping notes on his laptop. This was to be his last observed angioplasty. After getting approval at Grand Rounds that afternoon, the next step would be to launch the VHP.

"Mr. Patterson," Dr. Jensen said, her voice reassuring. "We are about to begin. If you experience any pain, please let me know."

"Alright," the eighty-year-old veteran said. "You're the doc. I trust you."

Taylor noted a tremor in the man's voice. Dr. Jensen stepped aside to re-evaluate the patient's admission EKG and the older man looked over at Taylor.

"I know you, don't I?" Patterson asked, a flicker of recognition in his eyes. "You were my doc in the Emergency room when I had my chest pain."

Taylor remembered Patterson from an earlier triage. "That's right, Mr. Patterson. I'm going to watch your angioplasty today."

"Yeah. I remember you. My wife, she loved you. Thought you were the greatest. Listen, I want you to do me a favor, if you don't mind."

"What would you like?"

"The missus. We've been together for sixty years now. She's in the waiting area. Somebody's going to have to be there for her if I don't make it through this."

Taylor inched towards the patient. "You'll be fine, Mr. Patterson."

"I know, I know. But still, I worry about her. Promise me you'll make sure she's okay for me, will ya? I don't want her facing this alone. Promise me, Doc."

Taylor thought for a moment of how he'd feel if their positions were reversed and he was lying on the table worrying about Sherilyn.

"I promise," he said.

Jensen returned. She glanced at the nurse.

"Heparin's in?"

"I.V.'s running," the nurse said. "3,000 units."

"We'll use a 6-French sized cannula," Jensen said. She placed a blue sterile towel around Patterson's exposed right thigh. The groin area had been prepped with Betadine and now glowed a dark orange. Sterile drapes covered the rest of Patterson's body. The nurse moved the overhead light into position, focusing the beam onto Patterson's upper thigh.

Jensen raised a skin weal of lidocaine, then pulled the angiocath off the sterile tray and readied the needle above the patient's right femoral artery. With a smile that was visible even through her surgical mask, she turned to Taylor.

"Are you sure you don't want to do this one?" she asked.

Taylor returned her smile. "I'll just watch and learn from the best."

"If you say so. You've watched me do so many, I believe you could do one in your sleep by now. No? How many has it been? Forty? Fifty?"

"Sixty-two," Taylor said. Sixty-two angioplasties. PTCA's as they were officially called. Percutaneous transluminal coronary angioplasty. Although Jensen had been joking, Taylor knew that in one essence she was right. He probably could do them in his sleep by now. And that was exactly his plan. He wanted to be so familiar with the procedure that when he finally did his first cyber-angioplasty with the Virtual Heart Project, he'd have an entire data base of experience.

"You'll feel some pressure in the area of your right groin," Jensen said. She slid the needle of the angiocath into the patient's femoral artery. A flash of blood filled the syringe. Carefully, she pulled the needle out and slid the catheter into the artery, guiding it towards Patterson's heart. "Relax, Mr. Patterson," Jensen said. "I'm going to take a few pictures now."

She turned towards the tech, positioned inside the control room adjacent to the cath lab. Witnessing everything through the lead glass separating the rooms, the tech was responsible for capturing all images of the heart in the computer system.

"Fluoroscopy?" Jensen asked.

"Ready," the tech replied.

"Let's go." Jensen stepped on the fluoroscopy pedal.

Instantly, an x-ray image of the patient's chest and heart flashed on the screen mounted over the operating table. The nurse turned the joystick, the cath table moving into position to perfectly center the image. The C-arm rotated around the bed with an audible whir.

"There's the tip," Jensen said, spotting the end of the catheter inside the aorta. "Let's move it forward." Jensen threaded the catheter up the large blood vessel, watching the x-ray monitor. "Steady." Moving her right hand in a circular motion, she guided the tip to the opening of the coronary artery.

"Let's look at the arteries now," Jensen said. She pushed on the syringe attached to the end of the catheter. A radio-opaque fluid, seen on the x-ray as black against a grey background, rushed from the tip of the catheter and filled the arteries, which radiated out across the heart muscle like branches on a tree.

Jensen focused her gaze on the monitor. "There's our problem."

Taylor nodded, seeing that one of the coronary arteries was constricted where the cholesterol plaque had built up against the sides like a wad of grease plugging a drain. "Looks like an eighty percent obstruction of the Left Main. The widowmaker."

"Exactly," Jensen said. "We caught this one just in time." She turned her gaze towards her patient, still awake and lying perfectly still. "Those chest pains were a good warning, Mr. Patterson. We've found the blockage and we're ready to remove it."

"Okay, Doc," Patterson said.

"Are you comfortable?" Jensen asked.

"Just fine."

"Then here we go," Jensen said. She maneuvered a flexible guide wire through the catheter to the site of the plaque. Taylor admired the skill with which she passed the thin wire into the blood vessel. Years of training. Thousands of cases of experience. Using fluoroscopy, she checked her position to make certain the tip was perfectly aligned at the point of obstruction.

"Ready for the balloon."

The nurse handed her the balloon catheter. Using the wire to guide her, Jensen threaded the balloon catheter into position inside the artery, to the exact site of the obstruction. Confirming with a glance at the monitor, she spoke calmly and firmly. "Here we go people," she said. "Start inflation now."

The nurse depressed the plunger on a second syringe and a rush of saline filled the balloon, inflating it to therapeutic size. The LED display on the syringe, activated the instant the nurse touched the plunger, read out the pressure inside the balloon and the time since inflation began.

"Two atmospheres," the nurse read aloud. "Four. Six. Eight."

"Hold it there," Jensen ordered.

"Holding at eight atmospheres," the nurse said. "Ten seconds so far."

"We'll go a full minute," Jensen said.

With the balloon fully inflated, the expansion inside the artery crushed the plaque, cracking open the obstruction. Taylor knew this was the most delicate part of the procedure. With the balloon inflated, this was when damage to the blood vessel could occur. He took a deep breath.

"Thirty seconds," the nurse said.

No one spoke besides the nurse. Jensen folded her arms across her chest and waited. Her eyes fixed on the vital signs monitor, studying the readouts. Oxygen saturation was normal. EKG steady.

"Forty-five seconds."

Taylor glanced at the blood pressure. It was holding.

"Fifty-five seconds."

Almost there.

"One minute," the nurse said.

"Come on down," Jensen said, exhaling.

The balloon deflated and suddenly Patterson's eyes grew wide.

"Uh oh," the nurse's voice was rushed. "We've got a problem."

Jensen shot her a glance. "What is it?"

"PVC's." The nurse pointed at the premature contractions of the heart on the EKG. "And lots of them."

Jensen glared at the monitor, confirming what the nurse had reported. "He's getting ischemic. Reset the fluoroscopy."

"Doc, my chest," Patterson said. "It hurts."

"I know Mr. Patterson," Jensen said. "I'm going to try and stop it." She turned to the nurse. "Oxygen at 4 liters and start some nitro." She glanced at Taylor. "Monitor his EKG. I think a piece of plaque broke off and closed the vessel."

Taylor pushed aside his laptop and stepped towards the cath table.

Jensen grabbed the syringe on the end of the catheter. "Injecting."

The image of the blood vessels filled the screen. "Damn it. Abrupt closure of the Left Main." Jensen pointed to the screen where a piece of cholesterol had broken from the main plaque and moved farther down the artery, closing it off. Completely.

"My chest, Doc! Feels like something's crushing it."

"Hang in there, Mr. Patterson," Jensen said, twisting her wrist clockwise, trying to maneuver the guide wire through the blockage.

"He's PVC'ing again," Taylor noted the erratic beating of Patterson's heart.

Jensen's breath grew sharp. She glanced at the monitor. "Damn, he's elevating his ST. He's infarcting."

The EKG alarm blared through the cath lab. "The pain, Doc," Patterson gasped. "I can't breathe!"

Taylor shot Patterson a quick look. His face was pasty white, the color draining from his cheeks. Without blood to his heart muscle, he'd have a massive MI in a matter of minutes.

"Can you place a stent?" Taylor asked.

Jensen jerked her head no. "It's a complete closure. I can't get the wire into it."

"My chest!" Patterson gasped. "The pain!"

Another alarm blared in the room.

"BP's dropping!" the nurse yelled. "90 over 70"

Jensen flipped the guide wire over in her hands. Fine beads of sweat glistened her forehead. "I can't get past the blockage. I can't get in!"

"BP's 80 over 60!" the nurse yelled.

"Get me another wire!" Jensen ordered, ripping the old wire out of the catheter. Blood splattered onto the sterile drapes. "Hurry!"

The nurse sprinted to the cabinet and pulled out another wire, opening it and handing it to Jensen.

Jensen inserted the wire into the catheter, trying to maneuver it through the clot.

"Come on," Jensen said. "Come on!"

Taylor's eyes fixed on the monitor. "We got more PVC's, in triplets."

"I'm almost there, if I can only get through. If I can only..." her voice trailed.

Suddenly, Patterson convulsed on the table, his legs splaying.

"Jesus Christ!" Jensen swore. "Call CT STAT. We need immediate by-pass!"

The nurse sprinted to the phone. Taylor glared at the monitors.

"Hang in there, Mr. Patterson," Jensen was yelling, leaning over the table to start CPR. "We're going to do surgery. Everything will be alright, just hang in there."

Jensen flashed Taylor a look. "Hurry up and get your VHP working," her words coming out in a rush. "We need it!"

Patterson gasped. Jensen pounded on his chest.

Another alarm shrieked.

CHAPTER 9

"Our guest today is Presidential frontrunner, Republican Senator Randolph McIntyre," Linda Fontana, the peroxide-blonde host of the CNN Washington Insider, was saying. "He'll be with me in the studio to take your calls and discuss the upcoming election." She turned from the camera and faced McIntyre. "Senator, welcome."

McIntyre settled into the leather chair situated in the center of Studio A of the Washington D.C. CNN News facility. He flashed his pearly-white smile. Camera 2 zoomed in for a close-up. With a subtle movement, choreographed by his entourage of media consultants, McIntyre turned to his left, lowering his chin, presenting his preferred three quarters profile to the American people. His salt-and-pepper hair, slicked back from his forehead, revealed his still youthful, non-surgically enhanced hairline. Botox hid the wrinkles. For this broadcast, his wardrobe consultants selected a dark grey single-breasted, three-button Versace, offset with a cobalt blue shirt and tie combination. The look designed to be dynamic and powerful, youthful and sexy; perfect to capture the 25–44-year-old voter demographic.

"Thank you, Linda," McIntyre said, careful to never lose his smile. "It's a pleasure to be here."

Linda reacted to the Senator's charm with a spontaneous smile of her own. "It's our pleasure, Senator. I look forward to an interesting call-in session with you. With only twenty-six more days until the Presidential election, and your commanding lead over Congressman O'Neil in the polls, the American people are very interested to learn more about you and your policies."

"Of course," McIntyre nodded. He listened while Linda recited McIntyre's personal history and political career, reading from a statement methodically prepared by McIntyre's campaign advisor. The camera shifted its focus from the host to McIntyre. The Senator clasped his hands by his mouth, a pose designed to suggest deep reflection. Strength yet humility. A warm feeling swept through him. He was in his element.

"Senator, tonight's subject is health care. No other issue seems to better define your campaign."

The Senator straightened in his chair. "No other issue so characteristically defines my campaign, Linda, because no greater challenge faces this country. People are worried about the economy right now, but what they don't realize is that it's the enormous cost of health care that is bankrupting our nation. It's as simple as that."

Linda gave a pensive look. "Politicians have been arguing over this for years. The bottom line is we need health care, and like any consumer good, it costs money."

"Health care is a necessity," the Senator agreed, "and it is expected to cost money. But, Linda, aren't you used to getting what you pay for?" He smiled, noting her Ferragamo shoes and Gucci skirt. "You look like a savvy shopper. When you pay for a designer purse, would you accept a $10 imitation? If you pay for a Rolls Royce, would you accept a used Yugo?"

Linda shook her head. "Of course not."

"But as a nation we do accept it with health care."

Linda's eyes narrowed. "But Senator, the United States has the best health care in the world. We have the best hospitals, best-trained doctors, best technology. How can you equate that with a bargain basement Eastern-bloc automobile?"

The Senator smiled inwardly. Either by design or chance, Linda was feeding him the exact lines he wanted. He squared his shoulders. "Do you know how much we spend on health care each year?"

"The last report placed it around $4 trillion."

"$4.3 trillion," the Senator corrected. "Over $4 trillion dollars each year. That's more than 17 percent of the GNP. The highest percentage in the world. No other country even approaches that. A close ally like England, only spends about 10 percent of its GNP on health care. We're nearly twice that."

Linda frowned. "But Senator, the British have a socialized medicine program that's fraught with problems."

"Our system is fraught with problems," the Senator interjected. "According to the World Health Organization, America places 37th in the world in performance of our health care."

Linda looked incredulous. "Did you say 37th?"

The Senator nodded, relishing Linda's reaction. "37th, we ranked behind the superpower nations of Malta, Andorra and Oman."

Linda shook her head, disbelieving. "But the average American believes that we have the best health care in the world."

"Of course, they do. Americans are used to thinking we have the best of everything. We're the world's superpower; the home of freedom and democracy. We're accustomed to believing that we take care of our citizens —but the numbers don't lie. Americans are spending Rolls Royce dollars to receive Yugo quality health care. Italy spends less than half of what we spend per capita, yet their healthcare was ranked number 2 in the world. England was 18th. France was even higher."

He turned from Linda and gazed directly into the camera.

"Once I'm President, my primary focus will be to correct this catastrophe. And that's what it is, a catastrophic waste of resource. Make no mistake; this is one of the gravest issues facing our nation today."

McIntyre paused to allow the gravity of his last statement to linger. He glanced towards the production booth at the front of the studio. Through the glass, Jennifer and Roderick looked on, beaming smiles branded on their faces. He knew what they were thinking. Game over! He'd hit this one clear out of the ballpark.

"The phones are lighting up," Linda was saying. "We'll take our first caller now. Chester from Utah, you're on with Senator McIntyre!"

"Did you say $4 trillion? Not billion, but trillion?" the male voice asked.

"That's right," the Senator said, his confidence beaming. "Trillion dollars, with a "T." With terrorists plotting to destroy every aspect of our way of life, we're spending five times our defense budget on healthcare."

"I'm 75," the crackling female voice from Arkansas came through the speaker, "and I got Medicare, but I can barely keep up with my co-pays. Now how am I supposed to eat when all my money's going to my drugs and my doctors?"

"I understand your problem." The Senator nodded. "You and millions of Americans. It's an embarrassment for our Nation. When you elect me President, this will be my first priority. With my plan for a single-payer system, our high costs of health care can be converted from a burden to an opportunity. By squeezing the fat out of the system, eliminating bureaucracy, contracting with drug companies, and putting a moratorium on hyper-biotechnology that our country simply can't afford, we can reduce the costs of our Nation's healthcare by half. Think what that will do for the economy."

With that statement, the phone lines at CNN lit up like a sky on the fourth of July.

The Senator looked into the camera and beamed. With each passing second, he could feel his power rising. He could feel the people hanging onto his words, clinging to his strength. It was the world's most powerful aphrodisiac. Their weakness fueled his passion. He could feel it all coming together.

Then in an instant, it all came crashing down.

"I heard you mention cutting back on hyper-tech to reduce costs," the male caller from Washington D.C. was saying. "But I read in the Post about a research project with some guy trying to perform surgery in virtual reality. It's all over the news."

The senator stiffened in his chair.

"Are you familiar with that research?" the caller continued.

The Senator glanced at Roderick in the production booth who shook his head. The Senator moistened his lips, strategizing how he'd handle this. He wasn't prepared to address the Abrahms project. Not yet. Plans had just been set in motion that would put a final end to this complication, but they needed more time. He had to tread carefully. If this was a plant from his opponent to bring out his family ties to that project, it would devastate the momentum he'd gained that day.

"I read the article," he said in a measured tone.

"Robots operating on people? This sort of thing must cost a fortune. Isn't this the exact type of hyper-biotech research you're trying to stop?"

A dangerous question. A trap, leading him to make a statement from which he couldn't escape? How much did the caller know? Had he made the connection to Abrahms? "It is," McIntyre said cautiously. "It may sound futuristic and advanced, but the simple truth is that the country cannot afford high-tech procedures that aren't cost-effective for the American people."

"Why are we spending money on this when millions don't have insurance?"

Another trap? Trying to set me up for the kill?

"My point exactly," the Senator said.

"Well, I couldn't agree more," came the caller. "I can't afford to pay my insurance premium and some yahoo in California is creating a medical video game!"

The Senator exhaled through pursed lips. He glanced to the production booth where Roderick's frown returned to a hearty smile.

His confidence returning, the Senator seized the opportunity. "This isn't a trivial matter. What you describe is indicative of the runaway spending that has destroyed our health care system. My opponent has no position on hyper-biotech, but I do. That Virtual Heart Project is an example of everything that's wrong with our medical system, investing our dwindling resources into a crackpot theory. And even if it works, it will cost the system much more than what we have today and equitable delivery will be a nightmare. As a nation, we can't afford this, not when our health care budget already exceeds the total we spend to educate our nation's children."

Steadying himself, the Senator gave a steely glare into the camera. He was keenly aware that Grand Rounds at SFU was about to get underway. He wished he could be there to see it for himself. A silent witness. To watch this problem, like so much detritus, get swept to the side of the road. The path cleared to the White House.

He held out a measured index finger and leaned in for the kill.

"Mark my words, caller" he said. "That project in California will never see the light of day."

CHAPTER 10

Taylor steadied himself, as he stood behind the podium of the Beckett Hall amphitheater on the Medical Center campus looking out over the packed rows of seats.

Grand Rounds, where unusual cases were presented and ground-breaking research reviewed, was a tradition at SFU. Typically, Rounds were scheduled to start at eight each Friday morning, but with the media attention focused on this particular session, the conference was pushed back to noon to allow for the camera crews to set up. All the major news networks were there; their lights and cameras aimed at the stage. IMVRA technicians focused their digital video feeds from the second landing.

"Ready camera two," Taylor heard a cameraman say to his left.

"Sound technician to the podium," he heard to his right.

Watching the rows of steeply banked seats fill with doctors, administrators and reporters, Taylor swallowed hard, his mouth growing drier by the second. Four hours had passed since the emergency in the Cardiac Cath Lab. After racing with Dr Jensen to Mr. Patterson's STAT cardiac bypass surgery, he'd barely had time to change from his scrubs before Rounds. His fingers still trembled from the adrenaline, his body emotionally and physically drained, but he had no choice but to compose himself and focus. Patterson was in the hands of CT surgeons now, and Taylor and the VHP had to get passed this Rounds.

"One minute," the sound technician said. He adjusted the microphone on Taylor's lapel, then handed him the wireless control. "Hit this button to turn it on."

Taylor watched the technician retreat to his control booth in the back of the auditorium. The podium rested atop a red-carpeted stage, adorned on both sides by flowing golden drapery. Near-blinding white light flooded the stage, glaring down from the news crews' spots. The auditorium boasted state-of-the-art audiovisual capabilities, including computer visuals and three-dimensional holographic image projection. Overall, the effect was a little ostentatious for a medical auditorium, but Andrew Beckett, the benefactor, had insisted on the best for his auditorium when he made the $5 million donation to the Medical Center.

"Standby camera one," a woman said.

"Standby camera three."

The rows of amphitheater seats climbed two stories to the rear. Sprinkled throughout the audience, Taylor recognized a few friendly faces; Mary and Peter from the ER in the upper right. Dr. Browne squeezed his ample frame into a seat near the first-tier exit. Dr. Lynette Jensen, her hair still disheveled with long strands breaking free from her ponytail, her face looking slightly older, lined and pale, sat two rows up to his left. True to her promise, she'd made it to Rounds, despite all that had happened. Taylor saw Malcomb slink into a chair in the back row.

But then he saw Ramona Fox, the hospital CEO, sitting up front, flanked by the frowning faces of Drs. Bennington Crawford and William Preston. White-coated faculty glared down from the higher seats with skeptical faces. The IMVRA officials were there, lost somewhere in the crowd. A nervous pit ate into his stomach. Since his best suit was stained from the

Chan resus in the ER, he'd had to pull his well-worn charcoal-grey, interview suit out of the back of the closet. He straightened his tie and pulled uncomfortably on his collar. *Too much starch*, he thought. The collar bit into the side of his neck like a guillotine, leaving the skin red and chafed.

He grimaced. *Just what I need before the most important presentation of my life, a starched cotton decapitation.*

The sound technician gave Taylor a hand signal. It was time to begin.

Taylor took a deep breath and cleared his throat. "Is this on?" he tapped on the microphone. A shriek of feedback reverberated through the auditorium. Taylor winced. *Nice start.* He straightened his laptop on the podium, collected his thoughts, pushing the drama from the failed Patterson Cath out of his mind, and forced himself to take that first step.

"Thank you for coming," he said, fighting against the tremor in his voice. "Today, I shall introduce something revolutionary. A new age. Soon, a new breed of doctor will emerge, not in surgical scrubs or white coats, but wearing a virtual reality headset and a sensor suit wired to a supercomputer. This new type of specialist, a virtual physician, will enter the environment of the human body, seeing and feeling, probing, cutting, and suturing all within the realm of virtual reality.

"This is the new, exciting world of medical microism."

The audience stared down at him with eyes fixed. Taylor gauged their reaction, taking it to mean he had their attention. His heart kicked up a notch.

"Cardiovascular disease is the leading killer in America. We've attempted to treat this with medicines, and when those fail, we move to angioplasty or cardiac bypass." An image of Patterson clutching his chest flashed through his mind. Taylor pushed it aside. "Despite these efforts, the death rate is climbing—increased by 60% over the last 30 years."

Taylor stabbed a button on the laptop.

"It's time for a new approach."

Instantly, a holographic image materialized on the stage next to the podium—a thin metallic headset, horseshoe-shaped, like Caesar's imperial wreath. The projection, ten feet across and four feet high, floated in space above the stage, rotating clockwise on an imaginary axis.

Whispers broke out across the audience. Taylor noted the news cameras focus on the hologram.

"This is the Neural Transcendence headset," he said, "the key technological advance of the Virtual Heart Project."

Taylor stepped away from the podium and walked to the projection, reaching out as if he could touch it.

"This is the next phase of virtual reality."

The murmurs in the audience increased.

Taylor stepped into the projection, standing inside the helmet which spun around him, slowly, rotating. The re-creation was remarkably vivid, each detail exact and precise.

"Ever since 1965, when Ivan Sutherland first envisioned virtual reality in his paper "The Ultimate Display", the goal has been to transport human beings into a computer-generated world. To do this, researchers have used head-mounted visual displays; placing pictures on small screens in front of their eyes, hoping it'll fool them into believing they're in a virtual environment."

Taylor shook his head. "It doesn't. Even with today's computing, the rendering of virtual reality is too limited, too primitive; all it creates is a blocky, staccato video game. You'll notice there are no LCD screens on the Neural Transcendence headset. No visual display of any kind. If I'm to operate on a human being, perform a true virtual angioplasty, I'll need more than that."

The whispering in the audience intensified. Preston tapped Crawford on the elbow and whispered in his ear. In the back row, Taylor saw Malcomb. He made eye contact and nodded. He took a deep breath.

"What I need is a direct neurologic link to the virtual world."

A cacophony of voices erupted in the audience. Preston stiffened visibly in his seat. He stabbed his finger towards the hologram. "Dr. Abrahms, are you proposing a direct BMI—a brain machine interface?"

"One that's never been done before," Taylor answered. He stepped further into the spinning projection which now wrapped around him like a cocoon. He looked up into the hologram. On the underside of the helmet was an array of flat-tipped electrodes surrounded by a horseshoe-shaped electromagnetic ring.

Taylor pointed to the electrodes. "Each electrode is strategically, sterotactically, positioned over specific regions of the brain."

Preston's gaze, and that of the entire audience shifted to the helmet.

"The human brain," Taylor continued, "has been studied and mapped for years."

A projected graphic of a brain flashed onto the screen behind Taylor. "Certain areas contain the centers for cognitive function, others for sensory. Brodman's areas 20, 21 and 37 of the temporal lobes contain visual-associated projections." As Taylor spoke, the mentioned areas of the brain glowed in red. "Areas 41 and 42 house acoustic perception. The occipital lobe controls sight—"

"I fail to see how this can be applied to medicine," Preston interrupted Taylor, his booming voice reverberating through the auditorium.

"But it will, Dr. Preston." Taylor pushed on. "In mapping these areas, researchers found that direct electrical stimulation of the temporal lobe could produce an onslaught of visual images and memories. People told stories of seeing childhood friends, long lost toys, a pet dead for years. This area is the house of memory; a virtual world inside the human brain."

Taylor spread his arms wide, reaching out as if he could grasp the horseshoe shaped helmet. "Instead of looking through VR goggles, with the Neural Transcendence helmet, detailed MRI and real-time TTE ultrasound scans of the patient's coronary arteries will be pulsed directly to the sensory areas in my brain, timed in perfect sequence with the virtual reality program, all coordinated with predictive analysis by AI."

There was dead silence.

"You're going to stimulate your brain to interact with the computer?" a voice called out from the back.

"Exactly."

Preston jumped to his feet. "This is absurd! The possibility of a BMI interface has been proposed for years. It's crackpot theory!"

"It's fact, Dr. Preston." Taylor was steady. "If the electrical impulses are properly aligned, I can stimulate my natural senses. My own vision and hearing will augment the virtual reality program. My own senses will give credence to the virtual world."

He tapped his right temple. "All of virtual reality will exist inside my mind."

Crawford reached up and put his hand on Preston's shoulder, encouraging him to sit down, but Preston brushed him aside. He thrust a finger at the stage, pointing at the helmet. "And you're proposing to use this—this game of yours to operate on patients? " He spit out the words. "That's preposterous, completely irresponsible!"

Taylor hesitated, taken aback by the force of Preston's tirade. He had expected serious resistance to his project, but not attacks on his medical integrity. Personal attacks in the midst of Grand Rounds were unheard of in scientific circles. Nothing was ever discussed except the scientific merits of the project at hand. He watched Preston's face glowing red with anger.

Out of the corner of his eye, Taylor saw Malcomb sink deeper into his chair.

Taylor righted himself at the podium. "Virtual reality is not a game, Dr. Preston. Computer Assisted Surgery has been used for years."

Preston's face hardened. "Would you care to explain that?"

"Currently, we use computer modeling to help surgeons make a diagnosis or manipulate 3D images to simulate the effects of surgical procedures. Brigham and Women's Hospital has an open-MRI scanner that allows doctors to continuously scan patients while they're operating, superimposing the three-dimensional scan over the patient's body. This, in effect, gives the surgeon X-ray vision inside."

Taylor paused to allow the audience time to absorb all that he had told them.

"Now, I will take CAS to its ultimate stage. I will operate entirely within the virtual image of my patient."

Taylor stabbed a button on the laptop. The image of the helmet vanished, replaced by a massive hologram of a beating, pounding, human heart. It rose ten feet tall, filling the stage, rotating on its vertical axis. Its glistening muscles contracting in syncopated rhythm. Pulsing. The heartbeat, the sound of the pumping ventricles, boomed through the Dolby speakers, *Ba Bum, Ba Bum*; the cardiac valves snapped open and shut as blood rushed down the arteries.

An audible chorus of "Ooh"s rippled through the audience. Crawford placed his hand on Preston's shoulder and Preston finally sat down. Crawford whispered in Preston's ear, and Preston responded by abruptly crossing his legs, thrusting his arms across his chest.

Taylor turned down the volume, the heartbeat still audible in the background. "This image was created by fusing Signa

CV/i diagnostic MRIs with real-time echo-T ultrasounds of the heart."

Taylor tapped another key. "Enlarge coronary flow." The image of the heart faded, replaced by a detailed view of a single coronary artery. The artery, as large as a drainage pipe, faced the audience, floating above the stage. Inside the artery, red blood cells flowed in orchestrated swirling patterns, streaming across the smooth-walled vessel lumen to supply oxygen to the pounding heart muscle. Farther down the artery, the lumen abruptly narrowed where stalactites of cholesterol plaque stabbed the vessel ceiling. At this point, the blood churned in chaotic eddies, swirling in unproductive currents.

"This image comes from phase velocity MRI mapping of the arteries," Taylor pointed. "You can see the plaque that's caused the heart attack in this patient."

"This doesn't prove anything," Preston sneered. "It's just a pretty picture."

"That's where you're wrong, Dr. Preston." Taylor could feel the heat rising in his cheeks. "What looks like a pretty picture to you is my portal to surgery of the 21st century."

Taylor took a sudden step to his left, now standing inside the virtual image of the coronary artery. The artery enveloped him. Blood cells, the size of beach balls, poured around his body. He spread his arms wide, his hands reaching out, running along the sides of the blood vessel as if he could feel them.

In the audience, Dr. Jensen gasped. A reporter blurted a quick statement into his microphone. A growing rumble of voices swept through the auditorium.

"With the Virtual Heart Project," Taylor said, "I will project myself into a virtual coronary artery just like this. The neural transcendence helmet will allow me to feel the nudging of these blood cells against my body. I'll be able to run my hands across the slick endothelial lining of the blood vessel wall. I'll feel the heat of the plasma. I'll feel the moistness of the blood."

Malcomb sat upright in his chair, his hands covering his mouth. A growing rumble of voices swept through the auditorium.

"Once inside the vessel, I'll navigate my way down the arterial lumen, just as if I was walking down a street, until I approach the plaque blocking the artery. Simultaneously, a micro-laser linked through the computer with predictive AI will follow each of my movements to the exact millimeter inside the patient's real artery."

Taylor stepped backwards into the hologram until he stood directly in front of the plaque, which hung from the vessel roof like a crop of stalactites above his head.

He held up his right hand. "In my hand, I'll hold a virtual laser, which I'll carry to the site of blockage."

Taylor aimed at the plaque as if he were holding a pistol.

"I'll focus the virtual laser at the plaque, while the real laser, inside the patient, will follow me with micro-robotics to the exact same location inside the patient's artery."

Projections of massive red blood cells soared around Taylor's body. The beating of the virtual heart pounded through the auditorium speakers. Intensifying.

Ba Bum, Ba Bum

"Disintegrate!" Taylor shouted.

Instantly, the plaque exploded, disintegrating into a microscopic plume of dust. The irregular currents of blood ceased, replaced by a smooth, life-giving flow, streaming through the vessel.

Taylor watched it all happen. "This is the future," he said.

The audience erupted in cacophony, questions pelting him from all directions.

"How does the laser get into the patient?"

"How does the laser move into position?"

"Do you really think this is feasible?"

Taylor allowed himself a smile. This is what he wanted, to capture their curiosity, fire their imaginations. He looked up and saw Dr. Jensen, smiling down at him proudly. Dr. Browne sat impassively; his face unreadable. The network cameras continued to roll.

Taylor walked out of the re-creation of the vessel. An image of the micro-laser flashed upon the screen behind him. Looking like nothing more than a fine wire, the projection detailed that the laser measured just a few millimeters in diameter.

"A cardiologist will introduce the laser through a femoral artery catheter, just like a standard angioplasty. Micro-robotics, based on fluid dynamics, move the laser upstream in the blood vessel. It's guided into position with instructions directly from positional feedback of my location in the virtual artery, routed through the computer's AI predictive analysis. The precision is exact."

Preston huffed, his voice blaring above the audience. "You're wasting our time, Dr. Abrahms. We've been doing angioplasties for years."

"Yes, you have, Dr. Preston," Taylor paused a moment as he thought of Mr. Patterson. "And patients have been dying for years. Some arteries are too blocked for standard balloon angioplasty. Blood vessels can be torn. Bits of plaque can shoot down the artery causing a heart attack. We need something better."

Preston stared at Taylor with cold, dark eyes, barely containing his anger. "This is ridiculous!" he sneered, then spun and faced the audience, throwing his arms open wide. "Are you going to support this? Is this how you want your precious resources spent?"

The auditorium erupted in a sea of voices. Taylor noted a reporter scribbling in a notebook. A news photographer snapped a photo, the flash momentarily blinding him.

"This must be stopped!" Preston was yelling.

Crawford, who had remained silent throughout Rounds, finally stood to speak. Immediately, a hush fell over the auditorium. Preston gauged the serious look in his friend's eyes and retreated to his seat and sat down.

Crawford cleared his throat. "You ought to be commended for your work and diligence," he began. "No one will argue that this is an incredibly advanced technical design that you've created, Dr. Abrahms. It's quite impressive."

Taylor was momentarily disarmed by Crawford's praise. "Thank you, sir."

"No thanks are necessary. Your research speaks for itself."

"My team has worked very hard on this."

"Clearly. Yet, you must realize that what you propose raises serious concerns about safety."

"Safety's always a priority," Taylor said. "That's why I'm proposing an investigative in vivo trial in the animal laboratory."

"Yes, in a pig model, I believe."

"That's right. Pigs readily develop atherosclerosis and the lesions closely mimic those in humans."

Crawford nodded. "Uhm-hmmm. Yet, animal studies don't always accurately reflect how the technology will perform in human beings, do they? For every new wonder-drug or wonder-technology that comes around, one thousand others fail in human trials. This trial-and-error approach to medicine costs society billions each year."

"We can't halt scientific progress because previous trials have failed."

"Indeed. Yet what you are proposing is more theory than fact. How can you rationalize investigating your project until you have proof that it's safe?" Crawford frowned, turning to face the audience. "We're not buying office equipment here, where upgrades can come at a later date. There's no room for error when human lives are at stake."

A few snickers of laughter rose from the audience and Taylor realized that, in his own disarming way, Crawford was teasing him. Taylor pulled on his collar. The guillotine was chaffing his neck.

"I've tested the Neural Transcendence system in the laboratory."

"To perform surgery?"

Taylor paused. "Not yet."

"I see." Crawford folded his arms over his chest. "So, what you're proposing is to allocate a portion of the Medical Center's dwindling resources to investigate your unproven, albeit interesting, theory?"

A few more snickers rose from the audience. A clump formed in Taylor's throat as he saw Preston grinning in the front row, his eyes laughing at him.

Taylor had to formulate his rebuttal effectively to win the audience back. "As imaging and computing techniques improve, virtual reality will become a mainstay of surgery. It's inevitable. Immersion technology will blur the boundaries between what is real and what is simulated. That ability alone will open new doors of medical treatment."

Crawford nodded slowly and rubbed his chin. "I have no doubt that this project will produce pretty pictures, but you seem to be eluding my main point." Crawford turned to take in the audience. "Rather than invest in outrageous technology, this Medical Center, and society as a whole, needs to direct its limited resources to providing quality care to those who need it now."

Crawford took a deliberate step towards the stage. "I'm sure you've seen the latest statistics from the World Health Organization. The quality of health care in this country is lagging far behind other nations because we value technology over quality health care delivery."

Again, a buzz of voices rose from the audience, heads nodding in agreement with Crawford's conclusions. A newsman, carrying a portable video camera, inched towards Taylor, the camera focused intently on his face.

"Cost is a concern with any new technology," Taylor countered. "But it shouldn't be the only concern. Rather than hide from new technology, we need to investigate technology that can improve patient care, access and equitable delivery, while simultaneously cutting costs. Medical virtual reality is such a technology."

The cameraman shifted to focus on the Chief of Staff.

"Your predictions are encouraging," Crawford said, "but, unfortunately, you are hardly an objective source. You see before you a wave of scientific discovery that can save medicine. I, on the other hand, am afraid that we will drown in it."

The camera swung back to Taylor. "Science must advance. Lasers, computers, microelectronics; they've all proven themselves and they will take surgery to undreamed of heights. Virtual reality is next. It's progress."

"What if that progress bankrupts the entire system?" Crawford asked.

"What if it saves it?" Taylor shot back.

Murmurs rose from all areas of the audience, the debate amongst the seats intensifying.

Crawford frowned. "I see you are a puppet of the technology imperative, which states that if the technology exists, we must use it."

The camera focused on Taylor.

"I'm not blind to the costs, Dr. Crawford." Taylor leveled his eyes at the Chief of Staff. "But you can't let the cost blind you. This technology can save lives. You can't hide your head in the sand in fear and wish for it all to go away."

"It's not fear," Crawford pursed his lips. "It's costs. Plain and simple."

Taylor paused and looked out over the audience. He gauged their reactions; the intent looks in their eyes, their lips parted slightly, as if anticipating his words. Just as he'd known it would, the issue all came down to cost. It wasn't about whether or not he could save lives. It wasn't about helping a veteran with chest pain get home to spend time with his wife of sixty years. It wasn't about his oath as a doctor to relieve suffering and cure the sick. It was all about cost.

And to that, Taylor could only think of one answer.

"I'm an Emergency Room physician," he started, sensing the camera zooming in on his face. "I spend all day watching patients get rushed in, clutching their chests, gasping for air, while their faces turn blue. And just as importantly, I see the wives of those patients, holding their children while they whisper that daddy will be alright. I see the wives clinging to their own words, wishing beyond hope, that if they say it enough times it may be true. Then I see the look of stunned realization in their eyes when I have to tell them that they are now widows and their children are fatherless because we don't have the ability to save a man dying from a heart attack."

Taylor stepped away from the podium. The news cameras panned across the stage, trained on his every step.

"I see this every day in the ER. And every day I ask myself the same question, and now I'm going to ask you, Dr. Crawford. You've become so concerned with the costs of medicine that you've lost sight of the greater picture."

The news camera flashed to Crawford. "And what would that be?"

Taylor felt all eyes upon him. The camera panned back.

"How much is a human life worth?"

CHAPTER 11

Taylor stepped out of the waiting room of the Cardiac Care Unit, on the sixth floor of SF City Hospital just before midnight. True to his promise, he'd gone to the CCU immediately after Rounds ended and stayed by Mrs. Patterson's side until her husband came back from emergency heart bypass and was admitted to the CCU for post-op care. Patterson had suffered a heart attack, but the bypass came in time to prevent extensive injury. It was touch and go for a while, but it appeared that Patterson would make it through the night.

Entering the elevator, Taylor wiped the fatigue from his eyes and punched the button for the fourth floor. He glanced at his watch. He'd promised Sherilyn he'd be home for dinner, but as the last few minutes ticked off before twelve, he knew that wasn't going to happen. There was still too much to do. Grand Rounds had drawn to a close with faculty members still hotly debating the merits of the VHP. Without a consensus, Crawford had called for a meeting of the Bioethics Committee to make the final decision. Taylor was allowed to proceed with his research until the Ethics meeting gave a final verdict, which was scheduled for Monday at noon.

It was victory by default.

That gave Taylor just over 48 hours to demonstrate positive results or risk losing it all. He'd already told Malcomb to prepare for initiation of the experiment tomorrow morning.

Tomorrow? Taylor glanced at his watch again. *More like today.* He ran his hand down his face. His return to the computer lab was only eight hours away. He knew he needed to get home and get some sleep, but there was something he needed to do first.

Taylor exited the elevator, walking through the double electric doors to the Intensive Care Unit. The image of Robert Chan's blown open chest and abdomen still dug deep into Taylor's mind, colliding with the incongruity of the paramedic's report. Something about the shooting didn't make sense. Taylor didn't know what he expected to find in the ICU, but for some reason he found himself drawn there. As if seeing Chan's body would ease his troubled mind.

Normally a hotbed of activity, the Unit was quiet at night. Arranged like a horseshoe, the glass-walled patient rooms formed an arc around the central nursing station. The Unit boasted the latest in critical care; computer-controlled respirators, automated medication dosing and high-resolution digital X-ray. A full complement of labs waited nearby; hematology, microbiology, cytology, blood gas. A central monitoring area allowed the nurses to track each patient's vitals, oxygen sats, and arterial line readings. Taylor noted the monitoring area was deserted; the staff reduced to bare bones for the night shift.

Walking deeper into the ICU, Taylor suddenly stopped. He glanced upwards. The security camera mounted above the nursing station had panned left with his movements, a high-pitch squeal emanating from its mechanical motor.

A knot crept into Taylor's gut and the hair prickled up the back of his neck. He'd been in the ICU dozens of times over the last four years, maybe hundreds, and never once could he recall the security cameras moving. In fact, he'd always assumed they were broken.

Taylor's fingers began to tingle, a cold chill inching up his spine. He squinted, studying the camera. All ICU's had security cameras to prevent narcotics theft. *Maybe they'd finally fixed the motor*, Taylor thought, *but if that was true, why would it squeak so much?* His gaze lasered on the camera, as if he could see through the lens into the eyes of whoever was watching on the other side. All he could see was a reflected image of the ICU in the blackened lens.

Taylor shouldered his concerns and walked deeper into the ICU towards Chan's room. Inside, the cardiac monitor beeped out a steady rhythm —slow, but steady. Taylor's eyes flashed across the digitized displays; blood pressure, mean arterial pressure, oxygen saturation, central venous pressure; each reading indicating that Chan was somehow clinging to life.

Taylor slid into the room, acclimating his nose to the medicinal sting of antiseptic. Chan lay immobile in bed. The foot-long thoracotomy incision, where the CT surgeons cracked open his ribcage, cut straight through the center of his chest, from the base of his neck to the end of his sternum. Multiple wounds crisscrossed his chest and abdomen. The edges of the wounds glistened with fresh blood.

A white hospital sheet draped across Chan's otherwise naked body, protecting his dignity; as if a thousand tubes and wires coming from every orifice left some dignity to protect. Around the bed, metallic poles supported the hanging bags of intravenous fluids, antibiotics and cream-colored nutritional supplements. These fluids dripped into his body and escaped from the other end, collecting into a plastic bag of yellowish fluid that drained from a catheter inserted in his urethra.

Taylor was silently pleased when he saw the half-full bag of urine. In the ICU, the yellowish bag was one of the first things a doctor looked for. Good urine production meant that the heart was functioning and supplying the kidneys with blood. Decreased urine output was the first sign of impending cardiovascular collapse. To the ICU doctor, that bag of fluid was worth its weight in gold.

Next to the bed, the respirator hissed, pumping a steady flow of oxygen to Chan's damaged lungs. The air passed through the tubing to the valve implanted in Chan's throat. The tracheostomy. Taylor nodded. It was standard procedure to trach all long-term ICU patients. It was another good sign. It meant that someone expected him to survive, at least a little longer.

Taylor crossed to the other side, his eyes never leaving Chan's chest. He picked up the ICU flow sheet, studying the readings from the Swan-Ganz catheter that ran through the patient's heart and into the pulmonary artery. Wedge pressure. Cardiac output. Mixed venous oxygen. The readings were erratic, occasionally dipping uncomfortably low, but not critical.

My God, he really might survive.

"What are you doing here?"

Startled, Taylor dropped the flow sheet and turned towards the door. A freckle-faced night shift nurse stood there, dressed in blue scrubs and a white jacket, holding a package in her hands. She looked like she was twelve-years old.

"I'm just looking at—" he started to say.

"Dr. Browne has specifically ordered no one be allowed in here."

"Dr. Browne—" Taylor began, then hesitated, his eyebrows furrowing. "I didn't realize this room was restricted."

The nurse smiled pleasantly, but firmly. "Well, it is, and I'm going to have to ask you to leave."

Taylor glanced at Chan. "How's he's doing?"

"That's privileged information between the doctors and family. Are you family?"

"No, but I'm—"

"Then you really must leave."

Taylor held up his hand, trying to get her to slow down. "I just want to know how he's doing."

"I told you, that's privileged." The nurse folded her arms across her chest. "Now, don't make me call security."

"Look, nurse." Taylor pulled his hospital ID out of his hip pocket. "I'm Dr. Abrahms. I took care of him in the ER."

The nurse's eyes suddenly widened. "Dr. Taylor Abrahms?"

Taylor nodded.

The nurse's cheeks flushed a brilliant red and she covered her mouth. "Dr. Abrahms, I'm sorry. I'm so embarrassed. I didn't realize it was you."

Taylor smiled wearily. It was no surprise that he wasn't recognized. With his face masked with fatigue and his disheveled suit, he looked more like a vagabond off the streets than the Chief ER resident.

"It's a pleasure to meet you," she added.

"It is?"

"Oh yes," the nurse said, smiling broadly. "We all heard about the extraordinary measures you took to save his life in the ER."

Taylor smiled politely. "Then I can stay?"

"Of course, you can stay. He was your patient after all."

"Thank you very much, nurse—"

"Stewart. Kelly Stewart," she said. "I'm his nurse this shift. And your patient's doing surprisingly well. His vitals have been stable since he came in from surgery." She crossed the room to the end of the bed. "I was just about to place these cards on his night stand." She pulled a stack of greeting cards from the package. "It makes such a difference, you know."

Taylor raised an eyebrow. "The cards?"

"Oh yes, the cards. I put them everywhere; on the tables, on the respirator, taped to the wall. It makes the room so much cheerier. It's much nicer to recover in a friendly room, full of good words from loved ones, don't you agree?"

Taylor nodded, thinking nurse Stewart had a little too much energy for this time of night. "Yes, I'm sure it does."

"Take this one for example," she held up a white card with a red rose stamped across the front above the words I HEARD YOU WERE SICK. "It's from his office. Since work is important to most people, I'll put it on the wall where he'll see it as soon as he opens his eyes. It'll make him feel good knowing that people at work care about him."

Taylor flashed Nurse Stewart a courteous smile and decided to leave Chan alone with his cards. He still didn't know why he'd been drawn to Chan's room. Perhaps it was the vividness of having held his dying heart in his hands, squeezing it to keep the lifeblood pumping through his veins that bonded them together. That Chan's life had literally been in Taylor's hands. Whatever the reason, Taylor had seen what he came for. Somehow, Chan had managed to survive. He was in the ICU team's hands now.

"Thank you, nurse Stewart," he said, looking over his shoulder as he walked towards the door.

The nurse called to him. "Before you go, could you do me a favor?"

Taylor stopped. "Sure."

She held out the GET-WELL card. "Could you stick this to the wall for me? There's tape on the back, but I can't reach up very high."

Taylor took the card from her and glanced across the room to the collage of cards stuck to the wall. He gave a weary smile. "No problem. Where do you want it?"

The nurse pointed, identifying an empty space above a card of a hippo holding a thermometer.

Taylor glanced at the card in his hands, reading the handwritten notes of well-wishes from his work colleagues.

Maybe she was right, he thought. Maybe it isn't million-dollar monitoring units or blood gas labs, but maybe it's cards that are the best medicine.

Suddenly, Taylor's eyes widened.

Seeing Chan's name in writing on the card stirred a vague memory from within the recesses of Taylor's brain. He knew that he'd learned Chan's name down in the ER before the resus, but seeing it on paper seemed different. Somewhere, he'd seen Robert Chan's name before. Not on a hospital chart or ER Sheet. But where?

Examining the card, Taylor's eyes shot to the company logo stamped across the bottom, printed in brilliant red letters. His eyes locked in place.

CYBERTECH SYSTEMS

"This guy worked at CyberTech Systems!" he gasped. "I recognize the name now. We use his AI programming paradigms for our research."

Nurse Stewart gave a sympathetic nod. "It's horrible, isn't it?"

Something felt wrong, very wrong.

Taylor shot the nurse a glance. "Have the Police found out what happened yet?"

The nurse shrugged. "They say it's a robbery."

"Robbery?" Taylor mouthed the word as if it was foreign. He thought of the tremendous amount of damage done to Chan's chest and abdomen. More than he would have expected from a random shooting.

This was no robbery.

"You just never know, do you? One day you're fine, the next some madman breaks into your house and it's all over."

Taylor nodded, but wasn't listening, her words an echo in some distant tunnel. Chan's connection to CyberTech was like a cold bony finger pressed to his spine.

He stuck the card on the wall, thanked the nurse and exited through the ICU doors. As he entered the elevators, a nagging edginess tugged at the back of his mind.

He'd gone to the ICU seeking answers, but was leaving with more questions than before.

A programming engineer at CTS gets brutally shot, Taylor thought. And we're using his CTS AI programming for our experiment starting tomorrow.

Rationally, Taylor knew that these events must be unrelated and that their occurrence at the same time was nothing more than coincidence.

But, as a scientist, Taylor had never believed in coincidences.

His mind raced back to the CTS logo on the card. The red ink blazed across his mind like a warning. He couldn't shake the feeling that something was very wrong.

As he stepped into the elevator, he never noticed the fourth-floor hallway B security camera panning left behind him.

CHAPTER 12

Inside the Chrysler Van parked on Bush Street, Edgar Ross replayed the video. Reflexively, he rubbed his palm and fingers across his freshly-shaved scalp while he searched for an answer. He was feeling uneasy, a sensation he hadn't felt in so long he could barely recognize it.

But tonight, something was bothering him.

It wasn't his usurping control of the Hospital Security system that worried him. A simple hack into the Security Center's Windows-based system gave him immediate access to the entire array of cameras. His notebook detailed that it had taken him only 17.6 minutes to complete the operation. Flashing between feeds, he could observe nearly every square inch of hospital space by tapping arrow keys to direct camera movement.

A captured image of target-one staring directly at the camera filled his computer, NORTHWEST ICU CAMERA 3 printed across the bottom of the screen. Ross had hesitated when it became apparent that the target had made the camera. His mind searched for an explanation, settling on the sound made from a faulty motor mechanism. Obviously, the hospital hadn't performed regular maintenance on the cameras. Probably too expensive, with little perceived return.

For a moment, the image of target-one staring at him through the camera caused Ross to pause. But he quickly realized that his position hadn't been compromised. The target had no idea who was monitoring the cameras. He'd naturally assume it was Hospital Security. Ross's trail through the security system was nearly invisible. Using an infecting rootkit, he'd seized control of a series of unprotected PC's, and laundered his internet proxy from one computer to another. He could never be traced.

No. Target-one making the camera wasn't what bothered him. It was something else. Ross made a meticulous note of the time in his log book, while the video flashed to a panoramic view of the ICU.

Ross's eyes tightened. There was the problem. Target-one's presence in the Chinese man's room had been completely unexpected. But more than the visit alone, it was the target's reaction that ate at Ross's gut.

Freezing the video on an image of the target holding a GET-WELL card, Ross grimaced. He zoomed in on the profile of his target's face, the image enlarging, zeroing in on his opened mouth and widened eyes. It was the look of shock.

"Fuck," Ross whispered.

Target-one had seen something in that card.

Ross knew that his employer wouldn't be happy to hear this. Switching to wireless LAN, his employer had to be alerted. Plans would have to be accelerated.

Finished typing, Ross grabbed his H&K and began polishing the barrel. Releasing the cartridge, he examined the bullets, each one spotless and shimmering in the monitor's glow.

His eyes shot to the monitor and locked on Target-one's face still frozen on the screen.

89

ENTRY

CHAPTER 13

Saturday, October 14th, 6:58 am

Taylor guided the battered MG through the morning rain, pulling into the parking lot of the Kelly Research Building, located on the Medical Center Campus, up the hill from Taylor's lab. A three-story concrete, 50,000 square-foot structure, the Kelly Building, was indistinguishable from the many similar buildings on campus. Nearly invisible, lost behind a grove of eucalyptus trees, only its red tile roof stood out, towering over the University below.

But despite its inauspicious architecture, the Kelly Building was world-renowned; the foremost center for innovative research on biological robotics. Housing a full array of research environments—including bird atria and deep-sea simulation tanks—Kelly scientists, armed with grants from DARPA and the Office of Naval Research, devoted countless hours of computer simulation, field investigation, and trial and error engineering to learn the basics of animal locomotion. Birds, fish, insects; every animal was studied, its locomotive principles broken down and analyzed, then reproduced in state-of-the-art robotics. Housing the largest animal research center on the West Coast, Taylor knew the Kelly building by its more commonly used nickname—the Farm.

Malcomb waited in the parking lot, standing besides his faded yellow 1970 Honda N360 two-door; a car was so small, every time Taylor saw it, he imagined a hoard of red-nosed clowns popping out and spraying each other with seltzer.

Taylor turned his collar against the rain and approached him. Malcomb wore a red polo shirt, green corduroys and his customary brown cardigan. He looked particularly pale that morning, his hair damp, glasses crooked.

"Why are you waiting out in the rain?" Taylor asked.

Malcomb looked down. "No reason."

Taylor laughed. "You didn't want to go in, did you?"

"Not without you," Malcomb mumbled under his breath.

"She doesn't bite, you know."

"She may." The she Malcomb referred to was Helen Yang, the bioengineer working on the Virtual Heart Project. "Besides, we've always met her at the library."

"Worried about meeting her on her own turf?"

"You never know what she has lurking in the darkness."

Taylor smiled. "White knight g1 to f3."

Malcomb rubbed his forehead. "Not now. Not just before we enter her lair."

"I like to attack when you're weak." Taylor's grin widened.

Malcomb pondered the chess board, his left lower eyelid twitching. "Pawn d7 to d6."

Taylor nodded. "Now come on, let's see which of Satan's minions awaits us."

They walked up the concrete stairs, opened the double glass front doors and stepped inside. Taylor found himself in a small vestibule, with slate floors and institutional white walls. A guard sat behind the security counter; the University Seal emblazoned on the wall behind him. Digital security cameras hung from the ceiling, panning the area in slow arcs. The walls were solid concrete.

Taylor approached the guard, Malcomb following. "I'm here to see Dr. Yang."

The guard looked up from his computer. "Which one?"

Taylor looked stumped. "Which what?"

"Look, buddy, I got six Yang's here. Philip, Robert, Helen—"

"Helen," Taylor said, interrupting.

"She expecting you?"

"We made an appointment for seven."

"Hang on," the guard said, tapping on his keyboard. He brought up a list of official guests for the day.

"What's your name?"

"Taylor Abrahms."

"And the skinny guy?"

"That's Malcomb Bernard."

"I'll need to see some ID."

Taylor and Malcomb produced their university ID cards. The guard took them and slid them through the scanner, reading the data tape on back.

The guard, a mountain of a man, with a shaved bald dome and goatee, looked like he'd be more comfortable on the back of a Harley than behind the security desk of a famous research lab. He handed Taylor a laminated guest badge and an electronic data board. Harley-man's hands nearly encompassed the entire board.

"Sign the bottom."

Taylor scrawled his name across the liquid crystal display and handed it back.

"Your fingerprints."

Taylor looked at the board and saw a small data square in the upper corner.

"Why do you need my fingerprints?"

"Military grants means military secrets. You want in, you give up your prints."

Taylor shrugged. He knew that a great deal of the research conducted at the Farm had military implications, but he hadn't anticipated security being this tight. He placed his thumb against the data square and a computerized image of his thumbprint appeared then transferred to the guard's desktop screen. The security cameras on the wall clicked off digital photographs of Taylor's face.

The guard tapped at his computer. When the computer beeped, acknowledging the download, he repeated the process with Malcomb.

"Okay. Yang's ready to see you now."

Taylor smiled and looked up from the desk. He scanned the vestibule, but didn't see a doorway, just the solid concrete walls.

"Where's the office—" he started to say, but stopped before the words left his mouth. The entire wall next to the security desk shuddered and pulled open with the soft whir of a hydraulic motor.

The guard smiled thinly and returned to his work.

Taylor's heart began to race. He pulled on his collar and walked through the entrance.

CHAPTER 14

Senator Randolph McIntyre took a deep breath.

Shifting his gaze out the window of his black Lincoln limousine cruising down Constitution Avenue, McIntyre's eyes flared, the only visible sign of his displeasure. Under normal circumstances, McIntyre loved this part of the drive, past the National Mall to his office in the Russell Senate Office Building. As the limousine made its way through the Mall, passing the twin fountains of the World War II Memorial, the moment would come when McIntyre would find himself perfectly centered between the Washington Monument on his right and the White House on his left. At that moment, a deep reverence for the importance of this city as the seat of democracy would overwhelm him. In the shimmering white stones of the monument, he could see the glory of the nation's past, and in the majestic beauty of the White House, the limitless potential of its future.

A future that included him in the Oval Office.

But that morning, McIntyre was in no mood for reflection. His campaign manager, Roderick Stevens, and personal assistant, Jennifer Langston, sat impassively across from him, sinking into their leather seats, doing their best to avoid his glaring eyes. Roderick poked at his Android Stylus phone, while Jennifer, her blonde hair pulled back into a tight bun, immersed herself in making adjustments to the Senator's schedule. The Senator's jaw clenched. His attention remained focused on the news coming across his cell phone.

The limousine crossed 15th Street. The White House passed from view and faded away behind him.

The morning had started well. McIntyre's address to military veterans, carefully staged at the base of the U.S. Marine Corps War Memorial at Arlington National Cemetery, had captivated the audience. With the drama of the six bronze figures driving the flag pole into the rocky crag of Mt. Suribachi on Iwo Jima, raising the stars-and-stripes in victory behind him, McIntyre spoke passionately about the challenges that faced the Nation; national security, a lagging economy and spiraling health care costs. With his arms spread wide, he orated that medical reform would be the foundation by which this country would right itself. How he was poised to follow in the great footsteps of the 7000 Marines who had given their lives on Iwo Jima, and lead this country back to its former glory.

The audience had hung on his every word. He had taken them up the side of the mountain and they had followed gratefully. The view from the top was astounding.

Then the phone call brought McIntyre crashing back down to earth.

"What do you mean it wasn't stopped?" McIntyre asked in a measured tone. "You said that there was no way it would get past Grand Rounds."

The voice on the other end of the phone pleaded its case, but McIntyre cut him off. "No, you listen to me. Yesterday I made a promise on national television that the Virtual Heart Project would be stopped. Now, with less than four weeks before the election, you tell me that it's still on? Do you know how impotent that makes me look?"

The veins in McIntyre's temples bulged. "You stop that project! I don't care what it takes. Do you hear me? It stops now!"

McIntyre terminated the call. The air in the limousine grew thick.

"Not good news, I take it?" Roderick deadpanned.

McIntyre glared at him. "Abrahms' research got the green light at Rounds pending an Ethics Committee review on Monday."

"What are you going to do?" Roderick's southern drawl seemed particularly acute that afternoon.

McIntyre bit his lower lip and rubbed his forehead. *That's the fucking million-dollar question, isn't it?* He knew that Grand Rounds had been televised nationally, and would already be picked up by the salivating jaws of the press. He could see their reports now. Since his health care reform included a moratorium on hypertech medical projects, they'd label it a weakness in McIntyre's health care plan. His Democrat opponent would latch onto this with the tenacity of a starving bear tearing apart a piece of fresh, bloody meat. McIntyre would look inept. Or worse.

So far, his daughter, Sherilyn, and her private life had remained out of the sights of the press, but that wouldn't last for long. Once the press made the connection between this research and McIntyre's own family, shouts of nepotism would blast from the AM talk shows and podcasts. A massive chink in his carefully-constructed armor would be exposed.

This one insignificant research project could blow up into my own Chappaquiddick!

The Senator fumed knowing he needed a plan. He searched his mind, reaching for a lifeline to pull himself out of this mire.

The election is less than four weeks away!

With the limousine cruising down Constitution Avenue, the National Archives Building passing by on the left, a vague memory stirred.

And then it hit him.

The Archives. The writings of our ancestors.

The Senator's eyes lit up. At first just a hint, then a smile stretched across his lips. An idea took hold. A flicker of hope sprung to life.

He glanced at Roderick. "Warfare is based on deception."

Roderick looked at the Senator like he was speaking Martian. "What'd you say?"

"Sun Tzu, *The Art of War*."

Roderick shook his head.

"The oldest military treatise in the world," McIntyre said, his gaze inwards. "A guide to waging war."

"War?"

"Even political war. All warfare is deception. As circumstances are favorable, one should modify one's plans."

McIntyre's mind locked in on the answer. Analyzing it, dissecting it, probing it for a weakness.

Roderick glanced at Jennifer, looking for help. She returned his befuddlement. "Are you going to start talking English any time soon?" Roderick asked.

McIntyre focused on his campaign chairman, taking in his bulbous nose and reddened face. "I've made a tactical error. We all have. We've put our efforts into hiding the connection between Abrahms and my campaign. We've been afraid of the embarrassment. Afraid that the realization could damage our momentum."

"Damn straight," Roderick ran his fingers through his thick grey hair. "You can't afford to have the media announcing that your own family is doing the very research you're campaigning against. It makes you look like a fool."

"No." McIntyre shook his head. "I look like a fool trying to avoid the connection."

Roderick looked nonplussed. "I don't follow."

"We all knew someone would find out that Abrahms is married to my daughter. It's public record. Any idiot who looks can find it. It's only a matter of time."

Roderick's look of confusion deepened.

The Senator's grey eyes narrowed. "Now is the time."

Roderick stiffened. "I have absolutely no idea what you're talking about."

"I'm talking about setting a new course. We have two choices. We either sit back and wait for someone to discover our dirty little secret and use it to destroy us or we take the offensive. Sun Tzu says that the clever combatant imposes his will on the enemy, but doesn't allow the enemy's will to be imposed on him."

Roderick nodded slowly, a glint of understanding in his eyes. "Twist the Abrahms connection to our advantage...."

"Every candidate has some embarrassment in their family. Carter had Billy and his beer. Clinton had a coke-dealing half-brother. Biden had his drug-addicted son. Now I have mine. We can survive this if we play our cards right. What we need to do is attack. Make this a target point of my campaign. Use the family connection to show I won't back down on my principles, not even for my own daughter's husband."

Roderick's face lit up. "Like Elliot Ness cleaning up the mafia."

"Exactly." The Senator turned to Jennifer. "Contact the media. Break the story with my displeasure at what Abrahms is doing. Tell them I'm furious that this research is being supported by a public university, much less from a member of my own family."

Jennifer nodded. "Got it."

He faced Roderick. "Cancel my speech in Massachusetts. Find an opportunity to get me to San Francisco."

Roderick's gaze turned inward while he searched his mind. "I can arrange a photo-op at the upcoming Google/NASA-Ames Anniversary celebration," he said. "We can set up a reception for the Republican ticket holders—"

"Fine. Just get me out there."

Roderick tapped out a note on his Android phone. He looked at his entry, uncertainty etched in his face. "Are you sure you know what you're doing?"

McIntyre closed his eyes and took it all in. He saw himself at the Google/NASA-Ames facility, reporters and voters surrounding him. With one wave of his hand, he'd set everything right. He'd transform this entire embarrassment into his killing blow. A rush of self-assurance flooded him. He was back in control, like the soldiers at Iwo Jima, reeling after a battle, but still rising to the summit for victory.

A stanza from *The Art of War* flashed through his mind.

Hold out baits to entice the enemy. Feign disorder, then crush him.

CHAPTER 15

A rush of air-conditioning and the smell of ozone belched from the entry chamber of the Farm. A short woman, barely five feet tall, stood in the hallway wearing a white blouse, black skirt and maroon flats, all covered by an oversized lab coat that draped down to her ankles. Her dark hair was pinned up in a bun, held in place with a pair of red lacquered chopsticks. Oversized black rectangular glasses perched on her nose. Despite being thirty-eight, her skin was flawless and smooth. Combined with her petite frame, she could have easily passed for a teenager.

"It's about time you got here," Helen Yang straightened the glasses on her nose. "I was about to send out a search party for the lost geeks from the computer lab."

Taylor stepped into the hallway, Malcomb following closely behind. The door hissed shut behind them. Taylor looked at his watch. It was 7:03 AM. They were exactly three minutes late.

"I didn't know security was so tight here. Taylor noted an armed guard standing three feet down the hall on the left. "Do you have the entire State police here?"

"No police. Just half the military. Now come on. Time's wasting."

She handed Taylor and Malcomb white lab coats. "Put these on. Who knows what you guys are carrying on you."

"Do we really need these?" Malcomb asked.

Helen snorted. "We can't have any stray fibers floating around. Some of the robotics we're working on aren't much bigger than a human hair, so one stray fiber could destroy the whole project."

Malcomb slipped the coat on. Helen flashed him a cold stare. "And for God's sake, no chocolate."

Malcomb shrank into his coat.

Taylor tugged on the coat's lapels. "This will hardly protect the environment."

"Don't worry. You're not going anywhere near the Microelectromechanical labs. That work is only done in the positive pressure zone, and you need full body containment suits just to get in the door. We're just going to the Aquatic lab and the coat will reduce your shedding. Now come on, I haven't got all day."

Turning on her heels, Helen shot off down the corridor. Malcomb gave Taylor a pleading look. Taylor smiled and cajoled him to follow.

Helen guided them down a long corridor. A series of rooms branched off from the main hallway. Drill presses, lathes, digital circuit boards and sine wave converters lined up in neat rows. Hydraulic pumps and pneumatic motors filled the shelves. Three engineers, dressed in blue jump suits bandied about, fitting hydraulics into a robotic leg. The smell of burning rubber stung the air.

"The heart of any robotics lab is the machine shop," Helen said without stopping.

"You make your parts here?"

"We have seven machine shops here in the Farm. Each one has its own specialty. Those we just passed are hydraulics. Digital and micro-engineering are farther back. The nanotechnology lab is still being built."

"Seven machine shops?"

"We can build anything our little hearts desire."

They passed into another, much larger hallway. Helen pointed to her left. A thick metal door was bolted into the concrete wall, black rubber gaskets sealing the edges. An armed guard stood at the entrance. Blazing red letters warned:

POSITIVE PRESSURE
ABSOLUTELY NO ENTRY
WITHOUT CONTAINMENT SUIT

"That's the positive pressure zone," Helen explained. "The nano-engineers and neurophysiologists have their labs there. That's where the security gets tight."

"Positive pressure?" Taylor asked.

"All the air in that part of the building is pumped through a series of micro-filters that clear out any fibers, bacteria, lint or debris. The air is heated to sterilize it, then cooled and recirculated back through those ducts." Helen pointed overhead.

Taylor looked up. A series of three-foot thick silver air ducts ran the length of the ceiling.

"The air is pumped back into the zone at a force greater than one atmosphere. The pressure blows debris into the filters, preventing contaminants from getting in."

Taylor nodded, taken aback by the level of technology in the building. "What are they working on?"

"Military projects and government grants. Mostly intel stuff. I don't know for a fact. The Army guys are a pain in the ass."

"The Army funds all this?" Malcomb asked.

"It's common knowledge," Helen harrumphed. "The Defense Department's Controlled Biological and Biomimetic Systems Program pumps tens of millions of dollars into research here and places like Case Western, Cambridge and the Leg Lab at MIT."

Taylor was impressed. "Why the interest in robots?"

"Simple. Our robots can go places humans can't, either because it's not safe or because a human can't get there. Like the surface of another planet, or into a fire, or a battle. Robots can maneuver over territory that even humans would have a hard time handling."

"You have robots that can do all that?"

"Sure. Like the robot lobster."

Malcomb snorted and burst out laughing. "A lobster?"

"This is the real deal," Helen said. "In 1990, the government tried an experiment to mount sonar on the backs of lobsters to use them to spy on underwater Russian facilities in the Black Sea. The problem was, lobsters aren't the most intelligent of all sea animals and they'd wander around and search for food and fight each other and get eaten without ever collecting any data."

"Why a lobster?" Taylor asked.

"Can you think of a more stable animal to crawl around the sea floor? Eight legs for balance. It can maneuver over any obstacle. Go forward, backwards and sideways. It's ideal for espionage."

"So, they contacted you guys to make a robotic one?" Malcomb dared to ask.

"It's a lot harder than it sounds. It's one thing to make a cute little robot that can walk around like a toy, but think about how you'd make one that can mimic all the complex behaviors of the original biological model. The lobster robots have to maneuver around rocks, crawl on the sea bottom, deal with tides and flows and do all this autonomously, under hundreds of feet of water. Just hope it doesn't turn up in your bisque. Now, can we move on or do you have any more annoying questions?"

Taylor shook his head. Malcomb's face turned pale.

"Good. We got lots of work to do and very little time." She shot off down the concrete hallway. After fifty feet, another corridor branched off to the left. Written on the corridor wall were the words:

WARM-BLOODED VERTEBRATE RESEARCH ENVIRONMENT

"The animal zoo is down there." Helen pointed. "That's where we keep the animals designated for digital motion capture and the research animals."

"Warm blooded vertebrates?" Taylor asked.

Helen gave him a perturbed look. "We have several animal environments here. Warm-blooded, cold-blooded, vertebrate, invertebrate, insect, aviary and aquatic. Each is designed to let us study how each animal locomotes in their specific environment."

"Is—is that where the pigs are?" Malcomb asked.

"Yeah. We got six of them, all bred to have atherosclerosis. They're expensive so try not to kill them, will ya?"

"Oh, I could never hurt a pig," Malcomb stammered. "I had one as a pet. They're very sensitive."

Helen looked at him, bemused. "You had a pet pig?"

Malcomb shrugged. "I'm allergic to dogs."

"Why doesn't that surprise me? Now come on, my lab's over here."

She led them through an open door. The sign read:

AQUATIC PROPULSION SIMULATION LABORATORY.

The hallway opened into a massive concrete room, bathed in yellow fluorescent light. Black slate lab benches lined the periphery of the lab, each table covered with robotic legs, eyes, wings and fins. Oscilloscopes and digital circuits filled the shelves above the rows of Mac supercomputers. A ten-foot-long taxidermist cast of a bluefin tuna hung above the doorway, while a stuffed barracuda and a reef shark were suspended from the ceiling, hanging by wires. Posters of fish filled every inch of wall space. The air was redolent of motor oil and salt water.

As impressive as the lab was, it was the water tanks that took Taylor's breath away. A series of seven clear acrylic aquariums dominated the lab, forming a circle in the center of the room. The biggest one, a six-hundred-gallon tank, sat in the center of the circle. Swimming in the tank, unaided by wires, was a two-meter-long robotic fish, made of an internal skeleton of motorized links with a skin of padded foam and lycra. Its vertical fin and tail swished from side to side propelling the robot to the end of the tank, where it circled and shot back the other way. Water splashed over the tank and dripped through drainage grates on the floor.

Taylor approached the tank, amazed.

"That's Charlie," Helen said.

"You built this?"

"Of course. I was studying the vortices that propel fish for our project."

"The what?"

"The vortices. The force of the water. If you think about it, when a fish swims, moving its tail back and forth, the vortices created could just as easily propel the fish backwards as forwards. The only way to understand fish propulsion is to build a model and break down each movement one step at a time."

"So, you built a pike?"

"It's a tuna."

"Sorry."

"Tunas are premiere long-distance swimmers. Their bodies are highly evolved to move water around them without producing drag or turbulence. Pike are faster, more agile. They're used to study acceleration." Helen watched Charlie reverse direction in the tank. The water splashed behind it. "My pike's in the next tank over."

"And the salmon?"

Helen looked at Taylor and frowned. "Don't be cute. It isn't working."

*****

Flapping overhead, a two-foot-long, robotic peregrine falcon, unaided by wires, soared around the lab, occasionally landing on a black slate table, cleaning its face with its wings then leaping back into the air. Its mechanical wings clanked as they flapped, filling the room with metallic clattering.

Taylor and Malcomb sat opposite Helen at the desk in the corner, Taylor studying the schematics for the micro-laser propulsion unit. He could hear the sounds of the tuna splashing in the background. Malcomb fidgeted in his chair. He avoided Helen's gaze whenever possible. Every so often, the robot falcon flapped overhead and Malcomb would duck his head with a jerking motion as if ducking for cover. His face was pale. Taylor thought that he needed some chocolate.

"Does that thing always fly around in here?" Malcomb dared to ask.

Helen gave a mischievous smile. "You have your pets, I have mine." She turned towards Taylor. "So, what'd ya think?"

Taylor lowered the schematics. "How's it functioning?"

"Perfectly, of course."

"Show me."

Helen rose from her desk and guided them to one of the lab tables. A black, Lycra glove rested on the slate, and a long thin fiberoptic cable.

Helen placed the cable underneath a microscope and gestured for Taylor to take a look. Taylor peered into the microscope. On the end of the cable, near the laser aperture was an almond-shaped servomechanism equipped with a series of miniature fins. The entire device was only 20 mm in length, about eight-tenths of an inch.

"The servomechanism is based on the same turbo fluidics that propels a shark through water," she said. "Since the goal is to move the laser up the blood stream, against the current of flow, it made sense to use that current to our advantage."

"And this does that?"

"There's an intake valve in the nose of this mechanism that will take in plasma and use the force of that flow to power the propulsion device. I call it our 'blood-shark.' Since sharks are drawn to blood, I thought the name was appropriate on many levels."

"Plasma is thicker than water," Taylor said.

"Accounted for. The intake filters small proteins from entering without clogging."

"Let me get this straight," Malcomb said. "The laser is going to swim up the blood stream?"

"Do you have a better idea?"

"No, no, I just—I mean, I—"

Helen waved him off with a flip of her hand. "Moving the laser up the blood stream required significant engineering. I couldn't create something that would crawl up the artery because contact with the blood vessel wall could irritate the lining and be dangerous. I couldn't use a propeller since it could create cavitation bubbles, and bubbles in the bloodstream could be deadly. Swimming seemed the most logical answer."

Taylor nodded, impressed. He couldn't believe Helen had crafted all of this into a robot not much thicker than a human hair. "And steering?"

"There are a series of paired fins; one on the dorsal side and one ventrally. These are for stability. In front, there are two pectoral fins for steering. Directional information from the computer is linked to the fin's micro-motors, allowing real-time adjustments."

"Instructions?"

"Sent from the computer, which analyzes your position in the virtual heart with predicative AI, then communicates that real-time to the blood-shark via a modem in its nose."

"How precise is it? It's got to be exact."

"Hey, I made it didn't I? Here, put this on."

Helen handed Taylor the Lycra glove. Silver wires, which recorded positional input on the location of Taylor's hand and fingers, branched out from each knuckle on the glove like a spiderweb. These wires formed a cable that ran to the port of a Reality Engine Ampere computer.

Taylor slipped the glove onto his right hand, wiggling his fingers into the tight spaces.

Once on, Taylor held the glove up. Helen typed at the keyboard. A graphic representation of the laser appeared on the screen, surrounded by a grid sectioned into 10-micron units, the image of the laser overlapped by a similar image highlighted in red.

"The robotics are designed to mimic your movements, but scaled down to 1/100th scale." Helen held the laser fiber upright for Taylor to examine. "Go on, try it."

Taylor moved his hand an inch to the right. There was no perceptible movement of the laser.

Malcomb's eyes gaped. "It doesn't work. It didn't move at all!"

"Easy," Helen sneered. "I said it scales down movements by one-hundredth." She turned to Taylor. "Come on, give me something to work with."

Taylor moved his hand two feet to the right. This time the laser cable made a noticeable movement, bending towards the right. Taylor glanced at the computer screen. The red highlighted laser image had moved off of the underlying image, in the corresponding vector direction. Its movement arc glowed bright red, the path of movement highlighted against the grid.

Helen gave a satisfied smile. "See?"

"Is it precise?" Taylor questioned.

"Do you have to ask?" Helen said, looking perturbed.

"Yes," Taylor said.

Helen's nostrils flared. She turned and read the data. "Your motion arc was twenty-four inches. That motion translated to 60.96 microns. Precisely."

"Let's check the movement in water," Taylor said.

"Sure." Helen walked over to one of the unoccupied 60-gallon tanks and lowered the entire one-foot length of laser cable into the water. "Try it."

Taylor took a step forward. Instantly, the cable responded, inching forward in the tank. On the computer, the screen flashed the data of Taylor's movement and the corresponding red motion of the laser.

"Forty-seven-inch movement in vector A," Helen said, reading the image on the grid. "119.38 microns. Exactly."

Taylor walked quickly forward, swinging his arm in a wide arc to the left. The cable bent to the left propelling itself in that direction.

"Bi-vector movement," Helen said. "Accommodated for and responded accordingly in both planes of motion."

Taylor sprinted forward, dashing to the end of the lab. The cable shot off simultaneously, swimming through the water towards the end of the tank. Taylor spun around and reversed his direction. The cable followed immediately, shooting off towards the other end. The image on the computer glowed red. Calculation of his movements flashed across the grid.

"Satisfied?" Helen grinned.

Taylor approached the lab bench, his smile beaming. "It's perfect."

CHAPTER 16

Edgar Ross swore as he passed the straight razor across his scalp.

Sitting cross-legged, naked, on the floor of his van, he wiped the razor on a towel, noting a streak of blood on the cloth. Seething, he polished the razor clean—it had to be clean—then went back for another pass across his left temple. He glided the razor over his skin with a carefully modulated stroke. Shaving his head was an obsession for Ross, one he did on every even-numbered day.

His eyes flashed down at the razor. A smear of blood stained the length of the blade. He brought the razor to his face, eye level, glaring at the crimson rivulets on the shimmering steel. He pressed the flat of the blade against his cheek, feeling the coolness of the metal against his flesh. With one deliberate motion, he ran the flat of the blade across his face, the blood smearing his cheek in the blade's wake. He turned it over, pressing the other side against his opposite cheek, wiping the razor clean with his skin.

It has to be clean.

A light flashed on his cell phone. Closing the razor, Ross hit the read button. The message was from his employer in response to his report of Target-one's presence in the ICU.

Dvd nd cnqr.

Ross mentally filled in the missing letters.

Divide and conquer.

Ross studied the message, divining its meaning. He took a deep breath and ran his fingers across the crusted blood on his face.

With the shaving cream and blood drying on his scalp, Ross moved to the van's observation console. The screen flashed and a black-and-white image of Target-2, Malcomb Bernard's computer desk and lab appeared.

Ross grinned. Installing the surveillance cameras in the laboratory had been a challenge, complicated by the presence of a security guard, the logistics of locating the lab lost in the bowels of the darkened basement, and the fact that Bernard rarely ever left the freaking lab. The Abrahms' apartment, on the other hand, had been a snap. Outfitted with a new fire alarm/sprinkler system in each room, Ross had simply pulled out the sprinkler heads and replaced them with the new C Series CT8823 pinhole cameras. Each camera came with its own fake sprinkler camouflage casing. Once installed, it was completely undetectable.

Watching Bernard's computer, Ross knew that his employer would be satisfied. Ross switched off the video monitor. Malcomb's image faded to black. Typing on his laptop he sent an encrypted message.

Payload delivered
Operation overload is go

Hitting the send key, Ross's eyes flared. He loved this moment; the rush that came with the start of a new job. He could imagine no other feeling like it. Adrenaline was like a drug, racing to his heart, driving his pulse, causing his fingertips to tingle. His entire body buzzed, begging for release.

Spinning his chair around, he picked up his briefcase, unclasped it, and pulled out a DVD labeled Target-3. He loaded the disc into the drive and hit the PLAY button.

A crystal-clear image of Sherilyn, dripping wet, stepping out of the shower, filled the screen. Sherilyn dropped her towel when she pulled on her bathrobe.

Ross hit the pause button, freezing her naked body on the screen. Her long bare legs glistened with moisture.

Leaning back, he ran his fingers across the dried blood on his cheeks then reached for his groin.

He was already getting hard.

CHAPTER 17

By the time Taylor arrived at the lab, tucked in the underbelly of Anderson Hall, he was practically flying. He beamed with so much energy he felt he could light up half of San Francisco. Helen's design had surpassed all expectations. Now, he was about to launch into uncharted territory. All that remained was Helen giving the signal that the pig was ready, and the Virtual Heart Project would begin.

Malcomb followed Taylor into the lab and without saying a word walked straight to his battered green metallic desk and climbed on top. He grabbed a bright orange crayon, and began sketching feverishly on the wall.

Damping Fields.
Elastic Deformation; surface vs volumetric.
$F(t) = mx'' + cx' + kx$

He lowered his crayon, surveyed his work then yelled out "Play." Mezzo-soprano Cecilia Bartoli emerged from the computer's Harman/Kardon speakers, filling the lab with the angelic opening chords of Mozart's "*Il Tenero Momento*". The Tender Moment. The instant in time when comes the realization of a dream. Malcomb gave himself a satisfied smile, his head weaving to the music, and returned to his equations.

Taylor watched Malcomb's quirks with his normal fascination, then drew a deep breath. Despite his excitement, he knew he had to throttle down, keep calm, proceed with caution. The Medical Center power hogs would be looking for any misstep to justify their interference. Any carelessness on his part would terminate the project and there'd be no second chance. Many a good medical idea had been decimated by a bad scientific trial.

At the same time, he didn't have much time to prove what the VHP could do. With the Ethics Meeting pending Monday morning, the project could still be halted. Stopped dead in its tracks. That gave him 48 hours. 48 hours to prove beyond a shadow of a doubt what the VHP could do.

48 hours to realize a dream.

Malcomb climbed down from his desk then froze in place, stricken. Taylor watched the color drain from Malcomb's cheeks. The air around him suddenly grew cold.

"Are you alright?" Taylor asked.

Malcomb didn't answer, taking one small step towards his desk. He reached towards his computer, but held his hand there, hovering above the keyboard, not touching anything as if it was poisoned. Taylor watched the twitching of Malcomb's lower eyelid accelerate to a frenetic pace.

"Were you in here last night?" Malcomb finally asked.

Taylor shook his head. "No. Why?"

Malcomb tore open a Nestle Crunch bar, his eyebrows furrowing. "Someone was."

Taylor glanced at the random piles of computers, printers and CPU units filling every square inch of the lab. "How the heck do you know that?"

Malcomb chewed in nervous bites, his mouth chattering like a chipmunk's. "This lab may look like a chaotic agglomeration of discarded parts to you, Taylor, but to me it is a carefully orchestrated symphony of electronics. I know when someone has been in here."

Taylor held up his hands. "What makes you think someone was here?"

"I don't think, I know. Someone was here. They rummaged through our equipment. They moved my computer mouse."

"They did what?"

Malcomb huffed. "On the rare occasions when I actually leave at night, I make certain that my mouse is lined up in the dead center of Mozart's forehead." Malcomb pointed to his mouse pad, a painted portrait of Wolfgang Amadeus Mozart. "That way I can tap into his genius."

Taylor looked baffled. "So, you can do what?"

"Never mind. Just know that right now the mouse is over his ear. Not his forehead."

"And you couldn't have 'eared' it by mistake?"

"Not a chance. Someone was here. They touched my mouse. And your pen is gone, the monogrammed one. It was right here yesterday."

"They took my pen?" Taylor ran his fingers through his hair. A warning ate into his gut. A scientist's lab was a private sanctuary. An inviolable space. No one should be rummaging through their lab, playing with their computer, on the eve of the experiment.

Taylor glanced around the chaotic room that was their workplace and tried to imagine why someone would be in their lab. *And my pen? Why in the hell would they take my pen?* A sudden image of the moving ICU security camera shot through his brain. The hair pricked on the back of his neck. The eagerness he had when he first arrived at the lab now replaced by something darker.

"Was anything else taken?"

Malcomb sat at the desk, typing. "I'm checking the files now. Everything seems normal, but I don't like it. No one should be in here snooping."

Taylor agreed. A memory of the CyberTech logo blazing across Chan's GET WELL card rushed into his mind. He hadn't told Malcomb that the man who wrote their virtual AI application was clinging to life in the ICU. He decided against telling him now.

Malcomb's eyes shifted from Taylor to his wall of equations. He took another bite of chocolate. "I have a bad feeling about this."

"I know," Taylor said. He scanned the shelves, looking for anything that seemed out of place. "Make backups of everything, physical and cloud, and take the log books home when you leave."

"If I leave, you mean."

Taylor managed a smile. "I'll ask the guard to keep a closer eye on our lab."

Malcomb nodded but looked only partially comforted.

Suddenly Helen's voice resounded through the computer speakers. "All set in the animal lab," she said. "The pig's been anesthetized and the femoral catheter is placed. MRI and ultrasound are ready. Are you guys planning on working today?"

Taylor spun towards the computer. His pulse shot off like a rocket. He couldn't believe this moment had finally come. He glanced at Malcomb, noting his face becoming drawn.

"Wonderful," Malcomb grimaced. "Now I hear her via Ethernet in my own lab."

"Are we good?" Taylor asked.

"Reluctantly," Malcomb nodded.

"We're ready Helen," Taylor said. He made his way through the web of wires to the back of the lab where three black partitions formed a small cubicle, a faded brown recliner in the center.

"Isn't that the La-Z-boy from your home?" Taylor asked.

"High-tech all the way."

Draped across the back of the recliner was the Sensory Immersion suit, the SIS made of black spandex to assure good contact between Taylor's skin and the sensors.

Taylor studied the suit. Conductors lined the inside, concentrated over the trunk, thighs, and arms. Designed to receive tactile information from the computer, these conductors transferred this information to Taylor's body by direct stimulation of cutaneous nerves, reproducing all sensations; temperature, moisture, object density and surface texture.

A wave of anticipation flowed through him. So close to stepping into a beating heart. He snapped his head towards Malcomb. "White bishop f1 to c4."

Malcomb glanced up from his computer. "I'll counter; bishop c8 to g4."

"What in the hell are you geeks doing?!" Helen's voice roared through the speakers. "I got a pig out cold on the table, a catheter stuck in its femoral, a blood-shark micro-laser just waiting to take a dive into a coronary, and you're playing chess?"

Taylor laughed. "Don't worry. I'm getting into the suit now."

"Well, it's about time. I'm getting old over here!"

Taylor stripped to his underwear and squeezed into the SIS, pulling it over his thighs and around his waist. It wrapped around him like a second skin. The conductors inside the suit pressed against his skin like a million pebbles stuck in a shoe.

Malcomb helped him stretch the torso of the suit to pull it over his shoulders.

"My God, it's tight," Taylor said.

"It has to be tight for you to feel the conductors."

Taylor nodded. "Help me to the chair."

Malcomb guided Taylor to the recliner.

"Be careful of the wires," Malcomb said. A strip of silver wires streaked down both sides of the SIS, extending from Taylor's wrists to his ankles. The silver strands fanned out at various points—his chest, groin, elbows and knees—to form a web of connecting cables. These cables merged to form one master cable that ran from the suit to the Velocity Engine; relaying Taylor's body position to the computer for instant adjustments to the visual images.

"I look like a marionette," Taylor said.

"Here's your helmet." Malcomb handed Taylor the neural transcendence headset.

Taylor turned the helmet over, examining the horseshoe array of electrodes. From each electrode, a silver wire ran through the headset, combining to form a master cable back to the computer.

Probing each electrode with his finger, Taylor made certain they were properly aligned and connected. He slipped the C-shaped helmet over his temples, which nestled around the back and sides of his head like a roman imperial crown.

With everything in place, Taylor sat in the La-Z-Boy, extending the footrest 45 degrees. Malcomb helped Taylor put on the two modified PowerGloves.

"On the palm of the right hand you'll feel a switch," Malcomb said. "The abort button. If you need to stop, for any reason, touch the switch. It'll halt the program."

"OK," Taylor said, only half listening.

Malcomb retreated to his desk and the computer fired to life. He hit the NEXT button on the MP3 player and Mozart's 'Symphony number 40' filled the lab.

"We'll start with a preliminary testing program to verify the suit's responsiveness," he said into a microphone on his desk. The deep resonance of his voice transferred through the helmet directly to Taylor's auditory cortex, booming inside his head like the voice of God.

"Fine with me," Taylor said. "Let's get this show on the road."

"I agree," Helen's voice echoed through the speakers. "Before the pig and I both die of old age."

"Remember you have the abort button in your right palm," Malcomb said. "I'll be monitoring your vital signs with the sensors built into the suit."

"You really are a mother hen, aren't you, Malcomb? I'm fine, let's go."

"Okay," Malcomb said, making a notation in his log. "Are you ready, Helen?"

"God, yes!"

Malcomb swallowed. "Then Virtual Heart Project, Experiment 1-1 begins now."

With a trembling finger, Malcomb punched the enter button. The computer whirled and the program booted itself and began to run. Lights flashed across the monitor as the screen image went black then flashed to life. Mozart blasted through the speakers, rising to a crescendo of strings and oboes, a symphony of passion, violence and grief.

Then, an electric pain ripped through Taylor's temples, his body spasmed, and all he could do was scream.

CHAPTER 18

Senator Randolph McIntyre walked through the northwest entrance of The National Gallery of Art Sculpture Garden, directly across Constitution Avenue from the National Archives. Originally gifted to the National Gallery by a private grant, the garden was created to give the American people the opportunity to enjoy the grandeur of twentieth-century sculpture in a pleasant garden environment. Walking past Oldenburg and Van Bruggen's nineteen-foot tall 'Typewriter Eraser, Scale X' sculpture, a monstrosity of painted steel and fiberglass, McIntyre scoffed at that thought.

He glanced at his watch. 1:15 P.M. He felt his apprehension rising, just as it did before each meeting he had with the man.

Turning, McIntyre walked down the garden path. The autumn carpet of fallen leaves crunched under his Bruno Maglis. He circled the central fountain towards the stone benches. In the winter, the fountain would be frozen to create an outdoor skating rink, but that wouldn't be until next month when the air turned cold.

After the election.

McIntyre allowed himself a smile. He straightened his Caraceni suit, sat on the bench under the shade of the linden trees and waited. The air was crisp, with an October chill; the fading scent of witch hazel and camellia lingering in the air.

Two Secret Service Agents took position on opposite sides of the fountain, their eyes scanning the garden behind mirrored sunglasses. It wasn't unusual for Presidential front-runners to command Secret Service protection—when requested.

McIntyre looked at his watch again. 1:17 P.M. He surveyed the garden.

Then McIntyre saw him, approaching from the northeast. The silver-haired man held up his hands while the Secret Service Agent patted him down and waved a metal detector across his hand-tailored suit. With a brusque nod, the man was waved through and granted access to the Senator.

McIntyre watched all this unfold, planning his strategy for how the meeting would proceed. Despite the travesty the curators considered art, the Garden remained McIntyre's favorite meeting place away from Capitol Hill. The Hollywood fantasy of secret meetings taking place in dark corners of underground garages was a myth. In Washington D. C., every garage was wired with an army of surveillance cameras. Any meeting would be taped from multiple angles. The reality of post-911 Washington meant that the best strategy to avoid arousing suspicion was to hide in plain sight.

And for that, the Garden was perfect. Far enough from the Russell Senate Office Building, it was unlikely that McIntyre would bump into a fellow senator or aide and the area was rarely frequented by tourists who preferred the Smithsonian or National Gallery. In the Garden, the Senator could enjoy a semblance of privacy.

McIntyre stiffened as the silver-haired man sat on the bench next to him. Reginald Erickson was a husky man, six-foot four, with the weathered skin of a frontiersman. He had the thick, calloused hands of a man who had built the CyberTech Systems empire one brick at a time, applying the mortar with his own sweat. It was only in the cloudy glisten of his eyes, that McIntyre could see a hint of his illness.

Erickson pulled a manila envelope from his suit coat and placed it on the bench between the Senator and himself.

"That's everything?" McIntyre asked.

Erickson coughed a smoker's cough and wiped his mouth with a handkerchief. "That's the original file."

McIntyre nodded. "No back-ups?"

"None."

McIntyre leveled his gaze. "Including your computer?"

Erickson met McIntyre's eyes with a hardened gaze of his own. "I don't believe I need to be questioned."

"If word leaks out—," McIntyre started.

"I have just as much at stake here as you do."

The two men glared at each other, the air thickening around them. Erickson coughed into his handkerchief, a dab of blood-tinged sputum staining the cloth. McIntyre picked up the envelope and placed it inside his coat breast pocket.

"This conversation isn't getting us anywhere," McIntyre said. "We both know what's at stake."

Erickson nodded. "Agreed."

"So where do we stand?"

"The final installment has been made. It will be deposited from six separate bank accounts, per our agreement. Each installment will be below the Federal limit on campaign fund contributions."

McIntyre listened. The autumn wind picked up, swirling the fallen leaves in whirlpools of frigid air. Across the fountain, a young child and his mother chased after a balloon that had slipped through the boy's hand, its string dangling just out of reach as the wind grasped it, pushing it upwards into the steel grey sky.

"And the Antitrust matter?" Erickson asked, watching the balloon sail away. His silver hair fluttered across his forehead.

McIntyre felt the temperature dropping around him. He shifted his eyes towards the oncoming storm clouds. "I've arranged a photo-op at the Google/NASA Ames facility in Mountain View next Friday morning. Being there, in the heart of Silicon Valley will be a perfect backdrop to raise the antitrust concerns."

"These concerns aren't mine alone," Erickson cautioned. "Your challenger O'Neil seems to recognize this. You'd do well to remember that."

McIntyre stiffened at the tone of the man's voice, the veiled threat hanging between them. His finger tips grew cold. He blew into his cupped hands.

"Once in office," Erickson said, "you've promised me the antitrust investigation will be tabled. I can't afford to have my company broken apart now."

McIntyre turned up his collar. "You'll be safe."

"Only if you get the White House." Erickson coughed a deep, forceful hack. His face grimaced with pain. "Have you controlled your situation yet?"

McIntyre hesitated. He tented his fingers under his chin, searching for the right response. *Was it controlled?* The last he'd heard from his contact at the University was that Abrahms' research was starting that morning. The news reports acknowledging his association with Abrahms were due to hit the wire by that evening.

"Let me attend to my own business," he finally said.

Erickson held up his hands. "I'm just reiterating my concerns. If this blows up, Randolph, we both stand to lose everything." He leveled his gaze. "And I don't have to remind you who will lose the most."

McIntyre shook his head in disbelief. *Dying of lung cancer and the old bastard is threatening me.*

The wind picked up. McIntyre watched the fountain, rainbows flickering in its spray. He felt Erickson's gaze boring into him. He closed his eyes for a moment, contemplating the plans already set in motion.

CHAPTER 19

Vision flooded his eyes.

Flashes. Red lights, blue, green... purple. At first, only ghostly images, silhouettes of grey, then slowly, the images cemented into form. Taylor spun his head around, fighting to orient himself. The electric pain in his temples lessened, dissipating to a dull ache. He tried to get his bearings. He found that he was standing inside a long tube, like a drainage pipe, ten feet tall. The wall was made of thousands of geometric sections, hexagons, each fitting together seamlessly, like the work of a perfect mason. He reached out touching the sides; his fingers running across the surface, smooth and moist. A thick layer of slippery mucous rubbed onto his fingertips.

It only took him a moment to figure out where he was.

"My God!" he screamed. "Malcomb, it works!"

Exhilaration raced through him like fire. He gulped a deep breath, spinning his head around to take it all in. The geometric shapes were the lining of the artery, huge endothelial cells, the size of floor tiles, forming the walls of the blood vessel. The artery surrounded him, enveloped him. His feet pressed against the soft vascular floor, while his hands ran across the smooth endothelial lining. Red blood cells, disc-shaped, the size of beach balls but shaped like massive frisbees, raced towards him, flowing past him with the current of plasma. He could feel the forceful nudging as the cells bumped against his body, then rushed by him, shooting down the artery. The plasma flowed over him like a rushing tide and smelled thick of iron and sulfur

"What do you see?" Malcomb's voice came into his head.

"Everything!" Taylor could barely find the words. "I see everything. The blood vessel, the red blood cells. I can actually feel it!"

A dim light filled the lumen, allowing visualization. Taylor swung his head from side to side. He could see the red blood cells shooting past him were soft and pliable, not rigid like he expected. To his sides, white blood cells crept by, undulating along the vascular walls like giant amoebae. Everywhere, around him, the massive *Ba Bum, Ba Bum* of the pulse, bellowed in his ears, pounding out like thunder. The arterial walls shuddered, vibrating with each heartbeat.

Ba Bum. Ba Bum. Thunder.

Incredible.

Taylor stood transfixed, his mouth agape. He'd known how powerful the system was, how advanced the visuals would be with real-time ultrasound updating, but he never expected this. The pounding heartbeat, the flowing red blood cells, the slickness of the blood vessel wall, the vibration of the vessel floor under his feet. The mucous, the smell. An entire world of senses existed within the program. Within his mind. Within the heart.

"How's the system responsiveness?" Taylor asked.

"Impeccable," Malcomb answered. "T-ultrasound update automatic. Visuals reformatting every 100 milliseconds."

"I wish you could see this," Taylor said. "I'm actually standing in a coronary artery. I'm actually here. I can't even describe it."

"How's your visibility?"

"Perfect. At this microscopic level, blood isn't red; it's about as murky as salt-water. It's like scuba diving with giant red cells swirling around my head."

"Sensation? Auditory?"

"Perfect. Helen, can you hear me?"

"Loud and clear," Helen said. "Sounds like you're having a good time."

"That's the understatement of the year. I'm going to try to move now. Is the blood-shark ready?"

"Primed and all systems go. It should track your movements precisely."

"Then I'm going to make my way towards the plaque. Keep me updated."

Taylor took a deep breath, composed himself, then took his first cautious step forward, concentrating on his leg as he lifted his foot off the vascular floor then lowered it. The arterial floor was soft, conforming to his weight, sinking under his foot like the canvas of a trampoline. He could feel the steady rumble of the heartbeat through the soles of his feet, his legs shuddering. He focused on the virtual image of his foot, watching as it lifted off the floor, then went back down. He moved one foot forward slowly, then the other, as if walking on the moon.

For a moment, he wondered what his real body was doing while he walked in virtual reality. Was it motionless? Were his legs flopping around like someone walking in their sleep? He lifted his leg again, watching his virtual foot rise from the vessel floor through the plasma. Then he lowered it.

800 million calculations, ten times per second. The computer was flawless.

The plasma rushed by, a steady current of warm fluid, flowing over him. Stepping forward felt like walking underwater, his movements thick and purposeful.

"Walking feels great," Taylor said. "I'm heading towards the plaque"

"Got it," Malcomb said. "System response optimal."

"Helen?"

"The blood-shark is following you. I have movement in three vectors. The pig is doing well, vitals stable."

Taylor took a few more cautious steps forward, straining to see through the murky flow of plasma. Upstream, maybe ten feet ahead, he could just make out a large dark mass clinging to the vascular roof. A few more steps and he was there.

"I have visualization," he said.

Before him lurked the cholesterol plaque, descending from the vessel ceiling like an ominous outcropping of greasy, yellow stalactites. At the base of the plaque, the arterial lining burned red with irritation. Blood cells, racing in the plasma, smashed against the plaque, rupturing upon impact. Platelets, the body's clotting cells, clumped together at the stalactite's base, like branches getting stuck in a beaver's dam. This was the source of blockage in the pig's artery, a heart attack in the making.

Taylor's mind raced to the next phase. With the blood-shark following his motions, guiding the laser into position inside the real artery, Taylor could now obliterate the plaque. Blood flow would be restored, preserving the hungry cardiac muscle. A heart attack would be abated.

The future of medicine was here.

Taylor's pulse raced. He steadied himself in front of the plaque.

"Prepare the laser for fire."

CHAPTER 20

William Preston stood fuming at the scrub sink of Operating Room 4. Crawford's words from yesterday danced in his head, teasing him like a mocking clown. *Maybe his project has merit.* He thrust his hands under the hot water and began scrubbing abruptly.

"Merit, my ass!" he said out loud. "If Grand Rounds isn't the time to stop his travesty, when is?"

He grabbed the scrub brush in his right hand and scoured his left palm, rubbing so roughly, he could see the skin turn red through the soap foam. Water splashed across the sink, splattering onto the floor. In his peripheral vision Preston could see the nurses sending him askew glances, but he didn't care.

Let them stare, damn it, this is my life on the line.

Grand Rounds was the forum to halt suspect research. Preston wasn't a great ethicist like Crawford was, but he did know that one fact. It was the official venue for debate—the forum for scientific inquiry. It was the perfect time to take Abrahms to the rails over the pitfalls in his project; yet Crawford had backed off.

Why? We had him hanging by a thread!

Preston had no explanation for Crawford's unwillingness to go for the jugular. And his insistence on securing an Ethics Meeting was unprecedented.

Looking through the glass that separated the scrub area from OR 4, Preston could see the nurses readying his emergency patient on the OR table. Angiography films displayed on the computer monitors, revealing the clogged arteries. An acute MI, non-operable by angioplasty, an emergent quadruple bypass surgery was needed to save the man's life.

Preston frowned and shoved his hands farther underneath the water. Crawford's question from the other day entered his mind. *Are you sure you're not just worried about your own department?* He couldn't believe that Crawford had had the audacity to ask him that. Of course he was worried about his own department.

I'm a surgeon, for God's sake!

Bypass surgery was what he did, more than 12,000 of them over his 30 year career. Bypass had brought him a hefty seven-figure salary that was now divided up in estate and alimony between his three ex-wives. Without bypass surgery, his career had no purpose, no income, no reason to exist. And now some young punk had come with a new hotshot technology that was going to make Preston's life work archaic. The day he first saw Abrahms' proposal, he saw the future. He knew that if the project was ever given the opportunity to succeed, his livelihood would disappear before his eyes. He'd be a dinosaur.

Preston scrubbed viciously at back of his right hand, running the scrub brush across his knuckles then between his index and second fingers. Soap bubbles gathered on his leathery skin, forming hidden patterns, then popped, disappearing into nothingness.

Just like my career, Preston thought.

There was no way he could sit idly and watch everything he'd spent his life creating be taken away from him.

With the violence of the back and forth scrubbing motion, Preston felt his necklace medallion bouncing against his chest.

Always tucked carefully out of sight, buried underneath his button downs or scrub tops, Preston thought of the medallion—a faded, round plastic tab, stamped in red with the number "22". He sneered when he thought about where the tab had come from—a small metal foot locker at the homeless shelter in the Mission District.

Preston remembered the shelter well, with its cockroach covered floors, lice-infested sheets and rat-filled showers. He was only ten years-old when that pit became his home after his father gambled away the family savings on a high-risk shopping center development. His mother, a good, strong woman, maintained a stoic calmness as her husband deserted them. For the next eight years, she did her best to raise her son, picking up odd housekeeping and factory jobs, but Preston still remembered the terrifying nights in the shelter, lying awake in bed, too scared to fall asleep; afraid that the foul-smelling drunk in the next bed would reach over and cop a feel. He remembered burying his ears under his wafer-thin pillow to cover up the sounds of the drug addicts fighting or yelling or sucking each other off and then retching in the corner.

He'd worn that locker tab around his neck every day of his life since then as a reminder of where he'd come from and a promise that it would never happen again.

Crawford's words burned into his brain. Preston sensed that time was running out. He knew he had to do something.

An overhead page called Preston to the Operating Room. He finished his scrub, heaving the scrub brush at the sink. It ricocheted out of the porcelain basin and bounced across the linoleum floor, scattering soap and water in all directions. Preston could feel his own heart pounding.

"We haven't played our last card yet," Preston said.

The nurses watched him as he kicked open the door to OR 4 and stormed inside.

CHAPTER 21

The laser floated before his eyes.

Looking like something from a Buck Rogers comic strip, Taylor reached out and grasped it. It felt solid in his hands, its data encoded in the program, running down the cables to the sensory conductors in his PowerGlove, firing his cutaneous nerves to feel it. Smooth and cold and heavy to his touch.

Taylor grinned. Malcomb could have programmed the laser to look like anything he chose. He'd had half-expected it to look like Mozart's baton or a giant Nestle Crunch Bar. But he'd chosen a Buck Rogers Atomic Disintegrator pistol.

With the laser gripped firmly in his hand, Taylor turned and looked down the artery. The computer adjusted his view as his head swiveled. Smoothly. Effortlessly.

It's come down to this, Taylor thought. Everything a surgeon needs, from the feel of the instruments to the distention of the tissues can be broken down into a stream of electronic information, fed into a computer and reconstituted with the aid of AI. Cells and organs are now just bits and bytes. Blood flow is a mathematical equation.

It's the age of the virtual surgeon.

"I've visualized the plaque," Taylor said. "How's the pig?"

"Vitals are stable." Helen's voice resounded in his head. "Blood pressure's good. Anesthesia is steady."

"And the laser?"

Malcomb's voice broke in. "Located 2.5 millimeters from the distal end of the pig's left main coronary."

"Perfect. Track the laser when I move in."

"Tracking."

Taylor stepped forward, inching closer to the obstruction. With each step towards the plaque, the plasma pulsed faster, the current raged around him with increasing fury. Like a boulder jutting out of a flowing river, the plaque transformed the current into a vortex of turbulence. Spiraling eddies gathered against the artery walls, the red blood cells spinning wildly, whirling out of control.

The force of the vortex was surprisingly strong. Taylor felt himself sucked towards the plaque. He tightened his leg muscles for support, bracing his quads against the current. He didn't know what would happen if he lost balance and was launched into the current downstream, and decided he wasn't about to find out.

"Laser movement?" he asked.

"Confirmed," Malcomb said. "You're looking good."

Taylor took a deep breath, adrenaline surging in his fingertips. "Helen?"

"The laser tracking is confirmed. The pig is stable."

So far, so good. Taylor leaned forward and studied the plaque, hanging down from the arterial roof before him. He scrutinized its coarse, irregular surface, looking alien like something from the moon. With his free hand he reached out, his fingers running across the surface. It was thick and oily. A gummy slime oozed between his thumb and index finger. The fatty slime of cholesterol.

He probed deeper, working his fingers into the crevices that cut deep into the plaque, searching for an area of weakness. The pounding thunder of the heartbeat sent tremors rippling through the artery walls. Plasma rushed by him. Taylor's whole world pulsated.

Ba Bum. Ba Bum.

Locating the plaque was one thing, obliterating it was another. If the plaque wasn't destroyed with absolute precision, pieces would break off and shoot down the artery causing a massive heart attack. If his aim was off, he'd burn right through the vessel wall. Either way, the experiment would be deadly.

"Start the Heparin," Taylor ordered.

"1,000 units per hour," Helen said, starting the anti-clotting medicine.

Taylor took another breath, trying to calm his own pounding heart. He decided the best course of action would be to work on the apex first then move to the base. Vaporize it from the tip to the foundation. He worked his fingers into a greasy crevice running diagonally, pinpointing his target.

Ba Bum. Ba Bum.

"Laser position locked." Malcomb said. "Ultrasound updates are steady."

"Okay," Taylor said. "Laser power?"

"Power set at 45 millijoules," Malcomb said.

Taylor took a long breath. His pulse buzzed in his ears.

"Helen?"

"All set over here."

"Then here we go," The excitement building in his voice. "Set the laser to discharge. The world's first virtual angioplasty is about to take place."

Taylor focused his eyes on the plaque. The plasma roared around him. His hand trembled with anticipation. Taylor aimed the laser on the crevice. The coronary artery pulsed faster, the thunder of the heartbeat booming like a canon in his ears.

Ba Bum. Ba Bum.

All of his years of work and training had come down to this moment. He wondered what would happen when he squeezed the trigger. Would the laser function as expected? Had the navigation system worked properly, guiding the blood-shark to the plaque and not the artery wall? Would the plaque disintegrate with the burst of energy or would the laser burn right through the artery? Would he save a life or take one?

His mind raced through the helmet schematics; the positioning of each electrode, the rendering speed of image update, the haptic cues of sensory input. All perfect and precise. It all came to him. Three years of his life, a childhood dream, all intersecting at this one point in time.

Ba Bum. Ba Bum.

"The laser's ready?" he asked one more time.

"We're go," Malcomb's voice responded.

"The pig is stable," Helen added. "EKG normal."

Taylor clenched his teeth, his jaw muscles tightening. He focused on the plaque, ignoring the distraction of the swirling red blood cells, the pounding heartbeat, the plasma. He fought against the pull of current sucking him towards the vortex of turbulence. He steadied his hand.

Ba Bum. Ba Bum.

Then he squeezed the trigger.

CHAPTER 22

The ringing of the CyberEscape phone nearly startled Sherilyn out of her skin.

With the debut issue of her cyberTravel magazine hitting the internet and travel agencies in less than two weeks, it wasn't unusual for her to be working alone in her Embarcadero Plaza office on a Saturday morning; especially with Taylor scheduled in the lab all day. Handling all of the pre-production work herself, she'd grabbed a Starbucks pistachio latte and lost herself in the tools of her InDesign publishing software. With her staff gone for the weekend, the office was quiet, the only sound being the tapping of morning rain against the window. She'd already completed a third of her layout, everything was proceeding perfectly.

The last thing she expected was a phone call.

Parking her coffee, she placed the wireless headset over her ear. "CyberEscape."

The voice that came back couldn't have been more unexpected. "I thought I'd find you there. I bet he's abandoned you for his laboratory again, hasn't he?"

Sherilyn's body immediately stiffened.

"Dad, is that you?" she asked hesitantly.

"Of course, it is," Senator McIntyre answered. "Don't you recognize the voice of your own father anymore?"

No, not really. Sherilyn rose from her desk and tried to recall the last time she'd spoken with her father. The Senator had been so vocal in his disapproval of her marriage that phone calls with the man had become unbearable. Rather than hear him raving one more time that she had to 'wizen up' and choose between her family and that man, Sherilyn had cut off communication with him completely. Whether the Senator liked it or not, if he was going to press her to the wall, her first loyalty would be to her marriage, and to the man she loved. She took a deep breath and tried to fight back her rising apprehension.

"What do you want?" Sherilyn asked carefully, waiting for the bomb to drop. She knew full well that whenever her father called, a hidden agenda was involved.

"Can't a man call his own daughter to say hello?"

And so, it begins. Sherilyn's eyes narrowed. "You gave up rights to a friendly 'hello' the day Taylor and I married. I believe it had something to do with you pulling me aside to lecture me that I was marrying the wrong man. Trailer Park trash, I believe you called him."

"Aren't we passed that yet?"

"It was my wedding day, father."

The Senator fell silent. Sherilyn fought the urge to hang-up. "So why did you call me?"

"You're right," the Senator finally said. "I was wrong to have said that. I was wrong to have pulled away my support on what should have been the happiest day of your life. I'm sorry."

Sherilyn hesitated, momentarily taken aback by the Senator's apology. In all her years living under the same roof with her father, she could never once remember the words 'I'm sorry' coming from his mouth. Now having heard it for the first time, she didn't believe it one bit.

"I'm sure you are."

"Can we move on now?"

"Don't we always?"

"How's your mother?" McIntyre asked.

Sherilyn regarded the question warily. "She's fine. Looking forward, I'm sure, to the day that she has to move into the White House with you and live the lie again."

"I know you don't agree with our arrangement, but it works for us. Your mother and I have an understanding."

"That you'll abandon her for your career?"

The Senator remained calm. "The life of a public servant requires dedication and sacrifice. Sacrifices that have to be made for the greater good of the country. You'd do well to learn that lesson yourself."

Sherilyn felt the familiar antipathy that accompanied conversations with her father. The only sacrifice she could see her father making was the human sacrifice of his own mother if it'd advance his political ambitions. She walked to the front of her desk, absently picking up a page of ad copy.

"Did you call to tell me how I should live my life?"

"No, dear. I didn't. And I don't want to fight."

"Hmmm."

"Have you seen the polls? The election's heating up."

"A ten-point lead as I recall."

"It's twelve points now."

"Congratulations. Is that what this phone call is about? Now that the White House is looming are you trying to create a loving family that can stand with you on the South Lawn for photo-ops and Presidential Christmas Cards?"

The Senator paused. "You cut me with your words."

Even through the phone, Sherilyn could sense his insincerity.

"Yeah, right."

"Okay, then, that is a part of it," the Senator said. "I'm about to become the President of the United States and I'd like to have my family around to enjoy it. Is that such a bad thing, to bring the family back together for a once in a lifetime event?"

The Senator's conciliatory tone caused Sherilyn to pause. It did make sense, after all. Now that he was on the verge of attaining his highest goal, maybe there was a part of him that had the insight to see the decimated remains he'd left in his wake.

Or maybe not.

"What about Taylor?" she asked.

"What about him?"

"Is he included in this grand family reunion of yours? Will his face be staring back at the American people on your Christmas card, or will he be hidden behind the statues of Rudolph and Santa?"

The Senator's voice lowered. "I've made mistakes with you and with him," the Senator said. "I'm ready to include him in the family."

"Uh-huh."

"I'm serious."

"Why?"

"Because he's your husband."

Sherilyn's anger pulsed. She stormed back towards the window. "Give me one reason I should believe you."

The Senator paused. "I just need to spend some time with the boy. Get to know him. I never had the time to talk with him."

"You never took the damn time."

"I'm trying to. Right now."

An awkward silence passed. Sherilyn didn't like this conversation and wished to God she'd never answered the phone. *Why did I answer on a Saturday anyways?*

"Listen, Dad," she said, with as much sarcasm as she could muster. "I don't have time for your games. What do you want?"

"I'm coming to San Francisco. Friday morning. I have a speech at Google/NASA-Ames, then the opera later that night. I'd like you to join me as my special guests."

"You're inviting Taylor and me to the opera?"

"Yes, say you'll come."

Sherilyn was at a loss for words. "You expect me to drop everything I'm doing and meet you for a campaign stop?"

"I'm asking for you join me as a family."

Sherilyn fought back the instinct to gag. "I don't know if Taylor's available. He's starting his experiment."

"Then he could use the break. Promise me he'll come."

A nagging uncertainly filled her. "I don't know."

"I'm asking you, Sherrybear," he said, using the nickname he called her when she was in nursery school. "This may be my last chance to be a father to you."

Sherilyn pondered his words, not knowing what to believe. Every ounce of her common sense screamed for her to hang-up. To fight off his lies and get back to the business of magazine design and ad placement and layouts without the intrusion of Senator Randolph McIntyre.

But one thing was clear, the Senator wanted something. She thought for a moment about the difficulties Taylor was facing trying to get the Virtual Heart Project started. If he had an ally like Senator McIntyre behind him, rather than against him, it all might fall into place a little easier. The thought made Sherilyn smile. Using the Senator to help Taylor's research. It almost made tolerating the man bearable.

"I'll see what I can do," she said.

"Great. I'll have a limousine pick you up at seven."

"Fine."

"And Sherilyn?"

"Yes?"

"Make sure Taylor comes. I'm looking forward to seeing him."

"I'll try," she said, but realized that the Senator had already hung up.

Sherilyn took off the headset, glaring at it as if it contained a demon. A bad taste lingered in her mouth and she suddenly felt like she needed a bath to cleanse the Senator's presence from her skin.

CHAPTER 23

A yellow beam of light shot from the laser.

Slicing through the plasma, the laser instantly sliced down the artery, hitting dead center on Taylor's target, deep within the diagonal crevice. On impact, the tip of the plaque exploded in an eruption of dust-like particles. Plasma rushed towards the plaque, swirling the debris into a thick fog of cholesterol dust.

Taylor couldn't see a thing. "I've lost visualization," he yelled. "Report!"

"Scanning," Helen replied.

"Image refreshing," Malcomb said.

"Tell me, people, what's going on?"

"It's coming," Malcomb said. "Updating."

"Tell me! If I burned through the artery wall—?" Taylor started to say, then his words suddenly stopped, his mouth freezing open.

The flowing plasma began to clear and Taylor found himself staring at what was left of the plaque. The laser burst had devastated the cholesterol stalactite, vaporizing the tip, cutting it down to half its previous size.

Oh My God.

Taylor's eyes grew wide. "Can you see it?"

"I see it," Malcomb whispered.

"Ultrasound confirmation?"

"It's real."

Taylor couldn't believe what he was seeing. It had worked. It really worked!

"Unbelievable!" Malcomb screamed.

"The pig?" Taylor asked quickly.

"Doing fine!" Helen called out. "Heartbeat steady."

"Laser discharge 45 millijoules," Malcomb said. "Intravascular ultrasound confirms reduction of plaque size by 53 per cent volume."

Taylor brought his hand to his mouth, suddenly overcome by emotion. After all the years holed up in the lab—the sacrifice, the time—

It really worked.

Hesitantly, Taylor stepped forward, studying the remaining stump of plaque. The edges were rounded, smooth, as if melted, where the laser had burned through the fatty cholesterol. Microscopic dust of plaque particles rained down from the vessel roof, swirling in the plasma like fish food being dropped into a tank. Taylor took a moment, to let it all sink in.

It was the greatest moment of his scientific career.

Then it all went suddenly wrong.

The plaque stump disappeared.

The visuals inside the artery flickered, strobing on and off, like a momentary loss of a television transmission.

"What was that?" Taylor asked.

"What was what?" Malcomb's voice came back.

Taylor's view inside the blood vessel stabilized, returning to normal.

"Are you alright?" Malcomb asked.

"I lost visuals for a second." Taylor's eyes squinted, studying the vessel; the plaque, the endothelial wall. Everything looked normal.

"Helen, is the pig stable?"

"We're good," she replied.

"And you?" Malcomb asked.

Taylor fought back a rising apprehension. Swallowing, he shook his head. "There was a disruption of visuals for a second, then—" Taylor cut off. The vessel image flickered again, blinking on and off. Faster this time. Strobing.

A rumbling sound gathered in the background, growing louder, coming closer.

Taylor perked his ears. "Do you hear that?"

Malcomb said. "Hear what?"

Taylor spun around looking down the artery. "I hear rumbling. It's getting louder."

"Repeat that," Malcomb said.

Taylor squinted, his eyes scanning, searching. "It's like the sound of an earthquake. Coming closer. And the visuals—"

The image flickered faster, alternating views of the artery with flashes of white light. The light getting brighter. Blinding.

Taylor squinted, shielding his eyes with his hand. The rumbling increased, growing closer.

"Taylor?" Malcomb asked.

Taylor started to answer—but stopped. The entire artery shuddered around him. At first a tremor, a quick jolt, then it increased in intensity, like an earthquake. Getting stronger.

Red blood cells scattered about wildly, bouncing off the vascular walls, ricocheting like pinballs. The plasma churned with increasing ferocity, like a storm tide crashing against the shore. Taylor's balance teetered.

"Taylor? Answer me? What's going on?"

The earthquake intensified. The vascular floor convulsed under Taylor's feet with increasing violence.

"I got major movement here," Taylor managed to say. His heartbeat burst in his ears. "The whole artery's shaking."

"Explain," Malcomb said. "The computer looks good."

A violent tremor rocked the blood vessel launching Taylor against the cellular wall, then falling face first to the vascular floor. Red cells poured down around him, platelets dropping like debris falling from a crumbling building. "I got an earthquake in here, Malcomb. Everything's moving. I can't stand!"

"Helen, is the pig causing this?" Malcomb asked.

"Negative," Helen shot back. "We're quiet here. The pig's asleep."

"Taylor, I don't have a problem on our end. Tell me what's happening."

The flashing intensified, increasing in frequency. Faster.

The vessel walls quaked.

"It's all going wrong!" Taylor said in a rushed stutter. Another upheaval launched Taylor like a ragdoll against the other wall.

"I've got to abort. Repeat. I'm going to ab—"

Then his vision seared to white.

CHAPTER 24

"What's going on in there?" Malcomb yelled into the microphone.

Malcomb's eyes shot to the La-Z-boy. Taylor's body, dressed in the SIS, thrashed about on the recliner, twisting and turning. His eyelids half-open, his eyes darted across the ceiling as if tracking an image in a nightmare.

"Taylor, talk to me. Are you alright?"

There was no answer.

"What's happening?" Helen's voice resonated through the speakers.

"It's Taylor. Something's gone wrong."

"What?"

"I don't know!"

Malcomb's panic was growing. He'd been monitoring Taylor's progress in virtual reality, keeping careful records of Taylor's sympathetic responses, heart rate, blood pressure, EEG readings. Everything had been normal until suddenly the readings flew off the scale. Taylor's heart rate shot through the roof, dangerously high, then his blood pressure and respiratory rate.

Malcomb raced through the cluttered lab, stumbling over discarded computers to reach the recliner.

"Taylor?" he screamed.

Taylor splayed out on the recliner, his body shuddering, his legs shooting outwards in convulsing spasms. The heart rate alarm shrieked. Malcomb flashed a glance at the monitor. Taylor's pulse topped 220, and climbing.

Malcomb paced in tight circles by the recliner. "If you don't abort now, I'm shutting you off," he screamed. "Do you hear me?"

Malcomb waited for an answer. "Taylor?"

"Talk to me," Helen said. "Tell me what's happening."

"His vitals are off the chart!" Malcomb yelled. "And he's thrashing around on the recliner in seizures. Something's wrong. Something's very wrong."

"What about the computer?"

Malcomb shot a glance towards his desk. "I don't see a problem. My screen shows him standing in the blood vessel. But—" Malcomb suddenly cut off.

"What?" Helen asked. "But what?"

"His heart rate. It's shooting through the roof. His breathing —" Malcomb's eyes widened. "His breathing is too fast. Respiratory rate is 34... 36. Jesus, his blood pressure—"

Suddenly, Taylor's entire body convulsed. His arms and legs shot rigid, then jerked. Taylor's back arched, shooting him upright in the recliner then he collapsed back down in a contorted spasm.

"Good God!" Malcomb shrieked. He flailed backwards from the recliner, tripping over a pile of modems and wires. He climbed to his feet and raced to the desk.

He shot his arms towards the computer, then punched the ABORT button.

The angioplasty program screeched to a halt.

CHAPTER 25

The Willard Intercontinental Hotel, poised on the corner of 14th Street and Pennsylvania Avenue, two blocks from the White House, was often called the Residence of Presidents. Lincoln had stayed there prior to his inauguration, his family watching the inaugural parade from the sixth-floor balcony. In the ornate lobby, where Senator Randolph McIntyre now sat, rumor has it that Ulysses S Grant coined the term "lobbyist," when he'd been constantly confronted by constituents seeking his favors, causing him to yell out, "get these damn lobbyists out of here!" And it was in this hotel that Martin Luther King wrote his impassioned 'I Have a Dream' speech, delivered the next day on the steps of the Lincoln Memorial during the March on Washington.

This sense of history wasn't lost on McIntyre. Much like President Coolidge had done in 1923, McIntyre maintained the Willard Federal Suite as his residence in Washington. McIntyre loved immersing himself in the history, soaking in the still-present ambiance of Lincoln, Grant, and King. Just like them, McIntyre thought of himself as a man of the people, a man of action.

A man of destiny.

"The micro-targeting in Iowa and Ohio looks strong," Roderick Stevens was saying, "But the RNC isn't moving along too well in the South."

McIntyre broke from his reverie and took in the ruddy face of his campaign advisor. The Senator sucked deeply on his Cohiba, enjoying the warmth of the Cuban tobacco. While smoking had been banned from most restaurants, bars and hotel lobbies in Washington D.C., it was still allowed in the Willard lobby as a courtesy to visiting statesmen from Europe and the world, where no social event was complete without a glass of brandy and a Cuban cigar.

"Talk to them." Smoke billowed over the Senator's head. "Move door to door."

"I've already done that. They've run into some roadblocks from regional Consumer Privacy Groups. They've had to shut down their computers."

McIntyre frowned. What Roderick referred to was the latest darling of the Republican National Committee, micro-targeting, which used a sophisticated computer program to digest reams of consumer data—magazine subscriptions, survey information, social media posts, DMV data, data collected by grocery stores with electronic discount cards—and spit out a personalized political proclivity score for each person in the state. According to the program, if you drank gin and drove a Volvo, you'd most likely vote Democrat; bourbon and Chevrolet meant Republican. Using this score, the RNC could target door-to-door encounters, bringing the election right to those voters on whom they could have the biggest impact.

"Ignore the consumer groups." McIntyre sipped his Remy Martin. "Until they get a court order demanding we shut that computer down, it's running day and night. We've only got three more weeks until the election, for Christ's sake."

Roderick nodded, acknowledging McIntyre's orders. He paused while a constituency of Iraqi delegates walked by, strutting across the richly-detailed marble floor. The newly elected Iraqi President was scheduled for a high-profile address before the Senate on Monday. His entourage surrounded him; stiff-backed men in pristine military uniforms. Secret Service agents fanned out around them, scanning the guests for potential threats. The Senator's own Secret Service flanked the lobby on both sides, while McIntyre held court in the semi-private vestibule in the lobby's northeast corner.

The Senator stretched out on the red leather sofa and took it all in. The Willard was a major player in the social and political life in Washington and McIntyre loved the buzz. His feeling that night was relaxed, enjoying his lead in the polls. He felt powerful, indestructible.

Presidential.

"Come on, this is beginner's stuff," the Senator said to his campaign advisor. "I expect you to handle this."

Roderick nodded again, but looked troubled. It was then that McIntyre noted the dark puffiness under Roderick's eyes. His skin seemed blotchier than normal, his nose even more red and bulbous.

"What's the real problem?" the Senator asked.

Roderick cleared his throat and leaned forward. "Have you seen the Post?"

McIntyre shook his head. "That's what I pay you for."

"Here," Roderick said, pulling the paper out of his briefcase. "But let me warn you, you ain't gonna like it."

McIntyre placed the newspaper on the couch, unopened. "Tell me what it says."

"It's about your son-in-law."

McIntyre nodded slowly, his gaze drifting down to the brandy snifter in his hands. He swirled the cognac in a lazy clockwise motion. "And...."

"It's started."

"What has?"

"The attacks."

The Senator's eyes narrowed. "No riddles, Roderick."

"Your opponent, O'Neil. The Democrats picked up the news we leaked about you being unhappy with the research in California. O'Neil has come back hard and heavy, lambasting you in his speech at the League of Women Voters. He did just about everything but call you an outright fraud, screaming about you cutting funding for hyper-biotech while your own family is spending dollars on that very thing."

The Senator nodded, expecting this response from his adversary. Snead O'Neil, the Democrat from New Hampshire, had always been a mundane, rather faceless politician, but a careful one. One who rarely made mistakes, clinging to the tried-and-true issues of the economy and defense. He straddled the fence so tightly on hot seat issues like abortion that the running joke was that the man needed to see a proctologist just to get the fence post out of his ass. The Senator knew that his public acknowledgement of the research at SFU would be all O'Neil needed to launch the most vigorous attack of his campaign.

He'd expected as much. He'd planned for it.

The Senator took a sip of his cognac and crossed his legs. "Is that all?"

"Is that all?" Roderick's eyes grew wide under his puffy eyelids. "He can bring you down on this one. You brought this on yourself by making that project an example for your campaign. Your entire flank is exposed and he's firing in for the kill."

"Is that all?" the Senator repeated evenly.

"Aren't you listening to me? This can turn the election. Attacks of fraud and nepotism aren't gonna fly three weeks before E-day. The Democrats are pouncing on this like coyotes in a hen house. The polls already show that."

With the last statement, the Senator stiffened. He leaned forward on the couch. "Tell me about the polls."

"It's just one, just an exit poll after O'Neil's speech at the League, but it hurt you. It definitely hurt. Your numbers dropped six points with just that one speech. Just wait until the damn New York Times and cable talking heads get a hold of this. It'll be fucking Research-Gate or Heart-Gate or whatever the hell 'Gate' they want to call it."

McIntyre placed his cigar in the ashtray and studied his Campaign manager, reading the emotion in his face, the fear. He could see that in Roderick's eyes the death knell had been sounded. The ship was about to go nose down.

"When able to attack, we must seem unable," McIntyre said slowly.

Roderick's jaw dropped open. "What'd you say?"

"When using our forces, we must seem inactive."

"Shit!" Roderick huffed, throwing his hands in the air. "We're about to go down in flames and you're spouting out that damn Chinese poetry again. Didn't you hear what I said? The shotgun's been loaded with buckshot and it's about to fire in all directions."

The Senators eyes narrowed to hardened slits. "I heard what you said," McIntyre said flatly, "And I'll ask just this once to watch your tone with me."

Roderick sank in his high-backed leather chair. "I'm sorry. I just saw this coming. It's gonna get messy. We got to be proactive. I'm rounding up the speech writers right now and we'll work to create distance between you and this."

The Senator shook his head. "You'll do nothing of the sort."

"Come on, Randolph. O'Neil's jumping all over this. It's as bad as we feared."

"Listen to what I'm saying." The Senator locked his eyes on Roderick. "When able to attack, we must seem unable. When using our forces, we must seem inactive. When we are near, we must make the enemy believe that we are far away."

"More Sun-tzu?"

"Everything is going as planned."

"But the polls—"

"Fuck the damn polls!" McIntyre snapped, his patience growing thin. "A tiny drop in an insignificant poll pales in comparison to what we'll gain. I know what I'm doing. Trust me on this one."

Roderick was shaking his head. "I don't know if I can, Randolph. I got others I have to answer to. Once the flack starts coming in from the RNC and Republican Congress, I don't know if I can stop it." Roderick spread his hands wide and shrugged. "It's on the table, Randolph. No amount of Chinese philosophy is going grease your ass out of this trap?"

McIntyre read the concern on Roderick's face and knew he had to handle this carefully. Three weeks before the election, with O'Neil breathing down his neck, he couldn't afford to lose the confidence of his campaign manager. With the situation in Abrahms' laboratory about to get dramatically messier, the wrong word leaked to the media at this time would be deadly for his campaign.

His best strategy was to reverse the burden of responsibility. McIntyre handed the newspaper back to his campaign manager. He spoke evenly, exuding confidence with each word. "Roderick, you're probably blaming yourself for this situation. Don't. I wanted this in the media to draw attention to the issue. The family connection at this point only focuses more eyes on the problem. I've been planning for this." McIntyre leaned back on the couch. "Where do we stand on the trip to San Francisco?"

Roderick frowned. "Randolph, I'd rather talk about—"

The Senator cut him off. "I asked where we stand on the trip."

Roderick sighed. Tapping at his computer he brought up the logistics for the upcoming visit to the Google/Nasa Ames Research Campus. "We have you flying out from Dulles at eleven Thursday night. We expect a huge turnout from the Silicon Valley executive and research crowds. But I don't see how this is going to solve our problems."

McIntyre inhaled deeply on his cigar and once again took in the enormity of his surroundings. He was keenly aware that it was also at the Willard that Julia Ward Howe composed "The Battle Hymn of the Republic," the ultimate Union fight song, sung as the soldiers of the North marched victoriously from battle, and chanted as slavery came to a long overdue end. Now, the Senator readied for his own battle, his mind racing forward as each step was slowly falling into place.

"What we're going to do is keep the pressure on Abrahms," the Senator said. "Don't do anything to create distance. Don't brush this aside as my family embarrassment. I want this to be a focus. The failure of Abrahms' research will bring unprecedented exposure to the issue. The family connection makes it stronger. Once his research fails my stock will soar."

"What if he succeeds?"

"He won't."

"But what if—"

The Senator cut him off with a steely glance.

"He won't."

CHAPTER 26

Taylor rubbed his eyes, demanding that they focus one more time.

He'd been going over the same computer program, time after time, for twelve straight hours, but he couldn't stop yet. Not until he had an answer.

Once again, he typed at the computer.

    /file:anatomy/scan
    /status: open

An image of a human male body flashed upon the screen. Taylor typed:

    /enhance file/ status
    /enlarge/file/open
    /animate

The image leapt off the screen and a three-dimensional holographic creation of a perfectly formed male body, floated inside the lab. The body glowed in pale blue light, x-y axis lines running down the length of its spine, z-axis lines encircling the torso. A dark blue grid projected across the skin, sectioning the form into anterior, posterior, dorsal and ventral segments.

Taylor studied the body, lying prone, hovering over his head. It rotated clockwise around a horizontal axis.

/command/exfoliate

Instantly, the virtual skin disintegrated, revealing the dense muscular fibers underneath. The body rotated above him, presenting different parts of the anatomy to Taylor's view: chest, left side, back, right side.

/command/DNL/open view

With the command, the musculature disintegrated. Taylor stared into the ethereal skeleton. The bones glowed in brilliant white. Encased inside the bony framework, each organ was intact, perfectly depicted in 48-bit color.

Stepping away from Malcomb's desk, Taylor walked underneath the rotating holographic image. He looked up. In the chest cavity, rotating above his head, the heart pumped steadily, its globular structure tightening with each contraction. Blood shot into the aorta with each beat, causing the main blood vessel of the body to shudder. The coronary arteries branched from the aorta, coursing around the muscular walls of the heart. The pericardium looked slick and moist, glimmering in the light.

/enlarge cardiac Image
/enhance coronary flow
/open

The body faded away, replaced by a massively magnified image of the heart, still floating above his head. Each coronary artery was as thick as a heavy rope wrapping around the bulbous organ. The sound of the heart beat reverberated through the speakers, the now familiar *Ba Bum, Ba Bum*. From Taylor's vantage point, he could see the blood flowing through his simulation. He could see the individual blood cells rushing down the arteries, carrying oxygen. He could see it all.

Now all I have to do is figure out how to get back inside.

Taylor looked at his watch and rubbed his eyes. It was 10:30 p.m. They'd been going at it since eight that morning. With the halting of the angioplasty, Taylor had emerged from the virtual reality program disoriented, like a man emerging from a bad dream. Pain, like an ice pick, drove into his temples. His body stung with fire, a million burning needles jabbing into his flesh. The SIS was glued to his body with sweat.

Helen had confirmed that the pig was unaffected by the disastrous end to the angioplasty. Whatever it was Taylor experienced in the virtual reality, hadn't translated to a problem with the pig.

While Helen signed off to care for the pig, Malcomb and Taylor set about searching for answers. Malcomb had dissected every step of Virtual Heart Project Phase One, experiment 1-1. Each of Malcomb's anti-viral scans had come back negative. The diagnostics had found nothing.

No virus. No errors.

There has to be an answer.

Turning from his projection, Taylor faced Malcomb. "We can't shut down. You know as well as I do, we don't have the time."

"But, Taylor—"

"Listen," Taylor said, walking out from underneath the floating heart. "I don't want a de Messier Syndrome any more than you do."

Malcomb nodded, knowing full well the details of Dr. Pascal de Messier's first attempted and failed telepresent operation. Halfway through a robotic coronary bypass, the artery burst open, covering the video camera with blood, the heart rhythm fibrillating. The robotics had to be abandoned to save the patient's life.

"What we need to do," Taylor continued, "is to go through everything again, break it down one step at a time. Logical progression. Go over every program command until we figure out what happened."

Malcomb took off his glasses and rubbed his eyes. "We need to flatten the entire hard drive and start fresh."

"Let's just solve the problem."

"I can't solve a problem I can't find!"

Taylor pushed on. "We know the angioplasty procedure was successful. Whatever happened occurred after laser initiation."

Malcomb ripped open a Nestle Crunch bar and let out a loud huff. He took a bite and started chewing. Chipmunk bites. "Agreed."

"And whatever occurred, happened in my reality only. The pig was unaffected and your monitor showed no trace of a problem."

"Agreed again."

Taylor mulled this over. That seemed to pinpoint the problem to the neural transcendence helmet. He picked up the helmet and sat on the edge of Malcomb's desk, turning the helmet over in his hands, studying each electrode. They were all perfectly connected and in proper place. His concept for neural transcendence came to him after learning of the MRI scanner at Brigham and Women's Hospital that allowed a surgeon to operate on a patient's brain while the patient was being continually scanned, allowing the surgeon to "see" inside the patient's brain. Now, Taylor's concept pushed this one step further. Beyond looking at MRI's while he operated, he'd created a system that put him inside the scans.

And it had worked.

Then, damn it, what went wrong?

Malcomb stood up, stretching his legs and back, loud pops emerging from his spine. "I'm not disputing what you think you saw, Taylor. But it's impossible for you to experience something that wasn't programmed. I've looked for an answer in the coding, but it's not there. There're no running inconsistencies."

"There has to be a virus."

Malcomb squinted. "The scans are negative. We've got firewalls on top of our firewalls. You'd have to be a genius to get through our security."

"Someone came in here before initiation. Maybe they planted a virus."

"There's no virus."

"But maybe the intruder installed a virus when he broke in."

"Taylor!" Malcom shouted. "There is no virus!"

Taylor fell silent. The cluttered lab felt smaller, the walls caving in. Air escaping.

Think, Taylor. Think.

"So where do we stand now?"

Malcomb stared at him blankly, opening his arms. "I have one theory, but you're not going to like it."

Taylor shrugged. "Let's hear it."

"The only rational explanation I can come up with is that the constant stimulation from the EM ring caused a momentary lapse in consciousness for you. In that altered state you had a very vivid hallucinatory experience."

Taylor raised an eyebrow. "You're saying I dreamt the whole thing?"

"Technically, yes."

"You're kidding? I didn't fall asleep. I was so excited I could barely breathe."

"It's the only explanation that makes sense. It must have lulled you into an unconscious state."

Taylor shook his head. "I wasn't dreaming." He thrust his index finger towards the monitors on the wall. "You have my physiologic readings there, look for yourself. My heart rate was erratic, pulse up to 220. My blood pressure, skyrocketing. Those aren't the patterns of someone who's sleeping; they're the patterns of someone who's terrified!"

Malcomb studied the monitors. The look on his face made it clear that he agreed with Taylor's point, but still he refused to acknowledge it.

"The fact remains, it's impossible for you to have a virtual experience other than what's running on the computer. It just can't happen."

Taylor directed his gaze to the helmet in his hands, running his finger over each electrode. None of this was making any sense

"I have an ER shift starting at noon Monday. We'll go back in before that."

Malcomb held out his hands. "We need to run another major diagnostic and recalibrate the system. Give me a week at least."

Taylor shook his head. "Crawford's ethics meeting is Monday afternoon. If they call us in and all we have is one partial success to show, we're finished."

"But—"

"We go back Monday, before my ER shift. We prove this can work. Before the ethics meeting."

"But it doesn't work!"

"We're going in circles here, Malcomb."

Malcomb recoiled in his chair, his eyebrows furrowing. He nibbled on his chocolate.

"I have a real bad feeling about this."

Taylor lowered his eyes and stared at the neural transcendence helmet. He understood Malcomb's trepidation. The truth was he didn't like it either. Something was terribly wrong. The angioplasty wasn't behaving the way it was programmed. But how? Malcomb had created the program himself and the thought of Malcomb creating a blunder of this proportion was absurd. Malcomb played the computer keyboard as effortlessly as Mozart played the piano and Mozart never banged out a concerto in the wrong key.

No. The error isn't Malcomb's. It's something else.

"Do you have another option?" Taylor asked. "One that can save our tenure?"

Malcomb squinted, thinking about this for a long while, his fingers tapping on his desk. He flicked an empty Nestle Crunch wrapper onto the floor. Finally, he spun towards his computer and stabbed the enter key.

```
Diagnostic run 16/ restart
/DIAGNOSTIC ONE (NB)
/Status= RUNNING EXT
/est=1.6 hours
/running
```

"I have a real bad feeling," Malcomb said.

CHAPTER 27

Sunday, October 15th, 9:14 am

The autumn wind whipped through Taylor and Sherilyn's hair as the MG maneuvered through traffic, weaving back and forth between the eastbound lanes of the Bay Bridge. Taylor drove, his hands locked on the wheel, his face pale despite the wind from the convertible buffeting his cheeks.

Yesterday's rain had ceased, but the dark clouds remained, hanging ominously in the sky, thick and heavy, pregnant with violence. Taylor thought that when the storm finally unleashed its fury, it would be one to remember.

The MG emerged from the east side of the Caldecott Tunnel into the vast expanse of the Diablo Valley, a once peaceful ranching and orchard region, now crushed under the weight of development. Taylor hadn't been in this valley for years. He promised he'd never come back, but the message he'd ignored earlier was from his father, asking to see him urgently. Taylor deleted the message the moment he'd heard his father's voice, but Sherilyn insisted he call. Too tired to fight, Taylor relented, and now found himself heading back to a home he'd long ago tried to forget.

Sherilyn sat in the passenger seat beside him, silent, not having said a word since the drive began—her way of expressing her anger at Taylor for once again spending the entire night in the lab. Her silence, combined with the thought of having to see his father, ate deeply into Taylor's stomach.

But there was something else bothering him that morning, something much harder to put his finger on. A nagging, lingering uneasiness. Something more than the failure of their first VHP trial or the thought of his father. Something troublesome, just out of reach. Something he'd felt since the VHP ended. He was on edge, tense, as if something was crawling under his skin, trying to claw its way out.

He fidgeted in the driver's seat, adjusted the rear-view mirror then toyed with the stick shift. He glanced at Sherilyn. The wind buffeted her amber hair, bringing a blush to her perfect cheeks. She didn't meet his gaze; her arms folded, her body shifted towards the window. Taylor could feel her pulling away.

Taylor knew what she was thinking, the pain he caused her with his absence, his hours in the laboratory. He knew she was ready to start a family, to have her husband home and create a life together. And he wanted to give her everything she wanted, be the man she wanted him to be, but he didn't know how. He'd devoted his life to this project since he first entered medical school. He had to prove himself. How could he stop now? Once the VHP was running it would change their lives, they'd be able to afford a house, a new car. Then a family. Everything Sherilyn wanted. Everything the Senator said she'd sacrificed to be with him.

They drove in silence, which became larger by the minute. Taylor wanting to say something, but still, no words came.

*****

Exiting off the 680 in Danville, Taylor headed down Sycamore Valley Road onto Camino Tassajara. As they drove east, the high-dollar housing developments began to fade away, returning to the last remnants of 100-year-old oak trees, fields of cattle, walnut orchards, and weathered barns. The MG sputtered as Taylor turned onto the familiar dirt road that led to his father's house, gravel crunching under the MG's tires. The orchard to the left, old man Doughtery's place, was still standing although ill-kept and in need of repair. The larger orchard on the right, where Taylor spent his youth packing walnuts, was quiet. A large SOLD sign hung from the rusted mailbox, swinging languidly in the dying valley breeze. Next to the mailbox was a brightly painted placard advertising this to be the future sight of the Tassajara Villa Luxury Homes.

Time moved on.

"This is it?" Sherilyn asked, breaking her silence. Taylor cut off the engine. He took in his father's dilapidated wood frame house. Chipped white paint peeled off the exterior, exposing large areas of dry rot in the underlying wood. Graying glass filled the rusted window frames. In front, the lawn had long ago died and turned brown, surrounded by a faded picket fence. Weeds grew out of control and engulfed the worm-eaten fence posts.

"Yep. This is home," Taylor answered, realizing that Sherilyn had never seen where he'd grown up before.

A cold wind picked up, scattering a cloud of dust, swirling off the dirt driveway.

"You okay?" Sherilyn asked, noticing the blank expression in Taylor's eyes.

He turned towards her, forcing a smile. "Let's see what he wants."

They climbed out of the MG and walked up the drive, the gravel crunching underneath their shoes. Sherilyn reached out to grasp Taylor's hand. They passed under the rustling branches of an ancient oak tree, a tire swing hanging from one of the branches, slowly circling in the wind.

Taylor hesitated when he reached the front porch. Perched on the back corner, in their regular spot by the door, were his father's shoes, his work boots, the same ones Taylor remembered as a child; the brown leather faded and cracked, the sides caked with years of gray orchard mud.

There was a time when Taylor loved seeing those shoes. When his mother was alive, Taylor would rush to the living room window each evening, scanning the porch for the arrival of those shoes, heralding his father's return home from the fields. It was a joyous time. It meant they could all be together.

But that was before it all changed.

Taylor pulled the screen open and knocked on the door. There was a hollow reverberation as his knocking echoed underneath the porch roof. Taylor reached up and knocked again.

"I'm coming, I'm coming. Shit, you don't have to knock the fucking door down."

It was his father.

CHAPTER 28

Malcomb was nervous.

Fidgeting with his glasses, he took them off, twisted them back and forth in his hands then put them on again. He knew that it was an annoying habit, one he'd carried with him since he was fitted with his first pair of coke-bottles back in Mrs. Whaley's class in second grade, but it helped him to think. And right now, as he twisted them around and put them on again, he needed all the help he could get.

His mind flashed back to the terrifying aborted run of the Virtual Heart Project; an image of Taylor lost in the virtual reality program, his body convulsing on the La-Z-Boy. With his body wrapped in the virtual suit with its dozens of sensory connector cables, he'd looked like he was a demented marionette dangling on a string.

And the computer was the puppeteer.

A mad, twisted puppeteer.

Around him, Mozart's 'Requiem' mass sprung to life, bursting from the speakers, filling the air with angelic voices, draping an ominous foreboding in the lab. Malcomb had always adored this particular piece by Mozart, sensing that it was his most spiritual work since it was written while Mozart was ill, facing his own death and pondering the everlasting love and mercy of God. Somehow, this seemed the appropriate selection to accompany his twenty-third review analysis of experiment 1-1, since Malcomb was also pondering the deep mysteries of the unexplained.

And how those mysteries could exist inside a computer.

The mad puppeteer.

"Any luck yet?" he heard a familiar voice say.

Malcomb jolted from his concentration, spun around, his eyes fixing on Helen Yang standing at the doorway, followed closely behind by her robotic falcon flapping near her head. Her usual white lab coat was replaced by an oversized scarlet turtleneck sweater and flared jeans. Her hair was down, flowing over her shoulders. She wore make-up, which Malcomb had never noticed her wear before.

Malcomb suddenly became conscious of his wrinkled cardigan and the fact that he hadn't brushed his hair in two days. He stammered. "What are you doing here?"

"Same as you. I came by to check on the experiment. But man, was it hard to find you. I walked around the basement for almost half an hour trying to find this lab. Could they have shoved you in a harder to reach corner, like Siberia?"

"Well," Malcomb shrugged, knowing that his Boiler Room-adjacent lab paled in comparison to the facilities at the Farm. "I get a lot of privacy."

"No doubt," Helen walked deeper into the lab, stepping over a stream of wires that ran across the door jam. A stack of hard drives teetered dangerously to her right.

"My God!" Her eyes opened wide. "This is where you geeks work? Could you possibly shove more stuff in here?"

Malcomb surveyed the clutter that covered every square inch of floor space. It suddenly felt very inadequate. Never in his career had he dreamed that one day a woman would step into his lab. An actual woman. He sank deeper into his cardigan.

"I like computers," he said sheepishly.

"And this?" She pointed to the vast mural of crayon equations that sprawled across the wall.

"Just some notes."

"Ever think of a chalkboard?"

"No, not really."

Helen nodded, smiling in amusement. "You definitely are unique, I'll give you that. Anyways, I wanted to let you know that everything is fine at the Farm. I checked on your pig and he was up and eating like, well, a pig. I still can't believe you used to have one as a pet."

"It really wasn't that unusual," Malcomb started. "With my allergies, I couldn't.... I mean... he really was lovable and..."

"Easy," Helen said, holding up her hands. "I'm just teasing you. I think it's cute."

Malcomb gulped. "You do?"

"Yes. Malcomb and his pig." She gave him a sly smile. "It sounds like a bedtime story. Besides, I know I'm just as weird, with this falcon following me everywhere I go." She instructed the falcon to take perch on top of a precarious stack of monitors.

"It's my motif," she said proudly. "Now, get back to work. If we're going back 'in' tomorrow, you better have that program figured out. So, tell me what're you working on?"

Malcomb gulped again. "You're interested in my work?"

Helen laughed. "I asked, didn't I? Why does that surprise you? We're not so different, you and me. We both like to tinker with technology. We're geeks in action."

"Geeks in action." Malcomb smiled. "I like that."

"So, are you going to show me what you're doing, or do I have to stand here in the computer avalanche zone all day?"

Malcomb nodded and waved Helen towards his desk. On the floor another computer station was running. "I'm trying to figure out why we had to abort the first run," he said. "So, I constructed an auxiliary system and programmed it to run a 'diff' utility."

Helen shrugged. "A diff utility?"

"A side-by-side analysis. The problem that we had was that Taylor encountered a computer experience different than what I'd coded. Antiviral programs search for known malicious coding segments. A 'diff' is different. It scans each line of code against my back-up of the original program, searching for any variations or inconsistencies."

"Has it turned up anything?"

"Not yet, but the answer has to be there. Computers are really pretty simple, they only do what they're told."

Helen agreed. "That's why I like my robots so much. They do what they're supposed to do. Unlike a lot of humans I know."

"Exactly!" Malcomb said, turning towards her. "I—I didn't think anyone else understood that."

"Of course, I do," Helen said, smiling.

Their eyes locked for a moment, Helen holding Malcomb's gaze with her eyes.

"So anyways," Malcomb said, suddenly feeling very warm. "I'm not an expert in system forensics but I should be able to root out this problem."

"You've checked for a virus?"

"That was the first thing I did. I ran six different antiviral programs and they all came back negative. I used intrusion detection/prevention tools also but nothing."

"Is that good enough?"

Malcomb nodded. "Believe it or not, standard antiviral software is pretty good. It can find about 99 percent of all infections."

"Then if it's not a virus, what else could it be?"

"I'm not sure yet," Malcomb said, sitting down cross-legged on the floor in front of the monitor. "But my 'diff' analysis is still running."

Helen was silent for a moment. "Sounds fun. Do you mind if I watch?"

"Not at all. Would you like a chair? I could probably find one if—"

"Nah," Helen said. Moving a printer out of her way, she plopped down, sitting cross-legged on the floor next to Malcomb, her eyes studying the monitor.

Malcomb looked at her for a moment, another surge of warmth racing through him. She was sitting so close that he could smell the floral hints in her perfume. He could never remember a woman sitting that close to him before.

Refocusing on the program, Malcomb typed at the keyboard, bringing up a subsegment for analysis, jotting down notes then bringing up another subsegment. The computer whirled and flashed while the diff program analyzed each line.

Five minutes passed. Then ten. Needing a chocolate fix, Malcomb opened up a fresh pack of Nestle Crunch bars, his second pack of the week.

He looked over at Helen. "Chocolate?"

"Love one." She took a bar from the pack. "When I'm in lab I go through boxes of these things. I can't work without chocolate."

"Me either. I always need—," But before Malcomb could finish, a warning beep resounded from the computer. Malcomb stopped, scanning the message, his eyes growing wide. He'd stumbled upon something that didn't make sense.

Helen noticed his reaction. "What's up?"

"I'm not sure," he straightened his glasses. "See this line?" He pointed to the screen. "I don't remember writing that." He jumped to his feet, ran to his desk and started shuffling through the debris.

Buried under a pile of papers, he found the notebook containing the original programming for the system. He studied the red Crayola on the wall, jotted down an equation, then jumped back to the computer.

He ran the program again; jotting down each line verbatim then compared it with his original notes.

"What's the problem?" Helen asked.

"I'm not sure yet, let me finish analyzing—"

He never finished his sentence. Malcomb gasped. He took off his glasses, wiped them with his sleeve and put them back on. He compared notes from his original programming to the data coming from the diff program.

Good God! They're different!

"What is it?" Helen asked.

"This isn't the code I wrote! The writing of the program has changed."

"But how can that happen?"

Malcomb felt a wave of panic. "Let's check another area."

He took another bite of Nestle and brought up a new subsegment to analyze. Referring to his programming journal, he memorized each line of original code then scrolled through the new segment.

They weren't close either.

Malcomb gasped and fought to swallow his chocolate.

"What is it?" Helen asked.

"There's another one," Malcomb pointed at the screen. "An entire line of code has transformed."

"Where? I don't see it."

"Let me show you this way." Malcomb quickly typed at the keyboard.

```
C:/csdiff vhproject
/cs3Dbinaries
/run
```

Instantly, a massive three-dimensional, multi-colored representation of his program projected onto the far wall of the lab, each line of code symbolized by foot-tall, three-dimensional, geometric shapes, glowing upon the wall in vivid shades of reds, oranges and greens.

Helen drew a breath. "Oh my God."

"You like it?" Malcomb asked.

"It's beautiful. What is it?"

"Something I came up with at MIT. I'm a visually oriented person, so I find it easier to interpret subtle programming errors when represented visually, as opposed to the endless written lines of code."

"Wow!"

Malcomb guided Helen towards the wall. Before them, holographic shapes cascaded down from the ceiling like a waterfall, green cubes and orange spheres and crimson pyramids, flowing in carefully aligned rivers of information. Each shape represented a line of code, organized by its command level, the procedure it instructed the computer to perform. While the 'diff 'program ran, the original code descended in a colorful river on the right, the problem code on the left.

Malcomb cupped his hands before his mouth and gave out a low whistle. When the program was projected this way, the problem became obvious. Line 245. A cube where a pyramid was supposed to be.

"There's the problem," he said. "Can you see it?"

Helen nodded slowly, amazed by the beauty of the colorful shapes spilling down the walls. "That cube?"

"Exactly."

"And there's another one."

"The sphere."

Malcomb nodded in astonishment. "And I see more. The program has completely changed."

"Do you know what caused it?"

Malcomb shook his head. A cold chill ran down his neck. He'd spent years working on the code, thousands of hours pounding it out line by line. It simply wasn't possible for it to change. But if there wasn't a virus, how could it have happened?

He took off his glasses and stared at the cascading river of shapes.

Another misplaced cube.

A pyramid.

Flowing by.

And it was wrong. All wrong.

CHAPTER 29

"You look like crap," Saul Abrahms said, surveying the thick, unshaven stubble on Taylor's face.

Taylor gave his father a hard look. "I've been busy."

Saul turned to Sherilyn. "You, on the other hand look wonderful. You must be Sherilyn?"

"Yes, Mr. Abrahms," she answered. "It's nice to finally meet you."

"Is this guy taking care of you?" Saul asked, stabbing his thumb towards Taylor. "In my day we really knew how to treat a lady. Flowers. Fancy perfumes. None of this slam-bam-thank-you-ma'am that passes for romance these days."

"He's doing well," Sherilyn smiled.

Saul harrumphed and ushered them passed the yellowing window panes leaking light into the hallway. They stepped into the musty air of the living room.

Taylor noticed that his father walked more slowly than he remembered, with no life in his once buoyant step. His hair was patchy and mottled. He'd lost a tremendous amount of weight in the ten years since he'd seen him, his blue overalls hanging limply from his once broad shoulders, his arms looked shriveled and decayed, the skin jaundiced.

Taylor and Sherilyn sat on the sofa across from his father who settled into his worn, plaid easy-chair. Despite the cold outside, the living room was warm and damp, redolent with the stench of spoiled beer. A pale beam of light filtered through the dirty windows, casting the room in shadows, swirls of dust floating in the light rays. Against the far wall, framed photos of Anna, Taylor's mother, rested on the fireplace mantel.

Saul opened a beer.

"Why'd you call?" Taylor went straight to the point, dispensing with formalities.

"What? I'm your father, I need a reason to call you?"

Taylor's eyes narrowed. "It's been ten years."

Saul looked downward, nodding. "It's been a long time."

"I made it clear at Jacob's funeral that I never wanted to speak to you again."

Saul gulped a long swig from the can. A small stream of beer ran down his chin, dripping onto his overall bib. "Ah yes, Jacob," he said, looking beyond Taylor, out the dusty window, his eyes unfocused. "He was a good kid. Always mindful of his father."

Taylor recoiled. "What'd you say?"

"I said he was a good boy."

Taylor's eyes flared. "What the hell did you know about him?"

"I was his father, I knew—"

"Bullshit, you knew!" Taylor lurched forward on the sofa. "You knew nothing about us. You never bothered to know us. You never gave us anything except a beating when we stumbled over your drunken body."

"Now listen here—"

Taylor slashed his hand through the air. "No, you listen, old man." Taylor thrust his finger forward. "The only reason I'm here is because Sherilyn insisted that I talk to you. So cut the crap and tell me what you want."

Saul stared into Taylor's eyes, matching the intensity of Taylor's glare with his own. Then, almost imperceptibly, he let go. His body sank into the chair as if he was shrinking, becoming smaller. He reached up and rubbed his eyes. The opened beer slipped from his hand, dropped to the ground and rolled across the floor.

Taylor looked at his father curiously. Sherilyn reached out and grasped Taylor's hand. Together they watched the old man sink into the plaid chair which seemed to engulf his withered body. The room dropped into an uneasy silence.

"I'm dying," Saul said finally, lifting his face out of his hands.

Taylor looked at him cautiously.

"My heart is failing and my liver's shot. The doctors say they can't operate."

Taylor swallowed hard and gazed at the ground. Beer continued to pour out of the toppled can, the puddle spreading across the wooden floor.

Taylor wondered what he was supposed to say, what he was supposed to feel. Was there supposed to be remorse for this bitter old man who sent him to the hospital three times with concussions? Who beat his brother so severely one night that he blacked out unconscious? Who drank both his and his family's life away?

"Is that why you called me?"

"Yes," Saul said. "I wanted to give you this."

He reached to the side of the chair and handed Taylor an old paperbound journal. The words THIS BELONGS TO JACOB ABRAHMS stenciled in green felt pen on the front cover, printed over the drawing of a '66 Ford Mustang.

Taylor stared at the journal; his mouth parting open. He ran his fingers across the dog-eared cover, his fingertips outlining the creases which coursed like a thousand branching rivers. He opened to the first page. The writing was faded and the page yellowed by time. The paper smelled old and mildewed.

He felt his chest tighten.

"This is Jacob's diary," he whispered.

"I thought you'd like to have it."

Taylor didn't know what to say. A watery glisten filled his eyes. He shifted his gaze to take in the old man.

"I know you and your brother were close, "Saul said.

Taylor winced, as if punched. Heat, stormed back into his temples. He leapt to his feet, his hands coiling into fists. "You knew we were close?" He spit out the words as if poisoned, not believing what he'd just heard. "You knew we were close? What kind of fucked up comment is that?"

"I just meant that—"

"You're damn right we were close." Taylor stepped closer, towering over the older man. "What choice did we have with a dead mother and a drunkard father?"

"Taylor—" Sherilyn said, reaching for his hand, trying to calm him.

Taylor shifted, pulling his arm away. He glared down at Saul, his anger rising. "We were close because we needed each other to survive this hell-hole you called a home." He thrust his finger at his father. "We needed each other to survive you, you bastard!"

Taylor grimaced, pain surging into his temples. He pinched the bridge of his nose, trying to drive the pain away, then glared at his father. He took him in. "So now you've finally drunk yourself to death, you call me. What do you want? Pity? You want me to forgive you? For the years of abuse? For driving Jacob to suicide? You want me to cry out, 'no daddy, don't go?'"

Taylor's eyes shot to the picture of his mother on the mantel. A faded Kodachrome portrait, the colors lost to years of sunlight and time. She looked about thirty, her auburn hair long and smooth, parted in the middle, cascading down the sides of her face. He remembered her then, her voice lulling him to sleep with song, the smell of chocolate chip cookies filling the house, the warmth of her arms.

So long ago.

He whipped his gaze back towards his father, his eyes seething. "Forget it, old man." He slashed the air with finality. "Life doesn't work that way. Fuck you, fuck your heart, and fuck your damn liver."

Taylor stormed out of the living room, kicked open the front door, and slammed it shut behind him.

The echo of the slamming door faded and the room fell into a painful silence. Particles of dust swirled in the dying rays of light. Saul stared at the faded photos of Anna on the mantle. The spilled beer spread over to his chair and soaked into his stockinged feet, staining his socks in pale yellow.

Sherilyn rose from the couch, righted the beer can, and placed her hand gently on Saul's shoulder.

*****

The view from Bear Tree was breathtaking, encompassing the entire San Ramon Valley below. Sherilyn approached the tree from the north, watching Taylor sitting in the low branches, staring at traffic snailing by on the distant 680 freeway. Bear Tree stood alone on the crown of the Las Trampas Hills, surrounded by sloping fields of dry wavering grass. Storm clouds, dark as river mud, marched across the valley, inching closer, like an army invading a new territory. Sherilyn shuddered against the cold.

On the base of the tree, bolted into the trunk of the ancient oak, Sherilyn saw a bronze plaque.

In Loving Memory of Jacob Abrahms.
A Child in Nature. Endless in Spirit.

Jacob's tattered journal rested on the ground by Taylor's feet, its pages fluttering in the wind.

Sherilyn covered her mouth, fighting to hold back tears. She stepped closer to the tree.

"Hello," she whispered.

Taylor managed a smile. "I knew you'd find me here."

"Are you kidding?" Sherilyn looked up at the solitary oak. "You spoke of this place so often I feel like I've been here a million times. It's so beautiful up here."

"And peaceful." He shifted his eyes towards her. "I'm sorry I walked out on you like that. I don't know what came over me."

Sherilyn looked at her husband. She'd never seen him with his father before, only heard the few stories that Taylor had shared on the rare times he talked of his past, and even then, she'd have been lying if she said she understood it all. Now, she was beginning to get a glimmer; the pain he'd buried, the endless hours in the lab trying to find something that could give him hope.

"I know how hard this is for you," she said.

Taylor shook his head. "I didn't know what to say." He paused, looking down at the ground, at the journal. "It just didn't seem real."

"Just be yourself. Let him know how you feel."

"I couldn't believe he talked about Jacob that way. Like he was still alive."

Taylor turned his head and looked at the plaque. "He was seventeen when he died. Christ, I'm nearly twice that age now."

Sherilyn's eyes followed Taylor's to the plaque.

A Child in Nature. Endless in Spirit.

"Do you remember him?"

Taylor shrugged. "I remember his voice. And his laugh. He had a great laugh, deep from his belly. A contagious laugh. Made everyone else in the room laugh along with him."

Sherilyn sat on the branch next to her husband. Despite her growing restlessness with their marriage, and the countless days she thought she couldn't go on playing second fiddle to his work, she knew, as a couple, they'd get through this. She'd be his strength until his spirit was strong enough to take care of itself.

She exhaled, allowing her pain to slip aside, and reached for his hand. His skin felt deathly cold under her fingers. The sensation frightened her. A sudden vision of her holding Taylor's hand while he lay in state in a casket stabbed into her mind. His face pale, lips white.

She shivered and willed the vision to leave.

"This was our spot." Taylor looked at the oak. "No matter how bad things got down below, we could always sneak up here and rise above it, the only place we'd be safe. It was only natural that I spread his ashes here. He'd have wanted it that way."

Sherilyn watched him brush a tear from his cheek. She held his hand tighter, willing it to become warm.

Taylor swallowed. "Did I ever tell you I was the one who found him?"

Sherilyn paused; her breath stricken. "No."

"It was October, just now" he said, his gaze lost across the valley. "I got home from school and there were letters addressed to me sprawled across the counter. The first one was from UCLA, offering me a full scholarship. I couldn't believe it. It meant that I had a chance to get out of that house. I was so fucking happy."

He paused and looked away.

"I ran out to the yard to show Jacob, but couldn't find him. I searched the house, the attic, even the tool shed, before I finally stumbled into the garage."

His eyes closed and he took a deep breath.

His voice trembled. "I found him there, hanging from a support beam."

Sherilyn covered her mouth. "Oh, God. Taylor, I'm so sorry."

"When my father came home, he found me crying in the bathroom. I couldn't even tell him what happened, I just kept screaming, 'in the garage, in the garage!'"

Sherilyn reached over and caressed his shoulder. "Maybe there's an answer in the journal."

Taylor shook his head. "I'm not going to read it. It's full of memories I don't want anymore."

"You don't want?"

"I don't want to remember him, Sherilyn."

"He's your brother," she said softly. "You can't forget him."

Taylor remained silent.

"You're not responsible for his death, Taylor."

He shook his head. "He read the letters before I did. He knew I was going away and leaving him behind."

"Taylor, you—"

He turned towards her, his face shadowed. "He couldn't bear the thought of being left behind to face that man alone."

Instinctively, Sherilyn pulled back. For an instant, she didn't recognize her husband, the darkness in his eyes. "It wasn't your fault."

"I should've seen how much he needed me. I should've known what would happen if I left."

"There was nothing you could have done," Sherilyn said more strongly.

He shook his head. "First my mother, then my brother." His voice cracked.

"Please, don't do this."

"And I didn't do anything to save them."

"Taylor—," she started.

But he wasn't listening. He jumped off the branch and walked towards the edge of the hillside. The valley hundreds of feet below.

Sherilyn watched him step closer to the edge, the wind blowing against his face, beating against his skin with the warning of impending danger.

The image of Taylor lying in the wooden casket tore back into Sherilyn's mind.

She closed her eyes and shuddered.

MADNESS

CHAPTER 30

Monday, October 16th, 6:23 am
A dozen reporters mobbed the entrance of Anderson Hall on the SFU Medical Center campus, microphones and plastic-bagged cameras bearing down on Taylor as he made his way from the parking lot to the front door. The incoming storm had finally opened its belly, battering the city with raindrops the size of quarters. The reporters huddled under umbrellas and foul-weather ponchos, jostling for position, shoving their microphones towards Taylor's face, pelting him with questions. Each of them clamoring for an opportunity to speak to Senator McIntyre's son-in-law about his controversial research, the Virtual Heart Project. Across the street, in front of the Science Library, medical students and PhD candidates lined up shoulder to shoulder, watching the chaos. Ever since the story of Taylor's relation to the Senator broke on the evening news, rumors flew around the campus with the ferocity of a cheetah hunting down prey.

Taylor pushed his way through the throng, brushing the microphones aside, elbowing a cameraman out of his path, and forced his way to the open door. Lawrence, the guard, stood there, one arm blocking the reporters from entering while he propped the door open for Taylor with the other. Taylor slid underneath Lawrence's arm and ducked inside. Shouting voices called out for comments as Lawrence locked the door shut behind him.

"Go on and get the hell outta here," Lawrence yelled through the glass. He turned towards Taylor. "Sorry about that. I couldn't force them to leave. Free speech and all."

Taylor smiled a thank you and headed down the stairs towards his lab.

"Did you like our welcoming committee?" Malcomb asked as Taylor pushed open the door. "This just keeps getting better and better."

Taylor stepped into the lab, dropped his backpack in the corner and brushed the water off his coat. He took a deep breath. Malcomb was right. Taylor had a hard enough time dragging himself out of bed that morning, the last thing he was prepared to deal with was the press. All he wanted to do was slither back home and crawl into bed with Sherilyn. But even that was problematic. Every time he'd closed his eyes last night, a nightmare drilled into his brain. His mother dying in bed from a failing heart. His brother's lifeless body swaying at the end of a rope.

Even when he wasn't sleeping, the visions came.

Taylor pinched the bridge of his nose, trying to drive out a dull pounding in his temples that had persisted since last night. "Sorry, I'm late. Had a bad night's sleep."

"Don't talk to me about sleep," Malcomb said, turning from the wall of crayon equations. His hair stood up on end like a bad modern sculpture.

He peeled open a Nestle Crunch bar. "I've been working on this non-stop."

Taylor looked at the chocolate. "Breakfast?"

"Of champions. My third this morning."

"So, what'd you find?"

Malcomb bit down on the chocolate. "It's bad, Taylor. Really bad!"

"Talk to me."

Malcomb finished chewing then pointed to the computer screen. "I found a coding change in the program, several of them. Things I didn't write."

Taylor glanced at the screen, not comprehending.

"Look here." Malcomb plopped himself down at the computer. He highlighted a line of code, drawing across it with his cursor. "There's a new line of code here, line 245, and I didn't write it. There are others also. Hundreds of them."

Taylor held up his hands. "Slow down. You're not making sense."

"Of course, I'm not," Malcomb swiveled his chair from the computer. "I'm not making sense because this whole thing doesn't make sense."

Taylor looked nonplussed. "How could this happen?"

"I don't know. It's as if the program is writing itself."

"Writing itself? Is that even possible?"

"John von Neumann theorized self-reproducing computer programs way back in 1949. But this is something far different. This is actually changing our program, mutating it like some complicated automata."

Taylor shook his head. "Forget theory, give me facts."

"That's what I'm saying. There are no facts. Just that there's corrupting data in the system. This must be what caused the problems you experience inside the VHP." He held up a portable hard drive, flipping it back and forth in his fingers. "I used the original back-up to rewrite everything."

Taylor closed his eyes and squeezed his temples. Half the San Francisco press was camped outside their doorstep itching for a story and Crawford's Ethics committee was in four hours. The last thing he needed were more problems.

"So, the question remains, what could have caused this?"

Malcomb shrugged. "I've searched for every type of malware I could think of, Trojan horses, worms, and crackers, but found nothing."

Taylor walked to Malcomb's desk and picked up the helmet. He wasn't going to let the VHP slip through their fingers, not when they were so close. "Then go over it again. Remove assumptions and don't go looking for zebras."

Malcomb raised an eyebrow in confusion. "What?"

"Med student 101. When faced with a patient illness that doesn't make sense, look for the obvious. Common things happen commonly. Don't go looking for zebras when it's probably a horse."

"And how does that help us?"

"This error you found, by your estimation could've caused our problem."

"Yes."

"And this error could have been caused by a virus?"

"Yes."

"Then we need to keep looking for a virus. Maybe one that's not known to us."

"That's the problem." Malcomb sighed. "It's one thing to scan for a virus that's known, but nearly impossible to scan for a virus that's unknown. Algorithmically speaking, it's not possible. How many times can I scan the same program?"

"Probably a million and not find the answer, because you're not looking in the right place."

Malcomb opened his mouth to speak, but no words came.

Taylor's eyes narrowed, feeling like he was zoning in on the issue. "Could the virus be hidden so well that you couldn't find it, like in the operating system?"

Malcomb took a bite of the Nestle Crunch bar, mawing over Taylor's words. "To do that, you'd have to be intimately aware of the details of our system." His mind raced forward. "You couldn't just stick it in anyplace; it'd stand out like Marilyn Monroe at a software convention."

Something in Malcomb's words reverberated within Taylor's mind, tickling a nagging memory. His eyes grew wide. His skin prickled, like a cold wind blew past him.

"What did you just say?"

"Marilyn Monroe. She was an actress—"

"Not that part," Taylor cut in. "About the virus."

"The only way someone could implant a virus we couldn't detect is if they knew the intimate details of our system. This wouldn't be just any old Microsoft virus, this would have to be specially engineered for us, incorporated into the very root of the program or the operating system."

Taylor's skin began to crawl. A memory came to life, tugging at the back of his brain; an image of Robert Chan lying in the ICU—the ventilation tubing attached to his tracheotomy, his chest a bloodied jigsaw of scars and surgical entry ports. He saw the GET WELL card pasted to the wall, the CTS logo stamped at the bottom and suddenly everything felt wrong.

Malcomb noticed the look on Taylor's face. "What's going on?"

"I'm not sure. Maybe nothing."

"You don't look like it's nothing."

Taylor looked up. "Do me a favor. Do some research on CTS and someone named Robert Chan."

Malcomb squinted. "And there's a reason for this?"

Taylor didn't want to tell Malcomb about Chan in the ICU and risk scaring him until he had some facts. He looked down at his hands, turning them over, back and forth, studying them as if he expected them to be still covered with Chan's blood, dried and caked, clotted under his fingernails. The memory so vivid; he could still feel Chan's heart squeezing between his fingers. Feel the muscle.

Open. Squeeze.

"CTS was the company that created our AI platform. Chan was the main programmer. See what you find." He wondered what Malcomb might come across. Something that might connect their problem to a man clinging to life in the ICU.

Malcomb nodded hesitantly. "I'll see what I can do."

"What about the virtual heart?" Taylor asked.

Malcomb shoved the last of the chocolate into his mouth. "I've reset the code."

"Then we're a go?"

"I'd protest more strongly, but I seriously doubt you'd comply."

Taylor nodded, giving a compliant smile. "Then one last thing," he said, tapping his temple. "White knight b1 to c3."

Malcomb closed his eyes and made phantom movements across his mental chessboard. "You're leaving yourself open. Black pawn g7 to g6."

Taylor registered the move then turned to the microphone. "Helen. It's Taylor."

Helen Yang's voice came through the speakers. "We've got a problem."

"I know," Taylor said. "The computer genius and I were just discussing—"

"Not that problem," she cut him off. "We got another one."

Taylor shot a glance at Malcomb, who shrugged unknowing. "What's up?"

"It's the pig," Helen said. "I went to the lab to prep pig number two for the trial."

"Did you have difficulty finding a vein?"

"Not with that pig, no."

"Then I don't understand—"

She cut him off. "That's not the pig I'm talking about."

Taylor's breath caught in his throat. "The first pig?"

"Yes. The one we operated on the other day."

Taylor felt his mouth grow dry. He closed his eyes. An image of Crawford meeting the hospital ethicist flashed through his mind.

"What's the problem?" he asked cautiously.

"The pig is dead."

CHAPTER 31

Dr. Bennington Crawford sat behind his desk in his fourth-floor office at the Medical Administration Building and lowered the morning edition of the San Francisco Chronicle.

There, on page one, six column inches wide, were printed Presidential candidate Congressman Snead O'Neil's comments made at the League of Women Voters, blasting the Virtual Heart Project. O'Neil was quoted as calling the project 'a bastardization of medical practice,' then launched into a full-scale assault against Senator Randolph McIntyre. The Senator was quoted in reply as being adamantly opposed to the project, regardless of the fact that the lead investigator was Taylor Abrahms, his son-in-law, but Congressman O'Neil insisted that the Senator's words were political maneuvering, accusing the Senator of nepotism. The only point the politicians agreed on was the fault of the University for allowing the project to proceed, their incriminating fingers pointed at Ramona Fox, the Hospital Administrator and the Chief of Staff, Dr. Bennington Crawford.

Crawford thought of his retirement ranch in Montana, his grandchildren, and his fly rods and the image never seemed so far away.

Before him, Dr. William Preston paced back and forth like a caged animal, nearly frothing at the mouth. His hands and arms flew about in a hurricane of activity, occasionally pounding down on Crawford's desk to punctuate a point. Crawford rubbed his forehead and wondered what he'd gotten himself into.

Ignoring Preston, Crawford rose from his desk and peered out the window. The autumn storm was rampaging in from the ocean to the west, devouring the Golden Gate Bridge, blanketing the city in a shroud of impenetrable grey. Whitecaps prowled across the Bay, the ocean's fury crashing against the wharves. Seawater shot over the boat slips, splashing onto Marina Boulevard. The weathermen said that this was just the beginning. In his thirty years at the University, Crawford couldn't ever remember a storm this fierce.

Despite the ungodly weather, a throng of demonstrators gathered at the Administration Building entrance. Amid the rain ponchos and umbrellas, signs waved back and forth, decrying COMPUTER CHIPS ARE FOR COMPUTERS, NOT PEOPLE and CARE FOR THE POOR, NO ROBOT MEDICINE. Mixed in the crowd, news cameras captured every angry outburst, every rehearsed speech, securing the drama for the evening news.

Crawford sighed. He knew that this political storm, like the weather, was only going to get worse.

"It's our goddamned last chance to stop this," Preston was saying. He paced, walking in tight circles. "I want to know what you've up your sleeve."

Crawford shifted his gaze to meet his colleague. "My intention is the same as it's always been. I'll present our case to the best of my ability."

Preston threw his hands up in the air. "That's it? That's your grand master plan? You'll present our case? Haven't you seen the goddamned paper?" he thrust the crumpled morning edition towards Crawford's face. "We're all over the fucking country!"

Crawford brushed Preston's hand aside. "What are you suggesting I do?"

Preston slammed the paper on the desk. "We need to take action. Expel him from the program."

Crawford shook his head, his eyes narrowing. He predicted Preston's response would be irrational, as always. Preston was a typical surgeon, a reactionary. He'd blow-up first, ask questions later. Not that Crawford blamed him on this one. His own heart had leapt into his throat when he saw the morning's headlines.

And the mention of his own name.

"I'll do nothing of the kind," Crawford said evenly. "This is an ethical decision. Not a personal one. We're an academic institution with procedures and guidelines. I'm not going to be bullied by politicians or reporters, and I certainly won't be bullied by you." He leveled his gaze at Preston. "I'll present our case and the research will be judged on its own merits."

Preston thrust a finger towards Crawford's face. "What if the ethicist doesn't stop this? What if she lets it go forward?"

Crawford shrugged. "Then it will go forward. This isn't the first project that's come along to test the PSCM resolve and it won't be the last. Regardless of what the papers say, this project is no worse than one thousand other projects happening at one thousand other medical institutions right now."

Preston faced his colleague, seething. "That's not good enough, Ben. Worse or not, we're the target. Don't you realize what this could do to the Medical Center? To our private benefactors?"

Crawford grimaced. Preston was right on that point. Benefactors, the financial lifeblood of any academic medical center, were notoriously sensitive to political issues involving the hospital. In the late eighties, donations had dried to a trickle when the Hospital Administrator had declined to open a private AIDS clinic despite overwhelming public support. In San Francisco, that was the wrong move. It wasn't until that

Administrator was reassigned to Texas and the AIDS Clinic opened that private donations came flowing back in.

"What do you want me to do?" Crawford asked, spreading his arms wide. "This is an academic center and we're challenging a young doctor's research."

Preston's face grew hard. "I want you to stop this, Ben. That's why I got you involved. You're the only one who can do it before we become a travesty in the eyes of the nation. Ramona Fox won't do it, she's too weak. It's your job. Hell, it's your duty."

Crawford met Preston's glare with one of his own, feeling his own frustration rising. He swore inwardly for ever letting Preston talk him into getting involved, then turned from his colleague to let his temper cool before he said something he'd regret.

Framed on the wall before him, adjacent to the bookshelf, was Crawford's medical diploma sharing a double mat with the Hippocratic Oath. Certificates and honors, including his many Professor of the Year awards, fanned around the diploma in a semi-circle, the fruits of at a long and illustrious career.

Walking away from Preston, Crawford approached the wall. The letters of the Hippocratic Oath were faded by age, but Crawford could still recite them from memory.

I will prescribe regimen for the good of my patients according to my ability and my judgment and never do harm to anyone. Through these actions, I will preserve the purity of my life and my art, and I may practice my art, respected by all men and in all times.

That seemed so long ago and medicine had changed so much since then.

He turned towards Preston. Outside the window, protest chants rose above the howling wind. A loud crash, a bottle breaking, shattered through the commotion. Violence was building.

"I will do my best, William. I want this to stop as much as you. For the hospital, for the cause. But I will not destroy this young man's life."

Preston's body stiffened. "Then you're destroying the hospital."

"Don't be so melodramatic."

"I have evidence that this research is more than just costly, it's dangerous. If the press gets hold of this, we're finished."

Crawford squinted. "What are you talking about?"

"It's deadly."

"What is?"

Preston gave a smug grin. "Abrahms is killing everything he touches in that lab. His first experimental pig died shortly after having the treatment."

Crawford looked surprised, then concerned. "How do you know this?"

"I know."

"But he just started the other day. How could you possibly know his results?"

Preston folded his arms across his chest. "I won't sit back and let one maverick resident destroy our hospital, Ben. Will you?"

Crawford studied the face of his oldest colleague, and paused. Thirty years of service, thirty years of teaching and caring, and now he was being picked out as the scapegoat for research he'd never even heard of before last week. He'd been thrust headfirst into the middle of a political battleground between two Presidential candidates, each more than willing to destroy the hospital and anyone's career if it garnered votes.

Crawford rubbed his eyes, trying to plan a strategy. Was Preston telling the truth? How could he know their data just days after the experiment began? The implication of Preston spying on Abrahms' lab was frightening, a violation of every ethical law, but if Preston was right, then the consequences could be dire. Being the center of attention for controversial research was one thing—the Hospital reputation could always recover once the project was completed—but not if the research was deadly.

Preston leaned forward until his face was mere inches from Crawford's. "You'd do well to join us, Ben."

Preston's breath was heavy, and even that early in the morning, thick with sourness of scotch. Crawford winced. "Join who?"

"Don't be naive."

"I generally try not to be."

"We're in the midst of a Presidential election and this research is a hot topic."

Crawford had a sinking feeling. "Join who?"

"This world is full of winners and losers, Ben. Do you know the difference?"

Crawford looked at his colleague impassively.

Preston's lips upturned slightly. "Winners know who they need to fuck to get ahead, losers stand by and watch all the fucking."

Crawford's skin began to crawl. "I fail to see how this involves me."

"Think about it, Ben. You're a black man, on the bad side of sixty. You could become a grand emissary for your race, the next Colin Powell. Maybe the next Surgeon General. All it takes are the right connections."

Like a warning, Crawford felt his body stiffen. In all their years of friendship, Preston had never referred to him as a black man. Crawford never assumed Preston was colorblind, no one ever was really, but he'd never figured him a racist either. Why was all that changing now?

"I still don't see what this has to do with me."

"You will, soon enough," Preston patted his comb-over into place. "Just know that there are forces that have a vested interest in seeing this project fail. You can be a winner or a loser, Ben. You can fuck or watch. The choice is yours."

Crawford couldn't believe his ears. Did his oldest friend, his career-long colleague, just threaten him? He pulled away, keeping the desk between them.

Preston's tone sent a chill racing down Crawford's spine. Outside, the growing mob of protestors chanted in unison, their voices gathering in strength. Someone was beating a drum, pounding out a steady war cry. The wind whipped up, buffeting the office with such force that the window rattled in the frame.

And through it all, Preston kept staring at him, a murderous detachment in his eyes.

CHAPTER 32

The heart pumped furiously.

Standing at the entrance to the aorta, Taylor stared into the cavernous chamber of the left ventricle which opened before him like a massive cavern. The leaflets of the aortic valve burst open before his eyes; blood rushing through the opened valve then snapping shut like two massive steel gates. The ferocity of the blood blasting through the valve amazed him. Red blood cells, like three-foot wide discs, shot past him as they raced down the aorta to deliver oxygen to the body. Carried along in the murky plasma, six-inch globs of proteins, hormones and Y-shaped antibodies churned in the flowing current, swirling past his head. The beating of the virtual heart reverberated in his ears as if coming from a massive loudspeaker.

Ba Bum. Ba Bum.

Taylor didn't think he'd ever get used to how amazing it was, to be standing inside a beating heart. As the current of plasma raced passed him, he braced himself to prevent from being swept downstream, tightening his quads to keep himself upright. His hands pressed against the slick aortic walls, his entire world shuddering with each contraction. He was still getting used to the concept that he could breathe while all of his senses told him he was 'under water,' bathed in the plasma. But each breath came easily. The smell of ferrous thick in the fluid, the warmth of the 98.6 degrees plasma flowing against his skin.

The aortic valve regulated the blood leaving the heart; opening when the heart contracted, snapping shut to prevent backflow while the heart refilled. Taylor whirled around; his vision in the VHP smoothly following his head movement as he watched the blood cells flowing down the aorta.

So far, all seemed to be working perfectly.

Ahead, he saw the tunnel-like opening where the coronary arteries branched off the aorta. Most of the blood cells soared past the entrance towards the rest of the body, but some detoured down these tributaries towards the heart muscle.

Taylor stepped forward, his feet pressing against the rubbery arterial floor. He took slow, deliberate steps until he reached the mouth of the coronary. The cholesterol plaque loomed downstream before him.

"Laser," he called out.

"Ready," Malcomb said.

Instantly, the hand-held laser appeared. Taylor gripped it tightly, and focused on the plaque. The death of the first pig had thrown their experiment into doubt. Taylor had no rational explanation. Helen had told him the pig had been perfectly well the day before, eating well, sleeping well. There was no obvious cause of death and no answers would come without a full autopsy.

They didn't have the time or resources for that.

What they needed were results.

Taylor took a deep breath and looked at the blood vessel floor which bowed under his feet, sinking with his weight. Eddies of plasma swirled around his ankles, the blood growing more turbulent the closer he stepped to the plaque. He ran his fingers across the stalactite of cholesterol. A piece of oily plaque squeezed off in his hand.

"I've found my site," he said.

"I'm ready," Malcomb's replied.

"Ditto," Helen said.

Taylor nodded. It felt good to be back at work. Being inside the artery felt natural to him, like it was where he belonged. He was still troubled by the nightmares and the headaches, but immersed in the blood vessel, focused on work, he could force those from his mind and concentrate.

"Prepare for laser activation."

"I've got you in position at the proximal end of the artery," Malcomb said.

A red light illuminated on the laser's barrel. Taylor focused on the plaque.

"Helen?"

"The pig is stable. Vitals are normal. Respirations steady."

"Okay, people," Taylor said, exhaling. He could feel his heart kick up a notch. "This is our last shot. We've got to get it right this time."

"Starting at 5 millijoules," Malcomb said.

"EKG normal sinus rhythm," Helen added.

Taylor could hear the energy in their voices. The anticipation. He felt it too. All of their careers rested on the success of this VHP run today. Their reputations as scientists. Their futures. The laser felt particularly heavy in his hand. He held it steady. "I'm focused on our target. Prepare for discharge in three... two... one—"

He tensed his finger, ready to fire, then stopped. Something caught his eye.

Movement. Quick and darting, not the fluid movement of a red cell.

Taylor spun around, his eyes searching down the artery.

Everything appeared normal. Plasma continued to rush towards him, blood cells spiraling in its current, racing his way. The vessel walls, faintly illuminated in a reddish glow, appeared smooth and slippery. The endothelial cells lining the vessel shimmered moist and glossy.

"Are you ready for discharge?" Malcomb asked.

Taylor lowered the laser, certain he'd seen something. His eyes scanned the vessel, but nothing appeared out of place. He shook his head.

Not enough sleep. Too many nightmares.

He turned and refocused on the plaque.

"I'm ready."

Taylor raised his right arm, again leveling with the plaque, aiming the laser at the first of the two crevices. The plaque shuddered and vibrated with each massive beat of the heart, the crevice moving in and out of his view in time to the pulse. Taylor had to synchronize his firing in perfect sequence with the heartbeat. He steadied himself, bracing his legs. His finger tightened on the trigger.

"Here we go," he called out.

"Ready," Helen said.

"Laser discharge in—"

Something whisked by. To his left. The laser dropped from Taylor's hand. He whirled around, his pulse shooting like a rocket. He knew he'd seen something this time, it hadn't been his imagination. A large, dark shape—like a man running.

But it couldn't be a man. Not in here!

What the hell?

He took a cautious step forward, peering around the plaque. He looked beyond, his eyes sharp. The hair tingling on the back of his neck.

"I'm waiting for discharge," he heard Malcomb say.

So am I, Taylor thought.

"Is everything okay?" Helen asked.

Taylor shot a final glance down the lumen. The blood cells raced towards him. The plasma flowed by. It all appeared so normal. Then what was it?

He took a deep breath and shook his head. "Enough," he whispered. "It's your imagination. Your nightmare-fueled, sleep-deprived, overly-amped imagination."

"What are you talking about?" Malcomb asked.

"Nothing."

"Are we going to do this any time soon?" Helen asked.

"Yes, I'm fine," Taylor said. He bent down and picked up the laser then straightened upright.

That was when he found himself standing face to face with another human being.

"Hello, Taylor," his brother said.

Taylor screamed and staggered backwards, falling to the blood vessel floor.

"What's wrong?" Malcomb asked.

Taylor couldn't answer, the words caught in his throat. He looked up, the image burning into his eyes of his brother, Jacob, standing over him, seventeen-years old, wearing his faded CAL BEARS sweatshirt and kneeless jeans. A frayed rope tied in a noose dangled down from his neck like a grisly necktie; his eyes ghostly pale surrounded by circles of blackened skin.

The air shot from Taylor's lungs.

"Taylor?" Malcomb asked. "Are you alright?"

Jacob halted, looming over him. His finger pointed at his neck where the skin was bloodied and raw.

"Why, Taylor?" Jacob asked.

Taylor's eyes gaped. He couldn't breathe. His heartbeat burst against his ribs.

"Why did you do this to me?"

Taylor fought to understand what was happening. His pulse pounded in his ears.

"Y-you can't be real," he stammered.

"Of course, I'm not real," Jacob said. "I'm dead."

"What's not real?" Malcomb's voice blasted down the blood vessel. "Talk to me, Taylor. Tell me what's happening?"

Then as suddenly as he'd appeared, Jacob was gone. Taylor fought to catch his breath. He cupped his mouth with his hands, his eyes widened in horror.

"Taylor if you don't answer me, I'm shutting down," Malcomb yelled. "Taylor?"

But Taylor couldn't speak.

CHAPTER 33

Dr. Bennington Crawford straightened his red Thom Browne tie, pulled sharply on his lapel and marched into the third-floor conference room, passing a sign that declared:

12:00 o'clock. Ethics Committee Meeting in Session.

Inside, he surveyed the room. Ramona Fox, the hospital administrator sat stone-faced on the left side of a U-shaped table; her flaxen hair pulled back into a bun, her eye make-up thick and blue, standing out in stark contrast to the drab grey of her suit. To the right, sitting at the head of the table, Agnes Walsh, the hospital ethicist, scribbled notes into a three-ring binder. Seventy-years old and wrinkled as a prune left out too long in the sun, Agnes peered up from her notes when Crawford entered, her gaze revealing nothing of her intentions for the day.

Crawford took a measured step forward. The room was large, dominated by the conference table. Fake Fichus trees stood in the corners, an attempt to add softness to the harsh angles. Glaring light streamed from the overhead fluorescents. A single window looked over Parnassus Avenue and Golden Gate Park in the distance, the bridge nearly lost in the clouds of the ongoing storm. The room smelled like Agnes, aged and stuffy.

The protestors that had descended on the hospital still gathered beyond the Administration front doors, roped off from the main entrance by a stream of yellow police tape and a security force. Chanting, "We need affordable health care, not video games," their voices carried up from three stories below.

Glancing to his right, Crawford was surprised to see William Preston, blue suit and grey tie, hair lacquered in place, sitting at the side of the table. Preston wasn't a member of the Ethics Committee; he'd never shown an interest before, having declined at least fifteen invitations to join. Yet, he found enough interest in the ethical process that Monday to cancel surgery, miss lunch, and take a seat at the head table.

Crawford gave a bitter sigh. His eyes flashed towards Fox. Since Preston wasn't a member of the Committee, the only avenue he had to gain attendance to this closed-door meeting would have come from Fox herself. Fox noted Crawford's questioning gaze and averted her eyes, shielding them under a thick veneer of mascara.

"Shall we start?" Agnes Walsh asked.

Everyone at the table nodded in unison. Crawford approached the table, standing before them, his shoulders stiff, his neck muscles tight.

"I believe we all know what's at stake here today," Agnes continued. "We've been asked by Dr. Crawford to judge the merits of a particular experimental protocol being conducted on our campus. One that has drawn the attention, dare I say ire, of a large portion of the country, not to mention a presidential election."

Fox nodded her head while Agnes spoke, her eyes fixed on Preston. Preston, in turn, directed his gaze at Crawford, his face unreadable. Crawford noted the exchange of glances and felt his stomach tighten.

Walsh pressed on. "Since you were the one who called for this committee to convene, Dr. Crawford, I'll allow you to make your opening statements."

Crawford cleared his throat. "Thank you, Agnes. Originally, I'd prepared my opening statement to piggyback on the words of Daniel Callahan," Crawford said evenly, taking in both Fox and Walsh. "Whose groundbreaking work in medical ethics I believe we're all familiar with."

With those last words, he shot a penetrating glance at Preston, knowing full-well that Preston wouldn't have the foggiest notion in hell who Callahan was.

Preston frowned and glared back.

"For those unfamiliar," Crawford continued. "I'd like to remind you of his address before the Congressional Subcommittee on Health Care Reform. He argued then that any effort to contain health costs would fail if doctors insisted that greater and more sophisticated technology would allow them to gain control over the human body."

He glanced at Preston. "You remember that speech, don't you, William?"

Preston looked caught off guard. "Of course," he stuttered.

"Excellent. Then you'll recall when Callahan stated that good quality care, not biotechnology, was the only basis for a fair and just health care system."

Preston nodded uncomfortably.

"Then can you tell us his conclusions?"

Preston's eyes grew narrow.

"William?"

"Enough with the games," Preston sneered. "You know damn well that I don't know that speech."

"Then why are you here, William?" Crawford shot back. "This is an Ethics Meeting, not your personal forum."

"I'm here to put an end to this. To see Abrahms expelled from this program and this research halted before it destroys our hospital."

Crawford turned his eyes surveying the other two occupants in the room. "And you? Why are you here? To put an end to this uncomfortable issue? Have you already condemned the man? Was the outcome decided before this meeting took place; the very second that the morning edition hit the stands?"

Ramona Fox shot an angry glance. "Dr. Crawford, I resent any implication—"

"And I resent this entire charade," Crawford cut her off. "I resent you wasting my time. I resent you humoring an old man that an important issue could be discussed calmly and intelligently, evaluating the merits of this young doctor's research and its ethical implications to health care. I resent you willing to throw all that out the door, Ms. Fox, because you feel pressure from politicians who have no bearing on the running of this hospital."

Agnes Walsh stood up. "Dr. Crawford, you are out of order. No decisions have been made before this meeting. We're waiting for you to make your point."

"The point is," Crawford said, "that Callahan never said that there was no role for biotechnology whatsoever."

With those words, Crawford could see Preston visibly stiffen. Agnes Walsh sat back down.

Crawford pressed on. "If used properly, biotechnology can add to the quality of care we offer our patients. It just has to be applied fairly and responsibly."

Preston sat bolt upright. "You endorse this travesty? With the national media, an army of protestors, and two Presidential candidates filleting us alive, you're supporting this?"

Crawford's eyes narrowed. "I said nothing of the kind."

"Then what are you saying, Ben."

"Yes, Dr. Crawford," Agnes added. "What is your point?"

Crawford looked at Agnes. "My point is simple. This matter, like all ethical matters has two sides, if not more. Nothing about this research is inherently bad nor good. It simply is."

"It's a travesty!" Preston shouted, rising to his feet. "It's a God-dammed, fucking travesty and it's going to bring the whole Hospital down!"

"No, William," Crawford held up his hands to quiet him. "We are the travesty. We're the ones who are willing to throw a young man's career away to avoid any political harm to our hospital." He shot a directed glance at Fox. "We are the ones who are willing to bow down to external pressure, willing to sacrifice one young lamb to the slaughter, if it means saving our collective ass."

Fox stiffened and glared back at Crawford.

Preston leaned across the table. "If you don't have the balls to stop this research, Ben, I will."

Crawford froze and took in the man who for so many years he'd called a friend. "Oh, I have the balls, William. I have the balls. What I don't have is the stomach to deal with you." He looked back at the other two in the room. "Or any of you who are so willing to throw away our objective process to suit your own needs."

Ramona Fox stood. "That's enough, Dr Crawford. I have an entire hospital to run. I have protestors cordoned off from storming my front door. I've had my reputation smeared across every major newspaper in America and I've had my hospital tossed into the middle of a Presidential election. All because of one project. Now, you can take your sanctimonious attitude right out of this room. I'm going to do what is best for this hospital."

"Even if it destroys a young man?" Crawford asked.

Ramona nodded evenly. "Yes." She straightened her spine. "I have more important things to worry about than the career of one resident."

Crawford took in her words, confirming his deepest fear. There would be no objective review of the VHP and no ethical debate on its merits or faults. This meeting was a sham, a thinly veiled justification for an academic lynch mob.

As much as Crawford was personally opposed to Abrahms' project, even he recognized its merits and potential lifesaving ability. Even he knew that what was happening at this "meeting" was wrong.

Crawford rubbed his mouth. He knew what he had to do. "You're right, Ms Fox," he said calmly. "I apologize for questioning you. You do have more important things to consider than the career of one resident."

Fox looked taken aback by Crawford's reconciliatory tone. "Thank you, Dr. Crawford. I'm glad that you're seeing things from my position."

"Oh, I am. Very clearly. I'm also seeing the media circus you'll have to face when they hear of the other problems you're having at the Hospital."

Fox stared at Crawford blankly. She shot a glance at Preston who looked just as confused.

"What are you saying, Ben?" Preston asked.

Crawford turned, fixing on Preston. "I'm saying I will no longer be a part of this lynching. I had my fill of it in the 1800's. But then you'd expect that of a black man, wouldn't you, William?"

Preston's face turned sour.

"You were the one who told me to 'fuck or be fucked,' as I recall. According to hospital policy, any recommendation by the Ethics Committee must be accompanied by a unanimous vote from a quorum of three, the Chief of Staff, the bioethicist and the Hospital CEO. Without any one of those members present, this issue will have to go to the Board of Governors for resolution."

"But we have a quorum," Preston said. "All three of you are here."

"Not your Chief of Staff." Crawford shook his head, leveling his gaze at Preston.

He took a deep breath, feeling good about himself for the first time since the Virtual Heart Project was dumped in his lap.

"As of this moment, I resign."

CHAPTER 34

The silence in the lab seemed infinite.

Taylor sat in the La-Z-boy, disoriented, his head pounding, feeling like he was going to crawl out of his skin. He cupped his face in his hands. The whole thing had been an illusion, he repeated over and over. An illusion. His brother hadn't just appeared before him, his neck stretched and raw. He couldn't have been standing inside a coronary vessel in a research trial, awaiting a laser pulse to clear the artery. Questioning him. Accusing him.

It couldn't have been him.

Taylor ran his fingers through his sweaty hair, desperate for an answer.

Malcomb had left the lab right after the aborted trial, sprinting to the restroom, and Helen had signed off to care for the pig, leaving the usually frenetic lab uncharacteristically still. Not since he was a child, could Taylor remember being so alone. He pulled his knees to his chest, wrapped them tightly, holding them close to his body.

"What in the hell's happening?" he whispered.

He rubbed his temples, trying to absorb it all. He'd spent the better part of three years designing the system. Now, after countless hours of work, the helmet visuals were working flawlessly. The problem was the program.

But Malcomb had checked it himself. He insisted that he'd reset the program. They'd checked for viruses, nothing. And his brother? If someone was trying to sabotage the system, why would they program intimate details of Jacob's death? How could anyone even know those details? He'd never told anyone, not even Sherilyn until yesterday.

It just doesn't make sense.

No matter how many times Taylor wrestled the problem in his brain, he couldn't find an answer. He was left with only one of two conclusions; either the program was hijacked by a hacker more skilled than either he or Malcomb could imagine.

Or else he was going insane.

He feared it was the latter.

He took off the Neural Transcendence headpiece and lowered it onto the arm of the La-Z-boy. He peeled the sticky SIS suit from his skin. Once Preston learned of this, it'd be over. Everything he'd worked for was about to be washed away, disintegrated like a sandcastle disappearing under the flood of an incoming tide.

What is going on?

*****

Arsenic. Cyanide. Strychnine.

As a student of the art of assassination, Edgar Ross kept an arsenal of the classic poisoning agents at his workbench, categorized and cataloged, neatly arranged in plastic racks bolted to the side of his van. Ross ran his hands across the vials, fingering the black plastic tops, feeling the potential of each deadly compound through the coolness of the glass. Of these, strychnine had always been his favorite. Arsenic was too slow, needing to be consumed over long periods of time to be fatal, and cyanide, unless ingested in sufficient quantities, was too unpredictable.

But strychnine offered real possibilities. Acting on the central nervous system, strychnine caused immediate and intensely painful convulsions, leaving the body rigid in rigor mortis, the face etched in agony. The opportunities to use it were limited, but the results were spectacular.

Ross allowed himself a smile. Maps and blueprints of Taylor Abrahms' apartment spread across his workbench. He studied them with intent.

As enamored as Ross was with the classic poisoning agents, practicality dictated that his skills progress with technology. He had the Eastern European penchant for poisoning political rivals to thank for the introduction of radioactive Plonium-210, dioxin and ricin to his armamentarium, each with its own world of possibilities.

Prussic acid mimicked the symptoms of cardiac arrest. For a mission in the Ukraine, Ross had fashioned a hydraulic system in an umbrella that crushed a vial of prussic acid and fired it into the face of his target, leaving him dead on the sidewalk in seconds. Plutonium dust left in the desk drawer of a senior politician in Bulgaria caused the development of virulent cancers, killing the target in a matter of months.

Both killings had been impeccably executed, masterpieces of his art. Definitions of his craft.

That was the moment he lived for. The kill. Adrenaline shooting through his heart, driving his pulse, making his fingertips tingle. He could imagine no other feeling like it. All of his senses heightened, driven by epinephrine to their ultimate animal peak.

It was a moment of ultimate presence. No regrets from the past, no thoughts of the future. For Ross, it was his moment of epiphany, when he would rise to the mantle of God, dictating the course of human life, giving or taking as he pleased. He was the Christ.

He was the Chosen.

His phone buzzed. His reverie broken. He looked down at the last message sent from his employer.

Nw assgnmt. Efftv immdtly

Ross let out a slow breath and deepened his focus. The instructions scrolled across his screen.

On his workstation sat the monogrammed pen he'd lifted from the lab in Anderson Hall. The name Taylor Abrahms inscribed on the shaft. A plan was already forming, taking shape in his mind.

Reaching up, his fingers danced across the vials.

CHAPTER 35

Bennington Crawford maneuvered his Volvo through the congested San Francisco city streets, heading down Parnassus Avenue towards the Presidio and the Golden Gate Bridge beyond. In his car trunk, carefully tucked away, was the box containing the awards and memories that used to adorn his Chief of Staff office. A lifetime of achievements and memories, now tucked away neatly into two banker's boxes in his trunk. Jazz legend, Sarah Vaughn's multi-octave voice belted out "Tenderly" through the stereo speakers—a melancholy farewell to his medical career.

The sun was setting low in the west, sinking beyond the Pacific horizon; the sky glowing pink and orange between the blackened storm clouds. Wind buffeted the Volvo as darkness fell. Crawford clicked on his headlights, wincing as the headlights flashed on from the car behind. Crawford adjusted his rearview mirror to divert the glare when he noticed the grey van following about two car lengths behind. The sight struck him as odd. Searching his memory, he could swear that he'd seen that van behind him several times as he wound his way through the city streets.

Crawford refocused on the bridge ahead, watching the Marin Headlands draw closer; the shoreline glowing orange in the dying traces of light. He knew Georgia would be home waiting for him. He'd tell her about the events of the day, drawing strength from her supportive arms. They'd share a brandy that night, and maybe a late dinner, losing themselves in plans for their future together.

Sarah Vaughn's voice rose to a swooping high as Crawford cleared the bridge and exited off the 101 onto Tiburon Boulevard. He turned right, heading towards Richardson Bay and his home in Belvedere. Looking in the rearview, he noticed the van exiting the freeway behind him.

Driving five miles above the speed limit, Crawford guided the Volvo towards the sparsely inhabited waterfront near the Audubon Wildlife Sanctuary then towards the rocky hills of Belvedere. He picked up his cellphone to call Georgia, let her know he was coming home, but never dialed the number. His eyes focused on the rearview mirror.

Normally, Crawford loved this part of the drive, when the road wound back and forth through the wooded cliffs of the Marin Peninsula, hundreds of feet above San Francisco Bay. At times, when Crawford rounded a corner, the views of San Francisco in the distance would be breathtaking. But tonight, he wasn't able to enjoy it. Crawford squinted as he noted the distinctive square shape of the van's headlights less than a full car length behind him.

"Go around me, buddy," he whispered.

Crawford adjusted the rear-view mirror to divert the glare, but kept the van in his view. His grip tightened on the steering wheel. The van didn't seem like it was trying to pass, so Crawford stepped harder on the accelerator.

The Volvo whipped past the Marina at fifteen miles above the speed limit. He sped towards the long sweeping right turn where the road reached the end of the peninsula near the crossing at Blanding Lane. There, only the darkness of the Bay waters would be visible ahead until the car pulled out of the turn and headed back towards Belvedere Avenue.

Sarah Vaughn's voice became irritating. Crawford turned down the stereo. He glanced again in the rear-view, his eyes focusing on the square headlights now just a few feet behind him. He didn't want the van tailing him so closely on that turn. Accidents happened there frequently, cars driving too fast, losing traction and leaping off the road, tumbling down the cliffs into the depths of the San Francisco Bay. Just last month one of Crawford's own neighbors had crashed on that bend at Land's End, barely escaping before her car sank into the icy waters.

"Back off, you idiot. Back off."

But the van didn't back off. If anything, it seemed to be getting closer, inching towards his tail. There was no place for Crawford to pull over until he passed that turn.

"God damnit, if you want to get by, then pass me!"

The blinding glare of oncoming headlights flashed into Crawford's eyes. He gasped. The Volvo had drifted into the lane of oncoming traffic. A car horn wailed.

"Jesus!" Crawford swung to the right. The Volvo jerked back to its lane, the oncoming car clearing him by inches, its horn wailing in the distance behind him.

Crawford exhaled, his breath hot. His heart raced. His gaze shot back to the rear-view. The van was growing larger in his view, the headlights glaring in his eyes. His face illuminated in a slash of light. Crawford didn't know what was wrong with this driver, whether he was drunk or just an idiot, but either way, he was too close. Swearing under his breath, Crawford gripped the wheel, willing his car to round the bend, away from the cliffs. Once he got around the corner there'd be a place where he could pull over and let the van pass.

He pressed on the accelerator. The tires gripping the asphalt as the Volvo entered the corner. The car gained momentum.

But the van didn't fall behind. It closed in on him, so close Crawford could swear it was touching his bumper. Lines furrowed Crawford's forehead. His palms grew moist. The waters of the Bay splashed below to his left as he entered the turn. His Volvo hugged the shoulder, his hands locked on the steering wheel, his fingertips growing white. He could almost feel the van's bumper grazing against his own.

But if it touched him now, while he was on the turn—

The thought suddenly raced through his mind, *Is this guy trying to kill me?*

He leaned to the right, willing his car to pull through the corner. The speedometer nudged higher, sixty miles an hour... sixty two... sixty four. The end of the turn was in sight. Crawford bit his lower lip, holding his breath as the straight-away grew nearer.

Still, the van came closer.

CHAPTER 36

"There's something I have to show you," Helen said rushing into the lab, gripping a 1T flash drive in her hand.

Malcomb stood at the projection wall, studying the massive 3-D shapes cascading before him, a sea of color, flowing in rivers of digital information. Six hours had passed since Taylor's last aborted run in the VHP, and still Malcomb had no answers. Mozart's "An Chloe" lilted through the speakers, but failed to lighten the morose pall that hung over the lab.

Malcomb turned from the raining spheres and cubes as Helen walked towards him. She wore blue jeans and a white tee-shirt, her hair pulled back into a loose ponytail. Malcomb took one look at her, her brown eyes gazing at him from behind her black-rimmed glasses. Behind her, the now familiar robotic Falcon flapped into the lab and took perch on one of the storage shelves.

Malcomb took in the seriousness on her face and a shudder raced through him.

He walked towards the desk. "What have you got?"

"You're not going to believe this." She held up the flash drive for him to see. "Where's your USB port?"

Malcomb took the drive from her hands. He reached behind his computer, pulled out a cable and connected it.

"What is it?" he asked.

"Just wait."

Malcomb raised an eyebrow, tapping his fingers while the computer read the data.

"Why the mystery?"

Helen nodded towards the computer. Malcomb clicked on the external hard drive icon.

"Hit that," Helen said, pointing to a video file.

Malcomb clicked the icon and the VLC media player loaded. "I wish you'd just tell me what's going on," he said. "I don't really do very well with surprises."

"Just hush and watch," she said.

The file opened and began to run.

"But really, if you'd only—"Malcomb started, then fell silent. "Is that—"he started to say, then stopped, his eyes gaping wide. He couldn't believe what he was seeing. Taking off his glasses, he wiped them clean. "Is that who I think it is?"

Helen nodded. "It sure is."

"Dr. William Preston."

"Yep."

"But what is he doing in your animal lab?"

"That's the million-dollar question, isn't it?" Helen said. "Just watch. This video is only a few hours old. I set up the digital recorder after the first pig died to monitor the rest of your pets, 24-7. I thought maybe they were seizing and dying late at night or something. I wasn't expecting this."

Malcomb stood by Helen's side, his mouth drawing open. He watched the image of William Preston enter animal storage room number 7 of the Kelly Research Building. The digital time on the video read 2:29 P.M., less than three hours after the second virtual reality run had ended. Closing the door behind him, Preston walked towards the cages where the VHP pigs were housed.

"How'd he get in?" Malcomb asked. "You've got Fort Knox beat with security."

"Anyone with a security badge can enter. He's done research there in the past. He's got clearance."

"Don't they track him once he's inside?"

"Not with his credentials."

"But what's he doing in our room?"

"Watch."

A shiver ran up Malcomb's spine as the Chief of Cardiothoracic Surgery walked to the locked cage of Pig number 2, the subject from their last aborted virtual reality trial. Turning his head from side to side, searching for anyone else in the room, Preston reached into his breast pocket and pulled out a syringe.

"What's that?" Malcomb's eyes grew wide. "What's he doing to our pig?"

"He's killing it," Helen answered. "You may not want to watch this part."

"No, no!" Malcomb said. He watched Preston uncap the needle of the syringe and inject its contents into the I.V. bag dripping saline into the pig's right front leg. Instantly, the pig convulsed, its legs kicking out spasmodically, then fell flaccid to the cage floor.

"He killed it," Malcomb cried. "He just walked up there and killed it!"

Helen nodded her head. "I'd bet Preston killed the first one too."

Malcomb looked at her perplexed. "But why?" he stuttered. "Why would he do this?"

Helen eyed him carefully. "Perhaps the better question is, is that all that he's done?"

Malcomb sat back as if punched in the gut, taking in the magnitude of her question. He thought of Taylor thrashing about on the La-Z-Boy recliner like a deranged marionette. The computer changing. Taylor seeing his dead brother inside the virtual reality program. He exhaled into his cupped hands, then reached into his desk drawer and pulled out a half-eaten Nestle Crunch bar.

Taking a nervous bite, he shot a glance into Helen's eyes.

"My God," he whispered. "What have we gotten ourselves into?"

CHAPTER 37

Gravel spit from underneath the Volvo's tires as Crawford guided the car to a stop on the rough shoulder of Belvedere Road. His hands locked on the wheel, he fought to catch his breath, adrenaline racing through his body.

Behind him, the grey van pulled to a stop on the shoulder, keeping its distance, its headlights still glaring into his pupils through the rear-view mirror. Darkness surrounded the van, steam bellowing from the exhaust like the breath of an angry beast. Crawford could hear the engine revving.

With fingertips tingling, Crawford wiped the sweat from his upper lip. His entire life, he'd been a man of reason, a man of words and compassion. But the events of the last few days were building inside of him. Like gunpowder in a keg, he'd felt like he could blow at any moment. Now the mysterious van with the damn headlights had lit the fuse.

Unbuckling his seatbelt, Crawford thrust the door open and stepped outside. The ocean wind cut him, salt air pounding his face, howling in his ears. His overcoat thrashed around him like a flag in a storm. He marched towards the van, the gravel crackling under his shoes.

Crawford squinted through the headlights' glare, shielding his eyes with his hands. "What the hell do you want?"

Waves crashed against the rocks below, ocean spray swirling in the wind. Crawford could taste the saltwater on his lips.

"Who the hell are you?"

He took another step towards the van, feeling more trepidation now. The initial rush of adrenaline had passed and suddenly he wondered what the hell he was doing; standing in the dark on a cliff high above the ocean, screaming at an anonymous van.

The van idled before him, looking more menacing, as if it was alive, a bull ready to charge.

Crawford realized how ridiculous he looked. He was a doctor, for God's sake, not an action hero. *Go home*, he thought. *Just go home.*

He took a cautious step backwards, retreating towards the safety of the Volvo, when something flashed to his left. He turned just in time to see a dark figure lunging from the darkness. Something clamped onto Crawford's wrists, spinning him around. Crawford felt his left wrist jammed backwards, up towards his shoulder. Excruciating pain shot through his arm. He let out a cry, the breath jolted from his lungs.

With another powerful thrust, Crawford's wrist was forced higher behind his back and he was certain that the bones would break. The strength drained from his legs. He collapsed to his knees onto the gravel.

"Who the hell are you?" he cried.

But the figure said nothing. A flash of light moved towards him with lightning speed. He could just make out the form of a plastic syringe then the piercing of a needle plunging into the right side of his neck. Bucking, he flailed out with his free hand, searching to make contact with his attacker, but fell short. He could feel the cold steel of the needle sinking deeper into the side of his neck, burrowing into through the muscle. Then pain, bursting like an electric explosion in his brain. Blood streamed onto his collar.

Panic seized him. He thrashed his legs, desperately trying to break free, but it was too late. He could already feel the acidic burning of the poison surging through his veins. A metallic taste shot into his mouth. Medicinal fire seared through his bloodstream.

Then his attacker let go and Crawford fell to the gravel. Fear seized him. *What did he inject in me? What?* As a scientist, his mind raced, desperately trying to predict the possibilities. Potassium Chloride? Decamethonium? Alfenta? His hand instinctively gripped his neck, applying pressure to the bleeding wound. He stumbled towards his car. Gravel kicked out from under his shoes and he fell to his knees. Staggering to his feet, he took a step then collapsed again, crawling across the gravel on all fours. The only thought in his mind was, *Get to the hospital, get the antidote.*

But already Crawford could feel his muscles starting to spasm. Jerky, fascicular contractions wracked his legs, making them useless. He collapsed to the gravel. Random nerve endings fired out of sequence, his arms, hands, shoulders, abdomen contracting, muscles seizing. Blinding pain filled every square inch of his being. His diaphragm convulsed; the breath burst from his lungs.

Then, as quickly as the spasms started, they passed, the contractions weakened, his body going limp. Every muscle medicinally paralyzed, every fiber flaccid.

The cold ocean wind buffeted Crawford's cheeks. He lay immobile, on his back, unable to move. He could feel the chill from the gravel bleeding through his overcoat; he could hear the crashing of the waves behind him. But he couldn't breathe, his diaphragm paralyzed, poisoned by the drug, incapable of drawing even the smallest breath.

Light from the van's headlights streamed into Crawford's pupils. A single tear leaked down the left side of his face as he felt the oxygen content in his blood fading; his mental need to take a breath beyond the point of gasping. But his flaccid muscles couldn't accommodate his brain's scream to inhale.

Crawford felt the coldness sinking into his skin. *Poor Georgia*, he thought. She'd be worried about him not being home this late. They'd planned on driving to their ranch over the weekend. Get things prepared for the grandkids' first fishing trip. He thought of her freckled cheeks and crooked smile and knew that he would miss her.

The light from the headlights continued to pour into Crawford's eyes until the light was the only thing left to see.

CHAPTER 38

Tuesday, October 17th, 5:29 am
FBI Special Agent Victor Ruiz walked across the gravel that lined the shoulder of Belvedere Avenue, pulled up his coat collar and frowned. Across the Bay, the night lights of San Francisco were fading as the morning sun began its ascent in the east; the barest points of light from the TransAmerica Pyramid still visible through the dense morning fog. The Pacific wind whipped across the Bay, carrying a nasty chill that cut straight through his suit coat like a chainsaw cutting through butter. He shivered in huge body-wrenching waves, his teeth chattering, his ample stomach jiggling.

A hell of a way to wake up, he thought, but realized when he glanced across the dead body lying in the gravel, that his morning could have started a lot worse.

Ruiz held his paper cup of Peet's black coffee in both hands for warmth, breathing in the steam. He was still annoyed at being roused from his warm bed with Marta out into the freezing morning to deal with another stiff. It was only 4:30 that AM when the call came in, the body spotted by a stock trader heading into the City to start oiling the day's money machine. Ruiz sucked from his cup of coffee and wondered why people couldn't have the courtesy of getting killed when the sun was up and the day was warm.

He shot a glance at his junior FBI agent, Justin Hart and felt his disdain rising. Even at 5:30 in the morning, Hart looked like he'd just walked off the cover of *Gentlemen's Quarterly*; his blue suit pressed, white tie impeccably knotted, ebony skin clean and fresh, hair close-cropped and body looking fit. It was a far cry from Ruiz's own wrinkled, off-the-rack suit and extra forty pounds.

Unconsciously, Ruiz tucked in his shirt. "What have you got?"

Hart glanced down to his notepad. Even his nails were manicured.

"Guy's name is Bennington Crawford. Apparently, he's a bigwig Doc over at SFU. Chief of Staff. Federal employee as head of the VA Hospital. That's why we were called in."

Ruiz nodded his head. "I've heard of him. He was in the news talking about all that robot medicine going on over there."

"Yeah, that's the one." Hart pointed to a pale, balding man, in a Versace suit standing by the side of the road, leaning against a silver Mercedes-Benz Maybach S-Class 580. "That's the guy who found him. Saw him lying on the side of the road on his way in to work."

"Does he know anything?"

"Just what his morning breakfast looks like."

Ruiz smiled. He was well aware of the how powerful the gag reflex could be after stumbling upon something as disturbing as a dead human body. It would certainly take your mind off the stock market. "Take his statement and let him go. From the looks of him he's gonna need a few hours at a couple hundred bucks per with his shrink to get past this one."

Hart nodded, looking at the car. "Looks like he can afford it."

The two men waked past the police cruisers on the side of the road, their red lights glowing like a parade in the dawning light, then under the yellow police tape that cordoned off the crime scene. Crawford's body lay in the gravel; face up, eyes open, mouth fixed agape in panic. Crawford's suit was dusted with gravel, his dead face glistening wet with morning frost. Tire tracks from two different automobiles crossed the gravel, but no cars were visible on the shoulder.

Ruiz took in his surroundings. Multimillion dollar homes jutted from the hillsides above, sequestered from the rest of humanity by stone entrance arches and iron gates. To his left the windswept hillside gave way steeply, plunging two hundred feet to the chilly waters of the Bay. Ruiz could hear the sound of water slapping against the black rocks of the seashore below.

"Hell of a place to get murdered," Ruiz said. "Guy out for a late-night walk after brandy and cigars?"

Hart shook his head. "Don't think so." He guided Ruiz towards the cliff and pointed. "There's his car down there."

Ruiz peered over the edge. He could just make out the rear end of a late model Volvo jutting up from the shallow waters at the shoreline.

"You ran the plates?"

"Yep. It's his."

"We got a body up here, but the car down below?"

"Yup."

"That doesn't make any sense."

"None at all. I figure the perp killed him, sent his car off the cliff to hide the evidence, then went back for the body but got interrupted. Maybe someone drove by. He got scared and hightailed it outta here."

"Sounds like an amateur. First time killer."

"That's my thoughts."

Ruiz nodded then turned back towards Crawford's body. Even in death, terror was still etched into the dead man's face. Sometimes a stiff looked calm, almost peaceful, as if death brought with it a great release. Not this time. Whatever had happened to Dr. Bennington Crawford was horrifying until the last second.

"Cause of death?" Ruiz asked.

"No gunshot or knife wounds. No evidence of strangulation or blunt trauma, but there's something here."

Hart led Ruiz back towards the body and hunched on his knees. He slipped on a pair of latex gloves and gently turned Crawford's head to its left side. "We got a puncture wound."

Ruiz leaned closer to the body. A small puncture wound, less than a millimeter in diameter, was visible on the right side of Crawford's neck, three inches below the ear. A single drop of dried blood clotted over the skin. "That's the guy's jugular."

"And we found this." Hart held up a plastic evidence bag containing an empty syringe. "It was lying in the bushes about a hundred feet or so down the road."

Ruiz grabbed the evidence bag, studying its contents, the morning sunlight glistening off the metallic needle. "Got a guess?"

"We'll know after the lab gets a hold of it."

Ruiz handed the bag back. "Jesus. When's the last time you found a stiff that'd been killed by an injection?"

Hart shrugged. "This would be the first."

"So, this wasn't random. The guy was targeted."

"Most likely. And there's more."

Ruiz furrowed his brow. Nothing about this killing was making any sense. He thought of Marta lying naked in their warm bed at home, bundled under three layers of blankets and wished again that he'd never received the call that morning. He took a long gulp from his Peet's cup.

Hart held up another evidence bag. Inside was a silver Mont Blanc pen, the engraved words clearly visible: *Dr. Taylor Abrahms, MD. San Francisco University*. "Found this lying underneath the body."

"Under the stiff?"

"Yep. Maybe he fell on it when he died."

Ruiz noted the scattered traces of two sets of shoe prints in the gravel, an area where the dirt had been kicked clear, revealing the ground beneath. "Maybe it fell out of the killer's pocket during a struggle."

Hart nodded. "That's my thought."

Ruiz took the evidence bag, scanned the monogrammed pen then shoved it in his coat pocket. Ten years on the force had taught him that rarely were murder cases as clear cut as they might seem at the time, but occasionally you got lucky. Looking at the pen, Ruiz envisioned wrapping this case up quickly and jumping back in bed with Marta before she even got dressed.

"Unless the pen's a plant," Ruiz said.

"I thought of that too," Hart answered. "I called around to a reporter friend of mine. She said that Abrahms was the guy at the University doing the research. The robot stuff that Crawford was arguing against."

"Sounds like they didn't get along too well."

"That's my thoughts, but there's something you need to know."

"What?" Ruiz asked cautiously.

Hart hesitated before he answered. "Taylor Abrahms is Senator McIntyre's son-in-law. He's married to the senator's daughter, for crap's sake. We're dealing with the family of the Presidential frontrunner."

Ruiz slapped his forehead. "Jesus Christ! You're fucking kidding me?"

"No. The name didn't click with me at first because I was focused on the stiff. It wasn't until a few minutes ago when I ran it by my reporter friend that it dawned on me."

Ruiz couldn't believe his rotten luck. "Just what I fucking need. And he's got motive."

A cold gust blew across the Bay, shooting up the exposed hillside. With the introduction of the Senator's son-in-law in connection to a frosty stiff in Belvedere, Ruiz saw any chance of crawling back into bed with Marta vanish before his eyes. He pulled his coat closed across his chest and chugged down the last of his coffee.

"I think it's time we paid Taylor Abrahms a visit."

CHAPTER 39

Taylor wiped the sweat from his brow and forced himself to concentrate.

It had only been five minutes since Mr. James Winstrom, the first cardiac patient of the day, had stumbled into the ER. He'd spent the previous night watching Monday Night Football at his local bar; his breath still stinking of cigarettes, beer, and salted peanuts. Yes, yes, he knew that he'd had two heart attacks in the past, and yes, he knew that he wasn't supposed to drink heavily or eat too much salt or fatty food, and yes, he was told by his doctor to lose weight and quit smoking, and he intended to do all of those things. Soon. Right after football season.

He swore, right after football season.

Well, football season was still several months from completion and Taylor seriously doubted that Mr. Winstrom would live to see the end of it. The EKG showed a huge S-T segment elevation in leads II, III and aVF, indicating that he was having a massive heart attack.

Taylor placed an oxygen cannula in his nose and ordered the nurses to give him nitroglycerin and morphine to control the pain. Mary, the head nurse, responded. Mr. Winstrom clutched at his chest and grunted. His skin looked ashen and pale, the color draining from his cheeks with each passing second.

He was still infarcting.

"Call the cardiac care ICU," Taylor ordered. "Alert them of his status."

Mary ran to the telephone at the clerk's desk.

Taylor flashed a glance at the beeping line on the cardiac monitor. The heart rate was too slow, much too slow. Damn. Cardiac arrhythmias were a bad sign during a heart attack, indicating extensive injury to the heart. Winstrom's blood pressure was too low and barely holding. Too much muscle had died. His heart wasn't capable of pumping enough blood to his body.

"Get another IV!" he called out. "I need one milligram of atropine STAT."

Mary placed the IV, piercing the needle through the vein on the back of the hand, and quickly injected the drug. No change. Heart rate was still dropping.

"Push it again," he ordered.

She forced more atropine into his bloated veins.

Nothing.

"Damn it! He's in sinus brady. His pulse is too slow." Taylor pulled his gaze from the monitor. "Get a central line tray. I'm placing a jugular line."

The nurses scattered, racing to the metal cabinets to retrieve the supplies.

Taylor swore under his breath. If the VHP was working, he'd be able to go inside Winstrom's heart artery right now, find the blockage and clear it away rather than sitting there pumping in useless medicines. But that was a mighty big if. He forced thoughts of the last failed VHP out of his mind and focused on his patient.

"Hold on, Mr. Winstrom," Taylor said, watching the plummeting heart rate. "The 49ers play the Raiders next week; you don't want to miss it."

Winstrom wheezed weakly and gasped in pain.

"Here's the tray," Mary said, rushing back with a sterile tray stocked with needles, catheters and sleeves. She placed the tray on a metal stand by the head of the bed.

"Prep the right side of his neck," Taylor ordered then turned towards the ward clerk. "Get me the on-call cardiologist. He needs tPA."

tPA, tissue plasminogen activator, was a wonder drug used in acute heart attacks that dissolved the clots clogging the coronary arteries and re-established perfusion to the dying heart. Unfortunately, the drug was dangerous; a patient could die from internal hemorrhage or stroke. As a resident, Taylor needed to get permission from a staff cardiologist before he could use it.

"Who's the cardiologist on-call?" Taylor yelled.

"Dr. Jensen," the clerk said. "I've paged her."

"He's prepped," Mary stated.

Taylor moved to the head of the gurney. He grabbed a large bore needle, placed it on a syringe, found his landmarks and inserted the needle into the side of Winstrom's neck. A sudden rush of blood flashed into the syringe indicating he'd successfully penetrated the jugular. Sliding the needle out, he threaded a catheter down the vein.

"Stabilize it," he ordered, indicating for Mary to bandage the catheter in place.

"Where's Jensen?" Taylor yelled towards the main desk.

The clerk frowned. "Still hasn't responded."

Taylor glanced at the monitors. The heart rate was plummeting. Forty-seven beats per minute. Forty-six. Forty-five. Too slow. Blood pressure barely holding.

"Damn it," Taylor swore. "He's in sinus brady. We've got to pace him. There's no time to wait."

"What are you going to do?" Mary asked.

Taylor turned towards her. "Get me a temporary pacemaker and prepare the tPA."

Mary stood immobile at the end of the bed. Taylor gazed up from the dying patient. "Didn't you hear me? I need a pacing wire and the tPA. Now!"

Mary still didn't move. "Doctor, you can't place the pacemaker without the cardiologist."

"The cardiologist isn't responding."

"But you can't do it. Hospital policy. Only a cardiologist can place a pacemaker wire."

"The cardiologist isn't here!"

"But I can't allow you to—"

"I don't care what you can or cannot allow me to do. I'm putting a wire in him. I'll take full responsibility."

"But I can't—"

"Then the patient will die!"

Mary looked stricken, immobile. She glanced toward the main desk to see if the cardiologist had responded. Nothing. Her eyes darted to the cardiac monitor. Beep... Beep. Forty-three. Forty-two.

"Okay," she said, and ran to get the pacing wire.

"Hold on, Mr. Winstrom," Taylor said. "Hold on."

Taylor positioned himself at the head of the bed, eyeing the monitor while he waited for Mary to return with the wire. What was taking her so long? Why didn't they keep those wires in each of the rooms? Winstrom wasn't going to hang on much longer.

There still was no word from Dr. Jensen.

Three more cardiac patients staggered into the ER, each clutching their chests and gasping for air. The nurses lined them up in adjoining rooms and prepared the oxygen, nitro and morphine. Taylor would get to them next.

One disaster at a time.

He scrutinized the emergency room as it grew more hectic, and crinkled his brow. An unusual tightness settled in his stomach. Something didn't seem right. He couldn't put his finger on it, but something was wrong.

Everything appeared normal, the nurses, clerks, dirty white walls, ringing telephones, stretchers lining the hallways, smell of stale urine.

But something struck him as being out of place.

What was it?

He shook his head and refocused on Winstrom. Mary ran to him with a package containing the pacing wire. He took it and placed it on a sterile drape at the head of the bed. He snapped on sterile surgical gloves and opened the sleeve on the catheter. He needed to carefully guide the wire through the catheter in Winstrom's neck, into his heart, then capture the wire in the muscular heart wall. Then he could administer an electric charge and the heart muscle would be stimulated to contract.

Taylor had only placed a wire a couple of times before, but had watched Jensen do several. With Winstrom's pulse plummeting, there was no other choice.

He grabbed the wire and twisted it in his hands, bending it backwards over his palm to create a smooth curve. This would make it easier to slide into the heart. Mr. Winstrom coughed, gasping for air. His heart rate was crashing, barely contracting at all.

Something flashed by in the hallway. Taylor caught a fleeting glimpse of something, like a child running. He turned, but the hall was empty. He looked at Mary questioningly, but she returned his look with a blank stare. Whatever it was, she obviously hadn't seen it. He glanced down the hallway again, making sure it was empty.

It was.

Taylor returned to Winstrom, now stretched out completely flaccid. He'd lapsed into unconsciousness from lack of blood flow to the brain. He'd be dead in minutes if something wasn't done quickly. Dr. Jensen still hadn't called. Taylor had no choice. It was now or never.

He took a deep breath and leaned over his patient, bringing the wire closer to Winstrom's neck. Holding his hand steady, he placed the wire inside the catheter, sliding it in slowly, one millimeter at a time. He concentrated on the EKG monitor, scanning the cardiac tracing for arrhythmias or premature contractions. He felt the wire nudge against the heart muscle and he knew he was almost there. Just another millimeter, he thought. Slowly.

Carefully.

That was when the voice came from behind him.

"Don't let him hurt me."

Hearing the words, Taylor spun around. He found himself staring into the teary eyes of a towheaded six-year-old, standing no more than a foot behind him. Fresh bruises swelled on the child's cheek; a trickle of blood dripped from his nose.

Taylor turned towards Mary. "Where'd that kid come from?"

Mary looked nonplussed. "What kid?"

"Right here, this child—" Taylor started, but cut off, his mouth hanging open in mid-sentence. He squinted at the child. Something about the little boy's face looked strangely familiar. Taylor leaned forward, crinkling his brow; the half-moon shape of the child's eyes, the crooked front teeth. He looked so much like—

No, my God, no! It can't be you!

Taylor's face blanched. His mouth dropped aghast.

It can't be!

The boy huddled behind Taylor's leg, squeezing it tight, holding it like he'd never let go. "Please don't let him hurt me. I'll be good. I promise I'll be good."

Taylor's breath caught in his throat. He stared dead-eyed at the blond-as-blond-could-be head of the child. He recognized the familiar cowlick and the patch of darkness on his crown. A reddened scar crossed the boy's forehead. Taylor knew it instantly. It had come at the hands of their father on a particularly drunken night, when a bottle of gin had been followed by a bottle of whiskey and then a bottle of rum. Taylor remembered his father stumbling into the living room, tripping over Jacob stretched on the floor watching TV. "Always under my feet," he'd screamed and lashed out at the boy with the butt end of a broom. Taylor remembered the hollow *whap* of the wood against Jacob's skull and the splash of crimson as Jacob's forehead split open. He'd jumped on his father that night to stop him and wound up with a sprained arm and blackened eye.

He remembered it all.

He glared down at the child holding his leg now, his eyes wide in horror.

But it can't be you.

"Doctor, are you alright?" Mary's voice called out.

Taylor snapped around towards her, his eyes wide and vacant, his eyebrows knotted in confusion. He tried to speak, but his voice stuck in his throat.

"It's—it's my brother."

"What are you talking about?"

"My brother, he—" Taylor turned towards Jacob, but the child was gone. The room behind him was empty.

Taylor's heartbeat burst into his ears. He jerked around, scanning the room. Everything was as it had been when the resuscitation started. The monitor beeped out a deadly slow rhythm. Oxygen hissed through the cannula in Winstrom's nose. The bright fluorescent light glared off the sterile white walls.

"He was just here," Taylor whispered, more to himself than to Mary. "I saw him."

"There's no one here, Doctor," Mary said.

Taylor could barely hear her. He spun around, looking down towards his legs, but there was no child holding him, and no evidence that there had ever been one. Could he have imagined it? There had been children in the waiting area; could he have overheard one of them crying to its mother and projected an image? Besides, Jacob was seventeen when he died, not a child. It didn't make sense.

Ignore it. He squeezed his eyes closed. *It couldn't be real. I'm going to open my eyes and I'll be in the ER and everything will be alright. It will all be alright.*

Slowly, he opened his eyes.

He saw Mary standing there, squinting at him, her eyebrows raised questioningly, a look of panic descending over her face. He could tell she was wondering what was happening. So did he. He righted himself and moved passed her, steadying himself at the head of the bed. The monitor sounded out a deadly slow rhythm. He took a deep breath and picked up the pacing wire. *Pace his heart,* he said to himself. *Just pace his fucking heart.*

"Doctor—?" Mary asked.

"I'm okay."

"But—?"

"Let's do this," he said.

Taylor readied himself by Winstrom's neck. Sweat beaded his forehead, glistening on his upper lip. He reached for the catheter. Fighting the tremor, he brought the tip of the wire to the catheter.

Then he heard the voice again.

"Please! Make him stop, Tay! Make him stop!"

Taylor froze. He now saw a nine-year old Jacob huddled near the end of the gurney, holding himself in a tight ball, knees to his chest, rocking back and forth. Before his eyes, Taylor watched a new cut appear across Jacob's cheek. A swath of blood. Tears filled Jacob's eyes.

Taylor stopped dead. He knew those eyes.

BUT IT CAN'T BE!

The wire dropped from Taylor's hands. He dashed towards his brother. Reaching the end of the gurney, he skidded to a halt. Jacob was gone and only the cold white floor remained. Taylor snapped his head around. He knew he'd seen him this time. It wasn't his imagination. He'd called him Tay. Only Jacob ever called him Tay. Pain drilled behind his eyes.

He was right here. My God, he was right here!

"Doctor!" Mary screamed.

But her voice barely traversed the confusion in Taylor's mind. He turned towards her, his eyes pleading, open wide.

Mary gasped when she saw his face, deadly pale, sculpted in panic.

"The patient! Mary screamed. "The patient!"

His eyes darted towards the monitor, but it was so hard to see. *Jacob was here. He needed me.* His temples pounded. He reached up to squeeze away the pain.

"The patient!" Mary screamed again.

Taylor forced himself to face her. Winstrom lay flaccid on the gurney, his blue, bloated face drained of all animation. Mary was screaming at him, but he couldn't hear her, everything lost in a swirl of confusion. Something deep inside of him knew that he had to fight this, that he had to pull it together and save Winstrom. Using all of his strength, he locked his vision onto the limp body on the gurney.

That was when the body sat up.

Taylor's eyes gaped. Winstrom was dying, his heart could barely beat. How could he be sitting up?

His gaze darted to Winstrom's face and he froze. It wasn't Winstrom sitting on the gurney.

"God-damn it, boy. Can't you do anything right?"

Taylor gasped. His father sat there on the edge of the gurney, his skin yellow and dried, hanging limply from his bones like a sheet draped over a clothesline. His face sunken and hollow, eyes deathly black. The catheter protruded out of his neck like a huge snake erupting from his body. Blood spurted out of its open mouth, streaming onto the floor, splashing against the walls, splattering around the room.

"You're supposed to be pacing me, boy. What the hell are you doing over there? I'm going to have to teach you a lesson again, ain't I?"

A scream erupted from Taylor's throat as he staggered backwards. He jerked around, stumbled over an oxygen tank, and fell to the floor.

"My God, Doctor, what's wrong?" Mary shrieked.

"Don't let him get me!" Taylor screamed, pointing towards the gurney.

"Who doctor, who? Don't let who get you?" Her panicked eyes flashed across Winstrom's prone body.

Taylor couldn't answer, his voice lost somewhere deep in his throat. He stumbled to his feet. His arms flailed and knocked over the instrument tray, scalpels and forceps shattered to the floor.

"Help me, Tay. Help me!" Jacob screamed.

Jacob was behind him again. Holding his tattered blanket in his arms. Tears stained his red and puffy cheeks. Suddenly, Jacob took off, running away from the Shock Room. He dashed towards the clerk's area, hiding behind her desk.

Taylor saw his father rip the catheter out of his neck. Blood gushed from the open wound, splashing onto his chest.

"Gonna have to teach you, boy."

Taylor staggered backwards, then bolted from the Shock Room after Jacob. The terrified clerk raced from the desk as Taylor ran towards her, looking like a madman. Mary sprinted to the phone.

"Call security!" she yelled.

No one else dared to move.

At the desk, Taylor reached for Jacob, but the little boy dodged him and dashed out the double glass doors of the Emergency Room. Taylor froze and took a panicked look over his shoulder. His father took a heavy step towards him. Blood streamed from his neck, painting his body a gruesome crimson. He took another lumbering step forward; his arms open wide.

"Come to Papa."

A scream burst from Taylor's lungs. He pushed away from the clerk's desk. Running blindly, he plowed his way through the group of stunned nurses and sprinted out the glass exit doors.

"Jacob," he cried out as he ran through the empty parking lot. "Jacob!"

CHAPTER 40

"I'm trying to understand," Dr. Norman Browne was saying, his large mass seated behind his desk. "Help me to understand."

Taylor paced back and forth across the Kodachrome covered floor of Browne's office, his right hand rubbing his face, his lower eyelid twitching. The gut-wrenching nausea that followed his hallucination was starting to settle, and it had been hours since he'd last vomited, but his legs still trembled with the weakness of a man teetering on the edge of sanity.

The nightmare in the Emergency Room had ended shortly after it began. Taylor 'awoke' to find himself huddled in the parking lot, clutching his knees to his chest; the nurses from the ER frozen in fear, staring at a raving lunatic.

He'd crawled to his hands and knees and thrown up bile onto the pavement. Then he'd huddled there, shaking like he had palsy, until a hospital guard helped him to his feet, half-escorting, half-carrying him to the holding room. Dr. Jensen had arrived simultaneously and resuscitated Winstrom, placing the pacing wire to steady his heartbeat, then cared for the other patients until a backup resident could be called in.

No one had died.

Except for a part of Taylor.

One nightmare had ended and now another was about to begin. Taylor had spent the early part of the morning in the holding room, huddled under a thin blanket, trembling under the weight of his hallucinations. Dr. Browne was phoned and came in at nine to sign for Taylor's release. Now Taylor had to convince Browne that he wasn't crazy, that these weren't paranoid delusions ravaging him, that he didn't need to be locked in a soft, padded room, wearing paper clothing and with no shoelaces, where he wouldn't be a danger to himself or anyone else.

But first, Taylor had to believe it himself.

Dr. Browne shifted in his chair. Mary stood by his side. Browne's office was on the administrative third floor of the Medical Center Building. An ash desk stood in the center of the room, every square inch of which was littered with piles of papers and patient charts. Pandemonium had struck the bookshelf to the right, textbooks and journals piled one on top of each other like a child's Lego project. A stack of patient charts rose to a height of six feet, teetering perilously in the corner while 35mm Kodachrome slides of X-rays, MRI's and ultrasounds littered the carpet. A small pile of rejected grant requests built up in the corner. Mary, standing to Browne's left by the door, had been called up from the ER to witness the meeting and give her side of the events. Dr. Browne positioned himself behind the desk, studying his protégé with a mixture of concern and condemnation.

Dr. Browne began again. "Please, Taylor. One more time. Tell me what happened. Tell me about your brother and your father."

Taylor stopped pacing and ran his fingers through his matted hair, still damp with sweat. He'd tried to describe the experiment and how it had failed, and how the system was changing, and how he was seeing hallucinations of his family, and how some demon was living under his skin scratching to get out, but every time he spoke, the words sounded crazy even to him. It was all so absurd. Computer programs don't change. His dead brother couldn't appear in the middle of the Emergency Room. None of this could happen.

He felt he was drowning in madness. How could he convince Dr Browne of his sanity when he wasn't sure he believed it himself?

Taylor took a deep breath and collapsed into a chair by Browne's desk. He buried his face in his hands.

"Taylor?"

He looked up. "I'm here."

"What happened?"

"It's so hard to explain, Dr. Browne. I don't know where to begin."

"Let's start at the beginning." Browne said calmly. "You said something about seeing your brother."

"He was standing right there behind me. Like he popped out of nowhere."

"But your brother is dead?"

"Yes, but I saw him in virtual reality."

"As part of your experiment?"

"Yes."

"In your laboratory?"

"Yes."

"Inside of a virtual blood vessel?"

"Yes."

"Then what was he doing in our Emergency Room?"

"I don't know." Taylor leaned forward, his eyes glistening. "God help me, I don't know. It has something to do with the program."

"The computer program?"

"When I first entered the virtual heart, everything was perfect. It was exactly as we'd planned. The visuals, the mechanics. It was perfect. Then it all went wrong. The virtual program changed, and since then I've been having these nightmares."

"Of things you're seeing in the virtual reality?"

"Do you understand? Tell me you understand, Dr. Browne. I'm not crazy. I can't explain what's happening to me, but I'm not crazy."

Dr. Browne gazed at his frazzled resident. He and Mary shot each other concerned looks. "I don't know what to think," he finally said. "All this talk of hallucinations and nightmares, it sounds delusional. If your tox screen hadn't come back negative I'd be worried about drug abuse."

"I'm not on drugs."

"That I believe." Browne released a sharp breath. "But I can't close my eyes and pretend this hadn't happened. A patient almost died. The liability is enormous. If something goes wrong with any of your patients and it became public that the hospital knew of your mental instability—I don't even want to think about it."

Taylor lowered his head, understanding. One thing doctors and administrators dreaded more than anything else were lawsuits. He could almost hear Browne's next words before they came from his mouth; still, hearing them came as a shock.

"I'm going to relieve you of all duties."

Taylor stiffened. "But Dr. Browne—"

Browne held up his hand. "This isn't open for discussion. I'll try to keep it out of the press, but I can't have someone in your condition working in my Emergency Room. I'll pull a resident from the VA to fill in. As of this minute, you're on suspension."

He looked at Mary. "He's not to go near the ER or see any patients."

"Understood," Mary agreed.

Taylor couldn't believe this was happening. His career, everything he'd worked for, being swept away. The walls of the office seemed to collapse upon him.

"Doctor Browne, you've got to give me another chance."

Browne's eyes grew stern. "I don't have to do anything but look out for the welfare of my Emergency Room."

Taylor sank back into his chair. He shot a pleading glance towards Mary, but the squint of her eyes revealed her position. There was no point in fighting. His own actions had condemned him. And could he blame them? He'd acted like a madman.

"I'm sorry it's come to this," he finally said.

"So am I, Taylor," Browne nodded. "You've always been my favorite, but you've been under terrific stress, with the research, the media, and your ER shifts. No one could take that for long. I think you cracked under the pressure. What I suggest is for you to get away for a while. Take your wife and get out of town, go spend a quiet night in the country. Get away from the ER and patients and just relax. Say you will."

"I will."

Browned scribbled a note to himself on a pad. "Next week, I'll have you see the staff psychiatrist. If you can convince her you're not unstable, we'll see if we can reconsider our position. Maybe start you back at half time. Will you agree to that?"

Taylor nodded, grateful that Browne was leaving the door open, if just a crack. But he knew a psychiatrist wasn't the solution. Whatever was destroying his life was linked to the computer, not his mental health. This wasn't something Freudian analysis or Skinner Behavior Therapy would solve. Somewhere inside the computer program was the key to understanding what was happening.

Taylor knew what he had to do. He had to get back to the lab and enter the system right away. The answer was there. He had to go back in to find it.

"And one last thing, Taylor."

Taylor turned. "Yes?"

Browne rose to his feet, placed his palms squarely on desk. "As of this moment, the Virtual Heart Project ends."

Taylor's eyes widened. "But Dr Browne... "

"No buts. You will promise to stay away from the virtual reality or I'll make your suspension permanent. Do you understand." It was not a question; it was an order.

Taylor sat silent, a million thoughts running through his mind.

"Do you understand?"

Finally, Taylor lowered his head. "I understand."

CHAPTER 41

Malcomb stumbled out of the Visual Computer Enhancement Laboratory in the basement of Anderson Hall, his bladder near bursting.

He locked the door behind him and headed down the corridor to the front stairs and the bathroom that waited on the first floor. The back hallway was bad enough in the summertime, Malcomb thought, moldy and damp, but in the winter, it was almost unbearable. With the rain, the extra moisture settled in the corridor, the halls filling with the stench of mildew. Maybe if they'd ever put some lights in here! He walked past the boiler room towards the rows of filing cabinets. He felt like he was working in the lost caverns of Tibet. Nothing quite like spelunking your way to work each day.

Helen had called ten minutes earlier. She was at the Farm performing an autopsy on the last pig. She'd planned a toxicology screen and analysis of the I.V. fluids Preston had tampered with. Malcomb still couldn't fathom a doctor of Preston's stature sabotaging their experiment, but the video evidence was irrefutable. Somehow, they'd become mixed up in something much more complicated than a simple run inside virtual reality.

This realization, combined with the obvious deterioration in Taylor's mental and physical condition, ate deeply into

Malcomb's mind. In fact, the only good that had come of the whole mess was the amount of time he was spending with Helen. As much as Malcomb hated to admit it, he'd missed her wit, her intelligence, her perfume after she left. He couldn't believe he was actually feeling this way about Helen, Beelzebub, the sharp-tongued she-devil.

Maybe, when this whole thing was over, he'd ask her out on a... a... date? Isn't that what people did? Go on dates? Malcomb scratched his forehead. He'd never actually been on a date, although once in third grade he did eat lunch with Elma Higgins by the see-saw. Of course, that didn't go too well when they started laughing and he snorted milk out through his nose, started coughing and had to go to the school nurse for his sinus medicines. He never had the courage to talk to her again.

He'd just finished climbing the stairwell when he heard voices filling the entranceway ahead of him. He poked his head around the corner.

A couple of men dressed in dark suits stood at the guard station asking questions; one a clean-cut black man, the other a stocky Latino guy flashing an ID. Their backs were stiff, chests puffed, shoulders square in a rigid stance of authority. From where he stood, Malcomb could hear their conversation clearly.

"—looking for a Taylor Abrahms," the Latino was saying, his voice thick and full of gravel.

The guard looked down at his registry, searching with his finger.

"Down in the basement, room 4."

The second man thanked the guard and together the two headed towards the stairs. Malcomb ducked around the corner.

"Hey, what does the FBI want with a science geek like Abrahms anyways?" the guard asked.

The two men ignored his question and continued towards the stairs in silence.

*****

By the restroom, Malcomb was having a fit. *The FBI! What are the Feds doing here?* He took off his glasses, fumbled with them, wiped them clean, put them on again. His bladder ached to the point that he thought he'd have an accident. He scrambled to the restroom.

Afterward he stood at the sink, washing and rewashing his hands, scrubbing and rescrubbing, trying to figure out what was going on. *Why would the cops be here? What could they want with Taylor?* Taylor didn't have any government grants that he knew of, and he'd never done work for the FBI. Why would they come to the lab? *Think, man, what else?*

"Calm down," he whispered to himself. "Calm down and think. What to do, what to do?" He hated this; he'd never been good under pressure. His sinuses began to ache and he had a terrible craving for chocolate, but his stash was down in the lab. Had he locked the lab? He thought so, he usually did. Had he this time? He couldn't remember.

His palms started sweating, so he washed his hands again.

Outside, he heard footsteps coming up the stairwell. He crept towards the door, opened it a crack and stuck his ear out to listen.

"—is the lab?" grumbled the gravelly-voiced one. "We walked all over the place down there and couldn't find any God-damned Room 4."

"That's the number the book gives. It's got to be down there somewhere."

"What about his partner, Malcomb Bernard?" The smooth-voiced cop asked. "Is he here?"

"Don't know. He'd be in the lab if he was."

"Why aren't there any lights down there?" The gravel voice asked. "I can't see a goddamned thing. Now why don't you get off your ass and—"

The smooth voice cut it. "I apologize for my partner's behavior. I know you're watching your post, but we need to get into that lab. How about escorting us down there and showing us where it is?"

"No can do," the guard replied. "I've never been there. I got no idea where it is."

"I don't think you understand the seriousness here. We need to get into that lab. You're about to interfere with a criminal investigation—"

"And you're trying to get into one of my labs without a warrant," the guard shot back. "Far as I know, Abrahms or Bernard ain't there right now, and I can't allow you to just prance into their private lab and conduct a search without a warrant. Last time I checked there was still a Constitution in this country."

The men whispered something to each other that Malcomb couldn't hear.

"Damn it!" The gravel-voice barked then stormed out the front door.

"We'll be back with that warrant," the smooth voice said. "I suggest you find out where that room is and be prepared to show us when we return." He dropped his card at the security desk, turned around and walked away.

The guard waited until the cop was at the front door, then picked up the card, ripped it in half and threw the pieces to the floor.

"Stuff it in your ear," the guard muttered.

Malcomb could hear the sound of the front door opening then slamming shut. He stood in the silence of the bathroom. He was just about to run back to the sink to wash his hands again when he heard a voice call out to him.

"They're gone, Malcomb. You can come out of the bathroom now."

Sheepishly, Malcomb stepped out of the men's room and walked across the hall to the security station. The guard, Lawrence, sat there with his feet propped on the TV monitors and a self-satisfied smile on his face.

"You knew I was in there?" Malcomb asked.

"Of course I knew. It's my job to know everything that goes on here."

"But you didn't tell the FBI where I was?"

"What? And help those smug bastards? Hell, no! I'll make them work their sorry Federal butts every step of the way. Going around with their fancy suits and sunglasses, thinking they're something special. I'll be damned if I'll be helping them out."

Malcomb looked confused. "Can't you get in trouble?"

"With them? Naw. They can't do nothing to me. I've dealt with their kind before, always thinking they're so superior because they have FBI badges. Well, I've got a badge too," he said, showing Malcomb the University Security patch on his shoulder. "And my badge says that I deserve just as much respect from them as they do from me. And they come walking into my territory, during my beat, and shoot off their Federal mouths like that? Uh-uh, no way. This is my house, and in my house I'm the boss, and they better be showing me some respect or they ain't never getting through my door."

"Uh, um... "Malcomb stuttered. "I see."

Lawrence leveled his gaze. "But you, well, you're a different story."

Malcomb looked up. "What do you mean?"

"They'll be back, like flies to a shit, they'll be back. And when they do, they're gonna have a warrant. It'll take them a while, but they'll get it, and then there ain't nothin' I can do. I don't know what it is they want with you guys, but I suggest you gather up whatever it is that you're working on in room number

4, down the back hallway, boxed in by the boiler room and water heaters, and hide it good, because they'll be looking."

Malcomb's brow furrowed. "You know where my lab is? But you told them—"

"Of course I know where your lab is. It's my job, remember. This is my house."

Malcomb looked at him dumbly, not understanding. He took a cautious step backwards away from the guard station. He felt pain building in his bladder again and retreated towards the bathroom.

In mid-step, he stopped and looked back. "Why are you doing this? Why are you helping us?"

The guard smiled, crossed his hands upon the roll of fat above his belt and gave Malcomb a sideways glance.

"Because you and me, Malcomb, we're two of kind."

That wasn't the answer Malcomb expected.

"We are?"

The guard gave Malcomb a wink. "You see, I have a Mac Pro M2 Ultra with an iRetina display at home. Nothing much, mind you, but I've been known to do a little hacking myself." He smiled a big, tooth-filled smile. "I've been watching you over the years, and I gotta say, I like your style."

"Um... my style?"

"Yeah, your style. Us computer geeks got to stick together, you know."

A smile emerged on Malcomb's lips.

He was beginning to like this man.

CHAPTER 42

Heading north towards Napa, Sherilyn watched as the concrete buildings of the City give way to wavering fields of dried grass. Strip malls and fast-food restaurants faded into oblivion, replaced by rolling hills and one hundred-year-old oak trees.

They took her car, a grey Honda; Taylor being unsure the MG would hold together for the drive. Sherilyn turned to take him in behind the steering wheel. At first, when he'd arrived home from work unexpectedly early, claiming to have arranged time off for them to spend together, Sherilyn had been excited. It had been months since they'd gone away, just the two of them. They desperately needed this, some time to rediscover who they were. Over the last week she'd felt more distance between them than ever. The irony of their relationship falling apart on the eve of her father's visit struck her like a slap in the face. But quickly, she'd realized that something was wrong. He couldn't arrange for time off, not when the ER was only staffed by a few residents, each pulling twenty-four-hour shifts. He was hiding something, along with the nightmares, the angry outbursts, and the growing bags under his eyes.

She didn't know how it all fit together, but she intended to find out.

But not today, she reminded herself. Today she was going to force those thoughts from her mind and enjoy being with him again; like when they were young and freshly married and the world seemed a large and beautiful place, stretching before them like some vivid watercolor landscape. She wanted to see the wide-eyed man she'd married, letting go of a lifetime of pain, reaching out, learning to love for the first time.

It was a beautiful day on the Bay as they headed towards the Carquinez Strait. The temperature nestled around sixty-five degrees, with the sun shining through the departing clouds. The water was as smooth as glass, dotted by colorful spinnakers flying from the sailboats cutting the water. Sherilyn looked back at Taylor's face, a little haggard and fatigued, but still handsome, strong, looking like it had been carved out of granite.

Yes, she thought, *today is just for enjoying.*

*****

Taylor pulled over in Napa at a general store to fill the tank. Climbing out of the car, he stretched, aware how good it was to be out of the City, breathing the clean air, feeling the warmth of the sun. He felt younger somehow; far away from the pressure in the ER, the cry of sirens, and the smell of death.

Away from the lab and the nightmares.

This will be good, he thought. His once rock-firm grasp on his life was crumbling. He'd been working too hard—consumed with the experiment. Maybe Dr. Browne was right. The fatigue must have caught up with him and caused the hallucinations. His body was telling him to slow down. His mind needed rest.

He removed the gas nozzle from the tank just as a grey Professional Perfect Plumbing van pulled to the pump behind him. Taylor noticed a man with a shaved head sitting behind the wheel, staring at him through a pair of mirrored sunglasses.

For a second, the sight of the man staring gave Taylor pause, but he brushed it aside and climbed back into the driver's seat. Sherilyn was munching on an apple and offered him a bite. He accepted and she playfully shoved the apple into his mouth, grinding it against his nose. Laughing, he took a huge bite, saliva dribbling down his chin.

"Let's find a B&B and tour the wineries," he said, his mouth stuffed with apple.

"There're some great country inns off highway 29."

He started the engine and pulled onto the two-lane highway, giving a glance in the rear view to confirm that the van stayed behind. They cruised north, passing the vineyards and manicured rows of grapes. They were at the tail end of the grape harvest and crushing season, which occurred from August to November, and the tang of fermenting wine draped heavily in the air.

They continued down 29 to Yountville. They'd just passed a small stone building when Sherilyn asked Taylor to stop. He pulled onto the shoulder.

"What's up?"

Sherilyn pointed. "That's Burgundy House. It's supposed to be fabulous."

Taylor smiled. He put on his blinker to pull the car around, but stopped as the plumbing van headed towards them on the highway. Taylor watched as the van drove by, the bald man's head turning as he passed. Taylor could almost feel the glare of the man's eyes through his mirrored sunglasses. Unexpectedly, a tingle shot up his neck. The van continued on, disappearing around a bend in the country highway.

"Are you ok?" Sherilyn asked.

Taylor nodded, dismissing his uneasiness. "I'm fine." He made the U-turn, pulling the Honda into the driveway. They unloaded their bags and walked through the front door into the rugged stone building. Inside a basket of fruit and a decanter of red wine waited on the bureau, surrounded by a bouquet of local wildflowers, chrysanthemums, marigolds and calla lilies.

Taylor dropped the bags, and called out, "Hello."

There was no answer.

"Nobody home," he surmised. He looked around the front lobby, decorated in 19th century antiques, the era when wine making first came to the Napa Valley. The air was laden with a potpourri of roses, jasmine and thyme.

"There must be someone here," Sherilyn said.

Taylor reached for the decanter. "Well, while we're waiting, my dear," he badly feigned a British accent. "Would you care for a spot of wine?"

"Why, yes," she replied with a smile. "That would be lovely."

He poured them each a glass and they walked out the back door onto the shaded patio. The backyard was quiet, with just the touch of a cool, autumn breeze drifting through the ivy-covered fence. A gentle hint of grapes in the air. Taylor breathed in the serenity of the courtyard, allowing himself a moment of peace. No hallucinations. No edginess.

Just peace.

"Hello," a voice said.

Taylor startled. He turned to see the innkeeper, an attractive woman of about fifty with long red hair, streaked with grey, walking towards them. She wore a period dress from the 1850s with a blue and white floral design, and she carried a platter with dried fruits and cheese. Her smile was warm and friendly.

"I'm Marina. Welcome to Burgundy House."

Taylor shook her outstretched hand. "I'm Taylor. This is my wife, Sherilyn."

"It's a pleasure," Marina said. "Will you be staying with us?"

"We'd love to," Sherilyn said. "If you have room."

"I believe we do, upstairs on the second floor. I'll get the registration book."

"Thank you," Taylor said, as Marina turned and walked back into the inn.

*****

Making love that night was passionate and intense. Taylor couldn't get enough of Sherilyn's body as they rolled across the quilt, rattling the fragile supports of the antique brass bed. The headboard banged so loudly against the stone wall he was certain everyone in the state could hear them. But he didn't care. It felt so good to be with her, surrounded by her, enraptured by her.

Outside, the wind tossed the oak branches against the window. Taylor rested under the flannel sheets, feeling Sherilyn's breath on his shoulder. At that moment, wrapped in her arms, he felt safe; protected from the haunting visions, the nightmare in the Emergency Room, the edginess that burrowed under his skin.

Everything was going to be alright, he convinced himself as he dozed off.

Everything was going to be alright.

But even he didn't believe it.

*****

In the gravel parking lot across the street, Edgar Ross took off his headphones and lowered the Sound-Pro unidirectional microphone. A recording of Taylor and Sherilyn's lovemaking played in the background, a sensuous symphony of moans and purrs, the rhythm kept steady by the clanging of the headboard against the stone wall.

Edgar Ross smiled and prepared his ritualistic journal entry. Ross had been twenty-seven years old when he'd killed his first man. Seventeen years later, the image of that kill was still resplendent in his mind like a freshly painted masterpiece. Every detail, vivid and precise. The pine needles stabbing through his Gortex as he crawled across the frozen Serbian hillside, his target centered in the crosshairs of his LPS high-powered scope. Frostbite burning into his flesh, the blood freezing in his fingertips. The hours spent controlling his diaphragm, reducing his breathing to the faintest exhale, hiding the plume of his frosty breath from the eyes of the sentries. And finally, the rush that shot through his veins as he watched the Serbian General's face explode into a satisfying mist of crimson.

To this day, he kept a handful of dried pine needles, carefully preserved inside a plastic sleeve, in his logbook next to the name, date, weapon and location of the kill.

Over the ensuing years with the Agency and then private employers, an additional forty pages of souvenirs followed, each one carefully categorized, cross-referenced and labeled in neatly filed plastic sleeves.

Flipping through the pages, he passed Dr. Bennington Crawford's gold AMA button, already neatly categorized next to the map taken from the breast pocket of the IRA double-agent. That memento was Ross's favorite; the bullet hole that tore through the center of the map, blood stains crusting the edges, making it more special.

Turning abruptly, he grabbed his Blackberry and re-read the last message.

PRCD PLN. FNSH JB.

Ross nodded, his resolution intensifying. His plan was already formulated. All he needed was a moment's opportunity.

In the meantime, Ross busied himself preparing the next entry for his logbook, noting the target's name in carefully scripted red ink.

Sherilyn's moans rose in the background.

CHAPTER 43

The knife froze in space, two inches above his stomach.

Taylor glared at it, struggling to free himself from its steely edge. His hand shot out to deflect the blade, but was brushed aside. He heard himself scream as the knife plunged into him, ripping open his abdomen, exposing his glistening intestines.

The pain shocked Taylor awake. He bolted upright in bed, gripping his stomach as if he could still feel the blade tearing open his skin. He doubled over, gasping, fighting to catch his breath, to let the nightmare pass. His heart pounding in his chest. Beads of sweat streaked his temples. The acidic taste of bile draped his mouth.

Jesus Christ! What the hell was that?

He slipped out of bed and staggered to the bathroom to rinse out the taste of bile. Nausea held his stomach in a death grip. He took a deep breath, trying to subdue the adrenaline racing through his veins. Gradually, the waves of nausea subsided and the sweat broke, leaving him trembling, but intact. It was only a nightmare. A vividly real, sick nightmare. He recognized the sight of his intestines exposed and bleeding as the same image he'd had of Chan's opened gut in the ER. Chan's connection to this nightmarish collapse of his life still hung heavy in his mind.

But what was the connection?

Taylor splashed a handful of water on his face. The cool droplets calmed his skin. He buried his face in a towel and took another deep breath. He glanced out from the bathroom towards the bedroom. The streetlamp trickled through the second story window, casting a flickering mosaic of light and shadow across the walls. He stared into the intermingling shapes, the disjointed union of light and darkness, and thought of the twisted pieces of his own life.

As much as he tried to stop it, the botched Winstrom resus played itself over and over in his mind. He saw himself, standing gape-jawed, yelling at the phantom image of his father. The pacing wire hanging impotently in his hands. He remembered the look of horror on Mary's face as she ran, distancing herself as if he had a disease.

Or gone mad.

Which he had.

Mentally, he ran through the events leading to his breakdown. He scrolled through the schematics of the virtual helmet, visualizing each circuit, then each electrode, reconstructing the helmet in his mind. He broke the system down into its separate components. He wondered if there couldn't be some external factor involved in the system's malfunction. He ran through the other variables: the power source, the fiber optic connection, the microprocessor.

The answer has to be there somewhere.

A heavy weight sank into his chest. He looked towards the bed at Sherilyn. The half-light illuminated her lips, making them appear fuller, even more beautiful. He sighed. All night, while they'd been making love, he could feel the hint of edginess returning, burrowing under his skin; the same feeling he'd had before his visit to his father, before his breakdown in the ER. Before the madness.

What the hell is happening to me?

Taylor drew a hand down his face. He wasn't going to get any answers tonight and he was too anxious to go back to sleep. He pulled the white cotton Burgundy Inn robe over his naked body, then tucked the covers over Sherilyn, giving her a parting glance. He'd put her through so much, yet she had stood by him.

"I'll make it up to you," he whispered.

He turned the brass handle and pulled open the door. The hallway was empty at that hour. Sabers of light pierced through the openings in the curtains, casting a pallid, haunting glare against the walls. There were no signs of life. All the other guests tucked away in their rooms; sleeping in peace—a feeling Taylor hadn't known in some time.

Quietly, Taylor headed for the stairwell. The wallpaper was silk, a floral pattern of crimson and evergreen to go with the blood-red carpet. Thick curtains draped the windows interspersed between framed portraits of 19th Century pioneers. Taylor walked slowly by the portraits, stopping to study one, a painting of an old man with a handlebar mustache and dark, angry eyes. His skin was ghost-white. The sight made Taylor uneasy. He didn't like the thought of those eyes staring at him in the darkness. He turned from the painting and walked down the hall.

When he was a child, Taylor had hated the night. The darkness was a beast that hid his fears in its womb. At night, he never knew when the door would fly open, his drunken father barging in with an open bottle of whiskey and a closed fist.

Sometimes, late at night, he'd hear the muted slap of his father beating Jacob in the room next door. With each thump of the hand against Jacob's body, Taylor would cringe. He'd squeeze the pillow tightly to his ears to mute the sound. But inside, he was always afraid that soon the sound would stop. As much as he hated to admit it, in some sickening way, the muffled thuds were comforting. As long as he heard that dull slap coming through the walls, he knew he was safe. It was only when the sound stopped that Taylor knew he'd be next.

Taylor had never forgiven himself for feeling that way. He doubted he ever would.

An owl screeched. Taylor startled, his heart leaping in his chest. His eyes scouring the darkness, he felt the air condense around him.

A little edgy tonight, aren't we?

Through the half-light, he could make out the polished banister at the end of the hallway. That was his destination. Go downstairs, out to the back garden, out into the spaciousness of open air. He remembered how peaceful the patio had been when they'd arrived, the flowers and cool breeze. He needed that peace now.

A creaking sound came from the darkness in the hallway before him, the unmistakable groan of aged wood giving under the weight of a human foot. Taylor hesitated, squinting through the half-light to see who else could be haunting the corridors at this hour. But the hallway before him was empty.

He stood there, frozen for a moment, each of his senses heightened as he listened for another sound. A raw tingle ran across his skin.

Another creak. He jerked his head toward the sound. It came from the stairwell.

Easy, boy. It's probably just another guest. Don't go imagining monsters.

He moved faster towards the stairwell, swallowing the fear in his throat. Reaching the banister, he could make out the shape of a woman, rounding the bend in the stairwell below, climbing upwards towards him.

It must be Marina, checking on the status of her boarders.

He reached the stairwell. The woman was on the midway landing. He paused a moment as she stepped towards him. The nerve endings bristled up the back of Taylor's neck. The woman's hair was dark and draped across her face, which seemed unusually pale in the dim light. She moved awkwardly, each step a struggle. She wore a long, white flannel nightgown, ankle-length, with a high collar. But something didn't seem right. The nightgown seemed two sizes too big and it hung limply from her shoulders. Her feet were bare.

A cold finger of fear pressed against Taylor's spine. He lowered his foot onto the first stair, the wood groaning under his weight. The woman stopped before him. Her head snapped upwards. With the motion, her hair parted revealing her face, sunken cheekbones, eyes darkened with shadow.

Terror shot into Taylor's throat. He didn't remember Marina's face being so sallow. Hadn't she been rather robust with rosy cheeks? He felt his chest tighten. His eyes locked on the woman as her arms, with slow, jerky movements, raised up before her. The sabers of light stabbed her skin which was dead-white and scaly. Her fingernails were blue and bloodless.

Taylor's eyes gaped, fighting to believe what he was seeing. His mouth too dry to swallow. The woman's head tilted to one side. She stepped one stair higher and the light streaked across her face.

"Come to me, my son," she said.

A shriek escaped from Taylor's mouth before he even knew he'd made a sound. Instantly, the pain returned, boring into his stomach. His pulse hammered in his head. He stumbled backwards, tripping over the top step and crashed to the carpet. He grabbed his temples and pressed them tightly, trying to drive out the pain.

"This isn't happening!" he screamed. "This isn't real."

His mother stepped towards him. Her eyes glossed; dead-marble white. The flesh hung loosely from the bones of her extended arms, sagging down like melting wax.

Taylor's scrambled to his feet, his legs moving before he even realized he was running. But he was running, as quick and fast as his legs would get him away from the horror on the staircase. He shot a glance over his shoulder and saw his mother lumber up the final stair.

He bolted passed the dark-eyed portraits and pushed open the door to his room. Sherilyn slept unknowing in their bed. Taylor wanted to run over to her, to shake her, wake her, drag her out of this house of nightmares. But he couldn't.

There was something else in the room.

Taylor froze in mid-step, his breath caught in his lungs. A dark figure hung there, suspended from the beamed ceiling. It circled in the shadows above their bed, dangling mere inches above Sherilyn head. The sound of a creaking rope rubbing against the wooden beam, like the sound of a casket being pried open in the dead of night.

A million thoughts raced through Taylor's mind. He wondered if he was dreaming, if this wasn't some insane, vividly real nightmare.

But he knew that it wasn't.

Taylor forced himself to step into the darkness, towards this thing dangling above his wife. The dark shape spun, rotating at the end of the creaking rope. The sickly-sweet smell of something rotting filled his nose.

Oh no...

The body continued to circle, its limp feet brushed against the side of Sherilyn's head, its decaying flesh rubbing against her delicate skin. He could make out the black and blue flesh of the person's twisted neck, then the bloated, anemic cheeks, then—

"Jesus, no!" he clasped his hand to his mouth. "No! No! No!"

Sherilyn jarred awake at the sound of Taylor's scream. She sat upright, her head brushing against Jacob's hanging feet. Taylor screamed again. He fixed on Jacob's eyes which had burst red and bulged from their sockets. Blood trickled from

Jacob's puffy lips, leaking down his chin, dripping onto the pillow by Sherilyn's head.

"Taylor?" she asked.

Taylor flailed his body backwards against the wall, arching and twisting his back. The hotel robe fell from his shoulders, leaving his body naked and unprotected. Panic filled his eyes as he clawed at the wallpaper.

"No!" he cried.

Sherilyn could barely see him in the darkness.

"Oh, my God!" she screamed. "Taylor! What's wrong?"

He didn't hear her. He collapsed against the back wall, his palm catching on one of the thick stones and tearing the flesh in a jagged arc.

"Taylor! What is it?" she cried.

His eyes widened in horror as his mother stepped to the doorway. She stood there, towering before him, her head limply twisted to one side. Her mouth gaped open, a black hole in her fish-white face. Her hands extended out towards him again, searching for one last embrace.

This can't be happening!

Taylor slammed his eyes shut, praying when he reopened them everything would be normal. The nightmare visions would be gone.

But they weren't. His mother stood there, closer than before, her dead fingers reaching for him.

"Come to me, son."

"This can't be happening!" he screamed. "This can't be!"

"Talk to me Taylor!" Sherilyn yelled. "What's happening?"

He couldn't hear her. He held his pounding temples. All at once, the room caved in on him. The hotel walls bulged and recessed around him like some circus madhouse. Pain drilled into his head and he cried out as he clawed at his face.

Sherilyn crawled to the end of the bed. "Taylor!"

He staggered to his feet, his gaze never leaving his mother, who's nightgown had fallen from her skeletal frame. She stepped towards him, naked, her breasts hanging limply to the sides of her chest, her stomach bloated and full and pasty white. The skin peeled from her bones like dried flaking paint peeling from a sunbaked wall.

Taylor could smell her, the sour stench of the dead. She took another lumbering step towards him. He could almost feel the sickening coldness of her flesh as she reached out to touch him.

"Hold me, son."

"Oh God!" he screamed. He had to get out of there. But there was no other exit, she was blocking the door.

I've got to get out! I've got to get out!

Then he saw the window.

Like a madman, he burst across the room, charging towards the window at full speed. He launched himself into the air, smashing through the glass amid a shower of crystal splinters.

Sherilyn screamed; her hands held in tight balls by her cheeks. Tears blurred her vision. She leapt from the bed, dashed to the window, and gazed in horror as Taylor crashed to the gravel driveway below. Bloody gashes covered his naked body like an insane jigsaw puzzle. She watched as he crawled to his feet, screamed again, then burst across the highway, losing himself in a vineyard.

"Taylor!" she cried through her tears. "Oh my God! Taylor!"

CHAPTER 44

Wednesday, Oct 18th, 8:41 a.m.

The local sheriff found Taylor the next morning, nearly catatonic, stumbling through a muddy field of grape vines. Blood caked his naked body. Shards of glass pierced his flesh. Sherilyn watched, her hand covering her mouth, as they lifted his limp body into the back of the ambulance and whisked him away.

The absolute blankness in his eyes terrified her.

At the Napa Valley Medical Center ER, she sat in the waiting area while the on-call surgeon debrided Taylor's wounds. She rubbed her hands together. Despite the hospital's heater, she felt cold, and couldn't seem to get warm. The sheriff, a balding, heavy-set man with a thick mustache, approached, handing her a cup of coffee.

"You look like you could be using this," he said, offering a sympathetic smile.

Sherilyn accepted the coffee with her trembling hands. She was terrified by Taylor's condition, and the two hours of waiting without word hadn't done anything to assuage her fears. Her whole body shook.

"How are you holding up?" he asked her.

"I'm not." She looked up at the Sheriff. "Is there any word yet?"

"Yeah. I just heard from the Doc. He says your husband's gonna be alright. Nothing too serious. Just a lot of superficial wounds."

Sherilyn exhaled. "Oh, thank God. Can I see him?"

"Not yet, but soon. We've got other things to talk about first."

"I want to see my husband."

"You will. First, we've got to process the paperwork."

"Are you charging him with something?"

"No crime, but—"

"Then why can't I see him?"

The Sheriff took a deep breath. "Listen lady, we've got a mental hospital here in town, the most famous one in the State, I might add, and I ain't seen too many of them crazies do anything as deranged as what your husband did."

"You think he's crazy?"

"Wouldn't you?"

An image of Taylor's naked body catapulting through the window drilled into her mind. Sherilyn squeezed her eyes shut and shuddered.

"My husband is not insane."

"I'm not saying he is. I just think for his own protection, we should admit him for a seventy-two hour stay. Let the headshrinkers take a look at him."

"No. I can't explain what happened to him last night, but he's not crazy. He was acting out some nightmare. Sleepwalking to some horrible dream."

"Does your husband make a habit of sleepwalking out a hotel window?"

Sherilyn lowered her head. "Look, officer. I know my husband. I'll vouch for his sanity. He's a doctor." She pulled a white ID card out of his wallet and handed it to the Sheriff. "Here's his Medical Center card. I can give you a whole list of references if you want. I'll take full responsibility, but I'm not going to let you lock him up."

"I think it'd be in his best interest."

"I said no. I'm taking him home. Now, may I see him?"

"I think you're making a mistake here."

"May I see him?"

The sheriff sighed and shrugged his shoulders. He pointed to room number eight. "He's right through there."

Sherilyn lowered her coffee and nodded to the Sheriff. She took a deep breath and steadied herself, then walked into the treatment area, entering the room just as the nurse finished giving Taylor a tetanus shot. Sherilyn's gaze fell on Taylor, sitting up, but hunched over on the gurney, draped in a blanket. His eyes were glazed, with no recognition in them. His skin was pale, covered with a montage of bandages and bloody gashes. Sherilyn felt her heart sink.

She stepped over to the gurney, brushing the muddied hair from his face.

"Oh, Taylor. What have you done?"

*****

Sherilyn checked him out of the ER and guided him to the car, settling his blanket-wrapped body into the passenger seat. Marina met her at the Hospital with their luggage. Sherilyn apologized, and asked Marina to bill them for the costs of repairs to the room. Marina nodded and hugged Sherilyn good-bye.

The drive home took an eternity.

Taylor sat silent in the passenger seat, staring into the distance. Every once in a while, his head would bob up and down when the car hit a bump in the road, like a spring-headed toy doll. He faded in and out of sleep.

Sherilyn felt ill. Looking at him hurt too much, so she tried to avoid it, but found her eyes constantly drawn towards him, like a passing motorist staring at a car wreck. She was terrified about what was happening. During his madness he had looked at her with eyes that had shown no recognition.

She recalled their wedding day, the Yacht Club on Hilton Head, decked out in $30,000 worth of flowers and wreaths. She was gorgeous, fully made-up and dressed in white lace, pearls and satin. She remembered stepping over to her father with a tear in her eye, for a last-minute kiss and a walk down the aisle. The guests were waiting. The music had already begun. Her father had looked at her sympathetically, almost in pity, as if she was about to throw her life away.

He reached out and held her arm. "There's still time to reconsider," he'd said.

Sherilyn remembered the anger that welled up inside her then. As a McIntyre woman, she was supposed to remain silent and respectfully submit to the authority of the male head of the family, but that wasn't her style. With a firm resolution, she withdrew from her father's touch, matched his glare with one of her own and said, "You have a choice right now. You can smile and walk me down the aisle as my father or you can walk yourself out the exit as a stranger. It's your call."

Briefly, she wondered what her father would say if he saw Taylor now. He was barely recognizable as the man she'd married. Her instincts told her that the VHP was the cause of his transformation; she'd seen the change in his personality since that first day the experiment began.

While Sherilyn guided the Honda onto highway 37, she made a decision. She didn't know what was happening, but she wasn't going to sit by and watch Taylor tear himself apart. She'd fought for their life together from the beginning and she was damn determined to fight now. First, she'd call Dr. Browne and enlist his aid. She'd tell him what happened and together they'd get Taylor to stop this madness.

Her head began to ache. Courtney, her young journalist, had left a pack of Virginia Slims and a lighter in the glove compartment. Sherilyn fumbled through the pack, pulled out a cigarette and lit it. She hadn't had a cigarette since college and the smoke burned her throat with each inhalation, but it gave her something to do besides look at Taylor. And right now, she needed something.

By the time they got home, she'd smoked nearly half the pack.

Sherilyn guided Taylor up the stairs into the apartment where she settled him into bed. Pulling the blanket over his chest, she leaned forward and kissed his cheek.

"Taylor," she whispered. "Help me understand what's happening."

CHAPTER 45

High above the plains of northern Nebraska, CyberTech Systems CEO, Reginald Erickson, gazed out the window of his Bombardier/Challenger 605 luxury jet. Two hours in route from D.C. to San Francisco, he'd be home at his massive Victorian on Nob Hill in less than four hours. He finished his jigger of fifteen-year-old Laphroaig and contemplated the frozen plains, forty-one thousand feet below.

As the jet sped along at Mach 0.82, an unusual feeling of solitude swept through him. Undeniably, he loved the new jet—the pinnacle of luxury executive private planes—yet, he found something disquieting about flying in it. With the ANVC System (Active Noise and Vibration Control) activated the sound frequency of the twin GE CF34-3B turbofan engines was nulled by the continuous emission of inaudible counter-frequencies. Though designed to make the cabin quieter, to reduce noise-induced travel fatigue, the effect on Erickson was akin to being sealed inside a glass box. With the two-member flight crew behind closed doors in the heavily-computerized cockpit, and the flight attendant aft in the galley, Erickson couldn't help but realize how alone he felt.

That didn't mean, however, that he was alone.

Across the cabin, his blonde traveling companion gazed at him seductively from the tan leather couch in the meticulously appointed cabin. Erickson watched as the blonde straightened her black skirt and steadied herself before the mirror on the table. She picked up the rolled one-hundred-dollar bill and pressed the end to the line of white powder. Inhaling, she made the line disappear. Her eyes closed slightly and she smiled. Erickson watched as the blonde reclined on the couch, her breasts straining against her tight blouse.

As beautiful as the blonde was, Erickson had no desire to be with her at that moment. With the election drawing near, and Senator McIntyre due to arrive in two days for his speech at Google/NASA-Ames, there was too much preparation to complete before he'd allow himself the luxury of the blonde's company.

His last face-to-face meeting with McIntyre had gone well. The information he'd received from Ross implied that everything was proceeding as planned. A few unexpected hiccups had developed, but they were manageable, and the problems had certainly been offset by the new opportunities that had arisen. As always, by design, McIntyre remained oblivious to the complexities in which he was now intimately involved.

Erickson coughed into his handkerchief, a heavy barking cough from deep in his lungs. He glanced at the soiled white linen cloth and grimaced when he saw the familiar blood-tinged sputum. The cancer was spreading, growing inside him, reaching out, like the tendrils of an octopus, expanding into deeper and deeper recesses of his lungs. He could almost feel his lung alveoli being systematically replaced by the invading tissue, filling his bronchioles, destroying his air sacs, shrinking his life.

He took a deep, labored breath. The election was still three weeks away, but to Erickson, it couldn't come soon enough. Although his body was still thick and burly, he'd noticed recently the first signs of weight loss. Since he never had any children, when he was gone, the company would be all of him that remained. Soon his vitality would start to ebb. He willed himself to live until the election. In order to cement the ultimate legacy of his company, and therefore the legacy of his life, he needed the antitrust case against him to be halted by the White House. Without it, his company would fall apart like so much high-tech detritus lost along the Silicon Valley highway.

Shoving the soiled handkerchief into his breast pocket, Erickson turned from the blonde and picked up the iridium SATCOM phone in the executive work area near the rear of the cabin. The spacious 605 provided Erickson a complete mobile office, outfitted with an Ethernet-based Cabin Electronic System, including bulkhead-mounted plasma video, LCD touch-screen video conferencing, high-speed Internet and on-board LAN.

Dialing the number, he leaned back in his leather executive chair and glanced out the window. Below him, square patterns of carefully planted fields of corn and wheat formed a jigsaw pattern across the open plains.

Pieces of a puzzle. All pieces of one big puzzle.

The phone was answered on the second ring.

"Are you prepared?" Erickson asked into the receiver.

The voice on the other end was thick and raspy, a telling sign of the countless speeches and news conferences, the endless hours of talking that went into a presidential election.

"I'll be better when my voice comes back," the man rasped. "Feels like a cold coming on."

Erickson frowned. This was no time for a presidential candidate to get sick. Three weeks before the election was the time for frenzied activity. Each talk show appearance, each town hall meeting, each photo-op and meet-and-greet took on unprecedented importance. While the rest of America was entitled to a few days off in October, as flu season made its rounds, that was a luxury a presidential candidate could ill afford.

"Are you slowing down the campaign?" Erickson asked.

"No. Not for the moment anyways. My people have planned out eight campaign stops a day for the duration. Ohio is the big swing state; we'll hit it hard this week. I'm living on vitamin C and Airborne until then."

Erickson allowed himself a smile. He turned back towards the blonde on the couch. She grinned at him, her fingers toying with the top button of her blouse which looked like it could burst at any moment. Her long red nails flicked and the top button snapped free.

"Are we on a secure line?" the raspy voice asked.

"Always. You know that."

"I can't be too careful. Not this close to the election. Is everything proceeding as planned?"

"Perfect," Erickson replied. "Everything is perfect."

"Does he suspect anything?"

"Not a thing."

Erickson continued to watch the blonde. The final button popped open and her breasts escaped. His pulse grew warm.

"When is the big moment?" the voice asked.

"Friday. At Google/NASA-Ames. During the speech."

The blonde stepped out of her skirt, one leg at a time. It seemed to take forever until the whole length of her leg was free. She leaned over the table and placed a long white cigarette between her lips. A spark flamed from a crystal lighter. She inhaled lightly, allowing the smoke to trickle from between her crimson lips.

The skin tightened over Erickson's cheekbones and he twisted his lips into a smile. Blood poured into his groin, heating him up, making him hard.

"During the speech?" the voice chuckled. "Damn, you're a cruel bastard."

"I promised you the Presidential election and I will deliver. After which, I expect you to keep your promise."

There was a moment of hesitation before the raspy voice answered. "Don't worry, you'll get an end to the antitrust investigation."

"And you'll be the next President of the United States."

"And nothing will get traced back to me?"

Erickson suppressed a cough. "How could it? He's all set to take the fall." He wiped the corners of his mouth with his handkerchief. "Everything is lined up. When this is over, his credibility will be so low that a fucking ant would have to look down to find him. Even when he figures out what we've done to him, no one will believe him."

The raspy voice sounded satisfied. "Good. I look forward to watching the show. It should be quite entertaining."

Erickson looked over at the blonde, a splash of powder under her nose, naked except for her black garter belt and stockings. The cigarette burned in her right hand while her left hand played with her breasts. She was waiting for him.

Erickson nodded to himself. "Get well," he said. "You need to get your strength back. There're still a lot of hands to shake and babies to kiss before you move into 1600 Pennsylvania Avenue."

"Understood. We'll talk later?"

"Yes, Congressman O'Neil." Erickson said. "We will definitely talk later."

CHAPTER 46

Taylor awoke several hours after Sherilyn had settled him into bed. His head pounded and his eyes ached as if someone had thrust a drill bit into his sockets. The nausea in his stomach had been replaced by a dull persistent burn.

He rose gingerly from the bed. With bloodshot eyes, he scanned his surroundings, trying to figure out where he was. Nothing was clear. The last thing he remembered was a vague image of running through a field, covered with mud and grape vines. He turned and gazed out the window at the familiar Golden Gate Bridge. The image confused him. How had he gotten home—hadn't he been in Napa? Suddenly, the realization hit him.

Oh God.

Another freak out. He grimaced as the certainty sunk in. It all rushed back to him, the ghostly images of his mother and brother; the manic leap through the window. It came to him with the suddenness of a man remembering a dream. Pain burned across his chest. He dreaded seeing what he'd done to himself this time. Delicately, he pulled the covers off and gaped at the zig-zagged slashes that cut across his chest and belly. Fresh blood streaked one of the bandages, leaving a crimson stain on the bed sheets.

He collapsed onto the bed. Defeated. He didn't know what to do. His life was spiraling out of control, each day sinking into a whirlpool of madness. He was already on the verge of losing his job, his research, now his sanity. What was left?

Then another thought raced through his mind.

Sherilyn.

Oh God! He'd been with Sherilyn when this freak out happened. She'd been there the entire time. She must have been the one who dragged him home.

The thought of Sherilyn seeing him like this was too much to bear. He had no idea how violent he'd acted during the hallucination. How crazy he behaved. She must have been terrified.

"Sherilyn?" he called out, his voice weak and craggy.

There was no answer.

The silence became overwhelming. In the back of his mind, he was certain she'd left him; that whatever she'd witnessed had been too much for her to handle. And could he blame her? She was living with a lunatic.

He called out her name again but still no answer.

Gingerly, he climbed out of bed, applying pressure to his belly to combat the feeling that his gut would rip open and his intestines fall out at any moment. He pulled a robe over his shoulders and headed to the living room where he found Sherilyn on the couch, her knees tucked to her chest, a cigarette burning in her right hand. She stared out the window, blankness in her eyes. Smoke filtered the light, cloaking the room in a hazy silence.

"Sherilyn?"

He sat beside her. She didn't look at him.

Taylor swallowed. "I didn't know you smoked."

"I just started today," she answered, inhaling deeply on her cigarette.

The brusqueness of her voice stung, but at least she was still talking to him. "Where'd you get the cigarettes?"

"I jumped out the window and ran naked and screaming down the street to the store," she snapped, turning towards him. Tears filled her eyes. "Taylor, what's with the questions? I should be the one asking questions, like what the hell happened back there?"

He recoiled on the couch and watched her as tears spilled onto her cheeks. She turned from him and drew again on her cigarette, wiping her eyes with her free hand.

"I'm sorry," she said, exhaling a plume of smoke. "I'm just angry and confused." She turned to face him. "Talk to me, Taylor. Tell me what's happening."

He took a deep breath and exhaled into his hands. He felt lost, like a child abandoned at a haunted house, left to face the shrieking demons alone. Talking about his problems had never been easy for him. How could he possibly explain this?

At the beginning, he heard Browne's voice in his mind. *At the beginning.*

He started at the beginning, from the Grand Rounds to the first phase of the experiment. He told her about the cyberangioplasty's failure and the grotesque appearance of his brother. He told her how the program had permeated his mind and was causing the visions to appear in real life, in the ER, the hotel.

He described the madness.

Sherilyn listened intently, trying to understand what had happened to the man she loved. She lit another cigarette and watched him carefully.

When he finished, Taylor sat back and looked into her tear-rimmed eyes, waiting for a response. He could see her confusion, trying to digest it all. He knew the story didn't make any sense to her. How could it when it didn't even make sense to himself?

"So, what now?" Sherilyn finally said.

"I need to go back into the virtual program."

"What?" Sherilyn exploded. "Are you crazy? You can't go back, it's killing you. My God, look at your body. You're a mess."

Taylor lowered his eyes. "I know."

"Then why are you talking about continuing this?"

"I don't have a choice."

"What do you mean you don't have a choice? It seems to me that you have every choice in the world. Don't go back into that damn machine."

"It's not that simple, Sherilyn." He looked up. "I need to finish this."

"And I need you here!"

Taylor grimaced. He thought of how he was going to explain this to her. His mind ran back to the day of his eighth birthday, standing at his mother's death bed, her fragile heart struggling to beat, her face growing more pale by the minute, lips bluish, body wasting. He'd tried to help her then, rushing to the kitchen to make a sure-fire, magic elixir of chocolate syrup and marshmallow cream. He was so certain it would cure her.

But by the time he got back, it was too late. He remembered the stillness that draped his mother's bedroom like a shroud. He stared into her lifeless eyes, the magic elixir dropping from his hands, unopened, to the ground.

He remembered the sucking void that ate into his chest then, draining the warmth from him. Leaving him cold and pale.

Her death was so long ago, he could barely remember her now. Her long auburn hair. Her skin smelling like molasses and cinnamon. She used to sing to him every night at bedtime.

Didn't she sing?

"I've worked my whole life for this," he finally said. "I've searched for some way that I could have cured my mother.

Saved my brother. Saved myself. A way I could make a difference."

Sherilyn inhaled her cigarette. "You're an emergency room doctor. My God, isn't that enough?"

He shook his head and looked off into the distance. Cigarette smoke obscured the sunlight filtering through the window. "Drug addicts and derelicts come into the ER. I patch them up and toss them back onto the streets. It's a never-ending battle, round and round, with no winners, only losers."

"And this is different?"

"It is. I finally have the chance I've been searching for." He looked down at his bandaged abdomen. "I realize I'm in trouble here, believe me, I know. But as scared as I am about what's happening, I'm more afraid of what will happen to me if I stop. Please tell me you understand."

"I don't understand." She stubbed out her cigarette into a glass. "You sound like you're willing to risk your life for this thing."

Taylor nodded. "I don't have a choice. I can't live with myself if I don't try."

"It's a computer." Sherilyn's eyebrows wrinkled in disbelief. "A God-damned computer! Why can't you just let it go?"

Taylor sighed. For a moment he remembered Jacob; seventeen years-old, his feet dangling lifelessly two feet above the ground. His head twisted to the side. Taylor felt the void returning to his chest, sucking him dry.

He looked at Sherilyn's glossy eyes and saw her pain. Her confusion. "I'm not trying to hurt you. That's the last thing I want to do. But I need to do this."

"And I need you. I need my husband, here at home, with me." Sherilyn shook her head. Mascara streaked her cheeks in shocking black patterns.

"Sherilyn, I love you. I—"

"This isn't about love," she snapped. "You're so mixed up you can't see what's real anymore. I know what you're talking about. You think losing yourself in this project gives you purpose, that it can bring you redemption, heal all the pain you've buried your whole life. But you're wrong. There's nothing you can do to bring back your mother or brother. You can't save yourself in that computer."

She moved towards him and touched his hand. "You're hiding, Taylor. Don't you see that? Just like when you were a child. You're still hiding. It doesn't take a strong man to lock himself away in a laboratory and pretend the world doesn't exist. It takes a strong man to stop running from their deaths, face the pain and move on. That's what we need to do now. Together."

Taylor fell silent. He looked into her eyes, the puffiness of her lids, her cheeks streaked with mascara. He wanted to hold her and tell her that everything was going to be alright. He wanted to believe her, and make love to her and return to their lives of take-out dinners and weekend trips and forget that this nightmare ever happened.

But he couldn't.

He thought of his father. His jaundiced skin. Puddles of beer staining his pathetic socks yellow. The man had been so vibrant once, so alive, until the void got a hold of him. It sucked him into a bottle and slowly bled him dry.

Taylor knew that he had to finish this or the void would suck him dry also. Its appetite would never be quenched.

"I'm sorry, Sherilyn."

Sherilyn lurched back as if bitten. She thrust her finger towards the door.

"Then go!"

"Sherilyn, please—"

She cut him off with another thrust of her finger. There'd be no more discussion, no point in trying to make her understand. Her pointing finger held firm with finality.

"Just go!"

CHAPTER 47

Senator Randolph McIntyre couldn't believe what he was hearing.

Lowering the telephone, he took a deep breath, pinched the bridge of his nose and sat down at his desk. Three weeks before the election, he wasn't prepared for the news coming from his contact at the Medical Center. He picked up his coffee cup embossed with a portrait of Harry S. Truman, and took a long sip, allowing himself time to think.

He straightened his tie, leaned forward and picked up the phone.

"What on God's earth were you thinking?"

On the other end of the line, Dr. William Preston stumbled for words. "I don't know. It—it just happened."

McIntyre fought to maintain his calm. He took a series of three breaths from deep in his belly, a meditation technique he'd learned from a former media advisor. Calm the breath, calm the body. Never let them know what you're feeling.

"It can't just happen," the senator said, his voice as cool as a glacier. "You had to go to that building. You had to show your I.D. You had to sneak into the laboratory and you had to kill those pigs."

"I know we should have discussed this," Preston stammered. "But they were on the verge of success. I only did what was necessary. We made a deal that we'd make sure the experiment failed."

"No, William. We made a deal that I would make sure the experiment failed. Your job was to provide intel on what was happening in the Medical Center. That's it. I never told you to kill the pigs."

"I know I overstepped my bounds, but it's done. I don't see the problem."

"The problem is you were videotaped."

Preston hesitated. McIntyre could almost hear Preston's face blanching. "But-but that's not possible."

"The Kelly Research Building carries contracts for the Department of Defense. Every square inch is under surveillance."

"I know that, Senator, but the animal labs are clean."

"Hers, isn't," McIntyre said with emphasis. "Helen Yang installed her own digital surveillance system to monitor her animals. She taped everything."

Preston's end fell silent.

"How do you know this?" he finally asked.

"How I know isn't important." McIntyre pressed on. "You could be plastered over YouTube any second now."

The door to McIntyre's office opened and his assistant, Jennifer Langston, walked in. She held a laptop in her hand, running Microsoft Outlook. "The lawyers are here to discuss the campaign finance issues—"

McIntyre cut her off with a slashing motion of his hand and pointed for her to leave. Stuck in mid-sentence, Jennifer, stepped backwards, and closed the door.

"Listen to me," McIntyre said, his tone revealing a hint of sharpness. "If that tape gets out, if it's made public in any way, my campaign will be severely damaged."

"It's me on the tape. How does that affect you?"

"Damn it, William," McIntyre said through clenched teeth. "Can't you see the problem you've caused? The press knows I support your PSCM group. They know I've thrown my name behind your platform and they know I've guaranteed the VHP will fail. It won't take a rocket scientist to make the connection. It doesn't even have to be proved. All it takes is the implication."

McIntyre ran his fingers through his salt-and-pepper hair. He moved his Truman mug to the side. The San Francisco Chronicle sat on his desk, the front-page lead off story, outlining the murder of Dr. Bennington Crawford. The Senator picked up the newspaper, glancing at the black and white photo of the former Chief of Staff.

"And now with Crawford's murder—" he drew a breath. "The press is going to have a field day with this."

Preston cleared his throat. "About Crawford," he asked. "Did he have to—I mean, was it necessary to—?"

Anger stormed into McIntyre's temples. His composure finally wearing thin, he slammed the paper on the desk. "What in the hell are you blathering about? Are you insinuating that I had something to do with Crawford's murder?"

"Well, no, but—"

"Listen to me, William. I don't know a thing about what happened to Ben Crawford, but I do know what will happen to you if you don't do something about that surveillance video. I won't go down alone. Am I making myself clear?"

Preston exhaled heavily. "Yes."

"Then get that video. I can't afford to have your bad combover streaming across the evening news while you're killing some helpless pig!"

"I'll do it. I'll get the video."

"There's still time to salvage this. But only if you don't cause more problems."

McIntyre slammed down the phone. He took a deep breath, restoring his calm, allowing his face to relax, to become impassive, a mask hiding all emotion. He hit the remote on the edge of his desk, activating a wall of OLED televisions. The screens flashed, McIntyre's eyes scanning from one to the next, CNN to NewsNation to FOX, taking in the subtext and captions, searching for a damage report.

The analyst on screen-one spoke. "—O'Neil continues to make ground in New England, the voters there responding to his claims of nepotism surrounding the McIntyre campaign—"

McIntyre shifted to screen-two. "—Senator McIntyre needs to make a dramatic statement as the election heads into the home stretch—"

Screen-three. "—heating up as the pollsters predict a larger than average voter turnout this year—"

Squeezing his temples, McIntyre sighed. All was not lost. So far, no mention of the video had turned up on the networks. The talking heads were blathering about O'Neil's rise up the polls. McIntyre still held the edge, but it was getting close.

He glanced back at the Chronicle front page. The murder of Ben Crawford troubled him, the timing couldn't have been worse. Crawford was a well-respected physician with tremendous political connections. Soon, the press would be snooping around the Medical Center like rats at a trash dump. That didn't give him much time.

McIntyre knew what he had to do. And it started with his upcoming speech at Google/NASA-Ames. Given at the center of the high-tech world, his daughter and son-in-law in attendance. That speech would spearhead the final push of his campaign.

All he had to do was keep it together until that speech. Just two more days and all of this would be washed away.

Feeling his confidence returning McIntyre turned off the volume on the televisions, straightened his tie then patted his hair in place. He picked up his coffee mug, drained the last gulp of caffeine and glanced at the photo of Truman. Below the picture, McIntyre's favorite Truman quote was embossed in gold lettering. *Carry the battle to them. Don't let them bring it to you. Put them on the defense. And don't ever apologize for anything.*

McIntyre hit the intercom button, connecting him to Jennifer's desk.

"Send in the lawyers," he said.

CHAPTER 48

Special Agent Victor Ruiz sat behind his desk, thumbing through the forensic report on the blood and tissue chemistry of the recently departed Bennington Crawford. He ignored the commotion of the Federal Building Central Station, the ringing phones, the rush of agents and analysts, and concentrated on the pages in his hand. Surprisingly, the blood chemistry was mostly normal, slightly elevated potassium, but that was about it. The tissue samples, however, were a different story.

Ruiz pushed his reading glasses up his nose and studied the data, trying to make sense of the stream of numbers and figures that unveiled before him.

Bis-quaternary ammonium compound—succinyl choline
Gas Chromatography/mass spectrometry
Detection threshold 5ng/g

      Muscle 5 pmol/g
      Kidney 1000 pmol/g
      Urine   650 pmol/g
      Eye   350 pmol/g

Ruiz had already flipped open his copy of the PDR, the Physicians Desk Reference, and studied the listing:

Succinyl choline. A depolarizing muscular blocker; used in anesthesia to cause a medically induced paralysis.

So what the fuck's it doing in my stiff's body?

With a sigh, he closed the book, looking up just as Justin Hart was striding towards him, two large manila folders tucked under his arm. As always, Hart's freshly pressed suit stood out in stark contrast to Ruiz's wearing-the-clothes-I slept-in-look. Ruiz huffed and motioned for him to sit down.

"What cha got?" he asked.

"I did the research on Abrahms and Bernard. I figure either one would have enough motive to off Crawford."

"Find anything?"

Hart pulled open the first of the folders. "Not much on Bernard. I ran a full profile. Computer genius since childhood. Cal Tech grad. Considered eccentric even by the research crowd. Apparently, the University just hides him out of sight and leaves him alone as long as he publishes. Which he does. 120 papers in the last ten years."

"Did you run him through ID yet?" Ruiz asked.

"I checked with them but came up blank. No arrests or warrants. Couldn't even find a recent picture. All we got is an eight-year-old driver's license." He handed Ruiz a picture of Malcomb posing stiffly before the DMV backdrop. "The University picture is even older. He's off our radar."

Ruiz looked the picture over carefully, knowing it wouldn't do him much good. Eight years was too long for a photo to be of much value. People's looks could change too much in that period of time, beards, hair loss, and weight gain. "Damn driver's license extensions," he muttered under his breath.

Hart shifted in his chair and ran his thumb across his manicured fingernails. "I hacked into the University computer system and got his user ID. I ran a report of his online activity for the last six months." Hart pulled another sheet from his folder. "The guy's amazing. He averages sixteen hours online per day. I don't know when he even has time to go to the bathroom."

"Sounds like a Unabomber."

"Exactly. And that's what bothers me."

"Go on."

"He's not the type to take on a victim face to face. He'd hack their bank account. Plant a virus in their work computer or some crap like that. Not kill them."

"Agreed." Ruiz nodded. "That leaves Abrahms. The senator's son-in-law."

Hart handed Ruiz the file he'd prepared on Taylor Abrahms. "This is where it gets interesting. The guy's record lights up like a Christmas tree in Union Square."

Ruiz opened the file and found a recent University ID photo. He memorized each detail of Taylor's face.

Hart spoke. "Most of this happened when he was a juvie. Records were supposed to be sealed when he hit eighteen, but you know how that is."

"So, what'd cha find?"

"Seems he has a history of violence. He's got a bunch of admissions to ERs with trauma. Grew up in a violent household. Father was a drunk, used to beat him and his kid brother. Seems Abrahms got tired of a taking it and dished it back at his old man more than once. Social Services were called to the house several times for family violence."

Ruiz rolled his eyes. It was a familiar story, an all-too-common byproduct of the social disintegration of America and the break down of the nuclear family. "What else?"

"His brother turned up dead 'bout ten years ago. Coroner called it a suicide."

"But it was never really known for sure?"

"You know how that goes."

Ruiz pulled on his lower lip. "Certainly, fits the profile better. He grew up with violence, is a bit of a hot-head himself,

comes up against an authority figure dissing his life's work....
that'd do it."

"But that's not all."

Ruiz raised his eyebrows.

"I ran a report on him, sent out a few feelers. Just this
morning he was admitted to an ER in Napa."

"Napa?"

"He was staying at a boarding house and freaked out."

Ruiz looked up. "Freaked out?"

"No other way to put. He flipped. Started hallucinating and
jumped out a second story window. They found him stumbling
in some vineyard."

"Psychotic?"

"Don't know. Wife wouldn't let them keep him for a 72. I
spoke to the Sheriff though and he said the guy was a stone-
cold goner. No lights on."

"Jesus." Ruiz let out a low whistle. "Sheriff let him go?"

"Yeah. He hadn't seen the report about Crawford."

Ruiz nodded, approving Hart's research. Even though his
sickeningly perfect appearance made Ruiz nauseous, he had to
admire the man's work.

"Now it's my turn," Ruiz said. "I got the lab report back." He
handed the paper to Hart. "Crawford was killed with an
anesthetic medication. Not commonly available on the
underground. Need to be a doctor to get it."

"Like our mad Dr. Abrahms."

"Seems like it."

"So, the question is; where is he?"

Ruiz closed the file and looked at his junior Agent. "I got the
search warrant for his lab," he said, grabbing his service
revolver. "Keep this out of the press. Make sure the Sheriff
keeps a lid on it. We can't let them start filling the front pages
about the senator's son-in-law until we get the facts straight."

"Got it."

Ruiz popped open the cylinder on his revolver, confirming it was loaded, then slammed it shut. "Let's find the bastard."

295

CHAPTER 49

The laboratory door creaked open.

Malcomb pulled himself away from the cascading wall of three-dimensional holographic shapes. He glanced at Helen who ceased typing at the computer, inhaled a sharp breath, and clasped her hand over her mouth. Together they watched as Taylor dragged himself into the lab.

He looked nearly dead. His hair a rumbled mess; caked with mud, some strands still clotted with blood. He propped his back against the shelves of discarded computers and his legs gave out beneath him. He slid down, collapsing into a plastic chair.

The smell of ozone hung in the lab, seemingly more unnatural than ever.

Taking in the condition of his friend, Malcomb spoke first. "Are you alright?"

"I'm still alive."

Helen grimaced. "Dare I ask what happened?"

"The program," Taylor exhaled, closing his eyes.

Malcomb's eyebrow furrowed. "But I recalibrated."

"It did the exact same thing. I saw my brother inside the Emergency Room. Then again with my mother in a hotel. It's in my mind, Malcomb." Taylor pounded against his temple with his fist. "The damn thing is in my mind!"

Malcomb fell silent. Their situation was worse than he'd imagined. He shot a glance at his computer. "I was afraid this would happen."

Taylor cautiously opened one eye. "What do you mean you were afraid? Have you learned something?"

Malcomb nodded.

"What is it? Tell me."

Malcomb swallowed. "Our program is changing."

Taylor stared. "I know. It's been changing since day one. What we've got to do is find out why. We're going to tear this thing apart and start over. We reboot the back-up. Recalibrate the zonal stimulation patterns—"

Malcomb shook his head. "I can't let you do that."

"What do you mean you can't let me?"

Malcomb held up his hands. "Taylor, listen to what I'm saying. The program is changing. It's mutating. I can't find a standard virus anywhere in the program, so it has to be something much more serious causing this."

Taylor crinkled his eyebrows. "More serious?"

"Helen and I checked the original notes and compared them to what's in the computer right now. The program is changing at an exponential rate. 174 coding variations per hour."

"What?"

"It's true," Helen said. "And it's growing each day. Soon we won't be able to recognize the original program at all."

"But how—how's that possible?"

"It's the AI." Helen said. "It's writing itself. I'm thinking it might be some advanced viral/rootkit hybrid."

Taylor squinted. "Then why can't you find it?"

"Because that's what these things do," Malcomb said. "They're nearly impossible to detect." Malcomb took in the look of confusion on Taylor's face. "You don't know what a rootkit is, do you?"

Taylor shook his head. "You're the computer genius, not me."

"A virus works by piggybacking onto a software program," Helen said, rising from the desk. "Say you're running a spreadsheet program. Each time the program runs, the virus runs also and can create whatever havoc it's designed to create. Viruses are easy to find because they're attached to a program and easy to eliminate."

"But a rootkit is worse," Malcomb said. "Much worse."

"A rootkit," Helen continued, "infects the operating system itself. The very root of the computer. They're nearly impossible to detect, because the operating system, designed to detect the rootkit, is itself compromised. It's like sending a corrupt cop out on the streets to flush out a drug scam, when in reality, he's the mastermind."

Malcomb agreed. "If you use the rootkit to plant a virus, it becomes part of the core operating system of the computer. It can do as much damage as it wants and we can't stop it."

Helen looked at Malcomb. "Show him what we mean."

Malcomb nodded and turned towards the cascading wall of code; the erroneous coding shapes now lit up in vibrant red. "This is a three-dimensional projection of the VHP. I've converted each line of code into a geometric shape based upon its operating principles. See the red cylinders?"

Taylor approached the wall. Massive brightly colored shapes cascaded downward, like rain trickling down a window. Each cascading line of cubes and pyramids and spheres was littered with glowing red cylinders.

Taylor inhaled sharply. "I see the red."

"Each red cylinder corresponds to a coding change," Malcomb said. "They shouldn't be there."

Taylor's eyes grew wide. "There must be hundreds of them!"

"Thousands," Malcomb said.

Taylor took a deep breath and exhaled into his hands. This all seemed so simple once. Play in virtual reality, create a test program, work on a system to augment surgery.

So simple.

When did it all go wrong?

"Were you able to track down the source of infection?" he asked.

Malcomb shoved a chunk of dark chocolate in his mouth. "Not yet," he chewed, "but this wasn't done by chance."

"Why do you say that?"

"We were targeted," Helen said. "A very sophisticated programmer who was intimately familiar with the virtual reality program created this."

Helen's words resonated in Taylor's mind. "Intimately familiar—" he whispered. A thought was awakening in his consciousness.

"Who would know our program well enough to do this?" he asked.

Helen brushed the hair from her forehead. "I've been wondering that myself. This is medical virtual reality we're talking about. It's pretty darn esoteric, not a high priority target for some deviant pounding out viruses in his basement of his mother's house. This isn't Microsoft Windows."

"No one would waste the time to do this randomly," Malcomb said. "This had to come from someone who engineered this specifically for us. Someone within CyberTech."

Someone within CyberTech? The GET WELL Card flashed in Taylor's mind.

"I know who," he whispered.

Helen squinted behind her thick glasses. "Do you know something?"

Taylor stared at nothing for a moment, searching for an answer. He faced Malcomb. "Did you research that guy, Robert Chan?"

"Boy, did I!" Malcomb spun towards his computer. Bringing up a fresh file, Malcomb pointed to his screen. "Take a look at this."

Taylor and Helen gathered around the computer.

Marina District man Wounded in Robbery

A.P. San Francisco—A young man was found critically wounded Thursday night, October 12, the apparent victim of a robbery/home invasion at his Marina District apartment. The man, identified as Robert Chan, works as a software engineer at CyberTech Systems, Inc., the Bay Area virtual reality and AI leader. He is listed in critical condition at San Francisco City Hospital. CTS president/CEO, Reginald Erickson, released a press statement, expressing his concerns to the family of the victim and praised Mr. Chan's years of service to his company.

Taylor recognized the date. "That was the night Chan came into the ER."

"How does this relate to us?" Helen asked.

Taylor stepped back. That was the question, wasn't it? The words from the article raced through his mind, colliding with the image of Chan in the ICU and Erickson's name on the GET WELL card.

"I think he's the one responsible for our virus."

Malcomb's eyebrows furrowed. "Why would you think that?"

"That night of the shooting, Chan's chest and abdomen were blown apart. It wasn't a robbery. He was targeted with hollow point bullets."

Helen let out a low whistle.

"How do you know all this?" Malcomb asked.

"Because I was the one who saved him."

Malcomb turned from Taylor. He unwrapped a Nestle Crunch bar, looked at it then threw it in the trash can, reaching instead for a bar of dark chocolate. He glanced at Helen, the fear growing in his eyes. "As bad as this is, we have more problems than just Robert Chan."

Helen stepped forward. "This you gotta see. I got Dr. Preston on video sabotaging our experiment at the Farm." She handed Taylor the memory stick. "It's all here. The video shows him entering our lab and injecting something into the I.V. bag of pig number 2. The pig died seconds later."

Taylor squinted. "He killed the pig?"

"I ran a tox screen," Helen continued. "The blood was sky high for potassium."

"Why is this happening?" Malcomb asked. "What's going on?"

Taylor shook his head. The shooting of programmers. Scientific sabotage. His own sanity crumbling. His job gone. His marriage. The targeted destruction of his life. It was too much to comprehend. His eyes darted to Malcomb's wall of scribbled technical equations. The Crayola drawings looked faded; the usual rush Taylor got when he saw the equations replaced by an overwhelming feeling of dread.

He faced the computer, the words VIRTUAL HEART PROJECT blazed across the monitor in eighteen-point font, like an enigmatic verse from scripture.

Or an epitaph.

As bad as things were, Taylor couldn't help but feel they were only going to get worse.

T.D. SEVERIN

END PROGRAM

CHAPTER 50

Electrode 16.

Taylor studied the computer screen. His fingers ran across the wound that slashed through his eyebrow. He lowered his hand, checked his fingers for blood then returned his attention to the computer. He could barely see through his bloodshot eyes, but managed to focus on the words illuminated on the screen as if they were a revelation from God.

Electrode 16.

According to the clock on the wall, it was 3:00 in the afternoon. He'd been at the computer for the last several hours, analyzing and re-analyzing. Despite his fatigue, Taylor felt more alive than he had in days. Working in the lab was a rebirth for him. It gave him a purpose, a sense of direction. His life had been spiraling out of control, pieces flying off in all directions like water spraying from a rapidly-spinning top; his career here, his marriage there. His sanity everywhere. He'd become a pawn in a game he didn't understand, but being back in the lab gave him the chance to prove that it wasn't going to get the best of him. He'd fight with every ounce of will to get his life back.

He rebooted the diagnostic program for a third analysis of the neural transcendence helmet. The first two test runs had returned with the same result.

Electrode 16.

While the computer began analyzing the amperes, voltage and synchronicity of the pulsed patterns with the program, Taylor retreated to the back of the lab. Pain rifled from the cuts across his torso. Grimacing, he arrived at the La-Z-Boy and lifted the helmet. He checked the positioning of electrode 16.

Left temporal region. Auditory stimulation.

A knot formed in Taylor's stomach. Grabbing the helmet, he returned to the front of the lab. It was 3:01. Helen was back at the Farm. Malcomb had gone to acquire a new external hard drive and was due back at 3:30. That gave Taylor twenty-nine minutes to figure out what was going on before Malcomb insisted on shutting down the program. Twenty-nine minutes to save his sanity.

The screen flashed white, indicating the end of the diagnostic program. Taylor shifted his gaze to the screen and fingered the cut running across his cheek.

*****

Malcomb arrived ten minutes early and was startled to find Taylor still at the computer. For some reason the sight made him shiver. So much bad stuff had happened since they'd started this experiment. Malcomb wished it was all just a dream that he'd awake from and return to his equations, programs, and Mozart. Seeing Taylor there confirmed for him that wasn't going to happen. He placed the new hard-drive on the rack of shelves then looked for solace in a chocolate bar.

Taylor glanced over. "Dark chocolate? You've given up on Nestle Crunch?"

Malcomb shoved a bite of Ritter dark into his mouth. "I'm so scared, milk chocolate doesn't do it for me anymore. I'm up to 72% pure cocoa. If this goes on any longer, I'll soon be eating raw cacao pods."

"That may not happen," Taylor said. "I've found our problem."

Malcomb swallowed the chocolate whole.

"I ran a phase two diagnostic on the helmet," Taylor continued. "There's an excessive amount of stimulation being directed through electrode 16."

Malcomb's eyes narrowed under his thick glasses. "The details of the helmet circuitry were your area of expertise. What's electrode 16?"

"By itself, nothing. A harmless little electrode positioned over the left temporal lobe. It's the mirror electrode of number 8 on the right side and together, under normal situations, they provide auditory stimulation for the program."

"Then, I don't understand how—"

"I said under normal situations."

Malcomb fell silent.

"On the underside of the medial aspect of the temporal lobe is a small area of the brain called the amygdala."

Taylor handed the helmet to Malcomb and pointed to the faulty electrode.

Malcomb shrugged. "It looks fine."

Taylor hit the enter button and a three-dimensional graph appeared on the screen.

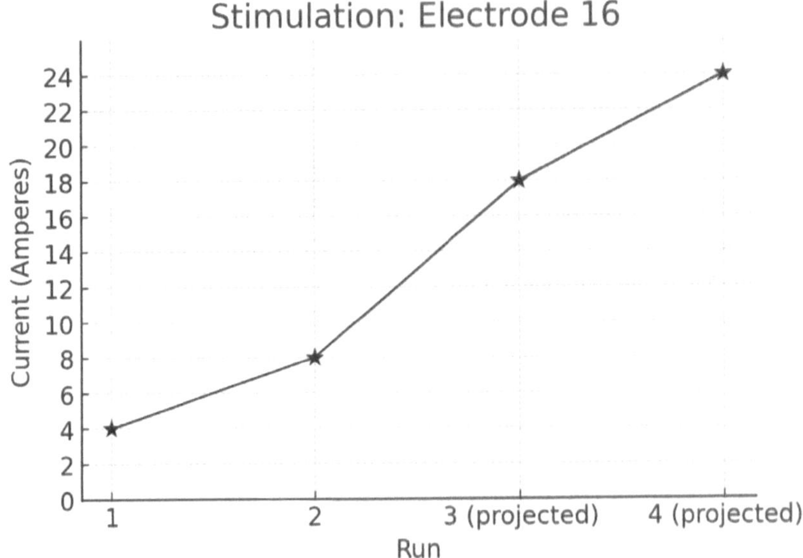

Stimulation: Electrode 16
Current (Amperes)
Run
1
2
3 (projected)
4 (projected)

"This graph depicts the levels of current stimulating electrode 16. With each entry, more and more current is being diverted to this area. During my last entry, that electrode was pumping out nearly 10 amperes. It's only designed to handle three!"

"You must have made an error in your calibrations."

"Three times the allotted power?"

Malcomb shrugged. "Then how do you explain the error?"

"That's my point. There is no error. This was done intentionally."

"Why on earth would someone increase the current to your auditory cortex?"

"They did it to drive me insane."

Malcomb wondered if Taylor hadn't finally lost it. Gone completely paranoid. "They're driving you insane by stimulating your hearing?"

Taylor tapped his temple. "Not my hearing, my amygdala. There's an intentional over-modulation of electrode 16 and direct stimulation of my amygdala nucleus."

"But I don't see how that could—"

"You don't know what the amygdala is, do you?"

"I just told you, I'm not familiar with that part of the brain's neuro—"

"It's the fear center of the brain."

Malcomb paused a beat. "The fear center?"

Taylor nodded. "And it's getting more stimulation than I ever thought possible."

Malcomb wasn't understanding. "I don't follow you. What does —?"

"The amygdala controls our experience of fear. If you remove it, the fear response is obliterated. If you stimulate it, you create unimaginable fright. It's our very own mental bogey man. It's the source of terror that races through us when a branch rakes against a window on a stormy night. It's the cause of every nightmare we ever had."

Malcomb frowned. "Surely you're being melodramatic?"

Taylor shook his head. "I'm not. Ever hear of post-traumatic stress disorder?"

"The returning Vietnam vets experienced it."

"It's not just a condition of vets. Say a person lives through some trauma, some unspeakable event, like war, or a plane crash, a rape or, in my case, the death of my family. That fear is imprinted in the neural connections of the amygdala. It becomes a part of the matrix of the brain. When a similar stimulus occurs, no matter how innocent, the amygdala kicks in an unconscious memory of the event, a flashback, and the person is overcome by fear. A vet freaks out and dives for cover when he hears a car backfire. A plane crash victim has nightmares about fires and crashes. The rape victim panics whenever someone stands behind her. With me, it's my family. It's all in the brain. In the amygdala."

"Are you saying that you have post-traumatic stress disorder?"

"Worse. My amygdala is being stimulated directly and repeatedly. It's creating a near psychotic break."

"But how? Why?"

Taylor shook his head. "That's what we need to find out. Whenever something in this reality triggers a memory, my brain is flooded with the images of my family. It's got me leaping out windows."

The color began to drain from Malcomb's face. Methodically, he unwrapped a piece of Ritter and placed the dark chocolate in his mouth, like a child reaching for a pacifier. The air in the small laboratory suddenly became thick and stifling.

Malcomb looked up, a far-away gaze in his eyes. "Madness. Amygdalas. Please tell me Taylor, what have we gotten ourselves into?"

Taylor could only shrug his shoulders and stare at the helmet in his hands.

He ran his finger across electrode 16.

CHAPTER 51

The ringing telephone pierced the silence in the lab.

Malcomb set down his chocolate and embarked on an expedition to find the phone. It had been so long since anyone had called that he'd forgotten he had a phone, much less where he'd left it. He fumbled through the mass of twisted wires hoping to trace the ringing to its source.

Finally, he found the receiver, buried under a battered ImageWriter II printer.

"Um, hello."

"It's about time you answered. Couldn't you find the damn phone?"

"Well, actually no, I—"

"Never mind. Just listen. This is Lawrence, upstairs. Those two Feds just drove up. I'm sure they got a warrant this time. You gotta go."

"Why do I need to go?"

"You guys are in some serious shit. I did some digging with some friends on the force. You're both wanted for questioning in the murder of Dr Bennington Crawford."

Malcomb's face went white. "Murder?"

Taylor glanced over.

Lawrence continued. "That's why they were here the other day. I know you well enough to know there's a mistake, but they don't. I'll stall them, but if they've got a warrant, I gotta show them where you're at. So, I suggest you get the hell outta there."

"But... but—" Malcomb stammered. "Where do I go?"

"How do I know? Here they come. Now move it!"

The phone fell silent.

Malcomb dropped the receiver, panicked. "That was the guard upstairs. The FBI just pulled up outside. They're on their way here!"

"Slow down." Taylor held up his hands. "What do the FBI have to do with us?"

Malcomb suddenly remembered that he hadn't told Taylor about the FBI's visit to the lab yesterday. It had seemed inconsequential in comparison to everything that was going on. It wasn't so inconsequential now. "They want us for murder!"

Taylor's eyes widened. "What? Murder? Who?"

"Crawford."

"Dr. Crawford? Dead? How can he be dead?"

"Lawrence said he was murdered, and they suspect us."

Taylor stood before the desk, his eyes darting towards the computer terminal, trying to make sense of this. ELECTRODE 16 still blazed across the screen.

"There's got to be a mistake. We didn't kill anyone."

"I'm not cut out to be a fugitive, Taylor, I do poorly on the road. My sinuses—" Malcomb stepped backwards, panic filling his eyes. An image of himself locked in a prison cell with a large tattooed inmate named Butch ran through his mind.

Taylor held out his hands. "OK, Calm down. I don't know what's going on here, but we haven't done anything wrong. We'll deal with the FBI and get to the root of this, but right now we need to get back into the computer program."

"Who cares about the computer? Taylor, the FBI are—"

"Now that we've found the problem with the system, we can correct it."

"But—"

"The over-stimulation of that electrode is tearing apart my brain, Malcomb. It's causing a feedback loop in my amygdala. It's driving me insane. We need to re-establish a normal electrical pattern. To do that, we need the computer."

"But—"

"One more entry," Taylor said. "That's all. One more entry to re-establish the proper neural stimulation, re-calibrate my brain, then I'll talk with the FBI."

Malcomb took a deep breath. His stomach felt like it was going to boil over. He rubbed his forehead. "One more entry?"

"Last one."

"Then we run?"

"Like hell." Taylor nodded. "Let's hide the system first. We don't know what they might confiscate. If they want to question us about Crawford, the VHP is the main connection."

Malcomb nodded then spun around and began to disassemble the computer. Taylor ran to the back of the lab, pulling the suit off the La-Z-Boy. He disconnected the sensor wires and rolled the suit into a ball then shoved it, the helmet and gloves behind a stack of computer terminals.

He dashed to the door and cracked it open. The tapping of footsteps echoed down the corridor.

Malcomb froze and looked up. They were coming.

Taylor shot back to the desk and helped Malcomb dismantle the computer. They stashed the components on top of the overflowing shelves, the necessary parts disappearing into the clutter of computers debris.

"Are you ready?" Taylor asked.

Malcomb heard the footsteps, growing louder. "My God, they're really—What's happening, Taylor?"

"You go first," Taylor said. "But don't go down the main hallway. Cut through the boiler room. Go out the back door."

"You're going to leave me?" Malcomb heard his own voice squeak.

"I'll be right behind you. Call Helen and have her meet us at my apartment in an hour."

"One final entry. You promise?"

"I promise. Then we'll sort this whole thing out."

Malcomb nodded. "Where are you going?"

Taylor took one final glance across the wall of crayon equations. "I'm going to see Robert Chan."

CHAPTER 52

Standing in the doorway of Robert Chan's ICU room, Taylor felt something was terribly wrong.

Scanning the white-tiled room, laden with stainless steel IV poles and monitors, he pondered the whereabouts of Nurse Stewart or one of her colleagues. The monitors were all functioning. The EKG, beeped out against the ominous silence, revealing a stable cardiac status; a normal P wave followed by the QRS complex, then finally the T wave. Rate 64 beats per minute. The respirator continued to hiss a steady stream of oxygen through the tracheostomy and urine continued to drip through the catheter and collect into the clear plastic bag dangling at the end of the bed.

But no one was around to observe this.

Where is everybody?

Taylor had come to the ICU immediately after leaving Malcomb at Anderson Hall. He'd cut into the Boiler Room just before the FBI agents rounded the corner to the lab, then circled to the back parking lot. He breathed a sigh of relief when he saw that Malcomb's Honda wasn't in its usual spot. That meant he got away safely. He looked at his watch. He still had 55 minutes until he was due to meet Malcomb back at his apartment. That left him just enough time to talk to Chan and try and get some answers.

He flashed a glance towards the nursing station. Two white-uniformed nurses gathered over a monitor, pens scribbling onto the daily flow sheets. One of them must be Chan's nurse he figured. Probably giving report. But the curtains to Chan's room were drawn. She wouldn't be able to see her patient from there and that wasn't appropriate.

What was going on?

Taylor stepped cautiously into the room. The medicinal scent of ammonia stung his nose. He crossed to the far side of the bed, studying Chan. Almost a week had passed since he'd last been in this room. So much had happened since then; his life turned upside down, his marriage destroyed, his career lost, his sanity ripped from his mind. All for reasons he couldn't begin to conceive. A systematic destruction of his life. Somehow, Taylor knew it all came down to this bloodied man in the ICU. He was the catalyst that had sparked a chain reaction of insanity.

He stepped towards the bed.

Taylor didn't know if Chan had regained consciousness, but he had to try. He reached out and touched Chan's left arm. Seconds passed. No movement other than the battered chest wall rising and falling in time to the respirator. Taylor poked him again, this time harder. Chan's body rocked against the pressure, but didn't stir. He lay flaccid as a corpse.

Taylor glanced at the monitors, reassuring himself that Chan was indeed alive. The beeping of the EKG confirmed it.

Taylor gave it one last try, prodding his arm while calling out his name. "Chan? Are you awake?"

Five seconds passed, then ten. Taylor began to lose all hope. The answer was here in this room somewhere, he was sure of it, but where?

He turned from the bed. On the wall was the GET WELL card he'd seen before. Reginald Erickson's name blazed across the bottom like a red-light warning.

A plan began to form in Taylor's mind. He needed to get more facts; find out why Chan had been shot, what he'd been working on, how this related to the VHP. His best chance was to get into the CTS computer and find Chan's files.

Lost in his thoughts, Taylor didn't see the twitching of Chan's eyelid or the jerky movement of his leg until the bed sheet slipped off Chan's abdomen and fell to the floor. Taylor caught this out of the corner of his eye and turned to the bedside.

"Chan, can you hear me?"

Chan's eyes opened and looked in Taylor's direction. By the lucidity of his movements, it was clear that Chan had regained consciousness some time ago and was merely sleeping when Taylor came in.

"Can you hear me?"

Chan nodded and pointed to his throat. He was unable to speak with the tracheostomy in his windpipe.

Taylor understood this. "I'm Dr. Abrahms. Taylor Abrahms."

Chan's eyes widened.

Taylor noted the recognition in Chan's stare. "Have you heard of me?"

Chan sucked air through the tracheostomy and nodded.

"Listen, I'm in trouble and I think you can help me—"

Chan's nodding confirmed Taylor's fears before he even had a chance to finish the question. Chan made an effort with his hands, mimicking holding a pen and writing. Taylor pulled a sheet of paper out of Chan's file and handed it to him along with a pen.

"Do you know what's happening to me?"

Chan nodded again. He struggled to position himself amongst the clutter of intravenous lines and monitoring wires. Taking the pen, he scrawled out a single word.

Erickson.

"Did he do this to you?" Taylor asked.
Again, Chan nodded.
"But why?"
Chan paused, sucking air through the tube in his throat then scribbled one word.

McIntyre.

"McIntyre? Senator McIntyre?"

pazsword.

"Password?" Taylor asked, suspecting the pain medications were affecting Chan's ability to spell clearly; confusing a 'z' with an 's' or writing one 's' backwards. "You want to give me your password?"
Chan shook his head emphatically.

No. *pazsword.*

"Your password has the answers? I don't understand. Give it to me and I'll—"
But Taylor never had a chance to finish his sentence. He heard the footsteps behind him only seconds before the voice stabbed into his ears. Instantly recognizable.
"I'm afraid, my boy, that is something that I just can't allow you to have."

CHAPTER 53

The voice was painfully familiar. Taylor's heart bottomed out even before he turned and saw Dr. Norman Browne standing in the doorway, a silenced silver 45-caliber in his right hand. Taylor's breath clenched in his lungs.

Browne stepped into the room, silently closing the door behind him. With the curtains drawn they were completely hidden from the nursing staff and the security cameras.

"The nurses—"

"Won't be coming in. Look at your watch, it's shift change. They won't be around for ten to fifteen minutes. We won't need nearly that much time."

Taylor's heart pounded against his chest. His eyes glared at the gun.

"To do what?"

Browne stepped deeper into the room. "Don't make this any harder on me than it already is, Taylor. You have no idea of what you've stumbled into. I tried to warn you to stay away. I begged you to get out before you got yourself in too deep, but you were too stubborn to listen."

"You—"

"Suffice it to say," Browne continued, "you've plunged yourself into the middle of a presidential election. There are forces out there that will do anything to see their candidate take office. Unfortunately, for you, your association with the Senator provided an opportunity for them to do just that."

Taylor's stared at the gun, trying to grasp what was happening.

"So now you're here to do what? Jesus, you're a doctor, not a killer."

"In desperate times, I can be both. Actually, you've made it quite easy for me. I came in here for Chan, but now I'll allow you to kill Chan before you kill yourself."

"What are you talking about? I won't kill anybody."

Browne twisted his lips into a smile. "Don't you know, my boy? You already have. At 9:45 this morning, an all-points bulletin was issued for your arrest. You're wanted in connection to the murder of Bennington Crawford. The FBI found a hospital syringe of succinyl choline next to the body. Not very nice of you."

"I had nothing to do with that."

"The entire University saw you two arguing at Rounds. We know he was planning on shutting your research down. He was killed with an anesthetic medicine obtained from a hospital. They found your pen at the scene. Everything points to you."

My pen? His mind flashed back to the day his pen went missing from the lab. It was the day they discovered that someone had moved Malcomb's computer mouse. He'd been set-up from the beginning.

"But—" he fought to make sense of this.

Browne continued, "Now when they find Chan dead, who do you think they'll suspect?"

The air caught in Taylor's throat. He felt he was spiraling down a whirlpool, deeper and deeper where the madness never ended.

"But why me? Why do this to me?"

"Wake up, Taylor. This is the new millennia. Presidents aren't made by policy or statesmanship anymore; they're made by the press and PR firms and news outlets. It's war out there and the victor is the last one standing with the least amount of mud on his face. Like John Kerry and his Vietnam service scandal, Dukakis and Willie Horton, or Gary Hart and Jennifer Flowers. One good scandal can break a campaign, all you need is one good fucking scandal. Your connection to McIntyre made you the perfect target. One call to Erickson and the seed was planted."

Taylor felt like an idiot. He'd never questioned Browne's decision to allow him to conduct research while working his ER shifts, and he was too blind to see anyone else's motives but his own. His eyes darted around the room, searching for an escape. He had to buy some time, keep Browne talking, stall him until one the nurses finished her report. The closed door would catch their attention. Once they saw the closed door—

"What does McIntyre—?" Taylor started to say, but the pistol thrusting towards Taylor's face, cut him off. Browne's eyes indicated that it was time for the questions to cease. Taylor froze, his chest pounded as he stared down the barrel of the gun.

Without saying a word, Dr. Browne stepped over to the respirator and flipped off the switch marked ALARM. The alarm mode protected the patient in case of mechanical failure of the respirator, sounding out a resounding beep if the pump failed or the tubing became disconnected. With the alarm switched off, the nurses would have no way of knowing of a pump breakdown.

"What are you—" Taylor started, but was hushed when Browne raised the pistol towards Taylor's face. Taylor's eyes widened as Browne shut down the pump. The churning of oxygen halted, the last few breaths hissing through the lifeless tubing. Chan's eyes grew wide, fear burning through his confusion as his chest began to buck and strain.

"Jesus Christ, you can't—" Taylor began. The gun rose in Browne's hand again, aimed squarely between Taylor's eyes. Taylor's gaze darted to Chan, his eyes starting to water, the color draining from his cheeks. His lips slowly turning purple. Without oxygen to his brain, he'd die in minutes. Taylor had to do something fast.

He reached for the only thing available, the bag of urine. Yanking it off the bedside, Taylor ripped the catheter from the bag and heaved the bag at Browne's face. The bag split open on impact, urine spraying into Browne's eyes. He screeched as the acidic fluid burned into his sockets, the smell filling the air. The gun dropped from Browne's hands and he clawed his eyes. Taylor leapt toward the doorway, thrusting his shoulder into Browne's gut. The impact lifted Browne off his feet and sent him crashing into the curtained window. The glass shattered and Browne's large frame catapulted through the window into the central hallway of the ICU.

The nurses at the station spun around just as Browne crashed through the glass, Taylor on top of him. Browne squirmed free and rose to his knees, screaming at the nursing staff.

"Stop him!" Browne pointed at Taylor. "He was trying to kill the patient. Somebody, stop him!"

Taylor froze in the corridor as all eyes fell on him. He wanted to scream that it was Browne who'd done it, but immediately he knew no one would listen. Browne was the head of the ER Department, a twenty-year veteran of the hospital. Taylor was a senior-resident that everyone saw freak out during a code and was now connected to the murder of the Chief of Staff. Who would they believe?

He spun towards the nursing station. One of the nurses had the phone to her ear and he could hear her calling security. Browne struggled to his feet. Suddenly, Taylor remembered the gun.

He lunged forward and kicked Browne squarely in the gut. The air burst from Browne's lungs and the older man collapsed to the ground. Taylor turned towards the nurses who visibly retreated under his eyes.

"The respirator in Chan's room has been tampered with," he yelled, pointing.

The nurses continued to step backwards.

Anger rose in Taylor's temples. This nightmare was never going to end. He was a faceless pawn in a game that he didn't understand; manipulated and deceived by those he trusted.

He yelled at the nurses again.

"I don't care what you think about me, but for God's sake get in there and save the patient!"

Browne grunted as he rose to his hands and knees. Taylor realized he had to get out of there. Security had already been called. It was only a matter of seconds before they'd arrive. He wanted to kick Browne again, make him pay for his betrayal, but there wasn't time. If he was going to save himself, he had to get out.

In that instant, his mind ran forward. He didn't know yet the full extent of this plot against him, but he knew that he had to blow the lid on whatever Erickson and McIntyre were doing. Once he found evidence he'd go to the cops and explain everything. Fight to get his life back.

"The patient!" he screamed at the closest of the nurses. "Save the damn patient!" The nurse stepped forward cautiously, working her way towards Chan's room. Her eyes never left Taylor, watching him as if he was a homicidal maniac, until she finally reached the door. Then she raced inside.

Taylor couldn't wait any longer. At the end of the hall, he heard the elevator chime. It had to be security. He leapt over Browne's body and sprinted in the other direction. Each floor had multiple stairwells, one at each corner, in case of fire. If he could reach the stairwell before security got him, he'd be able to get out of the hospital. The MG was parked in the ambulance zone. If only he could get to the stairwell.

The sudden impact of a fist against his cheek sent him sprawling against the wall. He turned, dazed, and stared into the eyes of a large Filipino medical intern, his fists clenched. Blood trickled from Taylor's nose onto his lips, the bitterness filling his mouth. The intern was trying to be a hero and slow Taylor down until security could get there. Taylor couldn't allow that to happen.

With all of his strength, he lunged at the intern, catching him full force in the chest. Both men smashed into a medicine cart, toppling it over and spilling bottles of injectables and syringes. The two men landed with a thud on the hard floor, Taylor on top of the intern, his shoulder buried in the intern's ribs. With the impact, Taylor heard a cracking sound and realized that one of those ribs had just snapped. The intern screamed in pain. Taylor staggered to his feet and stumbled backwards, slipping momentarily on the spilled medicine. At the end of the hallway, the elevator door opened and three security guards stepped out. Immediately, the nurses ran towards them, their fingers pointing in Taylor's direction.

Taylor regained his balance and sprinted for the exit. If he could only reach it before the guards, he knew he'd be safe. In that instant, a thousand thoughts ran through his mind. He saw images of his mother and brother. He thought of the hallucinations and the insanity. Then a different set of images entered his brain. His father. Sherilyn. At that moment he realized that he was a child of two worlds and that each world held a grip on him just as desperately as the other. The world of the past and the world of the present. It became clear to him; his life had been a futile battle for redemption, not from the hospital or university or medical research panel, but from himself. He remembered the tears in Sherilyn's eyes as he left the apartment.

He had to get back to her.

He had to get his life back.

The security guards raced in Taylor's direction, but he had a good head start. He reached the fire exit before they could even get past the nursing station. The alarm sounded when he yanked open the fire door.

Get back to the lab and grab the equipment, he thought. One last entry in the virtual world to clear the over-stimulation in his brain, get his mind back, then get out of there before the FBI arrived, or hospital security or whoever else was after him.

One last entry. One final question to answer.

The door slammed shut behind him as he raced down the stairs.

CHAPTER 54

By the time Taylor reached his apartment, Malcomb had already arrived, his tiny yellow Honda parked out front, sticking out a good two or three feet from the curb. Taylor pulled in behind him and turned off the MG's engine.

Taylor had doubled back to the computer lab after he'd evaded hospital security. Before entering the building, he scanned the parking lot for the FBI then bolted through the front door, racing down the steps to the lab.

He ducked under the yellow police tape sealing the lab entrance, opened the door and ran inside. His eyes darted around the lab, inspecting the shelves. Everything was just as they had left it, nothing confiscated. Taylor knew that the FBI would never be able to find anything in Malcomb's pigpen of a lab. Each computer component looked like the rest, each modem the same as any other. There was no way to tell what was important.

"I could shoot you right now for interfering with a crime scene."

The voice came from behind Taylor. Slowly, he dropped the virtual suit that he'd pulled from its hiding place and faced the door. Lawrence stood there, his revolver drawn and held firmly in his hands. Taylor studied the guard hesitantly, looking down at the drawn pistol. It was the second time he'd found himself staring down the barrel of a gun.

"It's a good thing I like you," Lawrence said, bursting into laughter. He holstered his gun.

Taylor exhaled a sigh of relief.

"That was pretty good thinking out there," Lawrence said. "Malcomb got out safely. What're you doing now?"

"Collecting the gear before they come back and impound the whole room."

"Why are they after you?"

"I have no idea, but I suspect this VHP project is at the root of it all."

Lawrence walked over and picked up the computer that Taylor had set on the desk.

"Let's do this quickly. You never can tell when the Feds will show up. They're kind of like a nasty old fart. You know, what I mean?'

"Uh, not really." Taylor squinted.

Lawrence smiled. "They're always lingering around."

*****

At the apartment, Taylor opened the door, carrying the computer and helmet inside. Malcomb sat on the couch, his hands trembling, holding a steaming cup of tea. Sherilyn sat across from him, her arms folded tightly across her chest.

Taylor glanced at his watch. He knew that it was risky coming back to his apartment. It was only a matter of time before the FBI arrived. But he also knew that there was no way that he could wait another day before he re-entered the program. Now that he was beginning to see the depth of the plot against him, he had to figure out the reason. The best weapon Taylor had to protect himself would be to discover the truth. But before he did that, he had to correct the amygdala over-stimulation. See if that would get the hallucinations to stop. Recalibrate his brain.

Ten minutes was all he needed. Ten minutes to correct the electrical misfiring and get his sanity back. Then he'd gather Sherilyn and Malcomb and go on the run.

Ten minutes, he thought. Just give me ten minutes.

*****

Sherilyn watched as Taylor laid the computer on the coffee table. Her skin was flushed and the lines on her face were deep and angry. Seeing him enter the apartment brought back a wave of hurt which tightened in her chest. She was happy to see him yet still angry that he'd walked out earlier. She could see him struggling with his own emotions as he glanced her way.

He walked towards her, his head low. "Hello," he said.

"Hello." Her voice was flat.

Taylor looked at Malcomb then nodded towards the door. "The rest of the stuff is in my car."

Malcomb nodded, getting the message, and stepped out the front door.

Taylor moved towards the window and sat in the chair next to her. Feeling him that close, she felt her whole body tighten. She wanted to let go, let the pain melt away, but she couldn't. He'd walked out on her. Given the choice, he'd chosen the lab over their marriage. Could she ever forgive him for that? The sun was beginning to set over the Bay and the fading light glared through the window.

"Hi," he said again, his voice timid.

"We've already done that routine, Taylor," she countered. "What are you doing here?"

"I had nowhere else to go. The FBI are after us. I think they want to confiscate our equipment."

"So, give it to them."

"Sherilyn, I can't. This whole thing has been rigged from the beginning. Dr. Crawford is dead. They've framed me for it. Browne is involved and so is your father. He set me up."

Sherilyn was incredulous. "My father? Set you up? For what?"

"I don't know. Right now, it's murder, but this whole thing is bigger than me. Some of the things Browne said... somehow this affects the whole country."

She eyed him carefully, then placed a cigarette between her lips, lit the end and inhaled deeply. A myriad of thoughts raced through her mind, all of them centered on his seeming lack of sanity. First the hallucinations, now the paranoia. Conspiracies, evil plots, deceptions.

"Still smoking?" she heard him ask.

"I haven't found a reason to stop," she said.

Silence.

"Look, Sherilyn," he said. "I've stumbled into something terrible. I know what you think of me right now, after what happened, but I'm not crazy and I'm not making this up. Browne tried to kill me. The FBI are after me."

She watched him carefully. Browne tried to kill him? Another delusion? More insanity?

"What are you going to do?" She finally asked.

Taylor hesitated. "We have to get out of here, but before I do, I need to go back into the virtual reality."

"Go back?" Sherilyn recoiled, not believing what she just heard. "You are crazy. By your own admission this whole thing has been a trap. It's been driving you insane."

"I know. But I've found the problem. I'm hoping that by going back in I'll be able to free my mind from the hallucinations."

She walked to the window and gazed out across the churning waters of the bay. The smoke from her cigarette filtered into a small haze over her head, further obscuring the waning daylight. She turned and winced as she looked at Taylor, his body ravaged by the effects of the experiment; cuts and bruises everywhere, his clothing disheveled, exhaustion eating into his eyes. She wondered what had happened to the man she loved.

She thought back to her wedding day and the conviction in her voice when she told her father how much she loved Taylor. Despite all that they've been through, she realized that the conviction was still there.

"I don't understand, Taylor," she finally said. "But I realize how important this is to you."

He looked at her. "You do?"

"Yes," she nodded. "You're just being you. Wearing your heart on your sleeve. Trying to do what you think is right. It's what I first saw in you the day I met you. It's why I love you so much."

"Sherilyn, I—"

"We'll talk about it later," she interrupted, holding her finger to her pursed lips. "There's a lot that we need to talk about, but if what you're saying is true, we don't have time for that now. Do what you need to do. I won't stop you."

He stood and walked towards her, taking the cigarette from her hand and extinguishing it against the window pane. The ash dropped to the ground. She felt the softness of his palms as he cupped her face in his hands and kissed her on the lips. His mouth was wet and warm.

"Thank you," he whispered.

*****

Malcomb returned with the last of the equipment and set it on the coffee table. Exhausted, he collapsed on the couch and sighed. He wanted to crawl away into some small hole and hide for forever, far, far away from any computers or police. Far away from Taylor and changing computer programs and amygdalas.

Malcomb's dreams of peace evaporated.

"No time for rest, Malcomb," Taylor said. "We have to get this back together."

"What?" he bolted upright on the couch.

"You heard me. I need to get back 'in' and I need to do it now."

"Good God man, have you lost your mind? What about the FBI?"

"That's exactly the reason. They think we killed Crawford. They'll be swarming all over this place. If I'm going to get us out of this mess, I need to clear away the over-stimulation. This will only take a minute."

"A minute?! By your own admission, they're searching for us, ready to pounce at a moment's notice and throw us into jail with Butch and you want to go back in?"

Taylor squinted. "Butch? Who's Butch?"

"He's our three-hundred-pound, bald-headed, tattooed cell mate!" Malcomb shrieked.

"What are you talking about?"

"Never mind, just please tell me that you weren't serious. You're not going back in, you were just joking, right?"

"I'm going back."

"Oh, I was afraid you'd say that," Malcomb whimpered as he collapsed onto the couch. He sighed deeply, resigned to his fate. Resigned to Butch. He gazed up towards Sherilyn, hoping to find a friendly face to commiserate with. She had moved from the window over to Taylor's side and now sat on the arm of his chair. The light from the window poured in around her and he knew she wouldn't be any help.

He exhaled heavily.

"Do you have any chocolate?" he asked.

*****

Sherilyn watched from the doorway of the bedroom as the two men set up the computer system on the floor and connected the sensor cables on the virtual suit. She watched Taylor strip down to his underwear and pull the tight black spandex up around his thighs while Malcomb connected the modem. Somehow, Taylor looked braver, more confident dressed in the suit. He moved like he had a purpose. She hadn't seen him like that in a long time.

She had done nothing but think about him since he walked out earlier. She was angry and hurt, but with time, the hurt subsided and she began to reflect on the situation. She knew Taylor hadn't intentionally hurt her. When he spoke of his experiment, this cyber-angioplasty, she knew that what he had done was finally focus his energy away from his troubled past and onto something that could heal him. In some strange way, he did need this. It was a way to reconcile the pain he kept buried all those years since his mother died. And then Jacob. And now his father.

She knew that she would never be able to understand everything he was going through, but she loved Taylor, and promised that she would be there for him in any way she could. Sickness or health. Good or bad.

Sanity or madness.

Now, as she watched him prepare to enter the computer program, her feelings of anger were replaced by fear. Doctors being murdered? The FBI chasing them? Her father involved? If all that Taylor had told her was true, then what was going to happen once he went back into the system? So far, the program had driven Taylor to the brink of insanity. What would happen this time?

While Malcomb fired up the computer, she reached for her pack of cigarettes, pulled one out and brought it up to her lips.

Stopping before she lit it, she looked at the cigarette, pursed her lips, then crumpled it in her hands, dropping it to the floor.

Taylor was home now. She didn't need to smoke anymore.

*****

Taylor finished pulling the suit over his shoulders then crawled on top of the cast iron bed in the master bedroom.

"How much time will we have?" he asked, positioning himself flat on top of the mattress.

"I'll use the modem to hook into the main system at the University," Malcomb answered. "The data transfer with fiber optics will be fast enough to run our program in real time. Figuring they're monitoring the system, they'll know that we're back online."

"And then?"

"It will take them awhile, but if they are good, they'll be able to figure out that this is an external connection and not a direct interface. They'll be able to trace us then."

"How long?"

"Maybe five minutes."

"That's not much time."

"I know. Their computer will be able to put an address to your internet provider number instantly."

"So how much time does that leave us?"

"We're looking at a total running time of ten minutes, tops. Can you do what you need to in that amount of time?"

"I guess I'll have to, won't I?"

"I'll disconnect you exactly ten minutes from when you first enter then we run before the cops get here."

"And save you from Butch."

"Yes, please."

Taylor nodded. "Agreed."

He looked over at Sherilyn standing by the door. She watched them closely, listening to their every word. He smiled at her and mouthed the words 'I love you.'

She nodded and bravely forced a smile.

Then Taylor lay down on the bed and closed his eyes.

CHAPTER 55

Pacing the plush carpet of his Embarcadero office, Erickson flashed a glance at the bank of digital screens that filled his eastern wall, taking in the striking image of Ross' shaved bald head and unreadable expression.

"Tell me what's going on," he said.

Reaching into his desktop humidor, Erickson selected a Chateau Fuente. He rolled the cigar back and forth between his fingers, watching the red seal and green ribbon flash by. At one point, when he was first diagnosed with metastatic small cell lung cancer, he'd vowed to quit smoking. But now, realizing that his time was drawing near, he couldn't see the point to giving up one of his greatest pleasures. In the end, it wouldn't make any damn difference. He removed the cedar sleeve from the cigar and glanced back towards Ross.

"Well?"

"I don't know what transpired," Ross said. "The sequence of events is murky."

Erickson's eyes narrowed. "I pay you to know."

"Understood," Ross said. "The scenario unfolded as I described it. Browne's effort to terminate the target in the ICU failed. I was unable to visualize the attempt through the security monitors, the curtains were closed. Putting the chain of events together, I think Browne went to the ICU, was surprised by Abrahms and then improvised. I don't know what he was doing with a gun."

"Neither do I. It makes things more complicated." Erickson paused to consider the situation. He placed the head of his cigar into the mouth of a double-bladed guillotine and cut the cap. "Where's Abrahms now?"

"At his house. With Bernard and his wife. I have them on surveillance."

Erickson rose from his desk, stepping to the window, thirty-four floors above the streets of San Francisco. Twilight was falling over the City, descending over the dark spires of the cityscape. He watched the red glimmering line of traffic as it crawled across the Bay Bridge towards Oakland and the suburbs beyond. Erickson pressed his cancer-filled chest against the window, feeling the coolness bleeding through his shirt to his skin.

Striking a wooden match, he rolled the cigar as he lit the end, the tobacco glowing red.

"What about Chan?" he asked, thick smoke streaming from his mouth.

"He's still alive in the ICU."

Erickson whipped around. "It's vital he be silenced."

Ross stared into the ferocity of Erickson's eyes. "Security has been increased since Browne's failure. Any attempts at this point will be far riskier"

"Just get it done. He mustn't be allowed to reveal what he's discovered."

Erickson shifted his gaze back towards the window. The City's lights flicked on one-by-one, illuminating the buildings and skyscrapers like a cluster of monstrous Christmas trees. He sucked on his cigar, filling his mouth with the flavor of cedar and coffee-tinged tobacco. He exhaled. All he needed was to keep everything in line until Senator's speech at Google/NASA-Ames. Two days, only two more days.

"I want you to proceed as we've discussed. First, deal with Browne."

Ross nodded. "Done. Anything else?"

"Get Abrahms and delete all traces of our program. I don't want any evidence linking us to him."

"Then what?"

"It's time to wrap this up."

"Remember, he's not alone."

Erickson sneered. The election was a little more than two weeks away. There was no way he was going to allow years of planning to fall apart now. He stamped out his cigar in the ashtray with finality.

"Then that's too bad for whoever is with him."

*****

Justin Hart pushed himself back from the dashboard of the Oldsmobile parked off Van Ness Avenue in downtown San Francisco. The notebook on his lap beeped and clicked. Victor Ruiz sat next to him in the driver's seat, his face buried in a dossier:

Murder: Taylor Abrahms.

"Yes!" Hart shouted.

Ruiz looked over cautiously. "Yes, what?"

"We've got him."

"We do?"

Hart smiled and faced Ruiz.

"He's back online."

Ruiz looked over Hart's shoulder, watching the junior Agent tap away at the keyboard. Numbers flashed and danced across the screen.

"When did he re-enter?" Ruiz asked.

"Just now. No more than two minutes ago."

"Where is he?"

"He's somewhere outside, hooked into the main system via DSL. I'm running a trace on the line right now. It should be coming up momentarily."

Ruiz tapped his fingers against the dashboard, stopping only long enough to swig a gulp of coffee from his Captain America mug, then he resumed tapping. He knew the first principle of detective work was patience, but God, he hated waiting.

"Have you got the stakeout at Bernard's apartment?" he asked.

"Yes, they've been there for two hours. No one has come in or out"

"What about his credit cards?"

"His cards haven't been used. No action on his savings or checking accounts."

"Any luck with that trace?"

"Almost. Here it comes," Hart said, studying the screen as a series of numbers took form. "Got it. Here's the phone number. It's here in San Francisco."

"Run the address," Ruiz ordered.

"I'm already typing it in," Hart replied, tapping on the keyboard.

"Well?"

"Got it. Private residence in Pacific Heights."

"Who's place is it?" Ruiz turned the key in the ignition, firing the motor to life.

"Wouldn't you know it, the guy's at home. Abrahms tapped in from his own fucking house."

Ruiz nodded in agreement. "Damn. You're right."

Ruiz slammed on the gas pedal and gunned the engine. The car screeched out of the parking lot and sped down Van Ness towards Pacific Heights.

CHAPTER 56

Malcomb ran about the bedroom in a flurry, racing to disconnect the system. He had already shut down the computer, severed the SPS connection and disconnected from the modem.

Taylor peeled off the spandex suit. His mind still groggy from the virtual connection, he shook his head trying to clear the cobwebs.

"Let's go," Malcomb said. "The FBI will have traced the outside line by now."

"I'm ready," Taylor answered.

"Hurry! They're on their way," Malcomb muttered to himself. "I just know they're on the way."

Taylor ignored Malcomb's whimpering and pulled on a pair of jeans, a worn tee-shirt, and some faded brown leather boots. His body was still coated with sweat from the SIS suit, his skin hot and sticky. Sherilyn stood by the doorway, a duffel bag in her arms.

Taylor glanced across at Malcomb. "Give me the program."

"I say we give them the program."

"Not until I know the hallucinations are gone."

Malcomb frowned and handed Taylor the external hard drive containing the VHP.

"Did it work?" Malcomb asked. "Do you think your mind is cleared?"

"I didn't see any visions this time, that's a start." Taylor studied the hard drive in his hands, amazed at how deceptively simple it was. So ordinary, like any other device containing any other program. There was nothing to belie its true nature.

Its deception.

His thoughts raced back to the start of the experiment. How could he not have known about Browne? Taylor was certain that there were clues he should have picked up, but he was so focused on getting the experiment started. He chided himself for thinking about that now. What happened in the past didn't matter. All that mattered was figuring out what was going on and getting his life back. Taylor knew that people were willing to kill for this. Who would be next?

He thought back to what Chan had written in the ICU. pazsword. Not password, just pazsword.

What in the world did that mean? pazsword?

A plan formulated in his mind. First, he had to get Sherilyn and Malcomb to safety. He knew of a place where they could hide, where neither Erickson nor McIntyre nor the FBI nor whoever else may be looking for them would find them. Then they'd hack into the CTS system and enter Chan's and Erickson's files.

The answer had to be hidden there, somewhere.

"Go now," he said to Malcomb.

"But where do I go?" Malcomb's eyes grew as wide as a lost child's. "They know where I live. They know my lab."

"You're not going home." Taylor handed him a folded piece of lined paper. "Here's the address. I'll call you there tomorrow morning."

Malcomb looked at the paper. "Whose place is this?"

"It's Lawrence, the guard. He'll hide you until we get things under control. We can trust him."

Malcomb shoved the address in his pocket. "What about the equipment?"

"I'll take it. We may need it later."

"What do you mean later?" Malcomb squinted. "Tell me there isn't going to be a later."

"Right now, I want you out of here."

"And what about you? Where will you go?"

"It's best I don't tell you."

"Right!" Malcomb nodded. He shot Sherilyn a look of shear panic, then raced out of the apartment. He left the front door open as he bounded down the stairs to his car. Taylor could hear the grinding of gears as Malcomb's Honda pulled away from the curb, it's little engine whining as it shot off down the street.

Taylor turned to face Sherilyn, taking in the lines of worry on her face.

"He'll be alright," Taylor said.

"It's not him I'm worried about."

Taylor exhaled into his hands. "I'll be fine too."

"I packed this for you." She handed him the duffel. "Clothes and toothbrush."

Taylor took the bag from her then ran to the closet and threw on his leather jacket.

"Get your stuff. You're coming with me," he said as he turned to face her. "It's not safe here."

Sherilyn shook her head. "I can handle myself. Besides, I don't know anything. All I can do is tell whoever comes that my husband conducted some bizarre experiment on my bed and I had no idea what it was. That's not too far from the truth."

"That's not good enough," Taylor shook his head. "I know what these people are capable of. Crawford's been murdered, a CTS programmer shot. Even Browne tried to kill me."

"You have too much to take care of without having to worry about me."

"But Sherilyn—"

"I'll stay at Courtney's until I hear from you."

Taylor hesitated, then nodded. He'd rather she stayed with him, but felt she'd be safe with her friend. He was tempted to tell her where she'd be able to reach him, but held his tongue. The less she knew the better.

He opened the duffel and stuffed his wallet between the pair of sweatpants and a clean t-shirt. The computer was piled at the end of the bed. One trip for his belongings and another for the computer and VHP gear then hit the road.

He took one final scan around the apartment, making sure he had everything he needed. His eyes fell upon the faded cover of Jacob's journal resting on the nightstand, the one his father had given him so many days ago, before the madness started.

If the virtual ordeal had taught him anything, it was how much he'd ran from his past. Tapping into his deepest fear, the virtual reality had brought memories of his family storming back into the center of his consciousness. Memories he'd spent his entire life running from. Now he knew that he couldn't hide any longer. Sooner or later, he'd have to deal with that pain.

He dashed to the stand, picked up the journal and shoved it into the duffel bag.

Sherilyn stood by the doorway, her gaze following him around the room. Taylor started towards the door then hesitated. His eyes shifted to hers. He looked at his wife and the quiet strength in her face. The pain in those lovely, watery eyes. He had put her through so much.

"Sherilyn, I—" he began then fell quiet. He realized that his words would only confuse things, turn the already opaque waters even more murky. He reached out and pulled her tightly to his chest and kissed her.

He broke away and looked into her eyes.

"I've always loved you," he said.

Sherilyn nodded as a tear fell onto her cheek.

"I'll be back," he said. "I promise."

Sherilyn squeezed his hand, then let go. Taylor took one step backwards then turned towards the door.

He didn't make it very far.

Dr. William Preston emerged from the shadows, his body blocking the doorway, a black Glock 9 mm pistol in his left hand.

"Back in the house," he said in a low voice.

Taylor stopped, staring at the handgun, the third one pointed at him today.

Intensity flared in Preston's eyes. Taylor's mind raced to Sherilyn. Silently, he damned himself for not getting her out sooner.

"What the hell do you want?" Taylor asked.

"Where's the video?"

"What video?"

Preston gave him a hard look. "I won't miss from here, Abrahms. If this gun goes off, you will die. Now, where's the video?"

Taylor hesitated; his brow furrowed. " I don't know what you're talking about."

"The video your little slant-eyed honey took at the Farm."

Taylor held up his hands. "I don't know about any video."

"Stop your fucking lies," Preston snapped. The pistol raised level with Taylor's head. "You have no idea how much trouble you've caused me. Now give me the God-damned video. I will count to three and then I will kill you."

Out of the corner of his eye, Taylor saw Sherilyn's body tighten. She was hiding behind the door, getting ready to pounce onto Preston's back. Taylor shook his head 'no'.

"One." Preston counted.

Sherilyn brought her hands up, to reach for Preston's gun. Taylor continued to motion for her to stop. If the gun went off, if he spun and faced her—

"Two."

Taylor felt his heart exploding in his chest. His mind raced forward. He had to stop Sherilyn before it was too late. But what could he do?

Preston's finger tightened on the trigger. His mouth opened to count 'three," the flesh of this forefinger starting to turn white from the pressure against the trigger, when a large metallic object flashed through the air towards the back of Preston's head. Taylor startled as the metallic object soared closer, barreling at high speed, then smashed into the back of Preston's skull. Taylor heard the muted thud as the metal cracked into Preston's occipital bone followed by Preston lurching forward. Preston's eyes rolled into the back of his head, and his body slumped forward, crashing to the floor.

Taylor stared, mouth open, as Helen Yang stepped through the doorway, her robotic falcon circling around the apartment before landing on her arm.

"I can't believe he called me your honey!" Helen looked down at Preston in disgust.

Taylor let out a deep breath. "Nice shot."

"Sorry I'm late."

"Your timing was perfect," Taylor said. He reached for Sherilyn and helped her step over Preston's fallen body. He pulled her into his arms.

"Are you okay?" he asked.

Sherilyn fell into his arms, trembling. "Jesus, Taylor. What have you gotten yourself into?"

"Something far bigger than I intended."

She glared at Preston's gun. "That man would've killed you."

"He's not the only one." He looked towards Helen, suddenly aware that they'd never met. "Helen this is my wife, Sherilyn. Sherilyn, Helen."

"You certainly know how to make an entrance," Sherilyn said.

Helen looked at her wryly. "I love drama."

Sherilyn buried her face in Taylor's chest for a long moment, then her eyes returned to Preston. She nodded towards his fallen body. "What do we do with him?"

"Grab the extension cord out of the closet, I'll bind his hands and feet."

Sherilyn shook her head. "The FBI are coming. You said so yourself. If they want you as badly as he did then you better get out of here." She picked up Preston's 9mm. "I'll tie him up and hold the gun on him."

"I can't leave you alone here."

"You don't have a choice. Get out of here."

Taylor paused. He hated the thought of leaving her. Two men, respected doctors both of them, had tried to kill him in the span of an hour. If whatever was happening was big enough to corrupt two hospital icons, he didn't know what would come next.

"Come with me, please."

Sherilyn shook her head. "Go while you still can."

Taylor took in the stubborn line of Sherilyn's chin. He'd seen that look many times before. It was pointless to argue.

He turned to Helen. "Malcomb got away, but things are worse than we thought. Preston was here after the video you made of his work in the Farm."

"My video? He was going to kill you for my video?" Helen sneered at Preston's fallen body. "What do you want me to do?"

"Go back to your lab. Check your email. You'll hear from me."

"Got it."

He looked up at Sherilyn and studied the determination in her eyes. She held the gun firmly without shaking, as if she'd held one a hundred times before.

Taylor grabbed the computer and the suit and carried them down to the MG. He ran back to the apartment and picked up his duffel.

"When will I see you again?" Sherilyn asked.

"I'll contact you."

"Be careful," she said.

Taylor nodded, glanced at Helen and bolted out the door, down the stairs to his car. He tossed the duffel bag into the backseat then started the motor. The engine whined, but came to life. He floored the pedal and shot towards Van Ness Avenue.

He knew that if he sped down Van Ness south towards Market Street, he'd be able to cut to Highway 80 and the Bay Bridge. Once he got to the highway, he'd be safe.

If he could only get to the highway.

CHAPTER 57

Ruiz and Hart barreled north up Van Ness towards Pacific Heights, disregarding all red lights in their path. Hart crouched in the passenger seat, griping the armrest with white knuckles, stamping his foot against the floorboards, slamming an imaginary brake. Ruiz stepped on the gas harder, cursing. Even flying through traffic, this was taking too long. He knew they were giving Abrahms too much time to get away. He kept in contact via cellular with the Field Office, where Bill, a heavy-set, foul-mouthed agent with a thick southern accent, watched the screen to monitor Malcomb's interface.

Five minutes ago, Bill had informed Hart that the outside hook-up had terminated.

Ruiz swore again. He'd missed Malcomb and Abrahms once, at the lab; he would be damned if he was going to miss them again.

Ruiz plowed through another red light at the intersection of Van Ness and Geary, careening through the crossing traffic. Drivers slammed on their brakes as their cars skidded to a halt, clearing a path for the speeding Oldsmobile sedan. Ruiz took off his sunglasses and threw them on the center console next to his forty-five-caliber service revolver. Jesus Christ, this was taking too long.

Suddenly, he snapped his head around.

"There!" he pointed at the oncoming traffic. "It's Abrahms!"

Hart turned just as Taylor hurtled by in his MG, his face clearly visible with the convertible top down. The MG knifed from the left lane to the right, shot past a slow-moving Toyota, then slashed to the left through a hole in traffic.

Ruiz slammed on the brakes. He twisted the steering wheel, sending the car into a controlled spin. Smoke spewed from the Olds's tires. The car slid one hundred eighty degrees. Completing the spin, Ruiz punched the gas, the engine roared, the tires shrieked, and the sedan shot off after the MG.

In his rear-view, Taylor saw a puff of smoke climb above the traffic then a sedan barreling after him.

Adrenaline shot through Taylor's veins. He stomped on the gas but there was no increase in the MG's speed, only a louder whine from the ancient engine. He swung to the right around a van and gunned forward. The light at the intersection ahead was green. If he could make it, he could lose them in the crossing traffic. He gripped the wheel and leaned forward, as it if would give his car more momentum.

But he couldn't pull away. The Oldsmobile sedan roared closer with overwhelming horsepower. Taylor downshifted into third, grinding the weak transmission, but picked up valuable momentum. The intersection was closer. Only a couple hundred more feet.

He had to make it.

The MG flashed past Turk street, barely making the yellow. The light changed behind him, crossing traffic flooding into the intersection. Taylor shot a rearview glance as a truck crawled into the intersection, blocking all lanes.

Taylor exhaled, believing he was safe, when a blast of smoke erupted behind him. His eyes darted to the rear-view just as the Olds launched onto the sidewalk, bounced off the concrete, swerved around traffic and crashed back to the street, barreling towards him.

Taylor threw the wheel to the left, thrusting the MG into traffic, trying to use the other cars as a shield. Market Street was still six blocks away, then another four blocks to the freeway. Behind him the sedan powered closer. Taylor's foot pounded the gas pedal to the floorboards but the Olds was still gaining.

Jesus, I'm not going to make it!

Taylor plowed through the intersection of Van Ness and Fell, running the red light. The MG's tires squealed as the car shot airborne hitting the dip in the road. Oncoming drivers pounded their horns and swerved, slamming on their brakes as the MG flew through the packed intersection and barreled down Van Ness. The Olds roared through immediately behind him, sparks spewing as its undercarriage careened against the pavement.

The two cars raced towards the freeway onramp, the Oldsmobile gaining. It pulled even alongside the MG. Taylor shot a glance over, the car racing just inches from his side. He stared into Ruiz's tight face and the service revolver aimed at Taylor's head.

"Pull over!" he heard Ruiz yell.

A thousand thoughts raced through his mind. He wondered what in the world he was doing. Trying to out run the FBI? The thought came that he should end it now, turn himself in. Maybe he could somehow clear his name and preserve some remnant of his career. Return to the University. Return to the hospital. Return to his life.

Then he thought of Browne and the deception.

"Get bent!" he yelled back, as he slammed on the brakes. Ruiz tried to stop but the sedan was moving too fast for a controlled spin. The Olds lurched outwards into oncoming traffic. Ruiz stepped on the accelerator, trying to break out of the spin, but couldn't control the tail of the sedan which continued to slide around. Suddenly, the rear wheels caught hold and propelled the car sideways where it rammed into the side of a delivery truck.

Taylor jumped on the gas and gunned the MG down Van Ness. In his rearview mirror he could see Ruiz struggling to restart the stalled sedan while a group of pedestrians gathered around.

Stifling a grin, Taylor sped up the onramp and lost himself on the crowded freeway.

CHAPTER 58

The Franciscan retreat at San Damiano stretched across the Las Trampas Hills, high above the town of Danville. The white walled, Spanish-style compound had been built in the early 1950's as a refuge for the brown-robed monks; a place to protect them from the commotion of city life. Not even many of the long-time residents of Danville knew of its existence in the wooded hills above town, but day after day, in the solitude of the valley, the monks walked along the cobblestone paths, tended to the small flower gardens and meditated in the St. Francis chapel.

Taylor exited off the 680, cruised passed the shops that lined Hartz Avenue, took a right on Prospect, and headed up Highland Drive. As a child, he'd come to San Damiano often, passing through its gardens every time he hiked the trail to Bear Tree. He'd come to know the grounds well, and remembered the groundskeeper, Mr. Starling, who he and Jacob would often share lunch with before retreating back down the hill to their father's house at the end of the dirt road.

Starling, a gruff old Scotsman with a pleasant, toothless grin, occasionally slipped a nip of whiskey into Taylor's tea, as he launched into tall tales about the haunted history of San Damiano. He told of the elderly monk who was murdered at the foot of the chapel by a couple of would-be thieves. Legend had it that his ghost became the protector of the retreat, each night voyaging out along the miles of oak-covered trails, guarding the meditation benches and crosses. Starling swore that one time he saw the monk's ghost and it gently touched him on the shoulder before wandering off into the moonlit sky.

Taylor figured it must have been the whiskey.

Taylor pulled the MG into the San Damiano parking lot and cut the engine. The car grunted to a halt amid a puff of black smoke. Taylor stepped out and surveyed the grounds. A tinge of oak and dried grass scented the air. A red-tailed hawk circled above his head, the fading twilight filtering through its tail which glowed with a crimson luminance. The faint sound of singing came from the chapel to his left. To his right, down a make-shift path, past the vegetable garden and the trickle of a Spanish fountain, was the small white stucco cottage that Starling called home.

Taylor walked down the path and knocked on the door. The wind rustled through the oak branches above his head. After a moment, the door creaked open and Taylor stared into Starling's familiar toothless smile.

"Well, I'll be. If it isn't young master Abrahms! Come in boy, come in. What brings you back into town?" He ushered Taylor into the small living room.

Taylor gazed at the old man. His long white hair protruded in all directions, looking like a Scottish Albert Einstein. He was dressed in blue denim overalls and a clean flannel work shirt. His aging body still proud and strong.

"I was in the neighborhood," Taylor said.

Starling eyed him suspiciously then smiled. "I'll bet you were."

Taylor returned the smile, suddenly realizing how much he'd missed the old man.

"I need a place to stay tonight."

"My home is your home. But what ails you? Have you got some trouble?"

"Nothing I can't handle."

"Well, why don't you try me? I may be able to give you a hand." He tugged on his overall suspenders. "I've got seventy-eight years in these old bones. I'm sure it's nothing I haven't had to handle before myself."

Taylor smiled, appreciating Starling's kindness, but knew there was no way to describe to the old man what had happened to his life.

"Just having your company is enough," Taylor said.

The old man gummed a smile. "Well, you stay here as long as you like. And if you stay too long, I'll put you to work in the garden. Now then, can I get you some tea?"

"That'd be great. Oh, and Starling?"

"Yes?"

"I'll take a little extra whiskey this time."

*****

Ruiz sat with Hart in booth number 28 at the Black Bear Diner on Camino Ramon Road in Danville. Taylor's MG had been spotted heading east on 24 by the Highway Patrol monitoring freeway traffic at the Caldecott tunnel. Even though the officer had lost him shortly thereafter, Ruiz thought that it was safe to conclude that Abrahms was heading towards Danville. A background check had revealed that Taylor had grown up in the old orchard town, and more importantly, he still had family there; a father who lived out Tassajara Road. Ruiz knew that when novices went on the run, the first place they headed was home. It was a gut reflex and as predictable as snow in the winter. They needed the familiarity of the surroundings to feel safe.

The night shift waitress, Brenda, was taking forever to bring Ruiz his fourth refill of coffee and he was more than a little impatient. His mood had grown fouler by the minute. He stared out the window as the wind blew through the oak trees out front, rattling the barren branches. The temperature had dropped a precipitous twenty-five degrees over the last couple of hours as darkness settled upon the valley town. Ruiz could feel the cold air bleeding through the window. Damn, he hated the cold.

Out of the corner of his eye, he spotted Brenda walking towards him, carrying the pot of coffee.

"It's about time you got here," he snapped when she reached the table. "I thought they chopped your legs off or something."

Brenda forced a smile and poured the steaming coffee into his mug. The cup overflowed and coffee spilled across the table, splashing into his lap.

"Shit!" he screamed, jumping to his feet as he wiped a napkin across his crotch. "You did that on purpose!"

Brenda feigned embarrassment and apologized profusely, then turned around and walked back through the swinging doors into the kitchen where the other waitresses greeted her with a celebratory round of high-fives.

Ruiz wiped at his stained pants then sat back down in the booth. Hart tried hard not to laugh.

"What are you smirking at?" Ruiz demanded.

"You certainly have a way with women, don't you?"

"Damn bitch, did that on purpose."

They drank their coffee in silence for a moment, each trying to sort out the facts of a murder case that was growing more bizarre by the minute.

"So, what have you learned?" Ruiz finally asked.

"Bernard never returned to his house," Hart said, tearing open a sugar packet and pouring it into his coffee.

"Can we trace him?"

Hart shook his head. "No cell phone on him."

"GPS in his car?"

"He's registered with a 1970 Honda. Definitely pre-GPS. He's off the radar."

Ruiz gulped the remainder of his coffee and looked out the window. "That leaves Abrahms."

"He ditched his cell also," Hart said. "It tracks to his home address. His car's even older."

Ruiz gave him a look. "Team One learn anything?"

Hart opened another sugar. "It's a delicate situation, her being the senator's daughter, and all. They questioned her but got nothing. Either she's the world's coolest chick or she really doesn't know a thing."

"Which do you think it is?"

"I think she learned how to lie from her father." He sipped his coffee, winced and reached for another sugar. "But I do have something for you."

Ruiz eyed the junior man suspiciously.

"Abrahms assaulted his superior in the ICU this afternoon," Hart said. "Eight nurses saw it. They say he tried to kill a patient also."

"Jesus Christ! What the fuck's going on at that hospital?"

"That's not all. When our team got to Abrahms' house, they found the unconscious body of another doctor hogtied on the floor. A Dr. William Preston. Mrs. Abrahms claims he'd invaded their house, fully armed. Tried to kill them."

Ruiz shook his head. "What is this, National fucking Doctors with Guns Week?"

"Seems like they all just went up and gone crazy."

"Nothing about this is adding up."

"I know what you mean. Too many cooks."

"And not enough broth."

Ruiz stared into his empty coffee mug, gazing at the dark swirl at the bottom as if he could read it like tea leaves. Nothing was making sense. The Chief of Staff of a major University Hospital murdered. Patients being set up to kill. Assault on another doctor. And the Senator's daughter? How was she involved? Ruiz had never liked politics and now it had been thrust right into his lap like a bomb with a lit fuse.

He looked at Hart. "So, the way it sits right now, is that this Abrahms, a respected doctor, the Senator's own fucking son-in-law, two weeks before the Presidential election suddenly up and goes crazy, kills one colleague, tries to kill another, then gets attacked by a third right in his own house."

Hart's lips pulled tight. "That's the way it sits."

Ruiz pulled on his right eyebrow, not buying it. Not one bit of it.

"Unless it's a set up," he said.

"A frame?"

"It's no more absurd than what we got right now."

Hart added a final sugar to his coffee. "But why?"

"I have no idea. But we got political Hiroshima just waiting to happen here. If the media finds out we're hunting the Senator's son-in-law for murder, two weeks before the election. Jesus, I don't even want to think about it."

Hart grimaced, his coffee still tasting too bitter. "What's our next move?"

"We need some answers and right now, Abrahms is our only lead. Whatever's going on, he's right in the middle."

Hart agreed. "What about the senator's daughter?

"Keep a tight eye on her. She may give us bargaining power with Abrahms."

"Pick her up?"

"Not yet. See if Abrahms tries to make contact with her. He's not a professional. He may make a mistake like that."

Hart nodded. "Abrahms' father's house?

"Cover it. Get an A.P.B. on his plates and run his driver's license through all the rental cars in case he changes wheels.

Check any security cam and traffic footage you can find in town."

Hart nodded. "There's another problem."

Ruiz grunted his disapproval. He'd already heard enough problems for one night.

"Senator McInytre is scheduled to give a private fundraising speech at Google on Friday, eight in the morning."

Ruiz's eyes gaped. "You're fucking kidding me? Why wasn't I informed?"

"I got the text while you were taking a whiz."

Ruiz rubbed his forehead in dismay. "Then it's time to talk to the Senator's people and the Secret Service. They need to know the manhunt's status. If Abrahms is indeed dangerous, we have to make sure he stays away from his father-in-law."

He poked at his half-eaten egg croissant like he was trying to revive a dead animal. What once seemed like a cut-and-dry, hang-it-out-in-the-sun murder case was rapidly descending into a toilet bowl morass of politicians and whacked-out surgeons.

The next President of the United States was coming to their town in less than 36 hours and all hell was breaking loose.

CHAPTER 59

"God damn it! Get out!"

Senator McIntyre's voice reverberated off the wood-paneled walls of his Election Campaign office as if projecting off the perfect acoustic tiles of a concert hall. Jennifer Langston, his assistant, lowered her head to avoid the barrage and retreated out the door. Even at two in the morning, not one of the Senator's staff had gone home. Flip Bosco, the slick-tongued press secretary and pollster Hugh Bittle examined the latest numbers in the adjoining conference room while Cassandra Williams manned the phones, overseeing her PR crew. The smell of sweat lingered in the air mingling with the burnt stench of stale coffee. With the election just around the corner and the polls tightening, work had become frantic.

McIntyre turned and faced Roderick Stevens.

"Go ahead. What were you saying?"

"That's all the news I have. The Secret Service wanted to keep us informed, particularly since it involves your visit to California."

McIntyre slumped in his leather chair. He closed his eyes and squeezed his temples. Wracking his brain, he tried to make sense of the news but still couldn't believe this was happening. On the threshold of the election! If the press got whim that the FBI were hunting his son-in-law, for a murder charge of all things, it would devastate his campaign. Not even the Teflon-coated Clinton could survive a blow like that.

"Is the evidence against him credible?" he asked.

"It appears so. He's directly linked to the murder of Dr. Bennington Crawford. There are a number of witnesses that saw him attack Browne and try to kill the patient."

"Jesus." McIntyre stepped to the mirrored wet bar, dropped two cubes of ice into a glass and poured himself a Glen Livet, watching the amber fluid pour into the glass as if it were a salve to ease his wounds. As much as he despised the trailer-park trash his daughter had married, Abrahms wasn't a murderer. Every gut instinct screamed that Crawford's murder was much more complicated than a medical resident gone mad. The question was how did it involve him and his campaign?

"When will we have more information?"

"Not until they bring him in." Roderick shrugged. "Have you tried calling your daughter yet? See if she knows anything?"

"Just voice mail." McIntyre threw back the whiskey in a single gulp then asked the question he really wanted to know. "Is the story out yet?"

Roderick shook his head. "Not yet. We've managed to squash it while the FBI cement their case. But we won't be able to hold the press down forever. The murder of a prominent physician will get headlines."

McIntyre pinched his temples. "And his relationship to me will get even more."

McIntyre felt it all slipping away. This situation was unprecedented in American politics. Jimmy Carter had had a beer swilling brother, Clinton a half-brother convicted of selling cocaine, and Roosevelt a nephew who married a Hungarian prostitute, but never could McIntyre remember anything resembling the political tornado that was facing him.

The son-in-law of the frontrunner for the presidency of the United States wanted for murder.

"We have some serious issues to discuss," Stevens said, his face solemn.

Serious? McIntyre scowled. *What could be more serious than having my campaign associated with a wanted murderer?*

McIntyre gave him a hard look. "What?"

"If they can't find Abrahms, we may have to cancel the Silicon Valley trip. We can't risk sending you out there if he's dangerous."

McIntyre tightened. He'd planned too long for this speech; it was designed to put the final nail into Abrahms' research and cement his own medical platform. It was what he and Erickson had been working for all these months. With the murder controversy brewing just under the press radar, now more than ever he needed to distance himself from his son-in-law.

He shook his head. "If we cancel, then we have to tell the press why."

"We could claim illness?"

"Two weeks before the election? They'd never believe it. They know I'd campaign if I had leprosy."

Roderick frowned, accepting McIntyre's argument. "It's too risky to expose you under these circumstances."

McIntyre remained silent for a moment, allowing Roderick's words to run around in his brain, searching desperately for an answer when suddenly, a thought flickered in his mind. A glimmer of hope.

"Unless—" he started.

Roderick's lips tightened. "Unless what?"

McIntyre's eyes fired to life, cementing his brain around a solution. The corners of his lips trickled into a smile. "We spin this to our advantage."

"That your son-in-law is a murderer?"

McIntyre shook his head. "Not that part, but its relation to my campaign."

"I don't follow."

"If we leak it that Abrahms killed his mentor, then threatened to kill me—"

"The press will eat you alive. It'll crush you."

"Not if we spin it right." McIntyre felt his momentum growing. "If it seems that the killings are motivated by my denouncement of his research. That his project was failing despite all of his bravado—" McIntyre let his words linger.

It only took a second for Roderick to catch on. "We could make it appear that Abrahms snapped because you were right all along."

"Exactly! He'd been under extreme pressure, fighting to save his failing project. With all the public scrutiny, he had a breakdown. Spin it so it reads that these researchers are so afraid of me and my opposition to their hyper-biotech they're willing to kill me rather than let me be president. Even my own son-in-law."

Roderick licked his lips. "We may even rouse up the sympathy vote."

McIntyre poured himself another Scotch while he thought through his plan. The FBI already had an APB for Abrahms, the dangerous fugitive. If McIntyre added to the litany of charges by filing a report that Abrahms had threatened to kill him, not only would it intensify the manhunt, but it would distance himself from his son-in-law in the eyes of the voters. It could make him appear stronger, a George Patton type; unafraid to stand up for his ideals despite the obvious danger. It could turn him into a hero.

It just might work.

McIntyre emptied the glass, realizing what he was about to do. Things were never supposed to have gone this far. When he first targeted Taylor's research, he'd hoped to shut down a frivolous project and perhaps drive a wedge between Abrahms and his daughter. Get her to see the error she'd made in choosing that man. But even with his disdain for Taylor, he'd never bargained on destroying the young man's life.

But what choice did he have? Things were out of control. The election was heating up. His once commanding lead had been reduced to a few percentage points.

He couldn't let the election slip away now.

"Make it happen," McIntyre said.

*****

Taylor huddled on the old camel-back sofa, wrapped in a tattered blanket, his feet hanging off the end, his body twisted onto the small couch like a circus performer. The aroma of English tea and Irish whiskey still lingered in the air, but couldn't calm Taylor's frenetic mind. Starling had wandered off to bed around eleven, leaving Taylor alone with his thoughts. He prayed Sherilyn was alright. He'd hated leaving her but knew she was right. If he hadn't gotten away, he'd be no good to either of them. He wished he could call her, but knew any call, any contact at all, could be traced.

His head throbbed with the viciousness of an invading army. A feeling of trepidation crawled through his skin. Each of his hallucinations had been preceded by a headache. God, he prayed it wasn't going to happen again. Rubbing his forehead, he needed something to occupy his mind. His eyes drifted across the room and landed on his duffel bag. Inside, somewhere, was his brother's journal.

Taylor rose from the couch, reached into the duffel and pulled out the faded book. It felt heavy in his hands—heavier than the weight of the paper and binding. An image of Jacob's body hanging from the ceiling flashed through Taylor's mind.

He plopped back down on the sofa and opened to the journal to the first page, his eyes growing wide, stunned by what he found inside.

CHAPTER 60

Thursday, Oct 19th, 5:45 a.m.

Dawning sunlight knifed through the curtains of Starling's cottage, stabbing into Taylor's tired eyes. He roused himself and glanced at his watch, blinking to clear his vision.

5:45 a.m.

Starling was still sleeping off the previous night's whiskey, his snoring reverberating from the bedroom. Taylor glanced out the window trying to focus. The morning sun strained to break through the canopy of clouds, shafts of light streaming down through the gray like searchlights coming from heaven. As if someone up there was trying to find him. The chirping of Fox Sparrows and California towhees filtered to Taylor's ears. He rubbed his face, dragged himself to his feet, and picked up the telephone.

He pulled a scrap of paper from his pocket and dialed the number.

"Hello?" the sleepy voice answered.

"Lawrence, it's Taylor. I need to speak to Malcomb."

"I think he's asleep finally. He was up half the night pacing around the apartment and eating chocolate."

"Who wasn't? Can you get him?"

The telephone dropped and Taylor heard Lawrence's footsteps tap across the floor. Taylor paced by the coffee table, stopping to stretch his back which popped like an aged symphony. He felt old. He wondered how much more of this his body could take.

Malcomb picked up the phone.

"Hello, Taylor. Are you in prison?"

"Of course not."

"It's only a matter of time, you know. Did you happen to see the late news last night? You were the star. Rogue doctor turned murderer. They're accusing you now of threatening to kill the senator."

"What?"

"Congratulations. You're the most wanted man in the country."

Taylor suppressed his reaction, remembering that it was all part of the carefully orchestrated deconstruction of his life. He had to keep focused.

"Listen, I have a plan."

"So, do I. It's called turning ourselves in and praying for our lives."

"My plan is better."

"I hope so. I'm not cut out to be a fugitive, Taylor. My nerves are shot, my gums are bleeding and last night I wet the bed. I haven't wet the bed since I was a child."

The anxiety in Malcomb's voice was palpable. Taylor needed to break Malcomb out of his thought spiral and get him to focus. Their lives depended on it.

"White knight f3 to e5," he said.

"The FBI are—"

"Can you remember the board?"

Malcomb hesitated. "Of course, I can."

"Then white knight f3 to e5."

The line fell silent. "I think you've finally lost it," Malcomb said. "The pressure's getting to you. I'll take your queen with my bishop, g4 to d1."

Taylor didn't miss a beat. "I need you to do something. Are your hacking skills honed?"

"I don't like the sound of this."

"I need you to hack your way into the CTS system."

"Are you nuts?" Malcomb squealed.

"Listen to me. The answer lies inside that computer system. We've been set up from the beginning, played like a couple of pawns and it keeps getting worse. Those phony news reports prove it. We have to find out what's going on."

"But why? What possible purpose could it serve?"

Taylor kept silent.

"You're not going to tell me, are you?"

"Are you sure you want to know?"

"No."

"That's what I thought."

Malcomb was quiet for a moment and Taylor knew that he was weighing the situation. "I can't guarantee I can get in. They'll have massive security, firewall after firewall."

"Give it your best shot. See if you can hack into Chan's files, or anything to do with the VHP."

"When do you want me to do this?"

"Now. I'll meet you at noon."

Malcomb gasped. "You can't be serious."

"I'm dead serious."

"Taylor, I'm exhausted. I haven't slept a wink!"

"There'll be plenty of time to sleep in prison."

There was silence. "How will I get to you?"

"I know a place. Have Lawrence call Sherilyn and ask her where the Bears scratch the trees. She'll know what he's talking about. Tell him not to mention my name. I'm sure our lines are tapped."

"What about you? Where will you be?"

Taylor swallowed. He reached into his duffel for a clean shirt. "Find out what you can. We'll meet at noon."

DEADLY VISION

*****

Taylor guided Starling's rust-bare, red and white 1961 AMC Rambler down the Las Trampas hillside and headed out Sycamore Valley towards Tassajara Road. Starling had stirred long enough for Taylor to thank him for his hospitality. He asked to borrow the car, knowing the FBI would be on the lookout for the MG. Starling nodded then rolled over, falling back asleep. He started snoring instantly.

The new day's sun had climbed high over the hills but failed to knife through the dense clouds—the landscape shrouded in an immutable grey. Taylor, sticking to the side streets, worked his way through town then onto Tassajara Road before turning into old man Dougherty's orchard, next to his father's house. He assumed the FBI would have done a background check by now, which meant they'd know where his father lived and would be watching. He guided the car behind Dougherty's dilapidated barn and parked under an oak tree, near the entrance to the Cold War-era underground bomb shelter that connected the two properties —built in the early 60's, when everyone was convinced Armageddon was coming any day in the form of a Russian missile.

Exiting the Rambler, Taylor shoved his hands into his pockets. His breath escaped in misty plumes. He dashed to the fence that separated Dougherty's property from his childhood home and peeked through a wormhole in the wooden planks, studying the weathered walls of his father's house—and the garage where he'd found Jacob's body.

He closed his eyes, squeezing them tight, as if he could drive out the memories. A vision of his brother dangling in the garage seared through his cortex, so real he could almost smell the odor of death. He remembered the hallucination in the

365

Burgundy Inn and willed himself to stay in control. He couldn't afford a breakdown.

Peering through the fence, Taylor could just make out the front half of a black sedan, parked fifty yards down the road. Two men sat inside, one eating while the other tapped at a laptop. They made no indication they'd spotted him. Taylor looked back towards Dougherty's driveway. It cut off the main road just before a sharp bend. From where they were parked, they couldn't have seen him pull up.

Taylor crept along the side of the fence until he was certain he was out of view then pulled himself over. He landed with a splash in a puddle in his father's backyard. He froze, forcing his mind to stay calm.

He dashed to the side of the house and peered around the corner at the black sedan. It hadn't moved.

He hurried back, took a deep breath and knocked on his father's backdoor.

"What?" he heard Saul yell.

He knocked again then crouched back into the shadows.

The backdoor opened and Saul stuck his head out. "What do you want?" he hollered to no one in particular.

Taylor stepped into the light. Saul's jaw parted and a weak smile tickled the corner of his lips. He looked fragile and had lost more weight since Taylor's visit; his cheeks were drawn, his skin anemic.

"We need to talk," Taylor said.

"We needed to talk ten years ago."

Saul stepped back, allowing Taylor into the kitchen. Empty beer cans littered the floor. Dishes overflowed the sink. The air was thick and oppressive. The whole place smelled like something had crawled away unnoticed into a corner and died.

"Let's go into the living room," Saul said.

"I'd rather stay here." The living room had windows that faced the street and the black sedan.

"Why'd you come to the back door?"

"I'll explain later. We need to talk first."

Saul pulled open the refrigerator door. He grabbed a beer and pulled the tab, releasing the carbon belch. He turned back to Taylor and took a long gulp.

Taylor took in his father. "You knew all along, didn't you?"

"I knew what?"

"About Jacob."

Saul wiped his mouth with his sleeve. "What are you talking about?"

Taylor grimaced, fighting to control his emotions. "You know damn well what I mean."

Saul met Taylor's glare with one of his own. A moment passed, the tension tightening between them, then slowly, he softened. His gaze drifted down. A cockroach scampered across the floor, racing towards the pantry. In an instant, it was gone, leaving the kitchen still.

"You read the journal," Saul said.

Taylor nodded.

"So now you know the truth."

"Jacob didn't kill himself because I left him."

Saul shook his head. "No, he didn't."

"He killed himself because he was sick."

Saul looked at his son and nodded.

"Jesus Christ, why didn't you tell me?" Taylor opened his hands, pleading. "My little brother was dying. And you knew all this."

Saul swallowed another gulp of beer. A thin amber stream trickled down his chin. His voice was a whisper. "You never understood, did you?"

"Understood what?"

"Your brother worshipped you," Saul said. "He idolized you. You were everything to him."

"But, Jesus Christ, couldn't you have—"

"No, I couldn't," Saul snapped. "We found out about a year before you left, but he was already too far gone. His system was shot. The leukemia was everywhere. We had a long talk and he made me promise I wouldn't tell you."

Taylor couldn't believe what he was hearing. "But there are treatments, drugs. We could have saved him."

Saul shook his head. "He had a rare form of AML, not curable. He was losing weight by the minute. I had to sponge him down each night to control his fevers. You just were never home to see it."

Saul's words slapped Taylor. He closed his eyes and inhaled sharply. His mind raced back to the days before he left for UCLA. He'd been so desperate to get out of that house. He'd shut out everything. Stayed away as much as possible. Had he really become so blind that he couldn't see his own brother dying?

"Why wouldn't he tell me?" Taylor pleaded. "I could've helped you. I could have been there."

"That's exactly why." Saul frowned. "He knew if he told you, you wouldn't go to college. You would stay and look after him. Which is exactly what you would've done. When your acceptance letter came, he saw it as his chance to end his suffering. He knew your future was secure."

Taylor turned and squeezed his eyes shut. Everything was turned upside down. Jacob had sacrificed himself for Taylor. The thought sucked the air from Taylor's lungs. He stared out the window into the overgrown backyard. The wind outside had died, leaving the air deathly still.

"All these years I thought he killed himself because I abandoned him. I thought that he couldn't stand the thought of being left alone with you."

"I know."

Taylor turned and faced his father. "I hated you for that! In my mind you as good as killed him."

Saul lowered his eyes. "I know."

Taylor's gaze softened. "You let me hate you all these years and you never said anything?"

Saul shrugged. "It was easier for you to deal with it this way."

Taylor said nothing. He stared into the old man's jaundiced eyes. The eyelids were wrinkled and hung down over his pupils like two sagging bags of grain. The whites had long ago turned pale yellow and glistened with water. He barely recognized the man.

"Why tell me now?"

"I'm dying," Saul said. "And I'm too old to keep secrets. The hate was eating you alive. I wanted to tell you earlier, at your brother's funeral, but you refused to talk to me. So, I waited until you could handle it." He paused. "You needed the truth to set you free."

The pit swelled in Taylor's chest, feeling like it would explode. He slammed his fist into a pile of beer cans, sending them scattering across the linoleum floor, their clattering echoing in the empty house.

"But you treated us so badly!" Taylor yelled. "You beat the shit out of us."

Saul's lips drew tight. "What I did was wrong. I know that. But in my own way, I was trying to do what was right for you."

"Beating us?"

"I never meant to hurt you. I just—I just didn't want you ending up like me," he slapped at his chest. "Tired and useless with no reason for living."

"What are you talking about?" Taylor furrowed his brow. "You were young. You had the whole world in front of you."

Saul shook his head. "When your mother died, I died with her. I didn't know how to go on. The sun didn't rise anymore."

"What about us?" Taylor thrust his thumb to his chest. "You were supposed to keep going for us. You were our father!"

"I wanted to." Saul looked up, pleading, his jaundiced eyes looking even more sunken. "Believe me, I did. I tried. But I didn't know how."

Taylor gave him a look. He thought of the old man, suffering the loss of his wife. Taylor had never really thought about how much pain his father must have felt when Anna died. How he didn't know how to go on.

"And now you're dying. You drank yourself to death."

Saul lowered his head. His lower lip trembled. "You don't know how much I loved your mother." His voice barely a whisper. "She was my breath of life."

The emptiness poured back into Taylor's chest. Moisture welled his eyes. "I always thought that you hated me," he whispered.

"I never hated you." Their eyes met, and held. "I just didn't know how to love you."

They stared at each other, deadlocked in silence. The wind ran through the oak in the back yard, its branches scratching against the windows like a phantom clawing to get in. Or get out.

Taylor studied the old man, and for an instant remembered the lively man he'd called father before his mother had died. He remembered tossing the football in the backyard, bedtime stories, and Halloween nights. He remembered him before the beer and the vodka and the beatings.

Suddenly, a knock pounded on the front door. Both men froze. Taylor whipped his gaze down the hallway. Through the door's beveled glass, he could make out the shaded form of a man.

Taylor's heart exploded in fear. He turned to his father. "I've got to go. Don't answer that until I leave."

"Are you in trouble?"

"Big trouble."

"How will you get out? What if they're watching the back?"

Taylor nodded. "They won't be watching the tunnel."

"The tunnel?"

"To the fallout shelter. Under our house, connecting to Dougherty's place."

Saul forced a smile. "You always did love exploring that, didn't you?"

Taylor nodded and for a moment he thought he saw the old familiar buoyancy in his father's eyes. He met his father's smile with one of his own.

Saul walked to the pantry, pushed aside a stack of empty beer cans and found a silver handle on the floor. Pulling it, a square floorboard popped loose amid a rush of stale air. A series of concrete steps was exposed leading down to the basement.

"There's no lights. How the hell you gonna see?"

"I've been through there enough. I'll manage."

The knocking intensified. Saul saw two figures at the door now. He turned towards Taylor. "Then go."

Taylor stepped to the cellar entrance. At the threshold, he turned and faced the old man. A thousand thoughts raced through his mind, but the words came slowly.

"I'll be back... father," he said.

Saul nodded and smiled through his jaundiced eyes.

"I know you will."

The knocking pounded on the front door.

Taylor ducked into the tunnel. Saul lowered the floor board, threw some empty beer cans on top then closed the pantry door. He swallowed a gulp of beer and grunted, staggering towards the front door.

The knocking pounded again.

"I'm coming, I'm coming. Hold your fucking horses," Saul muttered. "Jesus Christ, can't an old man have any peace in this world?"

CHAPTER 61

Sherilyn maneuvered her Honda through the crowded parking lot at Union Square Macy's Department Store. Pulling into a spot, she glanced into her rear-view mirror. The green Dodge Charger slowly cruised down the traffic lane and parked in a vacant spot behind her. It was the same Dodge that had followed her to the market and to the dry cleaners before that. She tried to catch a glimpse of the driver's face, but it was hidden behind a pair of mirrored sunglasses. Just a faceless shadow tracking her through town.

She cut off the engine and looked into her handbag, pulled out her compact, and freshened her make-up. It was time to play the game again. The same game she'd been playing all morning—driving around town pretending to take care of errands. She'd dropped off clothes at the cleaners even though they were freshly pressed. She'd picked up a gallon of milk even though an unopened gallon rested on the top shelf in the fridge. She did anything she could to convince her tail that this was just a normal day in the life of a small travel eMagazine publisher.

She'd formulated the plan shortly after receiving a call from Lawrence. He introduced himself as a member of Greenpeace and asked for support in saving the wild North American brown bear. At first, she was confused, but when he asked if she knew where the bears scratched the trees, she knew it was a message from Taylor. She offered her support. Lawrence gave her a number where he could be reached for future fund-raising. She assumed the FBI were tapping her phone or listening in on her cell, so she returned the call from the gas station on the corner.

The number Lawrence had given her matched a payphone at a pizza parlor in the Sunset. He told Sherilyn that he needed to get Malcomb to a meeting place with Taylor. Together, they discussed the situation. Sherilyn predicted there would only be one agent watching her; anything else would be a waste of manpower. If she could find a way to lose her tail, she'd be free to help.

Sherilyn closed her purse and glanced in the rear-view. The faceless cop sat in the car behind her, watching. It was time to see if the plan would work.

One more deception.

She opened the car door and stepped out, careful to leave the door unlocked. She left the key in the ignition. Diligently, she swept the wrinkles out of her skirt. She was wearing a grey business suit with a white button-down blouse. Something professional but not flashy. She threw her purse strap smartly over her shoulder, closed the car door and strode towards the main entrance, never looking back at the green Dodge.

When she'd been at the dry cleaners, the faceless one could see her through the window of his car, so he stayed behind the wheel, but at the supermarket, he tailed her inside, following her throughout the store.

She hoped that he wouldn't follow her into Macy's.

As she approached the large double glass door entrance, she could see the reflection of the parking lot in the glass. The faceless one was right behind her.

Time for plan B.

She entered in the men's wear department and scurried down the escalator to women's accessories and shoes. She turned left at the bottom and meandered to the back of the store to costume jewelry, where she eyed the bracelets and tried on a pair of earrings. She adjusted the tabletop mirror so she could see behind her. The faceless one had stopped by the purses, partially hidden behind the tall display rack.

She looked down at her watch. It was 10:45.

Five more minutes.

A friendly, terribly buck-toothed, saleswoman wandered over to Sherilyn and offered her assistance. Sherilyn smiled and told her about an upcoming night at the opera and how she didn't have any of the proper accessories and could she please help. The saleswoman's eyes lit up with the image of a big commission and she dashed to retrieve a tray of gold bracelets.

Sherilyn looked into the mirror again. The agent had strolled over to women's shoes and was holding a pair of black pumps, pretending to look for a price tag. He was about as subtle as a nuclear accident.

The buck-toothed saleswoman returned, carrying the velvet-lined tray of expensive bracelets. Sherilyn smiled and feigned excitement. She looked at her watch.

10:47. Three more minutes.

She tried on a gaudy gold and sapphire monstrosity and held it up to the light, pretending to admire it. She glanced to her right. Barely twenty feet away was the entrance to the restrooms. Next to that was the delivery exit to the loading dock.

10:48. Two more minutes.

She placed the bracelet back on the velvet and said that she couldn't make up her mind. It was so beautiful, but would it go with her black evening gown? She really had been thinking more of diamonds.

Dollar signs cha-chinged in the saleswoman's eyes. She dashed off to fetch a tray of diamond tennis bracelets. Sherilyn fidgeted with a silver necklace and looked up from the counter. Her heart was pounding.

Then she saw him. A large black man, wearing a University Security outfit, strutting towards her from the other side of the department. Without acknowledging her, he walked past women's accessories towards jewelry.

It was Lawrence. Sherilyn had never seen him before, but his self-description had been perfect, all the way down to the size of the belly roll overhanging his belt. Sherilyn watched him closely until she caught his eye, then she nodded towards women's shoes. Lawrence coolly walked by her towards the agent browsing in the shoe section.

Sherilyn gathered her purse and slid towards the end of the counter.

It was time.

The store was deathly quiet. It seemed as though time stood still.

"Hold it right there!" she heard Lawrence shout. She turned and saw him rush to the shoe section. The faceless one looked up from his black pump just in time to see the large security guard descending upon him.

"Hands against the wall, mister!" Lawrence yelled.

The faceless one's mouth dropped open in surprise. Words tangled in his throat. "What—?" he managed as Lawrence grabbed him and spun him towards the wall.

"I saw you pocket that watch back there, buddy" Lawrence said, twisting the agent's arm behind his back. "No one shoplifts when Big Daddy James is on shift."

"What are you talking about?" the agent protested.

"Shut up! I'll ask the questions. Did you think I wouldn't see you pocket the goods? You think I'm blind?"

Lawrence forced the man's arm higher behind his back. A small crowd gathered in the shoe department. The clerks eyed each other in bewilderment, wondering who in the hell the fat security guard was.

"Get your fucking hands off me," the agent yelled. "You're making a big mistake."

"You're the one who made a big mistake. Stealing on my shift? I just don't believe it."

"Goddamn it, unhand me. I'm FBI, you idiot."

"Yeah right, you're FBI and I'm Mother fucking Theresa. Keep your hands where I can see them."

"You moron," the faceless one screamed. He wriggled free of Lawrence's grasp, pulling out his Federal ID.

"I'm a FBI, damn it, I'm a FBI!"

He pushed himself away from Lawrence with one hand and swung around to face the jewelry counter. His eyes frantically scanned the store looking for Sherilyn.

She was gone.

The agent panicked and dashed to the walkway. He looked down the aisle then turned, searching the other way. He ran to the escalator then sprinted to the restrooms, kicking open the door to the Ladies room. She wasn't there.

She wasn't anywhere.

He whirled back towards women's shoes. The fat guard was gone also.

He'd been had.

*****

Sherilyn waited until Lawrence spun the agent towards the wall before she sprinted to the delivery entrance. She pulled open the door and jumped down the steps to the concrete holding area, then ran around the corner through the large garage doors.

Parked outside, just where he said it would be, was Lawrence's tan Ford Fairmont. She pulled open the driver's door and jumped into the seat. The keys were in the ignition.

376

She cranked over the engine and sped out the delivery driveway onto Powell Street.

She twisted and turned through town, weaving down one-way streets and alleys. Throughout it all, her eyes fixed on her rear view watching for the green Dodge.

A smile beamed across her lips when she thought of Lawrence, dressed in his best uniform, pretending to be a Macy's guard, arresting an FBI Agent in the middle of women's shoes. It must have been quite a scene. She definitely owed him a big favor if they ever got out of this mess.

She looked into the rear view one last time.

"It's okay now. We're safe," she said.

"Are you sure?" A voice came from the back seat.

Sherilyn smiled. "Come on, get up."

Malcomb pulled himself off the floor and propped himself onto the back seat.

"God, I hate this fugitive stuff."

CHAPTER 62

Being alone on the hill at Bear Tree, to Taylor, was like standing on top of the world. The Las Trampas hills fell away before him, dropping a thousand feet to the valley floor. The San Ramon Valley cut a path north to south across the base of Mt. Diablo, before vanishing into the horizon. The crown of Diablo, the largest mountain in the Bay Area, was obscured, buried behind the steel grey clouds that filled the eastern sky. A solitary turkey vulture soared through the clouds above.

Taylor pulled up the collar of his leather jacket, bracing against the coming storm. He exhaled into his cupped hands as he made his way to the base of Bear Tree where long ago, he'd mounted Jacob's memorial plaque.

He knelt in front of the plaque and ran his fingers across the raised bronze letters. Pulling Jacob's journal from his jacket, he placed it by the plaque. It seemed like the proper place to leave the journal. Returning it to its soul.

It was all so difficult for Taylor to understand. He'd never imagined his brother had been sick. That his father had kept such a painful secret so close to his heart.

The wind whipped across the hillside, scattering leaves from the massive oak. Taylor rose to his feet. The journal rested on its spine, its yellowed pages fluttering in the wind. He could almost see his brother's words being swept off the pages, carried away into the autumn sky. Floating free in the valley. Forever at peace.

He wiped his eyes and took a deep breath.

"Good-bye, Jacob," he whispered.

*****

At that moment, Edgar Ross maneuvered the grey plumbing van down Interstate 680, knifing the vehicle into the fast lane to pass a slow-moving truck. On his dash, the mounted windows-based GPS display beeped a steady holding pattern, a red circle impressed upon a digital map of the western hills of Danville.

The tracking system utilized British TACCS software, identifying the device he'd placed under the left front tirewell of Taylor's MG on day one of his Target Recce. After marking the beacon with an electronic warning fence, Ross knew that the MG had remained parked at the same location for the last eighteen hours; the top of Highland Drive. A quick run of the address through Google maps gave him the location.

The San Damiano Retreat.

The Police radio fed Ross a steady stream of updates on the manhunt for the fugitive. The hunt had narrowed to the town of Danville, but information was sketchy. There hadn't been a confirmed sighting. Currently, the FBI had no idea where the fugitive was.

But Ross did.

CHAPTER 63

Malcomb frowned.

"How do you expect me to do this?" He propped open his laptop and placed it on the table. "I've been trying to hack in for the last six hours and I've been blocked every step of the way. Unless you've magically figured out Chan's password, the system is closed to us. Do you hear me? It's closed."

Taylor shook his head, unwilling to accept Malcomb's answer, and gazed out the window. The sun was falling in the west, the autumn clouds bursting with orange. After a brief emotional reunion between Sherilyn and Taylor at Bear Tree, they got right down to work, setting up office in Starling's living room. Starling was in the kitchen, humming away as he and Sherilyn chopped up potatoes and carrots and threw them into a boiling pot with the enthusiasm of twin conductors leading a symphony. The giggles in the kitchen temporarily cut through the fear that hung like a pall over the cottage.

Taylor turned towards Malcomb, watching his lower eyelid twitch. He could almost see the images racing in Malcomb's mind.

"Is that all he said?" Malcomb referred to Chan's words scribbled in the ICU.

"We didn't have much time. Browne came in before he could finish."

"With a gun."

Taylor nodded.

Malcomb let out a huff. "Do your professors always carry guns?"

"Malcomb, let's get serious."

"Pardon me, if I ruminate on tiny details like murder," Malcomb shot back. He ripped open a Lindt dark chocolate bar. 78% pure cocoa this time. "Go over it again."

Taylor sat on Malcomb's left. "pazsword, with a 'z'. That's what he wrote."

"It doesn't make any sense. What the heck is a pazsword? Are you sure he wasn't writing 'password' and messed up? Groggy from morphine or something?"

"That's what I thought, but he wrote it twice. Deliberately. pazsword."

Malcomb typed at his computer. "I've finished foot-printing the CTS security posture, identifying their internet, intranet, remote access and extranet environments. They have significant intrusion-detection systems in place. Cisco Agent Watch. RealSecure Server Protection. eTrust Intrusion. These guys are good."

"Maybe what he wrote is his password. pazsword. Maybe switching the 's' for a 'z' is his trick. Try it."

"I've tried, it doesn't work. I've tried every permeation of the letters. Nothing works. I've run a copy of John the Ripper, a password-cracking tool. It didn't work."

"So, what are you doing now?" Taylor watched Malcomb typing at his computer.

"I'm trying a different tool to see if we can remotely guess a null password."

"A null password?"

"To get into the system we need Chan's username and his password. Most people tend to use the easiest password possible so they don't forget it. These are called null passwords because they really aren't a password at all. Something like password or administrator or CTS employee."

"Like my own password at the lab. Virtual."

"Exactly. It only took me two minutes to crack that one."

Taylor glared at Malcomb. "You did what?"

"Oh, don't look so shocked. I just wanted to see how easy you'd be. Turns out you were even easier than I expected."

"Glad I didn't disappoint."

Malcomb shrugged and began typing, letters flashing across the screen.

"Getting Chan's username was easy," he said. "At most companies, the usernames are a variation of the person's name and the company name, so it's easy to guess. Chan's is RChan@CTS."

"Great," Taylor brightened. "We're half way there."

"Not really. That's the easy part. Guessing the password is much harder. Sometimes you have to do it by brute force. Grind it out. This program I'm running is called SMBGrind. It sets up multiple grinding programs that run in parallel to see if it can turn up a null password. I'm writing it to check the entire CTS system. See if we can find any point of entry."

Taylor watched Malcomb type.

```
D:\>smbgrind -1 100 –I 192.168.2.7
Host address: 192.168.2.7
Cracking host 192.168.2.7 (*SMBSERVER)
Parallel Grinders: 100
Percentage complete: 0
```

"With this, I'm running 100 grinders, all working in parallel."

Taylor stared at the screen:

```
Percent complete: 25
```

"Do you think it'll work?" he asked.

Malcomb shrugged and tore the wrapper covering the last bite of chocolate. "It has to," he stuffed the chocolate in his mouth, his cheek pouching like a squirrel's. "Anything else will take far too long."

Percent complete: 50

Taylor frowned and shook his head. "The answer's in those files. The explanation to everything that's happened since the experiment started."

Malcomb pushed his glasses up his nose. "If this doesn't work, I may be able to find another way, but it'll take weeks. If I use a process called enumeration, I may find a point of vulnerability in older security software or some other point of entry."

Percent complete: 75

"We got hours, Malcomb. Not weeks!"

Percent complete: 99

"Then this better work," Malcomb said. "Here it comes."
Taylor's eyes shot to the screen, waiting for the results.

Failed: password: unknown
Percent complete: 100
Grinding complete, failed all accounts

"Blasphemy!" Malcomb whipped off his glasses. "Nothing."
Taylor grimaced. "We have to get in."

"What do you want me to do?" Malcomb threw his hands in the air. "We can't keep guessing. Every time I try, the system knows I'm there. It's only a matter of time before they trace the source back to my computer. This can lead them right to us!"

"Then let's don't guess," Taylor said evenly. "Let's take this one step at a time. Break down the word. What else could it mean; pazsword."

Malcomb shifted on the sofa. "It doesn't mean anything. Its root isn't Latin or Greek or even Arabic based. That's what I've been trying to tell you. It's not even a word!"

Taylor mulled over Malcomb's statement then his eyes grew wide. A flash of recognition shot through him.

"That's it! It isn't a word, not in English anyways."

"What are you saying?" Malcomb frowned.

Taylor pointed to the screen. "Look here. It's not one word, it's two."

"What? Where?"

"Here," Taylor pointed again, stabbing at the letter 'z.' "Break the word here."

Malcomb moved the cursor and inserted a space. pazsword suddenly changed into two words.

paz sword.

"Oh, great," Malcomb groaned. "That made it loads clearer."

"It did," Taylor countered, studying the screen. An idea formulated in his mind. "We assumed the password was in English. What if it's in a combination of languages?"

"I don't follow."

"Paz is Spanish. It means peace."

"Peace?"

Taylor nodded. "What if the password is peace sword?"

Malcomb scoffed. "What in God's name is a peace sword? And Chan is Chinese, why would write in Spanish?"

"Maybe he studied Spanish in high school. I don't know. Play with it. Try plugging it in as the password."

"I can't do that. I told you, if we keep guessing they'll know we're trying to break in. Another failed attempt could lead them right to us."

"But we've got to try."

"Not until we have our best guess. We've already run two programs. One more shot may be all we get."

Taylor bit his lip. He felt his breath accelerating. Taylor ran the letters and words through his mind, searching for a clue. What is a peace sword? Is it an anagram? An acronym? A word game?

Then it hit him. "Spanish uses word modifiers differently than English. paz sword wouldn't translate to peace sword; it would probably be Sword of Peace."

Malcomb squinted. "Sword of Peace? What does that mean? Is it a reference to the Middle Ages? King Arthur?"

"It's from Jesus," Sherilyn said, leaning in from the kitchen. She wiped her hands on a dish towel and sat next to Taylor.

"Jesus?" Malcomb looked up. "How'd you get Jesus from this?"

"It's from the Bible," Sherilyn said. "It's a passage, attributed to Jesus. 'Do not suppose I came to bring peace to the earth. I did not come to bring peace but a sword.' People often refer to that as the Sword of Peace or Jesus' Sword."

Taylor let out a low whistle. "Sounds like quite a warning. Chan must have used that as a message about Erickson."

"It would make sense based upon what you've been through," Sherilyn said.

Taylor nodded. "We must be on the right track."

"But how does it help?" Malcomb cried. "How does that give us the password?"

Taylor took a deep breath. "Maybe that is the password. Sword of Peace. Why don't you try it? Plug it in."

Malcomb hesitated, studying his screen. "With caps on or all lower case? Write it all one word or with underlines between the words? Dashes? The password is keystroke and cap sensitive. One mistake and we're done."

Taylor looked at Sherilyn, who returned a nervous glance. "We only get one more shot?" he asked.

"I'm sure their security has been alerted to us by now. They'll be running a log of failed logon attempts using Policies/ Audit. They may even have a Real-time Intruder Alert System. They'll trace our signal. One more shot. If we screw it up, we're blown."

Taylor rubbed his forehead. "Try all one word, no caps. Just do it."

Malcomb shot him an anxious glance. "Be prepared if this fails."

Host address: 192.168.2.7
Username:Rchan@CTS.com
Password: swordofpeace

He maneuvered his finger over the ENTER key, stopping to glance at Taylor one last time for confirmation.

"Are we sure?"

Taylor inhaled sharply and stared at the screen. swordofpeace. Why didn't it look right? Most passwords had letters and numbers. One more false step could alert their pursuers. But the answer was there, somewhere. The entire unraveling of his life.

swordofpeace.

He could feel his heart pounding. "Do it."

Malcomb took a deep breath. "Here goes."

Taylor watched Malcomb's finger descend towards the ENTER key.

swordofpeace.

"No, wait!" Taylor shouted.

Malcomb's finger froze in place. "What?"

Taylor turned to Sherilyn. "You said this phrase came from the Bible?"

Sherilyn nodded. "New Testament."

Taylor rubbed his chin. "If Chan's using this as a warning, he'd be more subtle." He faced Malcomb. "You checked Chan's background, didn't you?"

Malcomb nodded.

"Was he Christian?"

Malcomb thought for a moment. "I remember finding reference to The Chinese Christian Fellowship when he was an undergrad at Stanford."

"That must be it," Taylor said. He glanced at Sherilyn. "What passage of the Bible is this from?"

Sherilyn nodded knowingly. "Matthew 10:34."

"What?" Malcomb squinted. "How do you know?"

"You don't grow up a senator's daughter in the south without knowing your bible," Sherilyn said, raising an eyebrow. "I'm sure."

"Try it," Taylor said. "matthew1034. All lower case, no spaces. Write it just like that."

Malcomb bit his lip. "Are you certain?" he asked. "We've only got one chance."

Taylor nodded. "Do it."

Malcomb inhaled sharply and typed on his keyboard. Without looking up, he hit the ENTER key and waited. Beads of sweat bulleted his forehead. The seconds passed like hours.

"Well?" Taylor finally asked.

Malcomb looked up, a glint in his eye. "We're in."

CHAPTER 64

Edgar Ross turned off the headlights and let the Chrysler van drift to a stop in the parking lot behind the 1800's facade of the Danville Museum. The former Feed and Grain building, it now housed valley artifacts and exhibits, and on weekends the parking lot hosted the regional Farmer's Market. With the window cracked, Ross listened for the sounds of pedestrians: opening car doors, idle conversation, footsteps scuffing across the gravel driveway. Anything.

Once certain that he was alone, he grabbed his rifle case, slipped a woolen cap over his shaved scalp then pulled up the collar of his black turtleneck. He locked the van and slid silently into the night.

Inside the case, he carried a Heckler & Koch PSG-2 High Precision rifle, five shot, 308 caliber with a twenty-five inch barrel and a two-piece Kevlar stock. He'd equipped it with an ATN 4-12x80 day and night vision scope.

More than enough power to do the job.

Slinging his rifle case over his left shoulder, he headed towards Prospect Avenue and dashed off at a steady pace. After a quarter mile, he reached the fork where the road butted against the hillside. Sky Terrace Road shot up the steep hill to his right while Highland Drive meandered up the hill to his left. Without hesitating, Ross ran straight to the point of the fork, stepped off the paved road and began hiking up the grassy hillside.

Slipping on his PVS7 night vision goggles, he lost himself in the darkness of the scrub oak and California Bay trees; the world illuminated in glowing hues of yellow and green.

He glanced up the hillside. San Damiano rested 1500 feet away, up the densely wooded hills. Ross had studied the layout of the retreat from downloaded maps, memorizing the floor plans of each building. He'd identified all routes in and out of the compound, including all hiking trails and paths.

He'd already made his plan; he'd approach from below.

CHAPTER 65

After a hearty dinner of beef stew and potatoes, Taylor climbed into Starling's Rambler, started the ignition amidst a belch of black smoke, and headed towards town. He guided the Rambler down Diablo Road towards the Diablo Valley Bank, parking around the corner, out of sight of the security cameras. He wanted to keep the car he was driving a secret.

He walked to the ATM and stuck his card in the slot. With a sideways glance, he looked at the hidden camera, knowing that each second his face was being captured on black and white digital cameras.

He punched the PIN and the machine whirled. His accounts were open.

He withdrew three hundred dollars; enough for a hotel room and food if his plan failed. He pulled out his card and jumped back into the Rambler. He knew the FBI would trace the transaction, but there was no other choice. They'd need to have cash in case everything blew up in his face.

*****

By seven o'clock, the manhunt had contracted down to an eight square-mile area, extending as far east as Camino

Tassajara and west to the base of the Las Trampas Hills. All roads in and out of downtown were monitored.

Earlier, Ruiz and Hart had stopped at the Sycamore Inn, the only hotel in town, flashed their ID's and commandeered a room for their operations base. Hart unloaded his computers and set up the connection with the main system in San Francisco. Five minutes later he ran Taylor's bank number and discovered his ATM transaction on Diablo Road. He checked his map and smiled, realizing the bank was less than a mile away.

Ruiz, meanwhile, began canvassing the town with Johnson, a junior agent, marching door to door, flashing Taylor and Malcomb's university photos and a photo of Sherilyn. This portion of the search had to be handled delicately. The Senator's people had given the green light to release Abrahms' status to the media, but Ruiz knew involving the senator's daughter would be a nightmare. He referred to her only as a woman who may be in the company of the two fugitives, maybe a captive.

With their story straight, Ruiz and Johnson checked the Taco Bell, the supermarkets and the gas stations. An attendant at the ARCO remembered seeing Taylor's car, but didn't recognize the face. A clerk at Walgreens Pharmacy recognized Malcomb as a man who'd purchased nasal spray and some chocolate. Ray, at the corner Chevron, identified Sherilyn as the woman who gassed up about four hours ago. And yes, come to think of it, there was a skinny guy hanging out in the back seat.

Ruiz smiled. They were here. Somewhere in this freezing valley town, they were here.

CHAPTER 66

Malcomb fidgeted on Starling's couch.

A pile of empty chocolate wrappers, 85% pure cocoa, littered the floor at his feet. Black bags hung like sacks of potatoes under his eyes, his hair matted and clumped. Sherilyn had gone out for an evening walk around the monastery grounds, but Malcomb couldn't dream of joining her. He had too much to do.

"You doing okay?" Starling asked, noting Malcomb's haggard appearance.

Malcomb glanced up from his computer. "As well as can be expected, I guess."

Eyeing the mounting pile of wrappers, Starling squinted. "Hitting the candy a bit hard, aren't you?"

"You have your vice," Malcomb said, nodding towards Starling's flask of whiskey. "I have mine."

Starling chuckled and plopped into the easy chair across from the couch. "Are you all packed then? Taylor has you leaving at first light, yes?"

"That's right, Mr. Starling. Everything I own has been reduced to one fugitive sized carry-on handbag. I'm easily transportable."

Starling took a swig of whiskey. "You'll be fine."

"Oh yes, I'm sure Switzerland will be lovely this time of year."

Starling looked at him quizzically. "Switzerland?"

"I figure if I have to flee the country, Switzerland's where I'm supposed to hide, isn't it? Aren't they supposed to be neutral?"

"Aach, that was during the war," Starling scoffed. "I wouldn't hide in Switzerland. It's too cold."

"Where do you suggest I go?"

"Head to the Caribbean. Find a nice tropical island with a hammock and fruit drinks and half-naked island women with big bosoms to fan you."

Malcomb managed a smile. "Is this my hiding place or yours?"

Starling flashed his toothless grin. "I'm just looking out for you, son."

"I appreciate the thought. I'll be sure to send a postcard of the first scantily clad native I come across in the Swiss Alps."

They both smiled and rested in silence for a moment.

Finally, Malcomb spoke. "Taylor should be setting everything up right now."

Starling took another sip of whiskey. "He's really playing with fire this time, isn't he? I don't know too much about the trouble you've gotten yourselves into, lads, but can this plan of yours really work?"

Malcomb positioned the laptop on the coffee table and typed. The screen fired to life.

THE VIRTUAL HEART PROJECT
BY
MALCOMB BERNARD

Malcomb's eyebrows furrowed and then his fingers danced across the keyboard. He stopped and looked at Starling.

"I'm dead tired, Mr. Starling. I haven't slept in days and I've never been more afraid in my life." Malcomb paused. "But I believe in Taylor and I believe this will work."

Starling pointed at the laptop. "And what are you doing there with that thing?"

"First I need to break into the cellular phone switch and scramble our number."

"Why's that?"

"They'll be looking for us on cellular. They'll do what's called a trap and trace. But if I can monkey around in the cellular network, I can disguise our call. Make it look like a regular land line and not the cellular."

"A little bait and switch for the trap and trace."

Malcomb grinned. "You got it. Then I need to work on the program. Now that I've cracked Chan's files, it won't be hard to track down the rootkit/virus and delete it. From there, all I need to do is restore the original stimulation pattern to electrode 16 and test the system responsiveness. By restimulating Taylor's amygdala with the proper amps, we should be able to cancel the hallucination feedback loop. Effectively rewiring his cortex."

"Is that all then?"

"That's all. Other than praying that this thing doesn't blow Taylor's brain apart the next time he enters."

Starling took a long swig of whiskey and wiped his mouth with the back of his hand. "Sounds crazy to me. I sure hope you know what you're doing."

"So do I." Malcomb looked up at the old man. He reached out his hand. "Can I have a sip of that?"

"You want some whiskey?" Starling looked surprised.

"Let's say my vice isn't strong enough right now."

Starling belted out a hearty laugh and handed the flask to Malcomb.

Malcomb swallowed a large gulp, shaking his head as the alcohol burned its way down his throat.

*****

Neither man saw the darkened figure peering through the curtains.

Silently, the figure slipped back into the shadows towards the oak trees.

CHAPTER 67

Taylor stopped at the local Walgreens and picked up a pre-paid Tracfone loaded with 300 minutes of airtime, then headed to the Danville Public Library. It was risky going to such a public place now that his face was pasted across the evening news, but he needed to contact Helen and enter Malcomb's University email account, and there was no way he could chance his signal being traced back to Starling's address.

Inside the library, Taylor created a new Gmail address, then sent an email to Helen, outlining the plan and giving his Tracfone number for future contact. He looked at his watch. It was eight PM. The Senator's speech was scheduled for tomorrow morning, just over twelve hours from now. Everything he'd learned in the files told him that speech would be his last chance to fight back, clear his name, and reclaim his life. That left a lot to coordinate in a short period of time.

Would his sanity hold long enough? Taylor had no idea.

But he had to try.

Just keep it together a little while longer.

He left the library and stepped into the metal and plexiglass, 1970's payphone, checked over his shoulder, then dropped in a couple of quarters. The line was still working. He dialed the number for the San Francisco Federal Building.

The phone rang five times before Agent Jenkins, answered, his voice gruff and hurried.

"What?" He yelled into the receiver.

Taylor swallowed, fighting against his nerves. "Get me the Special Agent in charge of the Abrahms investigation."

"Ruiz's busy right now."

"I think he'll speak to me."

"You think he'll speak to—? Listen, we're right in the middle of a—"

"I'm Taylor Abrahms."

The phone fell silent. Taylor could almost hear the agent's heart racing.

"I'll patch you through."

Taylor stared through the Plexiglas payphone window. Evening traffic was tapering off, the rush hour slowing to a trickle. Every so often the flash of passing headlights caught Taylor's eyes. He felt exposed behind the thin sheet of plastic, vulnerable, like a deer on a highway. He slumped behind the phone casing, trying to keep his face hidden.

There was clicking as the telephone connection relayed from station to station until it finally reached Ruiz. Twice along the way, Taylor thought the connection had been severed but the muted ringing reassured him. He checked his watch and took a deep breath.

"This is Ruiz," a gravelly voice answered.

"I've got what you need," Taylor said.

"Who is this?"

"This is Taylor Abrahms."

Silence again. Taylor could tell that Ruiz had covered the receiver with his hands and was giving orders to his men.

"Don't bother tracing this. I'll be long gone before you get here."

"Calm down, buddy. No one is trying to trace you."

Taylor checked his watch. The transfer had taken fifteen seconds. He would only stay on for another forty-five seconds. Keep the conversation under one minute. Taylor knew that with current technology in caller ID and computerized telephone networks, phone calls could be traced instantaneously, all they needed was a connection to be made. But even if they did find the phone, he'd hightail it before they could find him. He gazed over his right shoulder; the onramp to Interstate 680 just around the corner. He'd be dead gone in seconds. Just keep the call short, so he could escape before they got there.

"I know who's behind Crawford's murder."

"You got my attention. Talk to me."

"I want to make a deal."

"No deals."

"Gotta go, bye."

"Wait, wait! Don't hang up. What do you want?"

"I want this game to end," Taylor said.

"Then turn yourself in."

"Only if you do what I say. I want you to clear our names. I want my life back I'm not a killer, I'm a doctor."

Taylor heard Ruiz chuckle. "With the shit you're in? I don't think so. A credible threat against the Senator. Murder and another attempt."

Ruiz's words made Taylor pause. "Attempt? That means that Chan lived?"

"So far."

That was the opening Taylor was hoping for. "Listen, if you've done your research, you'll know I had nothing to do with Crawford's death and I was there to help Chan, not kill him. Take a statement from him, he'll tell you. Norman Browne is the one responsible. Bring him up on charges."

"That's not possible."

"Listen to me, I'm telling you Browne did it. This is all part of a much bigger —"

"I'm not saying I don't believe you," Ruiz cut in. "I'm saying he can't be brought up on charges. He's dead. Blew the back of his head off with a .45."

Taylor froze. He sagged against the payphone window.

Finally, Taylor exhaled. "Dr Browne's dead? Suicide?"

"You're the number one suspect."

"What? That's crazy. I never—"

"There are ten witnesses who saw you two fighting in the ICU, including an intern with a couple of broken ribs."

Taylor's head began to swoon. When was this nightmare going to end.

"Listen to me, Ruiz." Taylor kept his voice steady. "I had nothing to do with Crawford's death or the attempt on Chan. I didn't kill Browne and I certainly didn't threaten the Senator. What's going on is much bigger than me. Talk to Chan. You'll get the truth."

"You're in no position to be giving orders."

"That's exactly the position I'm in. You keep chasing me, you're going to miss the biggest headline bust of your career."

There was silence before Ruiz answered. "Chan's back in a coma. We can't talk to him until he wakes, if he does. You've got no room to run, Abrahms. We know you're in Danville. We have units everywhere. Turn yourself in. If what you have is that good, I'll see what I can do to help you."

"Not good enough," Taylor said. "Call off your manhunt. Leave us alone. The Senator's Press Conference at NASA-Ames/ Google is tomorrow morning. Everything will be revealed there."

Ruiz coughed into the phone. "Why should I trust you?"

"Do you think I want you on my ass for the rest of my life? You'll get your evidence. I've posted a sample on the SFU Bulletin Board. Check under Malcomb's account. That should convince you I'm serious."

Taylor checked his watch.

"Google/NASA-Ames. Tomorrow."

*****

From his vantage point in the second branch of the 100-year-old oak, high above the San Damiano Retreat, Edgar Ross watched the red and white AMC Rambler pull to a stop in the monastery parking lot; the engine cut off, the headlights went dark, then the creak of the parking brake being applied. Ross brought his Heckler & Koch into firing position. Through the telescopic sight, he could see Taylor's face as he exited the car, clearly illuminated in night vision.

Ross estimated the distance to be 300 yards. He followed his target, tracking him as he walked through the parking lot towards the monastery courtyard. He fixed the crosshairs on Taylor's right temple, before losing him behind another parked car.

Taylor's advance towards the gate was at a steady, predictable pace. Ross estimated it to be two miles per hour. At that rate, he'd emerge from the cover of the parked cars in seven seconds.

CHAPTER 68

"Senator McIntyre! Senator McIntyre!"

Randolph McIntyre, dressed in a grey Versace suit, white Ralph Lauren shirt and red tie, marched with his entourage passed the mass of reporters that lined the tarmac at Ronald Regan National Airport, en route to his private jet. Jennifer and Roderick dashed up the stairs to the plane, while Secret Service agents flanked either side of the converted Boeing 737 MAX 8. Wheels up for San Francisco was scheduled for 11:30 pm. The roar of jet engines rumbled across the runway. A row of Washington D.C. Metropolitan P.D. vehicles, their red lights flashing, barricaded the plane from the clamoring press.

The Senator's salt-and-pepper hair, slicked back from his forehead, gave his face a sculpted look of determination. He wrapped the cashmere scarf around his neck, protecting him from the chill of the autumn night. When he reached the boarding steps, he stopped and faced the press. The barrage of questions hit him immediately.

"What does this mean for the future of your campaign?"

"—when did you first learn of the assassination attempt?"

"—reports are that your own son-in-law is involved, could you comment?"

"—talked to your daughter yet?"

McIntyre took two steps up the airstairs to elevate his position, making certain the police cars were not between him and the press cameras. He held out his hands like Souza leading a symphony. He flashed his friendliest smile and the flashbulbs popped like fireworks in July.

"I have time for just a few questions."

The commotion rose again, the reporters jostling to be heard. A bald man with a protruding belly emerged from the throng and stepped forward.

"Howard Michael, LA Times," he said. "The legal analysts at CNN are calling this the biggest political scandal of the decade. How do you see it?"

Senator McIntyre raised his hands again to calm the crowd. His chest puffed out and his shoulders squared, adopting what McIntyre referred to as his battle position. It was a carefully chosen posture, like the grin, designed to photograph impressively. Untold hours had been spent in front of a three-mirror dressing stand perfecting this pose. He had watched himself from every angle, analyzing the curve of his back, the sweep of his shoulders, the fall of his coat, his ¾ profile, until he had it perfect.

He started talking, his speech slow and direct, so each word could be transcribed with complete accuracy. Each sound bite clear and distinct. His eyes burned like fire.

"CNN is correct. When has there ever been evidence that suggested an assassination attempt on a presidential candidate by a member of his own family?" McIntyre paused then grinned. "The presidential forerunner, I might add."

"Senator? Senator?" the crowd began again.

"Have you spoken with him? With your son-in-law?"

McIntyre adopted a facial expression of grave concern. "Of course not. I rarely communicate with Dr. Abrahms. I've questioned the young man's ethics since the day of my daughter's wedding. And now I understand that my daughter has gone missing. I can't reach her. I have no knowledge of her whereabouts or safety. I can only pray that maniac hasn't harmed her."

"Senator McIntyre? Senator McIntyre?"

A young Japanese reporter stepped forward. "Can you please elaborate on your theory for why he's trying to kill you?"

"I think his motivation is clear. We're in a crisis. Health care spending is out of control. Over the next decade, one out of every five dollars spent in the United States will go to medical costs. One out of every five dollars! This will bankrupt the nation. Research like my son-in-law's is the first thing we need to cut. He knows this and knows that I am strong enough to do this. Does it surprise you he's threatened to kill me?"

A voice from the back. "So, you think he's acting like a threatened animal, striking out at his attacker?"

McIntyre smiled. "That's exactly what I think. He's frightened prey in my sights. His death threat is a testament to the strength of my campaign."

"Senator McIntyre? Senator McIntyre?"

The Senator held out his hands. "You'll have to excuse me. I'd love to stay, but I have a speech to make in San Francisco and my plane is waiting."

"You're going to push on with the speech?" a voice called out. "Despite the assassination attempt?"

McIntyre squared his chin, ready to deliver his carefully practiced reply. "It will take more than death threats to stop me from bringing my message to the American people."

Sound bite captured.

"Now if you'll excuse me." The Senator turned, climbing the rest of the steps to the private jet.

"Nicely done," Roderick said, handing the Senator a scotch when he boarded. "We should be able to play off this momentum all the way to Election Day."

McIntyre stiffened, his smile quickly fading. "Just get me to San Francisco."

CHAPTER 69

Pushing open the gate to the inner courtyard at San Damiano, Taylor spotted Sherilyn sitting on the stone bench in front of the Spanish fountain, bundled in a red parka and scarf, sipping a cup of tea. The sound of water trickled down the three terra cotta tiers of the fountain. A thousand stars shone overhead, crisp and dazzlingly in the October sky. Starling, sitting beside her, bundled in an ancient wool coat, had dispensed with the formalities of spiking his tea and was drinking the whiskey straight from the bottle.

Taylor headed down the path. With nightfall, the temperature had plummeted, Taylor's breath emerging in frosty plumes. He blew into his hands for warmth.

Walking briskly down the flagstone, Taylor passed the rose gardens then suddenly stopped. An unsettling feeling tickled the base of his neck. It was the same feeling he'd had before, many days ago in the ICU when he saw the security camera panning with his movements. He felt it just before he saw the dead image of his mother lumbering up the stairs towards him. It was in the eyes of the portraits. A warning, a lingering sense that someone was watching him.

Taylor knew that his grip on sanity was loose. The last thing he could afford was another breakdown, but he couldn't shake his unease. His eyes darted to the darkened oak trees towering above the monastery walls, scanning the black branches that reached into the sky like clawing fingers. He thought he'd heard something moving in the branches. But everything seemed calm. A frigid breeze ran through the tops of the trees. A scatter of leaves fell upon his path.

Starling saw him, called his name and waved him on. Taylor pulled his eyes from the trees, and headed down the path towards the fountain.

Starling greeted him, rising to his feet, and handed Taylor the bottle. "You look like you could be using a nip of this." He nodded his head towards where Taylor had been standing. "What was it? Did you see a ghost back there?"

Taylor gladly took the bottle. He downed a large swig, grimacing as the whiskey burned down his throat.

"Just my imagination." Taylor wiped his mouth. "How've you two been?"

"We've been great," Starling answered, retrieving the bottle from Taylor's hand. "Your wife's grown quite fond of me. She's been putting the moves on me all evening."

"Oh, really?" Taylor allowed a smile, feeling his tension ease a bit. He cast a glance towards Sherilyn who returned his smile.

"Certainly," Starling nodded. "Just because there's snow on the roof doesn't mean there's no fire in the oven."

Taylor sat on the bench and wrapped his arm around Sherilyn's waist. "Then I suggest you get your oven under control, old man. I wouldn't want you to hurt anything."

"Ach," Starling grunted. "Don't you fear. My body is made for loving. I'm a love machine."

*****

Edgar Ross held the rifle steady, watching the old man through the night vision scope, the aiming laser centered on the back of the old man's skull. He played with the idea of pulling the trigger just to watch the old man's head explode. But he didn't. Instead, he watched the caretaker rise from the bench and retreat down the path towards his cottage. Once inside, Ross swung the rifle back to the inner courtyard. His vision through the night scope flared in shades of green. He centered the aiming reticule in the middle of Taylor's forehead, the red laser aiming beam glowing like a tattoo on Taylor's skin.

From his vantage point in the tree, forty feet above the eastern corner of the courtyard, Ross was close enough to hear the water trickling through the fountain in front of Taylor's bench. Regrettably, the fountain provided a partial obstacle to Ross' line of sight, but the flow of water shooting from the top was steady and predictable. He didn't believe it would hamper his accuracy. Ross estimated the distance to be 200 yards. Not a difficult shot. He lowered the rifle, adjusted the scope's minute of angle and windage, compensating for the oncoming storm blowing in from the west, then returned the scope to his eye. Ross' finger rested against the trigger, maintaining a gentle pressure. Years of training took over and he began to suppress his breathing, calming his heart rate.

*****

Sherilyn watched Starling walk away. "He's quite a character."

"The best," Taylor agreed. "I'd forgotten how much I missed the old man."

Sherilyn stared into the fountain. Droplets of water splashed at her feet. She bundled herself in her parka, bracing against the cold. "Can you do this?" she asked, her face growing dark. "Can you really get out of this?"

The fear in Sherilyn's voice was palpable. Taylor felt it too.

"I've contacted Helen," Taylor said. "She's preparing the Farm. Malcomb should have the program ready." He took a deep breath. "If my brain can hold together, I think we can pull this off."

"Tomorrow? At the news conference?"

"That's the plan."

Sherilyn rubbed her hands for warmth. She glanced towards the darkened oak trees rising over the eastern courtyard. "I saw your picture on the news today," she said. "The Chronicle said this is the biggest manhunt in the Bay Area since the Zodiac Killer."

Taylor covered her hand with his. "I'm sorry to drag you through this with me."

Sherilyn bit her lower lip and forced a smile. "I think I'm beginning to understand."

"About earlier—" Taylor started.

Sherilyn interrupted him, placing her finger across his lips. "Not now. Someday we're going to talk about everything. All that we've been through. But not now. Right now, just stay with me."

Taylor nodded and looked at his wife. He recognized something in her that he hadn't seen before; an unwavering inner strength. Throughout this entire ordeal, she had stood strong, her love fueling him, nourishing him like water to an orchard. He inched closer and wrapped his arm around her shoulders. Her body heat penetrated through his clothing. He'd never had that before. A place of safety.

He glanced at his watch. "I have a treat for you." Taylor said, hoping to lighten the mood. He looked at his watch, then glanced towards the fountain. "Every night at this time, the lights come on."

As if on cue, the colored spotlights surrounding the fountain flashed on; brilliant red and green shooting through the trickling water, immersing the courtyard in a wavering spectacle of light. Rainbows danced through the prisms of water droplets, bouncing off the monastery walls.

Sherilyn covered her mouth. "It's so beautiful—"she started to say, but was cut off by the rifle blast that shattered the night.

CHAPTER 70

Edgar Ross winced.

Blinding light, white and red and green, poured through his night vision scope. Abrahms had been lined-up dead center in the aiming reticule when the fountain lights flashed on. The glare from the spotlights rushed through the scope, every photon magnified and intensified by the night vision amplifier, instantly bleaching his retinas, searing his eyes with pain.

Now, all he could see were bluish spots, his vision lost in the blazing afterimage of the fountain. Tears streamed down his face. He'd managed to fire one round just as the lights came on, but had no idea if his shot had found its mark. With the quiet of the courtyard shattered by his rifle blast, any chance of a second shot would be that much more difficult.

Damn it, did I hit the fucker?

Flicking off the night vision, he brought the telescopic sight back to his eye. He blinked to clear the afterimage still blurring his vision. He heard a rustling to his left. Lowering the rifle, he looked down to see the old groundskeeper rushing out of his cottage running towards him, carrying what looked like a 1929 Winchester M12 shotgun.

Ross frowned. He was in no mood to deal with an old drunk and his pre-WWII rifle and had no time to fuck with any more distractions. He swung his H&K around, bringing the scope eye level, the red laser aimed at Starling's chest, just above the fifth rib, 3 inches to the left of the sternum. Directly over the heart.

"I usually get paid for this," Ross said under his breath. His finger tightened on the trigger. "But for you, old fuck, I'm going to do it for free."

*****

"Oh God, no!" Taylor heard Sherilyn scream.

Pain seared through his shoulder where the assassin's bullet had torn his flesh, but Taylor realized his wound wasn't the cause of Sherilyn's cries. With him lying on top of her, covering her behind the concrete bench, there was no way for her to know he'd been shot.

As soon as the blast had erupted, Taylor had acted instinctively. Grabbing Sherilyn, he'd pulled her behind him even as the marksman's bullet had just ripped through the flesh of his left deltoid. He'd twisted Sherilyn around, covering her with his body then fell to the slate tiles behind the concrete bench.

Now, a warm fluid ran down Taylor's arm followed by searing pain. He clenched his teeth and followed Sherilyn's gaze out the courtyard gate. Instantly, he could see why she'd screamed.

From their vantage point, Taylor could see Starling, brandishing an old shotgun, racing towards the tree where the rifle shot had come.

"He'll get himself killed!" Sherilyn said.

Taylor knew she was right. Whoever had shot at them was probably the same killer who'd murdered Crawford and Browne. Probably the one who'd shot Robert Chan as well.

The one who started this entire mire of death.

Taylor winced, fighting the pain. Blood streamed down his arm, staining his sleeve in a growing darkness, before dripping from his fingertips onto the courtyard tile. His arm felt heavy, he could barely lift it, but he didn't have time to worry about the extent of his wound. Watching Starling rushing towards the tree, Taylor knew he couldn't allow the old man to be killed because of his mistakes.

Jumping to his feet, Taylor sprinted towards the courtyard gate. Starling had stopped about ten yards ahead, pulling the ancient shotgun into firing position. Taylor could hear the *chick chick* of the pump action cocking a shell into the barrel. Out of the corner of his eye, Taylor could make out a faint silhouette in the upper reaches of the oak, high above the eastern corner of the courtyard; a darkened mass against the starlit sky. He saw a brief flash of moonlight against metal.

Taylor sprinted as fast as his legs would carry him. His arm was dead meat, hanging limply at his side as he crashed through the courtyard gate. His breath came in sucking gasps, his heart hammering against his ribs. Starling steadied the old shotgun against his shoulder to fire. Taylor's eyes widened when he saw the assassin's red laser tattooed against the caretaker's chest.

With a final burst of strength, Taylor launched himself through the air, flinging his body towards the old man. He hit Starling in mid-dive just as the second burst from the assassin's rifle boomed across the hillside. The breeze of the bullet whizzing just inches passed Taylor's ear, its high-pitched whistle buzzing as it smashed into the earth in a cloud of dust.

Taylor and Starling hit the ground hard, both men rolling. Taylor twisted to absorb the impact, the earth leaping up to meet his ribs with Starling on top of him. The breath shot out of Taylor's lungs, then the snapping of a rib. Stabbing pain shot across his chest.

Taylor had no time to consider the pain. He knew that the assassin would be aiming to fire again, another bullet already in the chamber, the rifle's sight tracing them while they rolled across the ground. The two of them out in the open, totally exposed. Taylor's only hope was to strike before the assassin fired the next deadly shot.

Continuing his roll, Taylor spun on top of the old man, momentarily protecting him from the rifle's line of sight. With one swift movement, Taylor grabbed the ancient shotgun from Starling's grip and continued his roll.

Hitting the ground again, Taylor sprung to his feet. He aimed the shotgun in the direction of the rifle blast and pulled the trigger, pumping as much buckshot as he could into the upper branches. He'd never fired a shotgun before. The recoil was stronger than he expected, the gun nearly jumping out of his hands. But at that instant, it all came together, pumping the slide-action to load another shell, steadying the barrel, squeezing the trigger as fast as his finger muscles could respond.

The weight of the gun was power in his hands. Taylor exploded in fury. He'd had enough of being a target, manipulated and conned by those he trusted. He'd had enough of being helpless, slack-jawed, watching his life disintegrate before his eyes.

But not anymore.

"No more!" he screamed.

Four shotgun blasts ripped through the night, the branches of the oak tree exploding in a hail of wood chips and shredded leaves. A shriek came from the branches, followed by a darkened silhouette falling to the earth. It landed with an audible thud then was lost as it rolled down the wooded hillside.

But Taylor didn't stop. He continued to pump the shotgun and pull the trigger long after the loading tube was empty. He squeezed off empty rounds for a full ten seconds, screaming "No more!" at the tree over and over, before he finally felt Starling's hand upon his own.

"That's enough, my boy," Starling said. "I think you got whatever was out there."

Sweat coated Taylor's forehead. His breath came in gasps, his whole body shaking. Starling pressed down on the shotgun barrel, aiming it towards the ground. Finally, Taylor lowered his head. His hands still locked on the shotgun, his fingertips white with pressure.

"Looks like I kinda lost it," Taylor whispered.

Starling looked at the tattered remains of the oak tree, a hail of shredded leaves still falling to the earth. "I don't know," he surmised, "the trunk is still standing. Do you want to reload?"

*****

Sherilyn joined them, running from the courtyard to Taylor's side. Malcomb burst from the cottage, looking towards the darkened hillside. "Is he dead?"

Taylor shook his head. "I don't know, but we're not sticking around to find out."

He turned towards his wife. "Baby, take Lawrence's car. Grab Starling and get out of here."

He reached into his pocket and pulled out his wallet, extracting the cash he'd taken from the ATM. "Check into a hotel in Walnut Creek. Use Starling's name and ID; they'll be looking for you but they won't be tracking him. No credit cards, only cash."

Sherilyn took the cash. "What about you?"

Taylor looked towards Malcomb. "Grab some blankets and the computers. Load them in the Rambler."

Malcomb looked panicked. "Where are we going?"

"I don't know. We'll leave my car here; they'll be looking for it. Hurry, we've got to move before someone else arrives."

"Are you sure you're in any condition to be doing all that?" Starling asked, taking in Taylor's left shoulder.

Sherilyn's eyes grew wide. "You've been shot!"

Through the excitement, Taylor had forgotten the grazing shot that had torn through his shoulder. With the adrenaline pumping, he'd been immune to the pain. Now, with his heart calming down, a burning sensation crept across his left deltoid. He could feel the warm blood dripping down his arm. His broken rib began to ache.

Taylor tore his sleeve open, inspecting the wound. It was superficial, more a cut than a bullet wound. The round had grazed the meaty portion of his deltoid, tearing the flesh, but had missed bone. He'd need sutures, but it wasn't life threatening.

"I'll be fine. I'll sew it up later."

Sherilyn squinted. "You need to go to the Emergency Room!"

"All gunshot wounds are reported," Taylor said. "We'd never get out of there." He faced his wife. "Don't worry. I have my med kit in my car. I'll be fine. Now go."

Sherilyn nodded, but the fear remained in her eyes. Taylor could see she didn't want to leave him, but he also recognized the glint of understanding as she realized they had no choice. They'd just been hunted by a killer. More could follow. Not to mention the FBI. For them to get out of this alive, they had to leave now.

She and Starling ran towards Lawrence's Fairmont. She stopped at the driver's door. Moonlight glistened off her moistened cheeks.

"When will I see you again?" she asked.

Taylor exhaled. "Watch the news coverage of your father's speech. One way or another, this all ends tomorrow."

CHAPTER 71

Friday, Oct 20th, 7:55 a.m.

Sunlight knifed through the clouds over Moffett Federal Air Field, shimmering off the fuselage of the custom 737 MAX 8 parked alongside the main hangar.

A Marine honor guard flanked the red-carpeted path leading from the plane to the stage, providing all the pomp and circumstance a presidential front-runner deserved. With the alleged threat, security was maintained at code red status; six teams of Secret Service fanned out across the runway, while additional agents wandered amongst the throng of reporters and attendees, their blue Executive Protection Division lapel pins reflecting the sunlight, their eyes canvassing the crowd behind mirrored sunglasses.

Senator McIntyre squinted in the sun. He marched down the staircase to the tarmac, smiling and waving to the reporters, then ambled passed the marine flag-bearer. The Stars and Stripes whipped behind him in the Bay breeze.

Now there's a photo for the cover of TIME Magazine, McIntyre thought.

Security measures dictated that the stage be moved from the planned auditorium to an outdoor setting, nestled at the far end of the runway. Surrounded by open tarmac, all sniper vantage points were removed from the equation, all hiding places eliminated. McIntyre smiled when he saw the freshly-constructed stage, surrounded by dark blue risers, each draped with the American flag. Flanking the podium were two massive High-def OLED screens, connected to the computerized audio/visual center, programmed to project graphs, charts and photos of the American people in sequence with McIntyre's speech. Behind the stage, the sun sparkled off the waters of the San Francisco Bay; pinpoints of daylight reflecting like a million diamonds.

Taking in his surroundings, McIntyre felt his power growing. He'd learned his lesson from the Reagan presidency; even a B-rated movie actor would photograph impressively against that backdrop.

And the White House awaited.

*****

Taylor paced in circles around the hay bales that littered the abandoned barn. Located about thirty yards off the rarely driven rural end of Norris Canyon Road, it had been a perfect place to hide. Wrinkling his nose, he exhaled, expelling the overwhelming aroma of mildewed hay. The crumpled heap of blankets and pillows they'd gathered from Starling's cottage stretched across the corner of the barn where they'd spent the night, perched against a stale 50-pound bag of feed. Now, as the sun rose, a dim light filtered through the cracks in the worm-eaten wood.

"What's taking so long?" Taylor asked.

Malcomb was perched on a wooden plank before the bale of hay that served as a desk for his computer. In his hands, he fumbled with a Hormel Chili can, an N-type female connector, and some wire.

Slowly, Malcomb nodded his head. "Almost there."

Taylor pulled the virtual suit from his duffel bag. His eyes darted around the abandoned barn, searching through the holes in the faded planks for signs of movement from outside. He flashed a glance at his watch. 8:10 AM.

McIntyre's news conference was due to start in twenty minutes. Taylor bit his lip and shot a gaze towards Malcomb. This was taking too long. The FBI had been stepping up the hunt; news reports blared across the AM radio morning talk shows. The MG had been found in the retreat parking lot by police investigating the sounds of gunshots. Taylor's call, apparently, had only served to rile Ruiz.

"Come on, Malcomb."

"I'm hurrying."

Taylor tugged the SIS suit over his legs then grabbed the neural transcendence helmet. A flood of memories rushed through his mind. How long had it been since he'd first donned that helmet? Taylor thought back to Grand Rounds when this all began, only a week ago, but seemingly a lifetime.

He looked at Malcomb. As always, Malcomb's hair stood up like a bad modern sculpture and the signature pile of chocolate wrappers grew at his feet. Taylor noted that Malcomb was up to 90% pure cocoa now. Raw cacao pods would indeed be next.

For a moment, Taylor allowed himself a smile. After all he'd been through, he never would have made it without Malcomb. Despite his whining and whimpering, Malcomb was as good a friend as Taylor had. When his entire world began to collapse, Taylor was amazed at the strength Malcomb found to work towards a solution. While Taylor watched him at his computer, he couldn't help but notice that Malcomb somehow looked different. Sat a bit taller. More confident.

"Are you sure you can do this?" Taylor asked.

"Absolutely. Any computer geek worth his weight knows that a tin can makes for the best long-range Wi-Fi directional antenna you can buy."

Taylor watched Malcomb inspect the can. One end of the Hormel can had been opened, the chili eaten cold for breakfast, then the can thoroughly cleaned. The label had been removed, leaving the shimmering metal exposed.

"What are you doing now?" Taylor asked.

"Since you've managed to select a hideout halfway between nowhere and oblivion, I need to boost my computer's antenna to find a WiFi network we can hack into." Malcomb held up the can. "This baby is our answer."

"It's a can of chili."

"In your eyes. In mine, it's a miracle of modern technology."

Malcomb turned the can over. "The performance of the antenna is dependent upon the diameter of the can and the frequency we're trying to capture." Malcomb pointed to a hole he'd punched through the side, one-and-one-half inches from the open end of the can. "If my calculations are correct, this will work perfectly."

Malcomb guided copper wire through the N-connector, screwed the connector into the hole then connected the assembly to his laptop with a connector cable. He positioned the antenna on the bale of hay next to him.

"Got it!" Malcomb pumped his fist. He turned to face Taylor. "We're in."

Taylor nodded, impressed. Now the real challenge would begin. His plan depended on precise timing and coordination between him, Malcomb and Helen. It also depended upon his brain keeping the hallucinations at bay until they finished. That may be the biggest variable of all. He picked up the Tracfone, dialed Helen's number and prayed this would work.

Helen answered. "It's about time you called." Her voice was rushed, panicked.

Taylor looked at his watch. "I told you I'd call just after eight."

"We've got a major problem here."

Taylor's eyes flashed towards Malcomb, a sinking feeling boring into his gut.

CHAPTER 72

"Do we have them? Answer me, do we have them?"

Ruiz slammed his Styrofoam coffee cup against the table in room 214 on the second floor of the Danville Sycamore Inn. The dark liquid burst from the styrofoam, splashing against the already stained carpet. Ruiz stared at the now empty cup then threw it against the wall. He swore under his breath.

Hart tapped at his keyboard, trying not to let Ruiz's impatience rile him. He'd followed his trace on Helen Yang's phone through the University phone system. Schematics of the relay stations flashed across his screen, followed by an inset square of a magnified area of the system. He zoomed in on the inset and enlarged it then another more detailed inset appeared, then another. A square within a square within a square.

He followed the grid back to the point of origin. Finally, he smiled.

"Got it!"

"Cellular? I bet it's cellular," Ruiz said.

Hart shook his head. "Land line. Point of origin Stone Valley Road, Alamo."

Ruiz ran his fingers through his graying crewcut. His years with the Bureau had taught him to follow his gut instincts, and all of his instincts screamed cellular. Why would Abrahms be using a land line? And Alamo? How the fuck did Alamo fit in? All of their intelligence, as piece-meal as it was, pointed to Abrahms being in Danville, not Alamo which was a good six or seven miles down the road. If he knew somebody there, why would he put them at risk by connecting out of their house? It didn't make sense.

"I've got the address," Hart said. "I'll dispatch our units. We'll be on them like—"

Ruiz shook his head. "Hold that order."

"But Abrahms—"

"Is trying to fuck with us. Run a check on the local cellular stations; see if someone has messed with the incoming signals. I think this is a dead-end."

"What about the Alamo address?"

"Send a car over to check it out. Meanwhile, you track them down on a cellular."

Hart nodded and returned to his computer. Ruiz stuffed a handful of Tums into his mouth.

"God Damn it, Abrahms. What the fuck are you doing?"

*****

Sherilyn walked through the metal detector towards the final ID checkpoint at the Google/NASA-Ames Research facility. So far, she'd made it through security without a glitch. Using the press ID badge issued for her writer, Courtney Jones, and carrying nothing but a digital voice recorder, notepad and pencil, she'd been waived through two prior checkpoints with little more than a cursory glance and a pat down. The final guard ahead, a thick-necked Indian marine with dark eyes, looked like he might be tougher.

Sherilyn pulled up the collar on her wool overcoat, swallowed hard and took a deep breath. Despite Taylor's best intentions to keep her out of harm's way, Sherilyn was determined not to sit in a hotel room while her husband battled to save their lives. After making sure Starling was tucked away safely in Walnut Creek, Sherilyn headed to her office in San Francisco, retrieved the ID and motored to Moffett Field. She was thankful that the news conference had been moved outdoors. It gave her a good excuse to wrap her head with a red scarf and don over-sized sunglasses. She and Courtney had similar builds and features. With the faint disguise, she prayed they were similar enough.

She approached the guard cautiously.

"ID?" he ordered.

Sherilyn handed him her badge.

The guard studied it then glanced towards Sherilyn.

Her heart pounding, Sherilyn smiled as sincerely as she could, then lowered her sunglasses, to allow the guard to see her eyes.

"I'm sensitive to sunlight," she said, smiling.

The guard nodded brusquely, shot his gaze back at the ID then motioned her forward. "Have a good day," he said, before reaching out for the next person's ID.

Sherilyn let out a nervous exhalation and maneuvered towards the rows of folding chairs lined before the stage. She found an empty seat, three rows back at the end of the aisle.

To the side of the stage, she could see her father, the Senator, talking with one of his aides. The sight of him stole her breath. An overwhelming emotion of revulsion swept through her. Despite all of her father's failings, she'd never hated the man before.

But that changed once she saw the files hidden inside Robert Chan's computer.

Now, being this close to him made her skin crawl. It took all of her willpower to stop herself from strutting to the stage and slapping him across the face.

She looked at her watch. It was 8:20 A.M.

She watched the Senator stride towards the stage and prayed that Taylor would be able to pull this off.

*****

"Taylor," the familiar voice said over the telephone. "This is Lynette Jensen."

"Dr. Jensen?" Taylor was stunned. She was the last voice he expected to hear that morning. What was she doing at the Farm? Had Helen been caught? Was this a set-up? Was Jensen there to talk him into giving himself up?

"Don't worry, I'm not working with the police," Jensen said with her French-Canadian accent. "I know you well enough to know you did not kill those men."

Jensen's words calmed Taylor's fears, but still didn't explain what she was doing with Helen.

As if reading Taylor's thoughts, Jensen continued. "I contacted Ms. Yang because I needed to talk to you."

Taylor switched to speakerphone. He shot Malcomb a worried look. "This isn't a good time," he said.

Jensen hesitated a moment. "It's your father."

Taylor recoiled. "My father?"

"Your father was brought to the ICU last night. Apparently, the FBI were at his house yesterday. The stress was too much for his ill health. He's had a major heart attack."

Taylor inhaled sharply. The FBI had gone to his father's house searching for him. His father had run interference while Taylor escaped. If the stress had harmed his father's heart, Taylor had no one but himself to blame.

"He's dying," Jensen continued. "There is nothing I can do for him. His liver disease has destroyed his blood's ability to clot, making surgery impossible. He'd bleed to death on the table. The arterial blockage is too advanced for angioplasty, it would be too dangerous. Nearly impossible to get the stent through."

Taylor wasn't prepared to deal with this now. He covered his mouth with his hand. "There're no options?"

"There is only one thing that I can think of. One hope to save his life."

Taylor could tell where Jensen was going. "The Virtual Heart Project?"

"If we can cannulate the femoral artery without significant blood loss, I can insert the laser. We may have a chance. The laser can cut through the clot that I can't with my balloon. It is his only chance. Can you do it?"

Can I do it? Taylor rubbed his forehead, his breath quickening. *Operate on my father?* He'd intended on performing another angioplasty as part of his plan to expose the Senator's plot, but that was going to be on a pig. Not a human. Not his own father.

Not now.

He shot a glance at Malcomb, who looked back at him nervously, his face pale.

"There's no way. We're not ready."

"His liver is failing," Jensen said. "The blood is backing up in the portal system. His blood pressure is unsteady. He doesn't have much time."

"But we can't—" Taylor stopped, a million thoughts colliding in his mind. The Senator's news conference was due to start any moment. He looked at Malcomb, searching for an answer.

"The blood shark's primed," Helen cut in over the phone line. "I've brought the equipment to the angio suite. We should be ready to go."

Taylor squeezed his eyes. "But we're not prepared to work from the suite. We're supposed to operate from the Farm."

"It makes no difference," Malcomb interrupted. "The camera is in the laser, not the Farm. Wherever we insert the blood-shark, we'll have access to the visuals."

"But you're all missing the point," Taylor said. "We're not human ready. We've never successfully done a pig. I can't do this on my father. I might kill him. And besides, my—if the hallucinations start while I'm operating—"

"He will die if you don't try," Jensen said.

Taylor looked at his watch. The news conference was due to start in seconds. He had to start his plan. They'd never have another opportunity. But if this was really his father's only chance—

"Ok," he whispered.

"Your father has already been wheeled into angio and the scans needed for your visuals are completed. We're ready to start when you are."

"Is the connection established?" Malcomb asked.

"I've got your signal registered here," Helen answered. "You should have real-time control of the laser. I'll upload the ultrasounds on your command."

Taylor couldn't believe this was happening. He looked at Malcomb. "The news conference?"

"I've accessed the audiovisual. That was easy. Phase two is more dangerous. I don't know how your brain will respond to this. Whether it will correct the overstimulation or...." he let his words trail off, as if he was afraid to utter them.

"Be careful," Helen said.

"Understood." Taylor was aware of the risk he was facing, both for his own life and now his father's. If Malcomb had failed to clear the rootkit/virus, if Taylor's sanity gave way at the wrong moment in the middle of the surgery, if the FBI found them and interrupted the procedure—he didn't even want to think about the possibilities.

His whole body ached with trepidation. He took a deep, calming breath then turned back to Malcomb. "Bishop from C-4 to F-7."

"Do we really have time for this?" Helen asked.

"Now is the perfect time," Taylor said. "Malcomb?"

Malcomb nodded, understanding. "I'll move my King from E-8 to E-7."

Taylor registered the move with a nod. "Are you ready, Dr. Jensen?"

"The cannula will be ready when you are."

Taylor closed his eyes and whispered a prayer.

"Let's do this. Wish me luck."

Biting his lip, Malcomb ran his fingers across the keyboard. His index finger hoovered over the ENTER key. "Once I hit this button, we're going to need more than luck."

Taylor nodded and his eyes focused on Malcomb's finger. He drew another deep breath, calming his pounding heart. He couldn't believe this was happening. Operate on his father. His palms begin to sweat inside the SIS power-glove. He thought of each step necessary for the VHP to work. It was all coming together at that moment.

"One last thing," Taylor said.

Nervously, Malcomb looked up. "Yes?"

"Bishop from C-1 to G-5."

Malcomb squinted and mentally ran through the move. His eyes widened. "But that's—"

Taylor nodded then lowered the virtual helmet over his temples.

"Checkmate," he said.

CHAPTER 73

Senator McIntyre felt heady. He leaned against the podium, gazing out upon the sea of reporters, Silicon Valley executives, State Senators, and Republican donors. The presence of the crowd energized him; he felt his vitality swelling, the crowd clamoring, hanging on his every word.

"Ladies and Gentlemen," McIntyre began, "I'd like to thank you for coming this beautiful morning. I promise my message will be short and to the point. This nation is in a crisis; a health-care crisis of such magnitude it threatens to destroy the very fabric of our economy. What I am going to show you today will shock you, just as it has shocked me."

McIntyre paused while the two 103 OLED screens on either side of the podium flashed to life. Across the right screen the words AMERICAN HEALTH CARE: EQUAL OPPORTUNITY MEDIOCRITY projected above a graph depicting the latest study on deteriorating healthcare quality.

The Senator looked at his monitor, confirming the data. He paused, allowing the audience to digest the magnitude of the message. To his left, he spotted Reginald Erickson, the CyberTech CEO, sitting at a private table, surrounded by his Silicon Valley peers. McIntyre smiled inwardly, feeling an overwhelming sense of satisfaction, knowing that the plan he'd constructed with Erickson so many months ago was about to see fruition.

On the screen to the left flashed a security photo, depicting the senator's son-in-law, Dr. Abrahms, standing over the fallen body of a University Medical Center intern.

A rumble swept through the crowd. Sensing a major story, the reporters' eyes grew wide.

McIntyre seized the moment. "What I am going to show you, I will present without prejudice. I will give you the facts; the truth about the failings of our medical system and the role of my own son-in-law in a research project so wasteful and costly that it boggles the mind."

The Senator straightened and surveyed the crowd. Reporters leaned forward, like hyenas awaiting their chance to feed at a kill.

The Senator flashed his patented smile. "I will show you the truth about a project that is typical of the lavish ways our medical establishment spends money, pushing the boundaries of expensive hyper-biotechnology with no regard to societal cost. I will tell you the truth of how badly this one particular project has failed. A truth so devastating, yet so typical of our current status of wasteful spending, that it led my own son-in-law to plot to kill me, rather than allow me to go public."

The Senator scanned the audience, taking in the anticipation building in the crowd. He was in his element. As his eyes grandly swept across the sea of faces, they fell upon someone who looked vaguely familiar. A woman, her head wrapped in a red scarf, her eyes hidden behind—

Sherilyn?

The Senator shook his head, swallowing a brief moment of alarm. It couldn't be her. With the manhunt in full force, this would be the last place his daughter would dare to show her face.

The Senator exhaled, returning his focus on the audience, searching for the perfect words to drive home his message.

"In just a moment, I will show you a truth that has led to murder."

*****

The world rushed in white.

Taylor squinted through the glare, shielding his eyes with his hands.

It wasn't until Taylor heard the familiar *Ba Bum, Ba Bum* of the beating heart that he knew that he'd made it.

I'm in!

A rush of adrenaline seized him. Blood cells rushed by. He felt the warmth of the sticky fluid, the plasma, flowing across his skin.

Looking around, inside the blood vessel, it was just as real as the first time Taylor had entered the program. He felt the slickness of the endothelial cells, mucous sliding between his fingers. He saw the immensity of the arterial lumen, the swirling disc-shaped, red blood cells. The roaring *Ba Bum, Ba Bum* in his ears. He was back inside the heart.

But this wasn't just any heart.

It's my father's.

Taylor allowed that realization to sink in. This wasn't a trial run. Not a practice pig. This was a living, breathing human being. All the family he had left. He had one chance, and one chance only to save his father's life.

He spun around, focusing down the arterial lumen. Before him loomed the massive cholesterol plaque damming the blood flow of his father's coronary artery, a near total obstruction. Blood cells swirled in the rushing plasma, smashing into the plaque, rupturing upon impact, releasing their damaged contents into his father's bloodstream.

Taylor took a deep, steadying breath. In his right hand he held the laser, his movements translated to the blood shark, now positioned by Dr. Jensen inside his father's coronary artery. The discovery that the pigs hadn't died from the VHP fueled Taylor's hopes. There was a small chance that what Taylor was about to do wouldn't kill the man.

A small chance.

Taylor bit his lower lip. "I'm ready."

*****

Contra Costa Sheriff Deputy Peter Nordsmith first noticed the AMC Rambler at 8:17, on his routine patrol of Norris Canyon Road. A three-year veteran of the county force, it struck him odd finding the car outside the abandoned "Double R" barn since the property had been vacant since Robert Roy, the former owner, had fallen into bankruptcy. He was about to investigate, but recalled hearing something about the property being on the market. He reasoned that the Rambler must be the car of a real estate or bank agent and didn't give it another thought.

It was on his return at 8:39 that his suspicions arose. Noticing the condition of the 1961 car, the dangling bumper and rust-worn exhaust pipe, he wondered why a real estate agent would drive a clunker like that. Slowing down, he saw a figure moving through the broken slats of the barn's southern wall. He pulled into the gravel drive and ran the plates through this computer.

The computer fed him the name of Henry Richard Starling. Nordsmith studied the DMV information, scrutinizing the birthdate.

AUGUST 15, 1947.

This was no real estate agent.

Nordsmith was well aware of the manhunt for the murder fugitives. During the morning briefing, his chief had reminded all deputies to report anything out of the ordinary. At that moment, Nordsmith had no idea what the Rambler was doing parked at the "Double R", but he wasn't going to take any chances.

He picked up his radio and called for dispatch.

*****

Senator McIntyre gauged his audience. He could feel their intensity rising, waiting for him to impart his discovery like Moses descending from Mt. Sinai with the holy tablets. McIntyre drank in the moment, intoxicated by their attention. He straightened his back, his battle posture fully assumed.

"I will answer questions only after you've had a chance to see this report," McIntyre said.

With those words, McIntyre nodded. Both plasma displays flashed in white. The senator smiled, knowing that the security video of Taylor assaulting his professor, Dr. Norman Browne, on one screen, paired with a graph of data showing the outrageous public spending on hyper-biotech would grip the media's attention.

As he glanced towards the screen to his left, McIntyre's smile suddenly faded.

*****

Taylor steadied himself against the current of plasma, bracing his legs against the slick endothelial surface inside his father's coronary artery. He could feel the vessel wall shaking like an earthquake with each beating contraction of the virtual heart.

Taylor just received word from Malcomb that they'd gone live, now broadcasting to millions through the video channel at Senator Randolph McIntyre's news conference. It had only taken Malcomb a matter of moments to seize control of the conference's computer board while simultaneously patching the VHP feed through the television broadcast booth.

"We are live with every major news channel in the nation," Malcomb confirmed. "Every iota of data we confiscated from Robert Chan's computer is downloading onto screen-one while we have live video on screen-two. Oh, and we have live audio feed also. They can hear everything we say through our microphones." Malcomb paused and cleared his throat. "Hello Senator, are you enjoying the show?"

"That should get the nation's attention," Helen said.

"And the F.B.I.," Malcolm added.

"Don't celebrate yet," Taylor cautioned, knowing his voice was broadcasting through the senator's speaker system. "We still have to prove my esteemed father-in-law wrong. Show the world what we can do."

"All systems are go," Malcomb said. "We have perfect coordination with the laser. Movements are calibrated to within 10 microns and responsiveness is currently pegged at zero point zero seven microseconds."

"Helen?" Taylor asked.

"Confirmed."

"Do you have word from Dr. Jensen in the Cath lab?"

"I have her on speakerphone. She'll be locked in with your commands."

"And our patient?" Taylor asked. He paused a second, then added. "My father?"

Helen pulled away from the microphone then returned. "Dr. Jensen says blood pressure is holding but just barely. Pulse is slow. He's dying. It's now or never."

Taylor swallowed hard, his own pulse pounding. He stared at the massive clot before him, the laser trembling in his hands. He knew the whole nation, maybe the world, was watching, reporters transcribing every word, but that didn't matter. What he cared about was his father, dying on the table, his heart struggling to beat. Taylor thought of the irony; his father, the man who had given him life, now with his life in his son's hands. After so many years of strife, Taylor now fighting to save the man he once hated. And once loved. He pushed those thoughts aside.

I can do this, he repeated slowly, like a mantra. *I can do this.*

Taylor elevated the laser, choosing his spot in the cholesterol plaque, a thin crevice in the massive stalactite. The plasma rushed in disjointed currents. Blood cells smashed wildly into the vessel walls, spinning over his head. He realized that the video feed would project this stunning view across the nation. Across the world.

I can do this.

"Prepare for laser," Taylor said.

"Laser is ready," Malcomb said.

Taylor focused through the streaming plasma, his eyes locking on the target. His entire world heaved with each massive beat of his father's heart, each slowing, weakening *Ba Bum Ba Bum* of the ventricle. He steadied his legs, allowing himself to move in time with the pulse, keeping the laser level.

Steady.

Steady now.

His father's virtual heart skipped a beat. Plasma shot around him, flooding passed him. Taylor's finger on the trigger turned white.

Steady.

Then he fired.

*****

Ruiz answered the phone with a short, angry voice. News reports were flooding in about a computer hijacking of the audio/visual feed at the Senator's news conference. CNN was broadcasting live, an image of an in-progress angioplasty while describing the streams of pirated data projecting on the adjacent video screen. No one knew what was happening or what these private emails and log entries meant. The news stations were in chaos.

The last thing Ruiz wanted was to be disturbed, but his tone changed when he heard what the County Sheriff had to say about Deputy Nordsmith's discovery. At that instant, the deputy remained outside the barn, waiting for clearance to investigate.

"Do you want me to send him in?" the Sheriff asked.

Ruiz shot his gaze to the chaos on the television screen. He could see audio/visual engineers at the conference trying to re-establish control over their video feed. The reporters were in a frenzy. Suddenly, the screen on Hart's laptop sprung to life, reams of data streaming in parallel columns.

Ruiz studied the screen, his eyes gaping. "Holy crap," he whispered.

*****

McIntyre stared at the screens in horror.

On the screen to his left, he could see the video feed of the angioplasty moving forward in real-time. The image of the blood vessel in stunningly clear high-def. The cholesterol plaque, looking like Everest. A resounding *Ba Bum, Ba Bum* blared through the audio like the pounding drums of his Marine honor band.

But the real horror was on the screen to his right.

At first, the Senator had no idea what was being projected, why Taylor was grandstanding with posting of private entries from the CTS database onto his news conference. A steady stream of emails and private log entries, copied from the CyberTech Systems database danced across the screen. The name Reginald Erickson blazoned across the bottom of each entry.

Then it registered.

The Senator felt like he'd been sucker punched. The magnitude of what was being projected sank in. McIntyre shot a glance at Erickson, whose face blanched in shock, clearly realizing what was happening.

"Turn it off!" Erickson was screaming. "Turn the damn thing off!"

But it was too late. The world had already seen it. Detailed in each carefully logged email and diary entry, McIntyre's plan to fix the election with Erickson's help. The plan spread out, step-by-step. Erickson had contacted McIntyre, alerting him that his company was preparing the AI for Taylor Abrahms' experiment, and with a little creative code writing, could make certain the experiment failed. All Erickson asked was the guarantee of tabling the anti-trust investigation, and in return, McIntyre would ride his medical reform platform to the White House, using his own son-in-law as a scapegoat for the wrongs of the Medical Establishment.

The reporters flew into frenzy. Digital cameras captured the data flying across the screen. Voices rang across the tarmac.

"Turn it off!" Erickson kept screaming. Technicians pounded at the keyboard, trying to sever the data feed. "Unplug it, just unplug the damn thing!"

McIntyre watched all this unfold without saying a word. He was too dumbstruck to move. But it wasn't the public unveiling of his criminal action that shook him to the core. It was the second half of the log entries that took his breath away.

These entries described how, after locking in his arrangement with McIntyre, Erickson had left nothing to chance. Within days, Erickson had contacted McIntyre's opponent, Congressman Snead O'Neil, informing him of McIntyre's conspiracy to sabotage his son-in-law's research. Erickson promised O'Neil that with the evidence he had against McIntyre, and the addition of a few well-placed dead bodies, he could implicate McIntyre in a conspiracy so vast that his reputation would make a slug's look glorious. A branded criminal, he'd be forced to withdraw from the election, guaranteeing O'Neil the White House. In exchange, once O'Neil was President, all he had to do was halt the anti-trust investigation. Erickson had a man inside the hospital, Dr. Norman Browne, paid to keep tabs on Taylor and clean up any messes. It was airtight.

It was all there, streaming across the video screen.

McIntyre couldn't believe what he was reading. He'd been played a fool from the beginning. In the audience, the reporters were a whirlwind of activity, while somewhere, watching in his own muted prison of horror, McInytre knew that O'Neil was hanging his head in shame.

McIntyre's head snapped towards Erickson. Erickson didn't return the glance, instead his eyes locked on the video screen, his mouth gaping open. Holding his chest, Erickson suddenly fell to his knees, gasping.

McIntyre felt a hand tap his shoulder.

Spinning around, he stared into the mirrored sunglasses of a Secret Service agent.

"I think you better be coming with us, sir."

"No! It can't end like this. I'm the President of the United States. I'm the President, damn it!"

The agent shook his head. "No, sir. You're not."

McIntyre's staggered backwards. He glanced towards the projection screens, the laser successfully blasting within the blood vessel, the cholesterol plaque erupting into a cloud of microscopic fatty-acid dust. Blood flow returning in swirling, life-giving patterns. The sun-glassed agent stepped closer. Panic gripped McIntyre. He snapped a glance towards the audience, searching desperately for a friendly face.

Roderick. Jennifer. Anyone.

Then he saw her, standing amongst the frenzied mob of reporters. The woman with the red scarf. Slowly, she removed her sunglasses and peeled off her scarf.

His daughter's damning eyes staring back at him.

EPILOGUE 1

8 months later

The Doctor's locker room was empty.

Taylor walked inside and collapsed onto the wooden bench. Exhausted, he pulled off the virtual suit and breathed a sigh of relief. Performed in front of the watchful eyes of the University Board, the Heads of the Departments of Surgery and Cardiology, his first hospital-sanctioned virtual angioplasty had been an unqualified success. His patient, Mr. McAdams, had flown through the procedure, free of complications, his coronary arteries cleared of all plaque. His EKG normal.

Taylor took a moment to let it sink in. It was amazing how far his life had come. Reflecting back on the last days of his ordeal, it almost seemed unreal now. Some sick, demented nightmare from which he had finally awoken.

The aftershocks of the Senator's news conference still rippled through the upper echelons of Washington D.C. With both candidates embroiled in a conspiracy that included industrial espionage, election tampering, and murder, the election had been thrown into chaos. Robert Chan, still recovering in a San Francisco rehab hospital, was declared a hero for his role in uncovering the plot, and received the Presidential Medal of Freedom, the highest civilian honor, for his meritorious contribution to protecting the national interest.

Never before in American politics had both candidates been disgraced before an election. With no precedent to follow, Congress utilized Article II, section 1 clause 4 of the Constitution; there was no choice but to postpone the election. With the current President having already served two full terms, the Vice President stepped into the Executive chair until a new election could be arranged and new candidates selected.

History had been made.

Taylor smiled at the thought. At Taylor's hearing, Victor Ruiz had argued for amnesty and helped Taylor and Malcomb get reinstated at the hospital, where Taylor resumed the task of completing his residency and research. This time, however, Taylor handled his duties at half-time. It meant graduation would be pushed back for another year, but it gave him the freedom to engage in more important duties, like spending time with his wife and father.

Taylor opened his locker, pulled out his grey wool suit coat, reached into his pocket and pulled out his cellular.

Sherilyn's voice was warm and inviting. "Hello?"

"How's my baby doing?" he asked.

"Do you mean me or the one growing inside of me?"

"Both."

"I'm fine," she answered, "and your son is kicking like a future soccer star. I think he's been practicing with my kidneys all day."

Taylor laughed. "That's my boy."

"How did it go?" she asked.

"It was beautiful, Sherilyn."

Taylor could almost see her smiling on the other end.

"I'm so proud of you."

"I'll tell you all about it when I get home."

"Will that be soon?"

Taylor looked at his watch. "I need to give a press conference with Dr. Jensen downstairs. There're about a hundred reporters waiting to hear about 'robot surgery'. Malcomb and Helen should be over by five to celebrate with us. Once I'm done here, I'll swing by the Care Home, pick up my father, then meet you all."

"Don't you mean your dad?" Sherilyn asked.

Taylor's eyes crinkled as he smiled. His father had survived the angioplasty and was now staying in an assisted living facility in the City. Far away from the darkened house at the end of the dirt road. While Taylor knew his father was still going to die—it was just a matter of time—he'd pledged that he wasn't going to die alone.

"My dad," Taylor said.

"We're having Italian tonight," Sherilyn said.

"I thought my growing son preferred Mexican?"

"Your son doesn't care what we eat, he just wants you home. Remember, you promised you'd finish putting up the shelves in the nursery tonight."

A glowing warmth filled him. He'd be there to put up the nursery shelves, just as he'd be there to play ball with his son, and teach him about animals and mathematics and girls. He'd be there for soccer games and boy scouts and skinned knees.

Not just as a father, but as a dad.

"Well?" he heard Sherilyn say.

Picking up his briefcase, Taylor headed towards the door. He turned off the lights and the locker room fell into darkness. He closed the door behind him.

He thought once again of everything that had happened to him—the virtual world, his father, McIntyre, Ruiz—everything that had led him to where he was today. A warm smile graced his face.

"I'm coming home," he said.

EPILOGUE 2

The man with the mirrored sunglasses sat at the mosaic table on the terrace of the Bakal restaurant in Acapulco, silently watching as his mark strutted through the crowded cantina. Behind him, the ocean roared, crashing against the white sand, sea salt spraying in the Pacific breeze. The tropical sun descended into a sea of red and orange. A group of red-skinned tourists, smelling of coconut oil and alcohol, paraded across the terracotta floor, momentarily obscuring the view of his target.

Edgar Ross pulled the straw hat down farther over his shaved forehead and leaned forward, re-establishing his line of sight. He took a sip of water, wincing as he swallowed. Pain still shot through his jaw, a residual effect of the face full of buckshot he'd taken eight months ago. Ross rubbed his cheek, his fingers lingering over the scars carved into his face and neck. He hadn't forgotten Taylor Abrahms, and the personal souvenirs he carried of his failure, but for now that would have to wait.

The DJ faded out the reggae beat, bringing up a pulsing salsa number. The dance floor filled with writhing bodies. Ross watched his mark melt into the dancing throng, his groin rubbing against the bikini-tourist's rear. The dancers, lost in a fugue of alcohol and the pheromones of sex were oblivious to everything else around them.

That was Ross's cue.

Rising from the table, Ross grabbed a drink coaster blazoned with the café logo and slipped it into his pocket, a souvenir he'd process later. He gripped a syringe in his right hand; 10cc's of strychnine, and stepped towards his mark. Fading sunlight gleamed off the 25-gauge needle. The salsa beat pounded through the speakers, the bodies twisting and sweating. Disco lights strobed.

And Ross walked closer.

ABOUT THE AUTHOR

T.D. SEVERIN. MD. is an internationally renowned professor, physician, surgeon, and award-winning author of medical suspense, who has been publishing both fiction and non-fiction since 1994. His writing has appeared in national and regional magazines/journals around the world, while his first novel, *Deadly Vision,* was an award winner at the SEAK National Medical Fiction Writing Competition. Dr. Severin's wellness book on the fusion of eastern and western medicine, *TriEnergetics,* has been published in multiple languages, and now enters its 4th edition.

T.D. Severin has been named one of the Nation's Best Ophthalmologists by *Newsweek Magazine*, and has been honored to receive the prestigious Telly Award, the Oscars of public access television, for his work on medical television programming.

T.D. lives with his wife and two pups in the San Francisco Bay Area and Florida, where he is currently at work on his next medical thriller. A former radio disc jockey, he also runs the heavy rock record label Ripple Music: www.ripple-music.com.

Stay in touch with all things T.D. Severin at his website www.tdseverin.com and www.tdseverin.blogspot.com

Also join the conversation on Facebook at

T.D. Severin -Author

and

TDSeverin.substack.com.

HILLS OF COTABATO
BY
MARC SCHIFFMAN

Hills of Cotabato is the story of Eddie Finn, a United States security investigator for the American government who, after being stationed in Rwanda during the 1994 genocide, is three years later posted at the U. S. Embassy in the Philippines. He has been informed by his government to negotiate the release of three American Peace Corp volunteers, and a Chinese priest, who have been kidnapped by the Abu Sayyaf, a known terrorist group in the southern province of Mindanao.

This single event, the kidnapping of three American Peace Corp volunteers, sets off a series of unforeseen events with the culmination leading Eddie Finn to Cotabato City and the jungles of Mindanao. The question of loyalty, personal and official obligation, and the regional conflict of religion and culture incite a web of intrigue and revelation.

PENMORE PRESS
www.penmorepress.com

The Glass Guitar

By

Marshall Riggan

Walter Woodrow Pillow would have moved through life unremarked if he had not committed the most outrageous and traitorous act in American history. A young design engineer in a Texas bomber factory, he had become consumed with guilt and remorse for his role in designing the deadliest weapons system of the Vietnam era. So, one day, in 1965, he sabotaged the mighty bombers. Wally made tracks for the border, the FBI, the CIA and Interpol hot on his trail.The Glass Guitar is the story of Wally's efforts to elude government agents and along the way champion causes promoting peace, fairness, and justice in an imperfect world. He is joined by a number of kindred souls, including a beautiful prostitute known as "Angel of the Arroyos," an Italian movie director whose mother dated Mussolini, and a reformed explosives expert who penned the classic Ethics and the Firecracker. In its efforts to make right the wrongs of the world, this merry band of fugitive-reformers leaves a path of devastation across the social landscape. The story is a cautionary tale suggesting that there are often unexpected consequences for doing the right thing.

PENMORE PRESS
www.penmorepress.com

The Book Of

Invasions

By

Rod Vick

The Book of Invasions is a globe-spanning adventure, a romp through history and mythology, a grudging love story, and an all-in battle against an evil hidden in plain sight. The world is stunned by the inexplicable murder of a dozen climate scientists at a remote research station in Greenland. When twenty-six-year-old Ricky Crowe, sister of a slain researcher, unexpectedly comes into possession of a parchment map found in Greenland's 5,000-year-old ice, she attempts to set aside the demons of her own grief and alcoholism—and a terrifying past that has left her with an eight-inch facial scar—in order to determine whether the map holds a key to her sister's fate. Bringing it to experts at the foundation that funded her sister's research, she sets in motion a race with her new allies to unravel puzzles hidden in tombs in Egypt and Ireland, and in an obscure book of Celtic myth—The Book of Invasions—before the secrets are lost to the ruthless cult that has searched relentlessly for the world-changing evil the map promises since before the pyramids were built.

PENMORE PRESS
www.penmorepress.com

ASSASSINS OF ALAMUT
BY
JAMES BOSCHERT

An Epic Novel of Persia and Palestine in the Time of the Crusades

The Assassins of Alamut is a riveting tale, painted on the vast canvas of life in Palestine and Persia during the 12th century.

On one hand, it's a tale of the crusades—as told from the Islamic side—where Shi'a and Sunni are as intent on killing Ismaili Muslims as crusaders. In self-defense, the Ismailis develop an elite band of highly trained killers called Hashshashin...whose missions are launched from their mountain fortress of Alamut.

But it's also the story of a French boy, Talon, captured and forced into the alien world of the assassins. Forbidden love for a princess is intertwined with sinister plots and self-sacrifice, as the hero and his two companions discover treachery and then attempt to evade the ruthless assassins of Alamut who are sent to hunt them down.

It's a sweeping saga that takes you over vast snow-covered mountains, through the frozen wastes of the winter plateau, and into the fabulous cites of Hamadan, Isfahan, and the Kingdom of Jerusalem.

"A brilliant first novel, worthy of Bernard Cornwell at his best."—Tom Grundner

PENMORE PRESS
www.penmorepress.com

Penmore Press

Challenging, Intriguing, Adventurous, Historical and Imaginative

www.penmorepress.com